* * * * * *

In a motel swimming pool, a retired general is suddenly retired forever . . .

At a call girl's apartment, sex is replaced by savage torture . . .

A private airfield is transformed into a bullet-riddled battleground for expert killers . . .

At a heavily guarded Arizona missile base, a nightmare project comes true . . .

And even the President of the United States becomes the helpless puppet of—

ASTERISK DESTINY

"Unflagging momentum . . . You'll keep reading!"
—*Kirkus Reviews*

"Meticulously crafted suspense . . . real and vulnerable characters . . . a superb writer. . . . Treat yourself and read ASTERISK DESTINY!"
—*Hartford Courant*

Big Bestsellers from SIGNET

ASTERISK DESTINY

---

*

A Novel

by
Campbell
Black

A SIGNET BOOK
NEW AMERICAN LIBRARY
TIMES MIRROR

A BOOK FOR KEIRON

PUBLISHER'S NOTE

This novel is a work of fiction. Names, characters, places and incidents are either the product of the author's imagination or are used fictitiously, and any resemblance to actual persons, living or dead, events, or locales is entirely coincidental.

 SIGNET TRADEMARK REG. U.S. PAT. OFF. AND FOREIGN COUNTRIES REGISTERED TRADEMARK—MARCA REGISTRADA HECHO EN CHICAGO, U.S.A.

SIGNET, SIGNET CLASSICS, MENTOR, PLUME, MERIDIAN AND NAL BOOKS are published by The New American Library, Inc., 1633 Broadway, New York, New York 10019

First Signet Printing, June, 1980

1   2   3   4   5   6   7   8   9

PRINTED IN THE UNITED STATES OF AMERICA

Grateful acknowledgment is made to my friends who helped: Ralph Himself Jarson, who was in at the start, TeeJay, K Winchell, and Eileen, best of all.

asterisk: the character * used in printing or writing as a reference mark . . . or to denote a hypothetical or nonoccurring linguistic form

—*Webster's New Collegiate Dictionary*

1:

Saturday, April Fool's Day

IN HIS DARK-BLUE SUIT THE MAJOR GENERAL MIGHT HAVE been a businessman awaiting the arrival of a client. He sat at a table in the cocktail lounge, a place of plastic plants and stained polyurethane ceiling beams, some Tudor fraud, and sipped from a glass of Seagram's and 7-Up. He held a leather attaché case in his lap. He looked at his watch. 12:10. What could be keeping Thorne? He hated unpunctuality at the best of times but now, especially now, it was quite intolerable. He lit a cigarette, turned the glass around between the palms of his hands, gazed across the crowded tables of the lounge.

Muzak played. *The King and I.* He had once been very fond of it.

But it was past and dead like so many things.

He stared at the door that led to the street. Thorne would come through at any moment. By the same token, so could any of the others. Lifting one hand from the edge of the attaché case, he rubbed his eyelids. Then he replaced his dark glasses.

He smoked another cigarette, ordered a second drink. In the old days there wouldn't have been these nerves. But something gives; something in the body yields and after a time you just can't cut it. You looked at death and what you saw was no longer an old enemy but something that grew increasingly familiar. *Come on, Thorne, come on.* He raised his glass to his lips and noticed that his hand was trembling. It had been a long time since he had last seen that. Still, he thought. Keep still. He put the glass down, spilling some of the drink on the surface of the table.

1

The tape stopped.

He listened to the babble of voices from all sides. He watched the door. His heartbeat, as if there were some quite desperate thing trapped in the cage of his ribs, was explosive. It was twelve seventeen. Thorne's father, old Ben, would never have kept a man waiting. Punctuality had been a law for Ben. *If a man can't be on time then it means his life is a mess.*

But Ben was dead. That was one of the worst adjustments of growing old; one by one, your nearest friends had gone.

And me, he thought. Me. How do you think of something so inconceivable as nonexistence? The door swung open, closed again. A young couple, hand in hand, a pair of lovebirds. She was smiling and lovely, he was tall and cool and unflustered. The major general considered his wife a moment, the track of some memory. A specter. He was twenty years older than her; had there ever been a time when they'd looked like the couple that had just come in?

He closed his eyes. There was new Muzak now. The sound of voices drowned it. Dying, he thought. The fight didn't seem worth it now. He tapped his fingers on the attaché case. They said young Thorne was smart, trustworthy, a man Going Places. All he could hope was that something of the old man had rubbed off on his son. Honor. At least that.

The door opened again. A middle-aged man, heavily built, constructed like some retired football player, came in and looked across the tables. How can I be sure? the major general wondered. *Please, Thorne, please.* The middle-aged man found an empty table some distance away and sat down and took a silver cigarette case from the pocket of his maroon leisure suit. You hardly ever saw cases like that anymore, the major general thought. They had once been all the rage. The man turned his head a little in the direction of the major general who glanced once more, once more, at his watch.

12:24.

Thorne.

He ran the tip of a finger around the rim of his glass. The trouble with fear, he thought, is the fact that it quickly becomes a constant. It becomes the norm of your

life and not the exception. You live all the time on the
dark edges. Because you can't live anyplace else.

He looked across the bar. Waitresses, like small panicked birds, darted back and forth between the tables and
the bar, carrying trays, setting glasses down, flustered by
the noise, the unseasonable heat. If Thorne didn't come,
he would have to talk to one of the waitresses. That was
the only course.

He looked at the man in the maroon leisure suit.

Then down at his attaché case.

Somehow, one way or another, the world would have to
know.

A truck, a tanker of some kind, had slammed into the center strip of the highway and skidded about a hundred
yards on its side. The driver, seemingly unconscious, was
surrounded by medics; two cars of the highway patrol
were parked some distance from the truck, their lights
flashing. The ambulance sat sideways, blocking the fast
lane.

Thorne got out of his car and looked impatiently along
the highway. How long before they could get this thing
moving? Behind him there was a long line of vehicles. A
few drivers, like himself, had come out of their cars and
were trying to get a look at the accident. He felt the kind
of hopeless anxiety that goes nowhere but into some frus-
trated resignation. He got back inside his car and
drummed his fingers on the wheel. How much longer?

He switched on his car radio, rolled down his window.
The day was hot, the air uncomfortably humid. There was
a news item or two on the radio: the possibility of another
oil embargo, a coal-mine disaster in Kentucky, the un-
manned spacecraft was sending back pictures of the Martian surface. He turned the radio off and wondered if the
old boy would wait.

Up ahead now he saw the medics carry a stretcher into
the ambulance. The truck, like some surreal metal elephant, lay on its side; a posture of death. If it were important, the major general would surely wait. Besides, what
was the mystery? What was the reason for this meeting?
and why in some suburban restaurant? Thorne realized he
hadn't seen the major general in—what?—fifteen, sixteen
years? The last time had been at the funeral. He remem-

bered the small reassuring man in military uniform with a look of genuine sorrow in his eyes. They had shaken hands after the service, the only mourner, Thorne remembered, who had looked genuinely sad—apart from his mother. Having shaken hands, the major general had taken a handkerchief from his pants and blown his nose; his eyes were watery. *Your dad stood for something, John. He stood for a set of values that aren't so obvious anymore in this great country of ours.* And Thorne recalled the pain in the man's face, the obvious struggle to control his grief, the way the voice shook. It had been a rainy morning; rain had soaked the flag draped around his father's casket, it had fallen against the black veil of mourning worn by his mother, pressing it flat upon her face so that her shock, her loss, was apparent to anybody who looked.

Walking away from the graveside, the major general had put his arm supportively upon the widow's elbow, and something in the gesture had struck Thorne as incongruously *gentle,* something he would not normally have associated with a man in military uniform. But there it was—a certain softness, a consideration, a moment of compassion. It had touched him; it had helped alleviate, in a small way, the sorrow of the morning. On the way out of the cemetery, the major general had drawn Thorne aside and said: *Be true to his values, John. Try your best to be true.* A brief salute, one man to another, not a patronizing gesture made by a soldier to a kid. Then the small man had walked off into the rain, to the waiting car.

Every Christmas since then he had received a gift from the old boy—handkerchiefs, socks, an electric razor, and on the Christmas of his twenty-first year a wristwatch. It was always accompanied by a card whose message rarely varied: *I hope this finds you well . . . I hope the last year has been good and the next will be even better . . .* Occasionally he heard from his mother that she had seen the major general, usually by chance, and that the old soldier was anxious to impart advice—on financial matters, on her late husband's papers, whatever. It was almost as if the major general were keen to make himself a surrogate member of the family, anxious somehow to please the ghost of a dead man.

And then the call last night. Incoherent, scared, urgent. *We must meet and talk. It's vital. Vital.* Thorne saw that

the inside lane had been cleared now. A highway patrolman was signaling cars forward, passing them through
slowly. He put his Volkswagen in first. The clutch was
slipping. It had always slipped in first, right from the time
he had bought it. Vital, he thought. What could be so vital
to an old man on the edge of retirement?

He looked at the bored face of the patrolman as he
passed. He felt some sympathy: it was a dumb way to
spend a Saturday afternoon.

12:49. The major general rose from his table, wiped his
lips with a napkin, and called to the waitress for his check.
She was young, pretty, anxious to please. New on the job,
the major general thought. He took two five-dollar bills
from his wallet and laid them on the table. His check
came to three dollars.

"I want you to do something for me," he said.

She looked at the notes, then at his face, as if she were
encountering for the first time the kind of drunk customer
she had been warned about. But she smiled still. The major general placed the attaché case on the chair.

"I am about to forget my case," he said.

She raised her eyebrows.

Mad, he thought. She sees madness in me. Or senility.
He looked quickly at his watch. 12:51. Even if Thorne
were not like his father, whom else could he trust at this
stage of the game? He remembered a fifteen-year-old boy
in a cemetery. A day of grief, but the boy had carried it
well. He was hurting inside, he wanted to weep, but he
had carried it the way a man might. Was that what he was
trusting? A fading, fifteen-year-old memory?

"Why would you want to forget your case?" the waitress
asked. She was blond and had her hair bunched back and
behind the smile there was the edge of some suspicion.

"I'm leaving it for somebody, do you see?" the major
general said. It had to be enough for Thorne.

He looked across the tables. The man in the maroon leisure suit sat stiffly over a glass of beer which clearly he
had no intention of drinking. He was not looking in the
major general's direction. It could be anyone, he thought.
It could be more than one.

"Somebody called Thorne will come here," he said to
the girl. He was conscious of speaking too quickly. There

was a tightness in his chest. "He will ask for me. Burck-hardt. You will say that I had to leave. You will give him the attaché case."

"Sure, no problem," the girl said. She was looking from the case to the two five-dollar bills.

The major general nodded. "All my life I've been a great tipper," he said. He winked at the girl. She picked up the notes. He walked away from the table. It was a constant thing, he thought: you begin to worry when you don't feel menaced. He reached the front door and went outside. For a moment he forgot where he had parked the car, a rented Ford, nondescript. What color was it? What did the damn thing look like?

He crossed the parking lot. When he found the car he fumbled his keys from his pocket, opened the door, and got inside. He drove to the motel where he had stayed the previous night. He parked the car, stepped out, and looked around.

A young man stood on the edge of the diving board above the pool. He raised his arms over his head, then, in a series of burnished twists, he was gone. The major general heard him hit the water. He took out his key and went inside his room. It was cool, the drapes drawn, the air conditioner blowing. He sat on the edge of the bed and smoked a cigarette. The telephone, he thought. Yes. Why not? You never knew if there would be another chance.

He asked the operator to place a collect call to Mrs. Anna Burckhardt in Fredericksburg, Virginia. Your name? she asked. Who shall I say is calling?

Momentarily he hesitated. A shadow, passing on the outside, crossed the drawn drapes. Anna, he thought: too much has been lost, too much has simply leaked away. He put the receiver down: where was the point to it now? He walked to the window, parted the drapes a little way. He saw the colored parasols around the pool. A long time ago he had told the boy: Be true to those things your father stood for. Be true. Now he could hope. He dropped the drapes back in place.

It was the perfect bitch, Tarkington thought. Nothing is simple in daylight. But there hadn't been an encounter, at least he could tell them that. He had seen an expectancy of death in the man's eyes. It was what you grew accustomed to. You recognized it as such.

He sipped some of his beer, left a few coins on the table, then went outside. He found a telephone booth on the far side of the building. The number. His memory for numbers was pitiful. He took a small dark notebook from his inside pocket, leafed through the pages, made a call.

He heard Sharpe's voice, sleepy as always. You couldn't trust that, though. What was that joke around the place? Sharpe by name, Sharpe by nature?

"They didn't meet," Tarkington said. "Don't ask me why because I don't know."

"Where did the old man go?" Sharpe asked.

Tarkington looked across the parking lot. The white sun glinted on windows, mirrors. He had forgotten his shades. He was forever buying sunglasses and leaving them places. He squinted.

"It wouldn't much matter," Tarkington said.

There was silence. Tarkington could see Sharpe behind the desk in his office. A sterile room. Sharpe was a workhorse. Saturdays even. A man gets ahead. Tarkington felt the sun burn on his forehead. In the field, you tired easily: Sharpe had presumably forgotten that.

"Lykiard is with him," Tarkington said. "It doesn't make a lot of difference now."

"Loose ends is what I hate," Sharpe said.

"Loose ends is what you don't get with Lykiard."

An anxious-looking woman, chewing on her lower lip, fidgeting with her purse, was pacing up and down outside the telephone booth. She had the appearance of someone with an emergency on her mind. Locked out of her car, Tarkington thought. Needs a locksmith. Good luck, lady.

Tarkington put the receiver down and stepped out of the booth. The woman rushed past him and slammed the door behind her. He walked to his car. It's the waiting, he thought. Always the waiting. But it was Lykiard's baby now. It was a job for the human eraser.

He hadn't waited after all.

Thorne asked the hostess if a Mr. Burckhardt had left a message for him. She was wearing a long dress, suggesting this place had some claim to class. She looked like a forlorn bridesmaid.

"Are you Mr. Thorne?"

Thorne said he was.

"Your party had to leave," she said.

"Did he—"

"He asked us to give you this." She reached behind her desk and brought out a brown leather attaché case. Thorne took it.

"No message? Didn't say where he was going?" he asked.

"Sorry," she said. "Just the case."

Saturday, Thorne thought. The sheer waste of it. He smiled at the hostess, who was leaning against a sign that read PLEASE WAIT TO BE SEATED. He needed a drink. He was led to a table, ordered a gin and tonic, drank it slowly. He found a small key attached to the handle of the case by a piece of string. He opened the case, glanced inside. A manila folder containing sheaves of paper. What was it? The old boy's memoirs? An analysis of the faults of our defense system? He closed the case and locked it. He stirred his drink, then finished it. There are better things to do on a Saturday, he thought. Better ways of passing time.

He got up from the table, paid the waitress, and went outside. He walked to his Volkswagen, slung the case in back, and drove away. On Interstate 95 he saw a plane begin its ascent from the runway of Washington National Airport. A DC-9. Beyond, on the other side of the Potomac, there were disintegrating jet vapors in the sky above Andrews Air Force Base.

2

Marcia was sunbathing on the balcony of the apartment when he let himself in with his own key. He put the attaché case down, took off his jacket, shirt, and necktie, and stepped through the glass door to the balcony. She smiled without looking at him. She was staring up at the sky, her eyes hidden by sunglasses.

"Welcome," she said.

There was a pitcher of lemonade, in which the ice had already melted, on a small table. He poured a glass for himself and deliberately spilled a few drops on Marcia's stomach. She grimaced.

"Keep you awake," he said.

"I'm not asleep," she answered.

She was wearing a black two-piece swimsuit. Her skin was turning red. Later, it would darken to brown and she would look . . . terrific, Thorne thought. But then she always looked terrific. He sipped the lemonade, which was bitter. He remembered that lately she had begun a campaign against the use of sugar after reading a book in which sugar was said to be a killer. Now, when she wanted a sweetener, it had to be honey.

"Did you see your old warrior?" she asked.

She sat up, sliding her sunglasses down, leaving them balanced on the tip of her nose.

"There was an accident on the freeway," he said. "When I finally made it, he was gone."

"Ah," she said. She was clutching her knees with her hands.

"He left me an attaché case."

"The plot thickens," she said. "What's in it?"

Thorne shrugged.

"Why don't you look?" she asked.

"Later," he said. He felt a sudden exhaustion, drained by the heat, the humidity. He finished the lemonade and went inside the apartment, put some music on the stereo. It was late Bob Dylan. When he returned to the balcony, Marcia was making a face.

"What a goddamn dirge," she said.

"When I think of your lack of taste, I wonder what I see in you," he said.

She threw a book of matches at his head and he ducked.

"When I think of your lack of intellect, I wonder what I see in *you*," she said.

"Want me to show you?" he said.

"Here? On the balcony?"

"She's the shy, retiring sort," he said. "She never likes to screw in public."

He lay alongside her and closed his eyes. He could hear the drone of traffic from the freeway. He put his hand against the base of her neck, rubbing lightly. She turned over on her front and said: "Get some oil. Massage me."

"I can't fucking move," he said. "This heat paralyzes me."

"Do you know it's April Fool's Day?"

"I heard."

"Maybe your old warrior was playing a trick on you, huh?"

"I don't recollect him having a sense of humor," Thorne said. He opened his eyes. There was a merciless quality to the brightness of the sun and he longed to be cool, to immerse himself in water. He got slowly to his feet and went back inside the apartment. On the desk beside the stereo Marcia's books lay open. Eng. Lit. Wordsworth, Coleridge's *Biographia Literaria*. Shelley. There was a copy of *Frankenstein*. Ever since he had known her she had been trying to complete her doctoral thesis at George Washington.

He went into the bathroom and stepped out of his pants. He took his wallet from his back pocket and laid it beside the washbasin. It fell open: a flash of credit cards, gasoline cards, his social security card, his classified pass. He removed his underwear, got into the shower, adjusted the flow of water for lukewarm. The old warrior, he thought. He felt the cooling stream of water on his body and he shut his eyes. This was better, refreshing, away from the unseasonable humidity of April.

The glass door slid open and Marcia handed him a towel.

"Join me," he said.

He wiped drops of water from his eyes.

"In a minute," she said. "I think your old warrior was really goofing on you, John. A real April Fool's Day trick."

"How come?" He looked at her.

"I just looked inside his case—"

"And?"

"Come and see."

He threw the towel over the rail and followed her into the living room. The record was still playing. She picked up the briefcase and took out the manila folder.

"Take a look," she said.

He opened the folder. Blank. Page after page after page, absolutely blank. He took out one page, went to the balcony door, held it up to the light. There was only a watermark.

"See what I mean?" Marcia said.

"Yeah." Page after page: nothing.

"Was he senile?" she asked.

"Looks that way," he said.

"He drags you all the way out to the back of beyond just to leave you a pile of nothing? I call that prime dotage behavior."

He looked at her. She was standing with her hands on her hips, her legs slightly splayed. Her sunglasses were still balanced on the tip of her nose, pinching the nostrils.

"I guess," he said. "I guess he's finally flipped."

"Understatement," she said. "Unless, of course, the sheets are covered with invisible ink."

"Big joke," he said. He looked inside the attaché case, he put his hand in to feel the lining. Nothing. A manila folder that contained maybe twenty-five sheets of nothing. He put the folder and the papers back into the case, then locked it.

"Well? What do you think?" she asked.

"I think we get back into the shower," he said. "As a twosome."

"Deal."

He took her hand and led her into the bathroom. He turned the faucet on and undid the top of her swimsuit. She stood with her back against the tiled wall, parting her legs for him.

He listened to the roar of water, the rattle of drops upon the tiles, the sound of her quick breathing on the side of his face. She put her arms around him, the tips of her fingers digging his shoulder blades. He glanced at her face, at the exquisite distance in her eyes.

"Am I good," she said. "Am I good, am I."

"The best," he said. Yes, the best, definitely the best. Undeniably so.

The major general woke, startled by something. He'd had no intention of falling asleep. He was still fully dressed. For a moment he did not recognize his surroundings—the plastic room, the drawn drapes, the chain at the door. A motel, yes: a room that emerged in his memory like a Polaroid print. He went to the window, his limbs a little stiff, and he looked out. There had been a young man before, hadn't there? Someone diving from the high board? The sun was gone, the afternoon darkening down, twilight. He walked into the bathroom and turned on the light. An extractor fan grated in the ceiling as if a blade were bent.

They could be outside, he thought.

Or anywhere.

Anywhere.

He filled the washbasin, splashed handfuls of cold water on his face and eyelids, brushed his short hair. He looked at his reflection and thought of the others: Harley, Garfield, Wilkinson, McLean. Were they all dead? How many more? McLean had committed suicide in a hotel in Mexico City. Garfield had died in an auto accident. Wilkinson in a fire. Harley—but he could not remember. Harley now, he could not remember the man, his face, mannerisms, anything. Natural causes, accidents, suicides. They said. *They* said.

The slaves who had constructed the secret chambers of the Great Pyramids were said to have been killed. So that the secrets would be kept.

Asterisk, he thought.

He mopped his face with one of the antiseptic towels of the motel. He was tired. The sleep hadn't done much for him. A dream, maybe the edge of a dream, something fading away like old parchment. A tapestry of mind. It was Escalante. That was the place. The desert. Why was he having this problem in remembering? The fatigue, the fear.

Had McLean been afraid in his hotel room in Mexico City?

I could fight, he thought. In the past that is what I would have done. I would have fought like all hell. But then you couldn't make it after a while. The sinews failed you, the muscles let you down, your memory began its inevitable disintegration, and something in your dead center—soul, life—sagged.

He held his hands out in front of him. They were steady. He walked to the window, peered out. There was no sign now of the young man who had been diving earlier. He was beset by a consciousness of solitude, thinking suddenly of how hard he had tried to talk Morgenthau into coming with him and how the old man's nerve had failed at the last. I don't have what it takes to be a hero, Morgenthau had said. I wish I did—but I don't. Heroes,

Burckhardt thought. Why do they have to be so damnably alone? Do *I* have what it takes?

He sat on the edge of the bed. John Thorne. Thorne would know what to do with the contents of the case: Yes, Thorne would *have* to know. There was nobody else, nobody.

He sat for a moment, tired now. If he thought back on his life, if he went down the years with a checklist of rights and wrongs, he could at least tell himself: This is one right thing. This. Then he remembered the faces of all the others, faces seen drifting in firelight. How many of them had tried to break the silence? How many? *I want it broken.*

He stared at his suitcase, which lay open on the rug. His clothing was piled neatly to one side; on the other side lay various files, indications of order, of that kind of compulsion to tidiness a man might feel when— What did they say about putting your affairs in order? He bent down, flicked through the files. Certificates of existence, of the tiny scratches and indentations you make on your way through life. A file of insurance documents, another containing mortgage papers for the house in Fredericksburg, birth certificates, marriage—all that was missing was the one nobody ever saw: the death certificate.

And then, shaken, he let the files fall from his fingers. No, dear God no— He rummaged again through the pile of manila folders. No. How could it be? How could he have done this? Of all things this? He lifted one file, flicked through the pages. *Asterisk.* How could he have *done* such a damnably stupid thing? Telephone, he thought, telephone, call Thorne, tell him, tell him—whatever I left for you isn't what I meant to leave, I screwed it up, whatever you've got isn't what you're supposed to have, dear God—

He picked up the telephone. There was a noise at the door. He put the receiver down, listened. The racing of his own blood. The curse of his own fear, his stupidity. Someone was trying to turn a key in the lock. Outside, trying to come in. He stared at papers in the manila folder. Do something. Now. Quickly. For a moment, he couldn't move, he couldn't think, there was only the rise of some savage panic inside him. The scraping at the door. Oh dear Christ, Christ. He took the papers from the folder. Thorne—what did I leave for John Thorne?

He rushed into the bathroom. Cigarette lighter. A flame. He held the papers over the bowl, put the flame to the edge of the papers, watched the papers catch and curl and blacken, saw cinders drift into the water. His fingers burned. Flame darkened his fingernails. It was pain, but no pain. He stuffed cinders, charred paper, even the bits that had not caught fire, deep into the water and then he flushed the cistern. The papers rose up and for a moment he thought they wouldn't go away, they would simply float there, but then he saw them sucked downward as the water receded. He lowered his head, hearing the door of the room open. He stepped out of the bathroom and looked at the man who had come in, a dark middle-aged man, a picture of some mindless viciousness. And he couldn't move, couldn't make himself move. All he could think of was his own mistake, his own utter stupidity and, behind that, behind that on some other stratum of awareness, how everything now was so senselessly lost.

Sharpe's office was air-conditioned, a fact for which Tarkington was thankful. Sharpe had his feet up on the desk. His eyelids were heavy, half lowered, giving him the appearance of some kind of lizard. His mouth was tight, like a rubber band drawn to its limits. Tarkington looked at the green filing cabinets and wondered what they contained. Secrets. The reasons for everything. You took orders because of what passed across Sharpe's desk and went into those fucking cabinets. One day, Tarkington thought, I'd like to look.

He felt uneasy here. The inner sanctum. Sharpe by nature. You had to keep on your toes or else it was Shanghai or Warsaw or bloody Reykjavik. Tarkington had had his fill of faraway places. He rubbed his huge hands together and slipped a thumb inside the white belt of his leisure suit. Getting fat, he thought. Time for the rubber suit.

He gazed back at the cabinets.

"When he went to the restaurant what was he carrying?" Sharpe suddenly asked.

"He had a case. One of the small square kind. You know."

"When he left, what was he carrying?"

Tarkington felt a certain dryness in his mouth.

"Was he still carrying the case?" Sharpe asked. He had picked up a yellow pencil and was pointing it toward Tarkington.

"Sure he was," Tarkington said. "I saw him."

Reykjavik, he thought.

The restaurant had been crowded. The day hot. He had dreamed at times. He had watched the hostess. He had watched her tits and the movement of her buttocks beneath the long dress.

"Did you see Thorne arrive?"

"I was gone by then," Tarkington said. "I followed the old man outside. I called you."

Sharpe closed his eyes. He gave the impression of a man who has spent a lifetime suffering around clowns, incompetents, and plain old-fashioned jerks.

"Then Lykiard will get the case later?"

"When he goes through the room, sure," Tarkington said.

"Sure," Sharpe said.

Tarkington lit a cigarette, watching Sharpe's face for some sign of disapproval, and finding none. He relaxed a little. He hadn't seen the old geezer leave the cocktail lounge. He just hadn't noticed. A moment's distraction. You turn your head away, a split second. The balance is gone. He stared at the half-open slats of the venetian blinds. The sky over D.C. was growing dark.

Sharpe smiled unexpectedly, slyly: "Then it's going to be clean. Clean as a whistle."

"Sure," Tarkington said. He watched the smile fade, the soporific expression come back. Christ, he thought. You never know where you stand with this baby. A case, an attaché case, he tried to remember, he tried to sift the snapshots of the recent past. Zilch. Christ. He felt a sudden hopelessness. You go along, you take orders, you assume there's some sense, some deeper meaning, to them, you don't ask questions, you don't know, maybe you're curious and maybe not, but you do what you're told anyhow—then one time you look away. A girl's tits. The sight of her thighs. And you're screwed.

Let there be a case in the old man's room.

Sharpe looked at his watch again. He glanced at some papers in front of him, then at the telephone. Tarkington thought of Lykiard. Lykiard never asked any questions either.

They drank martinis and watched TV, but Thorne could not concentrate on the movie. It was something of Eisenstein's; dark shadows and melodramatic eye close-ups and surging music. He looked at Marcia. She was wearing cutoffs and a halter top, lounging on the sofa with her legs crossed. Earlier, after the shower, they had discussed marriage. It wasn't something either of them particularly felt they needed; and yet there seemed an inevitable drift toward it. He watched the black-and-white images change.

Marriage, he thought. *Should I get married, should I be good?* Who was it that had written those lines?

But it was Burckhardt who was uppermost in his mind. The old man had reached the rank of major general, but what was his history? Thorne seemed to recall that, during the war years, his father and Burckhardt had been involved in an intelligence-gathering agency. Later, after Truman had come into office and Thorne's father had been elected to the U.S. Congress for the first time, they had worked together on a committee responsible for financing and overseeing the success of Operation Vittles against the Russian blockade of Berlin. Burckhardt, at that time, had been a liaison officer between the congressional committee and the staff of Lucius Clay, the American commander in Germany. Later still, after Thorne's father had been elected to the U.S. Senate, they had continued their acquaintance, building it over the years into a friendship.

This much Thorne knew: the periphery of the major general's career where it came in contact with that of his father. But what about the spaces? What had Burckhardt done during the late 1950s, the 60s, and in recent years? What then? It would be relatively easy to find out—if he wanted. It would also be reasonably easy to assume that the major general had, as Marcia suggested, freaked out. Blank pages, after all. The suburban restaurant, the out-of-the-way rendezvous. You could see the shadowy outlines here of some imagined conspiracy on the old man's part. If that was what you wanted to see.

"Doesn't this flick interest you?" Marcia was asking.

"I haven't been following it," Thorne said.

Marcia finished her martini. "Seminal in the history of film, Philistine," she said. She got up from the sofa to mix fresh drinks. He watched her move around in the half-dark of the living room.

She brought him a drink. "Notice the olive impaled on the toothpick," she said.

"Which I loathe."

"Exactly." She sat on the arm of his chair. "I know what you're thinking. You're wondering if it should be a civil or a religious ceremony, right? It's befuddling your brain. How many guests, where do we honeymoon, crap like that."

"You're a regular mind reader," he said.

"Ah-hah." She touched him lightly beneath the chin. "The old warrior's empty manuscript, no?"

"Something like that." He tasted his martini.

She was silent for a time, watching him, the palm of one hand flat against the side of her face. "I never thought I'd love somebody like you," she said.

"Who did you imagine loving?"

"Dunno. A professor of English lit, maybe. You know the kind, spectacles, quiet manner, bookish. But a thunder-ball in the bedroom."

"Are you complaining?" Thorne asked.

"Uh-huh." She leaned forward and kissed him. She tasted faintly of vermouth, olives.

When she drew her face back she said: "Maybe the old guy was trying to tell you something. It's like how we students of lit are always being told to read between the lines."

"Except there aren't any lines," Thorne said. "There aren't any lines."

Now, now there was no more running, nothing to run for—beyond fear there was a vacuum, a place where you accepted your end. His assailant's eye, a bird's eye, the predator. He felt strong hands on his shoulders, a vise around his neck, and he was being dragged to the edge of the swimming pool. Survive, goddamn, survive. It came back, when you didn't need it and couldn't do a damn thing with it, when you had become resigned to an ending, it came back. He scratched, kicked, bit. Thorne, he thought— Thornethornethornethorne. It was useless.

The edge of the pool. Blue water. Parasols overhead, umbrellas tilting, the dark sky beyond, hazy stars over the city. Kicking, clawing. *Live. To die like this without a fight.* A rat, a dog, nothing more. And what had he left behind him but silences? His face was held beneath water and he was confused—had he been dragged out of the room? that iron hand clamped across his mouth? dragged, drawn, it was a dream, it was a nightmare of falling from impossible heights. A file, a folder, everything important just sucked away— His face was being held beneath water. Panic, the urge to fight, no strength left, nothing remaining. He opened his eyes. The underwater lights blinded with the intensity of fireworks exploding in his brain. Thorne— He attempted to raise his face from the water. No. Couldn't do it. No. Nothing left. He saw his own limp hands sink in swirls of foam under the surface, he felt himself drift and drift and dream—and the dream was taking him round the edges of some impermeable darkness toward which, inevitably, he was sinking.

Tarkington was looking through the slats of the blind at the night sky when the telephone rang. He turned around, saw Sharpe pick it up. Tarkington felt tense. He was aware of perspiration on his forehead, his upper lip. He thought: Stupid fucker. Screw yourself. What did they teach you?

Observe, observe, observe.

At all times.

There can be no relaxation of vigilance in the field.

He stared at Sharpe's knuckles. They were white beneath the glow of the desk lamp.

Sharpe said into the receiver: "You got the case?"

Tarkington waited.

Sharpe was quiet for a time, then he put the receiver down slowly, deliberately, as if he were afraid of missing the cradle.

"Lykiard?" Tarkington asked. He poured himself a cone of ice water from the cooler, watching the bubble rise and burst.

"Lykiard, right," Sharp said. "Lykiard. But no sign of the case. Anywhere."

Tarkington felt blank, dizzy.

"It's got to be somewhere, Jesus," he said.

Sharpe smiled at him coldly: "I wonder where, Tarkie."

2:

Sunday, April 2

THE MAN WITH THE HIGH-POWERED BINOCULARS HAD BEEN
waiting for the sun to come up and an end to the long, cold
desert night. He had lain most of the night in his down-
filled sleeping bag in the tent, shivering, now and then
sleeping, waking intermittently because the cold had gotten
through to him. When he emerged from his tent it was
dawn, the landscape beginning to fill with a soft red light.

He had camped in an arroyo. Now he scrambled up out
of the dry wash, binoculars hanging from his neck, his
hands gloved, a balaclava hat around his ears. He lay flat
on his stomach. In the east the rising sun was the color of
molten lava. But still there was no warmth. The saguaros
cast long flattened shadows that were strangely motionless
in a way that suggested they would never change, regardless of how high the sun might climb. A terrible landscape, the man thought. He had read books in praise of it,
he had read the works of those who had come to love
such a place, but he knew that he himself would always
feel alien out here. It was hostile. The only book he had
come to trust was the one he had in his backpack: *Desert
Survival*.

He looked through the binoculars.

Out of focus. He adjusted them for a time. The sun
climbed almost perceptibly. There was not a cloud anywhere in the sky. In the west there hung a fading moon
and beyond that the stars were one by one going out. The
sun and the moon together in the sky: didn't that mean
some form of calamity?

He looked through the lenses. He swung the glasses
slowly left to right, then back again.

20

Beyond the perimeter fence that lay some distance away he saw a stationary truck, a jeep, and a solitary figure in uniform stroll along the inside of the electrified fence. The man had an automatic weapon slung against his side, presumably an M-16. From this perspective he could not see the man's face but he could guess easily at the expression on it: bored, dutifully watchful, longing for his relief to come.

He trained his lenses now on the building beyond the sentry. Low, flat, painted white: no sign of activity. He was restless because for days there had been no special activity. Guards came and went. There was a black one, tall and powerful in his build. There was a short Caucasian who wore glasses. There was the one with red hair. But nothing ever seemed to happen around the building itself. There were no windows. The guards went inside. The guards came out. Night followed day and the sun and the moon appeared simultaneously in the sky.

He watched for a while, then went back down the slope to his small tent. He had a portable tape recorder with a casette of the sounds of desert birds. He had a book on the habits of the cactus wren and another on the vulture. He had a small loose-leaf notebook in which he was meant to record his observations of the behavior of these birds.

Precautions. Blinds. He was a bird watcher.

He boiled some water on a Coleman stove and made coffee. As he drank it, he thought: Thirteen days now. Thirteen days of nothing. I have begun to feel like Robinson Crusoe.

He sympathized with the sentries inside the fence, but they at least had the comfort of knowing for sure when they would be relieved. And presumably they existed on a more attractive diet than raisins, dried apricots, chocolate and coffee. He poured himself a second cup.

He had been told to stay fifteen days. After that, somebody else would come to take his place. Sometimes he wondered what would happen if nobody came, if Hollander simply forgot all about him. I sure as hell wouldn't hang out around here until I starved, not for one fifty a week, expenses, and a suntan.

He thought about Hollander and wondered if what he had heard on the grapevine were true—that Hollander had gone soft, lost his touch, that retirement from service had rendered him senile. Maybe there was something to it; maybe this desert jaunt was symptomatic of some kind of decay in Hollander. After all—where was the point to the exercise? The installation was a hard missile site, so why the fuck did Hollander want it kept under observation like this? Afraid the Russians might just sneak down like vultures from the great desert sky and wing off with a couple of nifty secrets? Or maybe Ted Hollander had had bad dreams of the Yellow Menace bellying across the dust to the perimeter fence and making away with a ICBM? You couldn't tell with old patriots, he thought: they went one way or another, especially when, like Hollander, they had time on their hands and not much to think about except a dead career and a bad marriage. Old patriots: it was either the hammer and sickle route or a lonely walk into a kind of madness.

Madness. I must be mad. Not Ted Hollander. This godforsaken place, this shitty desert. Christ, how he loathed Escalante.

Why had he ever allowed Ted Hollander to talk him into this?

He stared at the khaki walls of his pup tent, sipped his coffee, and lit a cigarette from his dwindling supply.

Why?

When Thorne woke, Marcia was already up. She had made coffee and was sitting at her desk in the living room, reading Coleridge. Thorne walked through and looked at her sleepily.

"Truth is the divine ventriloquist," she said. "Did you know that?"

He gazed at her a moment, scratched his head, and went out into the kitchen for coffee. When he returned she was sitting with her bare feet up on the top of the desk. He had often wondered how such a beautiful woman could possess such ugly toes. They were short and stubby and stunted. If they had been fingers, you would have guessed arthritis.

"I'm quoting Coleridge," she said. "When he was accused of plagiarism, he answered by saying that truth is the divine ventriloquist. It's charming. I wonder what he would have been like in bed."

Thorne sat down on the sofa. All night long he had

dreamed. Strange, jumbled images. His father dressed in robes and receiving an honorary degree from the Barber-shop Singers of America. His mother leaping off the Brooklyn Bridge. Marcia turning the pages of a book with blank after blank. What are you reading? he had asked. An interesting novel, she had said.

It was fading.

He got up and went to the balcony doors. The sky was gray, the morning drizzled rain. Marcia came and stood beside him and hooked her thumbs in the loops of her jeans.

"You snored all night, my love," she said.

"I never snore," Thorne answered.

"Last night you did." She put an arm lightly around his waist. "You look positively inelegant in the morning, you know that?"

He yawned, pressing his face against the glass.

He felt inexplicably depressed. The dream, the sense of something disturbing him, some revolt of the unconscious: it was as if he had dreamed the dream of a stranger. He glanced at Marcia, who was pushing her dark hair away from her face.

She was watching him in an anticipatory way that made him feel uneasy. At times it seemed to him that she had an uncanny capacity for seeing straight into his head, an ability to know what he was thinking or feeling; a creature of intuition. He reached for her hand and held it. Loving her had come easily to him, so easily that he could not remember with any exactitude the shape of his life before he had met her. He saw, stretching behind himself, a dreary texture of days, hours spent on one or other of the anonymous subcircuits that pass as Washington social life, the harmless cocktail parties and dinners that conceal, just beneath the surface, a curious sense of desperation—he had gone beyond all that now. Whatever emptiness, whatever absences, had existed before, Marcia had managed to fill.

He looked beyond her at the litter of papers spread across the desk, the pile of opened books, blunt pencils, the yellow felt-tipped pens she used to outline passages; he loved even this, the mess of her life, the incoherent traces she left lying around her.

She had turned her face away from him; she was looking through the glass at the gray day. He leaned toward her and kissed the side of her face. She smiled.

"What was that for?" she asked.

"It was a simple impulse," he said.

"Do it again," she said. "I like simple impulses."

He put his arms around her and held her against himself a moment. He was conscious of rain on the glass falling in slow lines, of the smell of her dark hair, of how her hands pressed against the base of his spine. He looked at the desk once more. Her books, her studies, they were somehow locked away from him—like secrets. It was as if there were an aspect of her life he didn't quite know how to explore.

And then he noticed, beneath the desk, the major general's attaché case. The sight of it surprised him in some way, almost as if he had expected it to vanish in the night and the enigma of the major general with it. He stared at it. For a moment he was tempted to pick it up and go through it again, but he resisted: he had done that whole bit already. The lining, looking for some secret compartment and feeling quite ridiculous. Nothing but the manila folder and the blank papers that had been so *vital* to the old man. What am I meant to do with it now? he wondered. Keep it until the old fellow decides he wants it back?

He walked to the window.

Marcia said: "I'm going to work for a bit. Do you mind?"

"I might go into the office, I don't know," he said. He felt the uselessness of a rainy Sunday all around him; Marcia trapped inside her books, incommunicado. A tourist could find something useful to do in this town, but he had seen it all. He shrugged.

"This damn thesis is beginning to feel like a kid that's been in my womb for five years," Marcia said, more to herself than to Thorne. She read, turning pages with her left hand, making notes with her right. He wondered where it would finally lead: an assistant professorship at Old Dominion University or a lectureship at St. Cloud State College? Whatever.

He turned once again to the balcony door. There were great rain clouds across the city and not a trace of sun; and yet there was heat compressed into the day and he had the feeling that sooner or later an electric storm might break.

Sharpe parked his car, a 1975 Buick, in the gravel driveway and walked up toward the house. It was pseudo Tudor and it depressed him. He expected the rain that now fell across the frontage to wash the black beams away. That was how they looked, as if they had been painted weakly on a white surface. He plunged his hands into the pockets of his raincoat. He went around the back of the house, feeling like a tradesman, like a boy delivering something.

He looked through the misted glass of the conservatory that had been built onto the house at the rear. He tapped lightly on a pane, waited, nothing happened, then he tapped again. He looked across the expanse of the back lawn and thought: Flawless. Flawless the lawn, the rockery, the fountain, the trees that stood like a great green screen against the cedar fence.

The conservatory door opened.

He went inside. He felt damp and miserable but he knew Dilbeck would not ask him to take his coat off or have coffee. Dilbeck wouldn't even invite him to sit down.

"Terrific weather," Dilbeck was saying. He was doing something to a plant. Sharpe encountered a whole world of ignorance: who cared about plants? Dilbeck was cutting, with the quiet precision of a surgeon, against the stem.

"Propagation by stem cutting," Dilbeck said. He wore glasses low on his nose, like some decrepit schoolteacher. His manner was similar. He lectured in a condescending way, as if everyone around him were mindless and incapable of even momentary concentration.

Sharpe watched him. He was old and stooped and he wore an unfashionable tweed jacket with leather elbow patches. From somewhere inside the house there was the sound of scales being played on a piano. There was an unmarried daughter, Sharpe remembered, an ugly girl with teeth beyond the assistance of orthodontia. She must have taken up the piano; probably because nobody had taken her up the aisle.

"Propagation," Dilbeck said. He put aside his knife and held in the palm of his hand a stem to which was attached a couple of leaves. What's the fuss? Sharpe wondered. He understood that, through Dilbeck's eyes, something of a botanical miracle was going on.

Dilbeck wandered through the plants. Trestle tables were covered with them, a regular jungle. The old man paused here and there, with Sharpe in dutiful attendance, indicating this plant or that. A pomegranate he had grown from seed. An unusual coffee plant already about to flower. What with the cost of coffee these days, Sharpe thought. Grow your own beans. An exquisite crossandra, a magnificent taffeta. *Do re me fa sol la ti do.* She was as awful on the piano as she was to behold. Clink, miss, clank, clink.

Dilbeck wrapped his new cutting in a moist plastic bag.

Sharpe watched rain slither down the conservatory windows. Miserable, miserable day.

"Something about an attaché case," Dilbeck said.

"Yes," Sharpe said.

"Your people are sometimes rather ham-fisted, Sharpe." Dilbeck took off his glasses, put them inside a case, snapped the case shut. "Don't you teach them how not to be bulls in china shops?"

Sharpe said something feebly inaudible about the quality of recruits. Can't get the men these days, not like it used to be, blah, blah blah.

Dilbeck listened in silence. Then he said, "We must get the damn thing back, mustn't we?"

"Yes," Sharpe said.

"The problem is that it is now in all likelihood in the possession of our young friend Thorne." Dilbeck frowned. He raised a hand and began to inscribe patterns in the condensation upon the glass.

"In all likelihood," Sharpe said. He had kicked Tarkie's ass, but the guy was superupholstered. Thick. You couldn't always make your point with Tarkie.

"It's simple, then," Dilbeck said. "We get it back."

Sharpe concurred by nodding his head.

"Then again, it's not so simple, Sharpe."

Sharpe, once again, agreed.

"Our young friend is well connected. That's always a problem. Bad publicity. Leaks. He has friends in high places."

Sharpe was beginning to feel suffocated, as if the plants were robbing him of something vital, strangling him.

Dilbeck smiled. He had beautiful white dentures. The piano went on playing. It was a joyless version of "The Harp That Once Through Tara's Halls" and every alternative note she hit was a bummer.

"My daughter," Dilbeck said. "Learning. A little hamfisted too."

Sharpe smiled now. He wanted to agree and at the same time to disagree. He wanted to say: She's coming along real fine.

"It should be no great problem to recover the case. I assume your people are capable of that?"

Breaking and entering, simple. "Yes," he said.

"That damned Burckhardt," Dilbeck said suddenly. He grinned. "Kept your people on their toes anyhow. I give him that."

There was a silence. Dilbeck continued to draw patterns in the condensation.

"But we don't know what the case contains, do we? We don't know what kind of information the old man passed along to our young friend. We don't know. We don't know what Thorne knows right now, do we?" Dilbeck turned his hands over, then rubbed them against the sides of his shapeless gray flannels. "There's a whole area of sheer ignorance here, Sharpe. How are my colleagues going to take it?"

Sharpe was tense. He wished himself miles away. He wondered vaguely if he had accumulated any sick leave, or if there was a vacation coming up.

"Simple breaking and entering," he said. "We'll get it."

"Yes," Dilbeck said. "But anything else, for the moment, is out of the question. You understand that? You must impress that on your people in the strongest terms. Am I making myself plain? No accidents, no accidents in swimming pools or automobiles, or anywhere else. Not for the moment."

Sharpe understood. He reassured Dilbeck. He would have gone down on his knees to reassure Dilbeck. Mercifully, the piano stopped. He turned and saw the daughter come into the conservatory. She was dressed in blue jeans with a blue cotton shirt that hung outside. She was plump, her teeth the kind usually referred to as buck, and she

moved with a strange self-consciousness, as if all her life
she had inadvertently bumped into things.

"Hi," she said.

Dilbeck said, "My daughter. Emily."

Sharpe nodded. "I liked your playing," he said.

"Really?" She smiled. It was as if her mouth came
leaping right off her face, a contortion.

"Well," Dilbeck said, "keep me posted."

"Certainly," Sharpe said.

The daughter went with him to the door. He realized
she was flirting outrageously with him, allowing her
breasts to rub his arm. He stepped gladly out into the rain.

"Come again," she said.

"I look forward to it," he answered and walked back to
his Buick. He drove away from the house as quickly as he
could even though, on account of a failure of the windshield wipers, he could hardly see where he was going.

No rough stuff, he thought. Just the attaché case.

And he wondered why it was so goddamn important.
Military secrets? Blueprints of a prototype bomber? In this
game, you worked as if your peripheral vision were irre-
parably damaged.

2

Across the park, a dark-green Porsche drew up in the
rain. The doors opened and Hollander, sitting some distance away on a damp bench, saw his kids get out. The
Porsche moved off slowly down the block and out of sight.
Hollander rose from the bench and began to walk in the
direction of the children. The sight of them caused him
more pain than usual. The architects of the divorce had
stipulated that he might have access to the children once
every three months—which had seemed needlessly harsh
to him. But the shit in the fan of legal maneuvering had
left him helpless. He wasn't, as the judge so rightly said,
much of a father: he was an *inveterate absentee*. It was an
unkind epitaph and one he might have answered by saying: But your Honor, I was busy keeping this country safe
for democracy. Ah, he might have said that.

Now, crossing the wet grass, feeling as if the weather
had conspired against him to make even this brief encounter a miserable one, he tried to keep from thinking that

this might be the last time, the very last time. The pain of
that prospect was sharp; it was like something about to
rupture in his brain. He approached them: they looked
small, abandoned, wretched in their colored raincoats. The
baby, Anna, six years of age, was holding Jimmy's hand in
the fashion of a child who sees only one anchor to the
familiar. The other boy, Mark, ten, was scraping his shoes
on the ground and looking dejected.

Hollander stopped. They hadn't seen him yet. There was
time, he thought. I could turn around, walk away; it
would be just one more rotten unfatherly act. He shivered
in the rain, turning up the collar of his coat. Anna had
seen him. She had broken free from Jimmy and was running across the damp grass toward him. When she reached
him he put his arms around her and lifted her up in the
air. She smiled uncertainly, wanting to be raised higher
but afraid of the fall. He held her close against him—the
smell of a small child, how quickly he had forgotten that.
It wasn't the sweet-sour scent of milk anymore, but of
soap and a suggestion of peppermint on the breath.

"Anna," he said.

She had the same bright blue eyes as her mother, the
same attractive mouth. Loss, he thought. It's all a cat-
alogue of loss, the dross of years, the drift of time, and
what is there left to show at the end of the game? Three
kids who barely knew him; three kids who, pretty soon,
wouldn't want ever to have known him.

Mark, followed by Jimmy, was coming across the grass.
Hollander wasn't sure: did you shake hands with a ten-
year-old son or did you kiss him? He felt a small, surprising panic, bewildered by his own indecision. Mark stopped
a few feet away, hands stuffed in the pockets of his raincoat. He looked briefly at Hollander, then away.

"Hi, Dad," he said.

Hollander caught his breath. If he had a favorite of the
three it was Mark; a sensitive boy, someone easily hurt,
someone Hollander had scarred in the warfare of his dete-
riorating marriage. He wanted to do something to make it
up to Mark—but what? Jimmy, the oldest, his face slightly
smitten with the acne of early adolescence, put his hand
out to be shaken. Hollander took it and held it a moment.
Jimmy was awkward, unsure of himself, and moved as
though there were no muscular coordination in his body.

"It's terrific to see you guys," Hollander said. "It's really great."

They were all silent for a time; Hollander looked across the park. The gray drizzling rain fell through the trees; there was an elegiac quality to the landscape. Hollander felt the sadness again.

"Okay, any suggestions about what we do?" he said.

"It's raining," Jimmy said.

"That's not news." Anna looked at her brother with some disgust.

"What can you do in the rain?" Jimmy said.

"Well—what do you guys want to do?" Hollander asked. He was thinking of the inside of a movie theater, the comfort of darkness, the lack of any need to communicate. For a moment he felt he wanted to say: *This is probably the last time. The last time.* No, he thought. Not that. He could feel the rain slither across his face.

"Ice cream," Anna said.

"Aw," Jimmy said. "That's all you ever think about."

"Mark," Hollander said. "What about you?"

Mark looked at his father a moment; and Hollander saw it in the eyes, the undeclared sentence: *You killed something in me.* Hurt, he had to look away from the kid's face. His heart was beating quickly, he felt dizzy, upset. What did I do to them? What am I about to do? Is there any more hurt left?

Mark stared down at the grass: "I'm easy," he said.

"A movie?" Hollander asked, hoping.

Jimmy said, "We went to a movie last time."

"I remember," Anna said. "*The Bad News Bears.* I'd like to see it again. Can we see it again?"

Jimmy mumbled something.

"Let's walk," Hollander said. "Then we can decide, okay?"

There was a duck pond, deserted in the rain. A few bedraggled birds, looking as if they had barely survived a tempest, floated bleakly on the surface. Hollander held Anna's hand. It was hot and damp and small and vulnerable. You could make out a convincing case, he thought, for the merits of self-hatred.

They paused by the pond. So far as Hollander could see there was nobody else in sight. It was a moment of ex-

traordinary emptiness, as if the day had been accidentally
inverted and all manner of living things spilled away.

Mark asked, "Are you still writing your book, Dad?"

Hollander looked at the boy. He had mentioned the
book last time and the kid hadn't forgotten. The child's
mind, he thought; like flypaper sometimes. He thought of
blank pages in a typewriter. The old intelligence operative
spills his guts. Tells all. Dazzling exposé of the dark underside of the law. Exclamation points. Even as you sleep,
America, your agents are frequently performing scummy
deeds. Even as you snore.

"It's slow," he said.

"I guess," Mark said.

"Do you think ducks like Juicy Fruit?" Anna asked.

They continued around the pond. Anna tried to feed a
stick of chewing gum to a duck, who circled it warily before swimming away. The rain increased. They went inside
a shelter and sat silently on the bench. Mark looked at the
graffiti on the walls.

"How's your mother?" Hollander asked.

"She got a new hairstyle," Anna said.

"Is it nice?"

"It's okay," Jimmy said. "She's okay."

Hollander was silent. He stared through the rain, thinking of Myers out there at Escalante, the sunshine. Myers
was a risk, he supposed; but so was everything connected
with Asterisk. So was everything. He had to be sure. They
had moved it once before, in the darkness they had
transported it from Oscura, New Mexico, to Escalante.
And if they moved it again, he wanted to know where it
was being taken. But it was a risk. He looked at his
daughter and realized she had been asking a question he
hadn't heard. Myers, he thought: I have to find somebody
to relieve Myers pretty soon.

"I asked why some birds swim and some don't," Anna
said.

"I don't think I know the answer," Hollander said. "Do
you, Jimmy?"

Jimmy shrugged. He picked up a pebble and threw it
toward the pond. There was a bird in flight, a small dark
bird heading for the trees.

"Nobody answers my questions," Anna said.

Hollander put his hand on her shoulder and squeezed

gently, conscious all at once of the child's fragility. Easy to break, to wound. She laid her head against his arm, closing her eyes a moment. He was aware of the sound of rain in the trees, the slow movement of a wind: the noises of solitude, uneasy, uncertain. He reached inside his pocket and took out a pack of English Ovals and stared at the emblem on the lid of the box.

Asterisk, he thought. And he imagined waking one morning to find the planet aflame, everything lost, cindered, swept away in a final rage of violence. These kids, these vulnerable kids . . . He was afraid all at once, afraid for himself, afraid because of the innocence of children. *It could happen,* he thought. *That was the trouble.* Sometimes, sometimes in the worst of moments, he would see himself as an actor in some play that is turning, inexorably, to reality, something more sharp, more dreadful, than mere fantasy. And sometimes he would wake shaking in the mornings. He put his arm around Anna; she moved closer to him.

"Rowley never does that," she said.

"Doesn't he?"

"Well, he's not a real father anyway," she said.

Mark began to whistle quietly, then broke off. There was a long silence. Then Jimmy said: "Rowley's all right."

Mark scuffed his feet on the ground and said: "It's a drag just sitting here. Why don't we go to a movie?"

Hollander looked at the boy. He felt a sense of jealousy suddenly—an unexpected sensation—at the thought of Rowley embracing these children, trying to behave like a father toward them; and the feeling had been quickened by Jimmy's defense of the man. *Rowley's all right.* Sure he is, Hollander thought. He's got my wife, my family, everything—what am I left with? Nothing save for some mad sense of mission. Why me? why do I have to deal with it? Why not somebody else?

Self-pity, self-hatred: how much further down the ladder could you slide? And now Mark had suggested a movie for the same reasons, Hollander suspected, that he himself had made the suggestion before. For the darkness, the safety, the blinding of any awkward sensations.

"Well? How about it?" Mark asked.

"Let's put it to a vote," Hollander said. "Who wants to see a movie?"

Jimmy was the last to put his hand up.

"Okay, it's settled," Hollander said.

They walked out of the shelter. He was conscious of how, as they walked through the rain, the kids seemed to cluster closely around him, as if he were a form of protection for them. He held Anna's hand and wished, with the kind of wishing that is a futile mental exercise in regret, that he had done more for them—been a better parent, a better person, perhaps even a value that they might hold up for themselves in the times that lay ahead. But it wasn't going to be anything like that. The only prospect he could see was their denunciation of him, followed by the protective veneer of amnesia.

I'm going to betray my country, he thought.

Since I've betrayed everything else, does it make any difference now?

Anna tugged her hand away. She paused to scratch her leg. Then she looked at him.

"You look nicer when you smile," she said.

He watched her a moment. And then he smiled.

3

Thorne didn't go to his office. While Marcia worked, he lazed in front of the TV and idly watched some of the action of a women's golf classic. Sunny California. It was tedious. He tried the other channels. A rerun of *Lucy,* a religious drama produced by the Paulist fathers about an alcoholic wife, and on the public channel a dreary analysis of the Martian surface. Outside, it continued to rain. He stood on the balcony for a while and watched it fall, possessed with the notion that it was somehow better than Sunday-afternoon TV.

When Marcia announced that she had had enough of Coleridge they went out to eat. They drove around for a while in his VW, debating restaurants. She wanted Chinese, she didn't want Chinese. French then? American? Greek?

They ended up at a MacDonald's, eating hamburgers and french fries in the car.

"I wonder how much sugar there is in a Big Mac?" she asked.

"They don't put sugar in Big Macs," he said.

"They put sugar everywhere," she answered. "You just can't escape it."

"You're out of your mind," he said.

"The book was called *Sugar Blues* and I suggest you do yourself a favor by reading it, buster." She licked her fingers.

"Cranks," he said. "Health-food faddists and three almonds every day will prevent cancer and you don't dare eat more than two eggs a day because of the fucking cholesterol."

"What a world," she said. "Pretty soon they'll leave us nothing."

They drove out toward Andrews Base.

He parked the car. They got out. Marcia pulled up the hood of her raincoat. In the gathering dark they could see the distant lights of planes and beyond, through spaces in the rainclouds, the occasional star.

"Do you know the names of the stars?" she asked.

"In grade school I did." There were thin, silvery vapor trails. He put his arm around her shoulder. She was shivering slightly.

"Twinkle, twinkle," she said. "I'm beginning to freeze my ass off."

"Let's go home then," he said.

They got back inside the VW. The clutch slipped in first and he promised himself he would have it repaired. Tomorrow, maybe. Or the next day.

Do something right, Tarkington thought. There is such a thing as making amends. The door was no problem. What was the problem was how it had to look good. He stood in the darkness. No lights, he thought. He had never been quite able to overcome the curious sensation of trespassing, no matter how many times he did this kind of thing. A sense of intrusion. But orders, after all, were exactly that. He was thinking of Sharpe and how Sharpe's face had had the look of thunder about it. One day he'd like to tell Sharpe: Go fuck yourself, buddy. Just stick the job up your ass. You could easily console yourself with thoughts like that. Sharpe turning white as a sheet. Sharpe having a coronary occlusion. Before Sharpe, there had been Hollander, and even if Hollander had been a bit of a disciplinarian in his own way at least he had been human. He understood that you sometimes caught a cold or you had a grandmother who had just died and was about to be buried, things like that. But fucking Sharpe worked on the assumption that you weren't human and you had no human attachments.

I had a wife one time, Tarkington thought.

He gently knocked a desk over.

He opened drawers.

He scattered clothing around.

He put a portable typewriter into his canvas bag. He took the electric percolator. The stereo receiver. He didn't fuck with the records, they were too bulky. I wish Hollander was in charge again, he thought. I wish Sharpe would come down with mono or something. He took a china vase that he knew to be worthless. He dumped flowers and water on the rug. *An amateur job,* Sharpe had said. *Shouldn't be too hard for you to do that, Tarkie.*

When he was finished he left without closing the door behind him.

The two uniformed cops were blasé. They had been in too many burgled apartments and listened to too many irate citizens and now they took notes and made noises they had been trained to make.

"My goddamn thesis," Marcia said.

"Thesis?" one of the cops said. "Can you describe it?"

Thorne wandered around the apartment. The stereo was gone. The Olivetti. It had been battered pretty much anyhow. In the bedroom a few drawers had been rifled, but nothing was missing.

Marcia was sifting among the papers that lay on the rug. The desk had been overturned. Thorne wondered why. What was he—or they; maybe more than one—looking for? A wall safe? The two cops were listing the missing articles. Marcia began to put papers together.

"God damn it," she was saying. "It just isn't right."

One of the cops agreed. "Lady, we get an average of three like this every night of the week . . . you know? And I ought to tell you confidentially that the chances of getting your merchandise back, well, they're pretty slim."

The other cop stuck a slab of pink chewing gum in his mouth. He masticated audibly. Thorne went to the balcony and looked out. It was still raining.

"I don't give a shit for merchandise," Marcia said. "I'm only interested in my thesis."

Frantically, she was piling papers and books together. Thorne watched her. He had never seen her so upset.

"Has it been taken?" the cop chewing gum asked.

"How the hell will I know until I get this goddamn mess straightened out?" she said. She looked at him with exasperation. He scribbled something in his notebook.

"You make a list of what's missing," the other cop said. "Make a complete list. Serial number of the stereo, the typewriter, you know? Make a complete list."

When the cops had gone, Marcia flopped down on the sofa. Her fists were clenched.

Thorne sat beside her. "Okay," he said. "Okay, relax, relax."

"Shit, it pisses me off to think of some creep coming in here while we're gone and just . . ." Her voice trailed off.

"I know," Throne said. "Why don't you relax and I'll straighten things out?"

"You mind making me a drink?"

He mixed her a scotch and soda and one for himself. He sat on the arm of the sofa and looked across the mess. He could understand burglary; it was your ordinary larceny. But he couldn't understand the destruction that went with it. The mess, the chaos. What made somebody want to do that?

"I was fond of that Olivetti," Marcia said. "I was attached to that typewriter."

"I'll get you another," he said.

"Pica, not elite," she said.

He was silent for a time, looking across the apartment. A stranger, he thought. It made him uneasy. He couldn't imagine a face, a shape, someone forcing the door. Then he laughed.

"What's so funny?" she asked.

"I just realized he took the major general's case," he said. "Can't you picture his disappointment?"

"Yeah," Marcia said, and finished her drink.

3:

Monday, April 3

IT WAS IRRESISTIBLE. YOU COULD TRY TO BE SKEPTICAL about it, even cynical, but it remained irresistible. And Thorne had not become accustomed to the curious, somewhat discreet sense of power, the odd hush of history, that hung over the place. His own office was tiny, tucked away at the end of a corridor, but even when he closed his door and sat behind his desk he could feel the vibrations of the building, as if the center, the Oval Office, were the heart of a web from which all the strands were being spun. It wasn't as if he were familiar with that particular office, since he had been inside it only once and had talked directly with Foster only once, but the sensation—from the moment of passing the guard, showing your pass, entering—remained the same.

He had once tried to explain all this to Marcia. But so far as politicians, especially presidents, were concerned, she was a committed cynic. It's all greed and fear, she had said. *What you think is the reverence of history comes down to the crummy business of getting your ass reelected.*

It was more than that, he had tried to say.

It was much more. But he had begun to feel foolish in front of her. He had dried up. *Just don't let it go to your head, kiddo.*

When he got to his office on the morning after the burglary, the newspapers had already been stacked on his desk by Miss Grunwald, who came in at some ungodly hour and who took some perverse delight in staying as late as she could at night. Fiftyish, her gray hair dyed purple, she had survived the comings and goings of administra-

37

tions. She dated as far back as Eisenhower. Then she had
been a junior secretary in the typing pool, a mere stenog-
rapher. Now she was Bannerman's own private secretary
and, in that capacity, she was virtually the assistant chief
of staff.

She didn't like Thorne; nor did Thorne have any special
affection for her. She was a martyr, a complainer, she always worked harder than anybody else and for small
thanks. In her eyes was the light of some profound belief
in a sacred mission: that of keeping the White House running. He knew it gave her a personal pleasure to have the
morning newspapers on his desk long before his own arrival at 7:30. It was a task she could easily have delegated
but didn't.

Thorne took his jacket off, hung it on the back of his
chair, took out his notebook, and began to go through the
newspapers. The secretary from the adjoining office, Sally
Winfield, came in with his coffee.

"What's new in the news?" she asked.

Her regular greeting. He watched her set the coffee
down. She was a skinny, pretty girl of about twenty-two
who thought it was "a riot" to work in the White House.
It was said she had slept with someone over in Justice,
who repaid the favor by recommending her for this
position.

"More of the same," Thorne said. He was opening an
advance copy of *Newsweek*. There was a long article critical of Foster's handling of the economy. Inflation, unemployment. The same old song. He didn't even bother to
abstract it because he had sent it up before and Bannerman himself had called to suggest he might save himself
the trouble of such summaries unless—as the great man
put it—it was something "bright." He flipped through
Newsweek, marked an article about the proposed price
rises in steel, then opened *The New York Times*. A critical
article on the op-ed page: "Does Foster Understand Black
Africa?" He cut it out, put it to one side, read the letters.
Foster sometimes liked to look at stuff from correspon-
dents: the compliments from Out There. *I'm delighted to
see we have a president strong enough to stand up to the
OPEC countries,* one of them began. He began to snip it
out; it would make the Old Man happy.

His telephone rang. It was Farrago, the press officer.

Droopy Max, the corps called him; his sartorial inelegance had prompted the name—floppy bow ties that belonged to the dark ages of the polka dot fad, pepper-and-salt tweeds of the kind you might only encounter these days on the bodies of retired missionaries.

"You got the summaries?" Farrago asked.

"Just about," Thorne said.

"Lazy fart," Farrago said. "You guys that live in sin misdirect all your energies."

Thorne put the receiver down, and picked up the *Star.* Joseph Donaldson's syndicated column regularly machine-gunned the administration. *It has sometimes crossed my mind that our president's secrecy in government, despite all the fanfare and hype about openness, is almost a match for the furtive machinations of his near-namesake in South Africa. Take the recent strange decision to cut $3.3 billion from the defense budget* . . . Thorne finished reading, skimmed the *Post,* then called Sally Winfield back when he was ready to dictate.

She sat with her slate-gray dress hitched up her thigh; her small breasts were always highlighted by tight sweaters that suggested to Thorne some atavistic longing for the fashions of the late 1950s. He watched her take shorthand and listened to the sound of his own voice droning . . . *Campaign promises . . . trust . . . already broken . . .* When he had finished it was already 9:30 and Farrago was on the telephone again.

"Quit fucking around, Thorne. Bannerman's been chewing my ear off."

"She's typing right now," Thorne said.

"Is it true she can turn out eight words a minute if she's really hammering?" Farrago hung up.

Thorne walked into the adjoining office and watched the girl type. On a wooden stand beside her desk there was a bottle of nail polish, a nail file, two apples in a plastic bag.

"You better hurry it," he said.

She looked at him lazily: "It's not my fault if it's late, is it?"

He shrugged and went back to his own office. He stood at the window and watched a Secret Service agent playing with his walkie-talkie, moving along the edges of the lawn and muttering into his device. Overhead, a helicopter with the Air Force seal came into view. Thorne saw it hover a moment and then go out of sight.

He sat down behind his desk, put his feet up. Later, the provincials would start to come in. The Old Man always liked to know what was happening in the sticks and would read the summaries before going to bed. But the pressure's off, Thorne thought: it's off for a while. He closed his eyes, tried to relax. He could hear telephones ringing, the persistent clatter of IBMs, voices from the corridor. At times he found himself struggling with a sense of some weird incongruity, moments of uneasiness when he wondered what he was doing in this place at this particular time and where, in the long run, it might all be leading. If somebody had told him a year ago that he would be working in the White House he would have consigned this prediction to a category of things that included belief in a flat earth, the notion that the moon was made of Gorgonzola, and the idea of coming one fine day to love the poetry of S. T. Coleridge.

There had been two blurry years at Harvard doing law: what could you say about that? Humdrum: anathematic to him—the stifling weight of legal judgments, the dust of dilapidated precedents. It was followed by the obligatory year of doing Europe in a VW bus; a drifting time, a fragile existence at best, one day shading pretty much into the next. There was a lack of adhesive, of a glue that would hold the experiential things together. And what he had come to realize, almost as something of a shock, was that he needed an epoxy of some sort to keep the passages of time together in a purpose.

A purpose.

He went to the window. The Secret Service agent, as though he anticipated an outbreak of demons, a plague of protesters, appeared to be crouching in the shrubbery, his face turned in the direction of Penn Avenue. Thorne watched a moment; the raincoated figure stood suddenly upright and moved off in long exaggerated strides.

Journalism, he wondered: what had attracted him to that?

He had done the upstate New York newspaper bit—funerals, flower shows, Eagle scout awards, graduations, weddings: the minuscule events that were finally sandwiched between the ads that paid for the paper. He remembered long hours, bleak snowy winters, a dreary sense of a system enduring in a vacuum. Where was the outside world? the real world?

His telephone was ringing.

It was Duncannon, one of the legal aides, suggesting a lunch. Thorne declined. He knew the nature of these lunches, the floating conspiracies, the tiny struggles for position, for power, for the opening that would suggest a foothold on the Way Up. He put the receiver down and thought: *What am I doing here?* What part do I have in the whispers in the men's rooms, the quiet words in nearby restaurants, the confidences—both false and true—that are exchanged in the mess?

What indeed?

You had to be ambitious to make it around here; you had to want it badly, you had to *hurt* for it. Where the hell do I fit in this scheme of things? he wondered. Where do I fit? where do I go from here?

He had been in Albany, doing some press work for the Democratic Party, when Max Farrago had called. Out of the ether. It's basically a scissors-and-paste deal, Farrago had said, but keep in mind that it's White House scissors and White House paste. It was a tough thing to decline: the only thing that mystified him now was why *he* had been singled out. His father, of course—the recommendation of some old family friend, some power broker, whom he had never been able to identify. Even the dead, he thought, don't necessarily lose their touch.

He sat behind his desk again and idly picked up the *Post*. He leafed through the inside pages.

And there it was.

There it was.

An inside page, lower left column, no more than a couple of dark inches of type.

He read it once, twice, a third time.

Then he picked up his telephone and called Marcia.

She answered yawning, still half asleep.

"Did you see the morning paper?" he ask. "My old warrior apparently killed himself in a swimming pool at a motel."

She was silent for a time. He could see her stretched across the bed, the telephone in her hand; he could feel her fumble for something to say. What *do* you say? he wondered. *Suicide by drowning.* By drowning, he thought. *Major General Walter F. Burckhardt had had a long and distinguished career in the Air Force.* He picked up his scissors in one hand and thought: Do people choose that as a way out?

"I'm sorry, John. Was there family?"

"It mentions a wife somewhere," Thorne said. Drowning: what kind of fucking sense did that make?

"I'm sorry," she said again.

He mumbled something, hung up, snipped the item from the newspaper. Why? Jesus, why? Why did anybody want to kill himself? Loneliness, despair, the end of a long line of rejection, intolerable humiliation, dishonor—were any of these applicable to Burckhardt? He saw a small middle-aged man at a funeral. A handshake on a rainy dying day. A clap on the shoulder, a touch. Gentle, solicitous, sincere. Of all things, sincere. *Ben Thorne was a great man.* It was misty, uncertain, the intangible web of a memory. You step to the edge of the pool, then what? Do you jump in? or do you walk the steps at the shallow end and just keep on strolling? What state of mind? Christ almighty, what state of mind?

And the wife, the wife he had never seen. Had she been with Burckhardt in the motel? had she discovered him lying in the pool?

He shut his eyes: a man floating in the fake aquamarine of a pool, a corpse drifting through filtered chemicals, what condition of the heart, what poisoned state of mind, what emotional disintegration, spiritual decay—madness?

It's vital I see you, John.

Vital, he thought.

Well: it couldn't be vital now, could it?

He fingered the clipping and looked at the photograph of his father that hung near the window. It was a stern portrait taken some months before the senator's death. The eyes were humorless, lifeless, the expression in them numb and at the same time vaguely inquisitorial, as if the man had spent his life asking questions to which he knew there were no answers. It wasn't the man Thorne remembered. He had been upright, moral, qualities that might have been tedious in themselves, but they had been offset by a sense of humor.

The only thing Ben Thorne had never been heard to

joke about in his life was the Constitution of the United States. He knew the document backward, forward, sideways, by heart. Thorne remembered how, as a child, he had been obliged to listen again and again to the historic background of the document . . . a memory burned into him like a cinder in his brain. The question-and-answer sessions. The quizzes. *Who was the first postmaster of the United States? Who printed the Declaration of Independence? Why was Sam Adams not chosen to be a delegate to the Philadelphia Constitutional Convention?* Even now the names were imprinted in Thorne's mind, indelible, heroes all to his father: Patrick Henry, Roger Sherman, the giants Paine and Jefferson.

His father.

The slow demented dying of the man, the profound disintegration, the long and terrible nights of pain when it had seemed to Thorne that no one person should be allowed to suffer in such a way. Touching the cold hands, seeing the hollow cheeks, wiping saliva from the corners of the mouth with a handkerchief, listening to the monotonous, crazed monologues that had been prologues to dying. Christ: the death was a relief, the tears a release, the loss an end to anguish. I watched him, Thorne thought, I watched him die, I saw him go down, I saw a man I loved sink, a man who was at times a stranger, at times a friend, but always loved, always that. The old man . . .

He turned away from the photograph. He picked up the clipping again. The fading of old warriors, he thought. The senator and the major general: what kind of young men had they been? What had they hoped for? what disillusionments had they lived through? A man walks into a swimming pool fifteen years after his close friend has succumbed to the misery of brain cancer. Finished, done with, over.

He put the clipping down. The garbled voice on the telephone had been trying to tell him something. And maybe, just maybe, if I hadn't failed to keep the appointment, if there hadn't been an accident on the freeway, the major general would be alive now. No: you can't blame yourself. How could you predict the urge to self-destruction from a few hasty words on a telephone? You needed a special kind of clairvoyance for that.

He looked once more at the picture of his father, almost

as if he felt the photograph were accusing him of something. He put the clipping in his wallet and sat without moving for a long time. Then, finally, he shrugged, made a phone call, and arranged a lunch date and a favor.

2

In the Sunday edition of *The New York Times*, which he looked at propped up against a Heinz ketchup bottle, Hollander surveyed the usual front-page despair. There was fresh evidence linking the CIA with insurgency in a South American republic. Communism and bananas, Hollander thought. An indefatigable combination. Sleep easy, America. There was a story about President Foster's press conference of the day before. *The American people deserve open government. We don't want government by secret in this country.*

He looked through the window of the restaurant into the street. A truck had stalled in the center of the road and irate drivers were banging their horns.

He turned back to the newspaper.

Photographs of the Martian surface. No apparent sign of vegetation. Tough titty, he thought. You spend millions to send some flimsy craft out there only to discover a Sahara with rocks. The taxpayer was John Sucker. *We're still receiving pictures, still analyzing the data.*

Hollander doused his one remaining pancake with artificial maple syrup. The Russians were making noises in Africa while Amin was continuing to sever heads. The Cubans were discussing nothing, as usual, while supplying troops to cheapshit kingdoms in unlikely places. Without a sense of balance, Hollander thought, and a touch of humor, you could go whacko.

He drank some of his coffee, which tasted as if it were brewed entirely of chicory, and then he sat back and lit a cigarette. He watched the street again. The truck hadn't budged from the center of the road and the driver was giving the finger to the motorists behind him. A waitress loomed up at his table, a plain girl with intense acne.

"Everything okay?" she said. Her lapel badge said her name was Theresa.

"Just dandy, Theresa," he said.

She smiled and passed on to the next table. Hollander

looked at the faces of the other diners. There was a mindless quality to them all. They shoveled and chewed and swallowed. Sometimes you had to remind yourself that they experienced pain and sorrow and grief as well as joy and buttermilk pancakes. Only a humanist had the right to detest the species. He folded his newspaper over and wondered why it was so bulky. It could be reduced to a couple of sheets if it weren't for Bloomingdale's and Altman's and all the others. He opened the book review section, flipping the pages to the best-seller list. He hated this: it reminded him he had a contract with a New York house for his memoirs. He hadn't written a single page. He wasn't likely to. He hated the idea of words as mirrors.

As soon as you write about yourself, he thought, you start to wonder who the fuck you are.

He closed the book review, finished his coffee, lit another English Oval. Through the window, across the parking lot, a neon sign said PANCAKE PALACE.

We meet in the most hideous places, Hollander thought.

He looked at his watch. It was almost ten. Myers would be in his little tent. Probably masturbating. Myers had the slightly gray, somewhat jaded look of the inveterate jerker.

"I'm late. Sorry."

The man who sat down facing Hollander was tall, almost bald. What little hair he possessed was smeared with brilliantine and combed back flat and slick. He had long, anemic fingers. Hollander knew he could pass himself off as an undertaker. *This way to the crypt, Ladies and Gentlemen.* He wore a black coat that sparkled with raindrops.

"A few minutes," Hollander said, and shrugged.

The other man studied the menu. "Is a pancake like a blintz?" he asked.

"Try it and see," Hollander answered.

"And maple syrup," the man said. He looked questioningly at Hollander, one eyebrow arched. He had hollow cheekbones and the complexion of a worm. The All-Slavic Boy. I keep strange company, Hollander thought.

The other man, whom Hollander knew only as Brinkerhoff, called to the waitress. He ordered a short stack of buttermilk pancakes with butter and syrup. He put his hands flat on the table, one alongside the other, and studied them a moment, as if they were not his own and might at any second leap up in the air.

The truck was being towed away outside. There was the flashing orange light of a breakdown vehicle. Brinkerhoff watched it for a time.

Then he turned to Hollander and said: "Your position strikes me as slightly strange. As indeed it strikes my superiors. Your motivation, to say the least, is highly questionable."

A world of cynics, Hollander thought. Everywhere you went you collided with the disbelievers and the skeptics, who wouldn't recognize a logical position if they saw one.

"I made my position plain, I think," he said. "I haven't changed."

"What you have to offer . . ." Brinkerhoff paused. His pancakes had arrived. He stared at them.

"Everything okay?" Theresa asked, smiling. She replenished Hollander's cup with a brown liquid that he looked at distastefully.

Brinkerhoff bit into the pancake. He suggested somebody sampling wine. Hollander put out his cigarette. "You've had my credentials checked, of course."

"Of course. They are as they say. Your credentials are not what concerns us."

Hollander waited. He thought of Myers again inside his pup tent. April; the cold desert mornings would be freezing his ass.

"It's altogether vague," Brinkerhoff said. "You promise us—"

"Revolutionary information, was the phrase—"

"Naturally, you don't specify. That is fair enough at this stage. Why give something away for nothing?" Evidently tired of the American delicacy, Brinkerhoff pushed his plate aside. He inserted a finger into his mouth and picked at something.

"Your own position is what puzzles us," he went on. "You ask for no money. You run the risk of being called a traitor. All you want from us is the assurance that we will allow you to come to the Soviet Union. Why doesn't it add up?"

Believe, don't believe, Hollander thought. He was suddenly tired. There was too much tension. He could feel a tightness in his chest. I didn't give up the job just because

I wanted to run into more of that old hypertension, I wanted peace.

"Perhaps it's your apparent idealism that troubles us," Brinkerhoff said. "I think we are suspicious of that label. I sit here, I look at you, and I keep thinking to myself, Is it possible? Maybe something inside me has become hard, Hollander. But an idealist?"

The old hero complex, Hollander thought. Sometimes he felt he was insane, out of it, blown quite away. Was it idealism? You don't look around the Pancake Palace at the blind faces of the munchers and think good thoughts. You don't sit in plastic enclaves and undergo this deep love of your fellowman; by the same token, you don't want to perpetuate the crassness of a synthetic society. It was balance, he thought. Balance. There was a structure that worked because of the balance. It was often uncertain, but so far nobody had started throwing nukes at each other. *Do I want to be a hero?*

"Information is usually bought and sold, Hollander. We're not children. We are not, as you say, wet behind our ears. People who have information, in this world at least, offer it at the highest price. You think we are naïve? All you ask is a place in Soviet society? No money? No hard-cash payment?"

Hollander said: "I want your assistance in getting out of this country—"

"You will have to prove something. You will have to show us something." Brinkerhoff stared at the tips of his fingers. "We have been caught before now. We have every reason to be cautious. Put yourself in our shoes for a moment. What if you have been planted? What if your purpose is to mislead?"

Hollander shrugged. "You want a little evidence, of course."

Brinkerhoff nodded.

"I'll be in touch." Hollander, picking up his newspaper, folding it under his arm, stood up. Brinkerhoff watched him.

"What are you, Hollander? The idealist? Or just some common spy?"

"I'm a nut," Hollander said. "An average, everyday, common or garden candidate for the funny farm."

Puzzled, Brinkerhoff stared at him: "You lose me, friend. You lose me."

Hollander left the Pancake Palace and stepped out into the rainy day. You want to sustain some equilibrium in this crazy world. Alone, you think you can provide the documents that will do just that thing. You could burn for it.

You must be pretty fucked in the head.

Tarkington said: "You asked for the fucking attaché case, that's what I bring you, so now you tell me I fucked up again."

He was walking up and down Sharpe's office, trembling with annoyance, conscious of his layers of fat in motion beneath the maroon leisure suit. He knew he was going too far with Sharpe, but he had done this thing by the book and was it his fault, was it his fucking fault, that the attaché case contained only stupid blank paper?

The manila folder was open on Sharpe's desk, the papers strewn all across it. Sharpe sat with his eyes closed and thought: A game, some joker's playing a game. But who? The major general or our young friend Thorne? You would have to work Thorne with kid gloves.

"Okay," he said. "Take it easy, Tarkie. Just sit down and take it easy."

"I mean, hell, I did the goddamn job," Tarkington said.

"A case filled with blank papers," Sharpe said. Blank papers. This couldn't be what all the goddamn fuss was about, that was for sure.

Tarkington sat, his legs splayed out. He closed his eyes and put his hands to the side of his face. Weariness, the weariness. When did he last have a good night's sleep? Come to that, when did he last get laid? He opened his eyes, watched Sharpe, waited for something to happen. Sharpe, staring at the blank pages as one might at the recalcitrant clue of a difficult crossword puzzle, was thinking of Dilbeck. Back to that fucking plant kingdom, he thought.

Tarkington could feel waves of sleep press in on him. He struggled against them. I done this by the book, he thought. They can't hang me for that.

Sharpe gathered the papers together, stuffed them back in the folder, shoved the folder into the attaché case, locked it, and stuck it in the bottom drawer of his gray metal desk.

"Thorne's a special case, Tarkie," he said. "You understand that? I don't want Lykiard near him, you follow me? I don't want Lykiard so much as to breathe on the guy. But day and night, day and fucking night, Tarkie, I want to know where he goes, who he screws, when he takes a shit. You got that?"

Tarkington thought, I'm going to need some speed about now. I'm going to need a chemical assist. Wearily, he got out of his chair. His shoulders sagged and he felt as if his legs might buckle. He looked at Sharpe; Sharpe thought of a large, overweight dog searching for cold water on a hot day.

"What do we do this for?" Tarkington said.

"It passes the time, Tarkie. Always remember that."

Myers watched the sun as it rose and, lying flat on his belly, beat at a fly that had come buzzing in against his face. He lifted the binoculars and trained them on the site. There wasn't any movement. You couldn't count the guard, because he was like part of the landscape. The sun dazzled on the white wall of the structure and glistened on the wire perimeter fence. Somewhere inside that fence they had the means of blowing away some major cities of the Soviet Union. *Blam blam blam.*

He rubbed his eyes.

From a distance, faintly at first, he heard the sound of a chopper. He scrambled down into the arroyo toward his tent. He went inside. The sound of the helicopter grew louder. He heard it reverberate. And when he saw how the walls of the pup tent shimmered, blown by a wind, he realized it was directly overhead.

Jesus Christ. Any minute now his tent would disappear. He stepped out, shielding his eyes, and looked up at the chopper; it was a vast sunstruck mantis. I'm bird-watching, he thought. A cactus-wren freak. A voyeur of buzzards. My feathered friends.

The helicopter was descending, coming down on the crest of the slope above him. He watched its blades spin to a halt. A man in a white helmet jumped out of the cockpit and stood looking down the arroyo at him.

"What the fuck you think you're doing, friend?"

Myers, his eyesight fettered by the sun, watched the white blur of the helmet.

The man came down the dry wash toward him.

He was black, he had the armband of an MP, and an automatic pistol, a .45, in his holster.

"What you doing?"

Myers looked nervously at his tent. "Bird-watching."

"Yeah? I guess this area's just brimming with them," the MP said.

"If you look, it is," Myers said. "You got to know where to look."

The MP stared up the arroyo at the helicopter. There was a second figure in the cockpit. Myers could not see him clearly.

"You know this place is off limits?" the MP said.

"Off limits," and Myers shrugged.

The MP stared at the tent, pulled the flap back, looked inside.

"I didn't see any signs," Myers said.

"Bird-watching, huh?" The MP took the pistol from his holster. He leveled it at Myers. He smiled; against the dark of his skin his teeth were an impossible white. "How long you been camping here?"

"Couple days," Myers said. "What's with the gun, mac?"

"I got myself a bird," the MP said.

* * *

Thorne waited in an obscure seafood restaurant called the Shrimp's Hideaway for his lunch date. It was a place festooned with nets and harpoons and posters of old whalers. You were meant to feel nautical here; they hammered you with it. But the effect was wrecked by the gingham dresses of the waitresses, who looked like unwanted partners at a country square dance. He ordered a Campari and tonic from a waitress whose badge said *Hi, I'm Cheryl.*

He sat near the window, watched the street. A rundown neighborhood, old storefronts and awnings, rusting fire hydrants, unemployed men lingering on corners with a kind of resigned irritation at the world. Most of the tables in the place were empty. Candles flickered bleakly in glass jars.

When Erickson entered, looking like a store-window model in his dark three-piece suit, his hair fashionably long but not yet unruly, he came straight to the table and sat down. He was carrying a brown envelope under his arm in a rather protective fashion; he placed it on top of the table, laying his hands over it.

"Like this place, John?" he said.

Thorne shrugged. "Is it where you people of fashion hang out?"

"It's where we come when we don't want to be seen, baby," Erickson said. He asked for a scotch from Hi I'm Cheryl and he slid the envelope across the table to Thorne. Thorne took it, slipped it into his briefcase, locked the case.

"Do we go through the charade of actually eating?" Erickson asked.

"We don't have to," Thorne said.

Erickson sipped his drink and looked around: "I feel seasick. What is this? A goddamn trawler or something?"

"You chose it," Thorne said. "Remember?"

Erickson played with his solid-gold cuff links a moment. He was smooth, a well-oiled machine, a young man on the rise. He was personal assistant to Senator McLintock, who served on the Air Force Appropriations Committee.

"What in the name of God do you want with that record anyhow?" Erickson said.

"The guy interests me," Thorne said. "An old friend of my father's."

"And recently dead, as I understand," Erickson said.

"Right."

They had two more drinks. Thorne watched a cop car slide down the block, cruising.

"He was pretty batty," Erickson said. "I gather they thought he was something of a radical. You know the kind. Old major general. Gets close to retirement. No more promo for him. So he either goes the hard-line conservative route—letters to the editor, sees commies under the bed, or they flip out like Burckhardt and get a little touchy."

"Like how?"

"He was always writing to Air Marshal Howard, for

one thing. Critical shit. This plane's going to be obsolete in a year, so why build it? That kind of stuff. They had him pegged as a malcontent."

"And was he?"

Erickson fingered the rim of his glass. "Your guess is as good as mine. What's radical in the service is pretty tame outside. You know that."

They were silent a moment. Thorne finished his drink.

"You've got photostats in that envelope," Erickson said. "I don't want to know what you need them for, so don't tell me. When you're through with them, scrap them. They'd bust my balls if they knew."

Thorne understood. "Another drink?"

"You kidding? I've got McLintock all afternoon. He's in a vile mood. I think he's going through male menopause. Plus he's teetotal. I'm going to suck LifeSavers."

Erickson stood up.

"I owe you a favor," Thorne said.

Erickson smiled, clapped him on the shoulder. "I won't forget it, either. Bet on it."

Thorne watched him go. He ordered another Campari and a plate of fried shrimp, picked at them, finished his drink, and left.

A Pontiac Catalina, an insipid green in color, picked up his red VW on Memorial Parkway and followed it to the White House.

Tarkington said to Lykiard: "No jokes with this mother. You got it?"

Lykiard nodded.

3

The night was clear, starry, a slight wind blowing away the haze that had hung all day over the city. Through the lens Dilbeck had a clear view of the crater Copernicus and, to the north, the area known as Mare Imbrium, the Sea of Rains. It was amazing, sometimes, the clarity of vision. Beside him on the darkened lawn Sharpe's cigarette glowed intermittently red.

"Take a look," Dilbeck said. "But don't touch the adjustment."

Sharpe put his eye to the telescope that stood on a

tripod. The moon appeared to shimmer, as though it were a large silver coin immersed in moving water. Very impressive, he thought.

"I built it myself," Dilbeck said. "I'm working on a stronger one now."

"It's really something," Sharpe said, straightening, stepping back from the instrument. He looked across the lawn at the house. The lights in the conservatory were pale; the shadows of a thousand plants pressed against the glass. There was no sign now of the daughter. No piano playing. In the darkness, Dilbeck sighed.

"So," he said. There was a suggestion of finality in the way he said the word, as if he were concluding a lecture and something necessary had just been proved beyond doubt.

Sharpe held his cigarette, not knowing what to do with the butt. He somehow knew that Dilbeck thought of his lawn as one might value a Persian rug. Dilbeck moved in the direction of the house and Sharpe followed a pace or two behind. They went inside the conservatory. It smelled musty. Somewhere in the middle of all these healthy plants, Sharpe thought, there's one rotting away.

"We have a slight puzzle," Dilbeck said.

Sharpe stared at a pale fluorescent tube that glimmered on the far wall. Something exotic was being cultivated beneath it. He wondered if Dilbeck talked to his plants.

"Thorne's mind," Dilbeck said. "A man's mind is private by nature. We live our lives locked away, don't we? What are we ever sure of? What are you ever sure of, Sharpe?"

What is this? Sharpe wondered. Philosophy 101?

"Are you sure that you're always doing the right thing?" Dilbeck asked, turning to face him, seeming to loom over him in such a way that the question was no mere rhetorical cant.

"I go by the book," Sharpe said.

"Because you think the book is right?"

"It's the only book I know."

Dilbeck moved away in the direction of the fluorescent light. On a small table there was a glass case of the kind that housed tropical fish. Inside was a small plant.

"Brazilian edelweiss," Dilbeck said.

Sharpe looked at the glass, the reflection of light.

"Was there something other than a blank manuscript in that case?" Dilbeck said.

"Every move Thorne makes—"

"Let's be interested in every *thought* Thorne thinks," Dilbeck said. "A man's observable behavior can only take us so far. How do we begin to learn what he thinks?"

Sharpe put out his hand as if to touch the glass case, then he remembered he was still holding the stub of a lit cigarette. How the hell do I get rid of this?

"Pressure," Dilbeck said. "When the time is right. If the time is *ever* right."

Sharpe watched as Dilbeck moved down the tables.

"In your book," he was saying, "in your book pressure usually means one thing. But there are other kinds. More subtle kinds."

Sharpe thought of Tarkington slumped asleep behind the wheel of a car.

"Your predecessor was a man of some finesse," Dilbeck said.

"Hollander?"

"He would have understood this situation rather well," Dilbeck said. "But as he grew older he began to develop certain sensitivities. In your job, a poet is the very last thing you need to be. He had ceased to have the soul of a cement mixer."

Sharpe felt the butt burn into his thumb. He had met Hollander only once, during the changeover. He had no particular impression of the guy. Quiet, withdrawn, too well liked by the people in the field. He had lost his sense of distance. But apart from that—what else? Nobody really knew why Hollander had quit anyhow. Tired, maybe, just plain worn out.

"I liked Ted Hollander," Dilbeck was saying. "As a matter of fact, I still do. But liking isn't the whole kettle of fish, is it?"

Sharpe waited until Dilbeck had turned his back, then he surreptitiously dropped the butt and stepped on it.

"The soul of a cement mixer, that's what you need," Dilbeck said, and looked around. "No fears, no regrets, no attachments. Only an awareness of *grinding*. Do you follow me?"

"I think so," Sharpe said.

Dilbeck picked up a potted plant and held it to the

light. One leaf was touched by brown spots. He ripped it away from the stalk and crumpled it in his hand and looked at Sharpe.

"Why didn't you ask for an ashtray?" he said.

There were perhaps fifty people in the lounge. Some sat on chairs, others squatted on the rug in front of the dais. Marcia took Thorne's hand and raised it to her lap and let it settle there, smiling at him quickly as if to say: *You'll like this. Be silent and listen.* The poet, a fat young man with a slight beard and a dark beret, began to read from a poem called *Auschwitz*. Thorne barely listened. This was Marcia's world and he wondered why he had agreed to be dragged along when, in the briefcase that sat now between his feet, there was Burckhardt's file—a fact that was burning a hole in his attention.

The young poet had a droning delivery. Marcia listened carefully, her head inclined slighty forward. Sometimes she made notes in the margins of the program; sometimes she shook her head from side to side, as if she disagreed with a line, a phrase, a meter. *The barracks here are always gray,* the poet said. *It rains. My mother stands in a doorway wearing a white apron.* Thorne opened the program notes. The poet's name was Roger Weleba—a curious name, Thorne thought. As he listened he played anagrams in his head. Weelba. Blewea. Baleew. *I remember, but memory is no exit.*

He was becoming restless. Marcia squeezed his hand tightly and whispered something to him. He couldn't catch it but didn't want to ask her to repeat it. There was an awful quietness, the kind of stillness he experienced in the reference rooms of public libraries: the turning of a page could have the timbre of a sneeze in a place like this. The poet finished. There was scattered applause, more of politeness than enthusiasm. The poet started another. It was called *The Death of a Soldier on the Russian Front.* He droned. Thorne reached down and touched the clasp of the briefcase. Then he picked up the program and drew sunglasses on the photograph of the poet. Marcia stared at him a moment, then looked back in the direction of the platform.

When the reading was over, Thorne was introduced to a couple of people in Marcia's department. A young man in a leather waistcoat whose specialty, it seemed, was *Moby Dick*, and who spoke with a nervous enthusiasm that suggested he had just come fresh from a seminar with Melville himself; an ancient hippie, behind whose features you could detect an aura of academic middlebrow respect-ability: beads and beard, Thorne thought—he must have been introduced to mescaline on his fiftieth birthday; a skinny woman with protruding teeth and plum-shaped am-ber decorations at her throat. Thorne understood that she was running Christopher Marlowe through a computer to assess the quantity of his vegetable imagery. Hands were shaken; the poems were discussed. Weleba's contribution was considered minor, it seemed. Thorne tried not to yawn. The briefcase, he thought. The goddamn briefcase. Compared to the major general's file, this gathering was slightly more than unreal. He thought: A man drowns in a swimming pool in a surburban motel and a poet writes of a concentration camp he didn't experience: there was a division of possibilities here, a kind of concussion that resulted from a head-on collision of the significant and the minor.

Outside, as they walked to the VW, Marcia said: "I think you're a Philistine."

"I beg your pardon," he said. "It was altogether a mov-ing experience for me—"

"Moving, my ass."

He took the car keys from his pocket. "Did you *really* enjoy it?"

She looked at him, smiling slightly, tossing a strand of hair back from her face. "Weleba just got a Rockefeller."

"That's an evasion."

"Some people think highly of him—"

"What do *you* think?"

She leaned against the car in a manner that he knew was calculated to be deliberately provocative: "I think they throw Rockefellers around, love. Like Frisbees. He isn't exactly my cup of java, if you must know."

They got in the car.

"My problem is I don't like poetry," he said. "I never liked it. Even in school."

Marcia said nothing.

"Weleba, I figure, is on a par with Valium," Thorne said.

She laughed. She laid the flat of her hand against his leg. He turned the key in the ignition; momentarily the headlamps dimmed as the motor labored.

"As for your colleagues," he said.

"What about them?"

He edged the VW slowly across the parking lot. At the entrance to the street, he turned to look at her: "How do you put up with them?"

She stroked the side of his leg and said: "I've developed a certain immunity. They practice their eccentricities and I practice mine. It's simple."

"What are your eccentricities?" he asked.

"I get these overwhelming urges to commit oral sex in automobiles. Except it makes for dangerous driving."

There was a red light just ahead; something that Thorne almost failed to notice.

In the green Catalina Tarkington was saying: "I wander lonely as a cloud."

Lykiard, driving, nodded.

"Shelley," Tarkington said. "I got an A in junior high for Shelley."

Hollander climbed the last narrow flight of stairs to his apartment. He fumbled with his key, unlocked the door, stepped inside the darkened room, and turned on the lights. It was tacky. It was what the realtor called a studio apartment; Hollander had come to understand that this meant it had one window somewhat larger than average. He sat on the edge of the sofa and undid his shoelaces and he remembered Rowley in the green Porsche, the shadow behind the windshield, the way the kids had scrambled into the car after the movie, how their faces had been faint shadows thrown upon the glass, their hands raised in stiff gestures of farewell . . . Shaking his head, he went into the kitchen. When he turned on the light the congregation of roaches dispersed, scuttling for the darker places. He opened the refrigerator, took out a can of beer, pulling it from the plastic collar of the sixpack. He popped the tab, took a couple of quick swallows, then returned to the other room and lay down on the sofa. After a moment it came, it came as it always did—a stranger, yet familiar to him in its own dreadful way. Loneliness. He got up from the sofa—as if movement, any kind of movement, might defeat the specter—and walked to the window, passing the typewriter in which there was a piece of paper with the sentence: *My career began, unexpectedly, in the winter of 1949.*

We want drama, the editor of the book had told him. What we don't want in this kind of book is any moralizing or philosophy. We want a lot of action.

Action, Hollander thought.

I could give them action.

He looked from the window at a street of tenements. In some windows there were lights, shabby lights, as if they originated from bulbs that hung suspended inside frayed shades. Over the buildings the sky was impenetrably black.

He suddenly wished he had never seen the Asterisk file. He wished he had never known.

But you couldn't go back.

Once you had knowledge you couldn't go back to ignorance.

If I had been a different kind of person, maybe . . . He stared at the dark sky in the manner of someone who expects to find solutions to problems in the patterns of stars. It's the only world we've got, he thought. And who were you to trust? Hungry presidents, crazed generals, the hawks of that calcified crew known collectively as the Joint Chiefs of Staff? No. Emphatically no.

He walked around the apartment, thinking now of Brinkerhoff's overlords. They weren't any different from the rest, they listened to the same frenetic melodies of global paranoia, they were eager participants in the same race to destruction. Build the bombs, build them bigger and better with more and more megatons, more and more of the bleak capacity for violence. He sometimes thought of his own kids blown apart. The worst part. And then at other times he imagined that his mentality was still in some way hooked to the notion of a cold war, that he was stuck in a repetitive groove of thinking—he was being alarmist without any reason.

Balance, he thought. Yes. The equalization. One side light-years ahead of the other was a true prescription for disaster. He couldn't let that happen. He couldn't. He would give Brinkerhoff everything. The whole damn thing. If history ascribed treason to him, then it was too bad.

He sat down on the sofa, drained the beer can, looked around the bare walls of the room. They menaced him: they were bare in the way he associated with rubber rooms in sanitoriums, padded cells where you could scream until you no longer heard the sound of yourself. Impulsively, he picked up the telephone. He dialed a number: he needed to see the girl.

"I'm busy, Ted," she said. "Why don't you call me back in a half hour?"

"Okay," he said. How old was she? Eighteen? nineteen? He put the telephone down.

He went to the window. In the blackness of the night sky above the tenements he could see, in a faint way, the stars, the smear of the Milky Way. The sources. Beginnings never mattered much to him, only endings, only how things turned out.

He drew down the blind. Loss: that was what lay at the heart of loneliness. A sense of loss.

At the kitchen table Thorne opened the file and looked at the stats. Marcia hovered around him, looking over his shoulder.

"What's that?"

"Burckhardt's file," he said.

"I shouldn't be looking, right?"

"I shouldn't be looking either," he said.

"All that secrecy junk," she said. "Sometimes I don't see any difference between how this country is governed and how the Freemasons run their lodges. You know that? The cult of secrecy."

He glanced at her, then he began to flip through the photocopies. They felt greasy, as if the letters might come away in his hands.

Walter F. Burckhardt. DOB 2.2.20.

Rank, current: Major General.

Marcia said: "Why the interest?"

"It's my kind of poetry," he answered.

"Seriously," she said.

Thorne looked at her. Why indeed? "I want to find out if he really was deranged or . . ." He let the sentence trail away into silence. Or what? What was the alternative? The doomed man's last testament: work it out from twenty-five pages of nothing. It was a hell of a thing to leave behind if you knew you were going; a suicide note without purpose.

"He was an old friend of Daddy's, after all," she said. "Boys must stick together, huh?"

"You know what they say about sarcasm," he said. "Put this down to my curiosity—"

"And your upright sense of duty," she said. "Yours is the kind of head that hates loose ends. I think the word is fastidious."

Fastidious, Thorne thought. It sounded strangely dull; it was an adjective he associated with female career librarians, a life spent lurking in the bookstacks where the gothics and the romances met in some nebulous area of the heart, and where all your passion was distilled in a single drop of perfume placed in the folds of a lace handkerchief that you continually wanted to let float down to some man's feet. Fastidious.

"You're saying these terrible things all because I thought the poetry reading was dull," he said.

"Thank you for ascribing motivations to me—"

"Thanks for calling me fastidious—"

"But you are, my love," she said. "You're the kind of person who can't sleep at night unless he knows that the mothballs are still operative in the wardrobe where he keeps his suits. Just the thought of lint in your navel makes you cringe."

"That's how you see me?"

"Part of the picture," she said. "Because of some perversity of nature, though, you're also warm and kind and loving, et cetera. I like that."

He watched her a moment. She was standing by the stove, her hands in the pockets of her jeans. Her legs were parted slightly; her left eyebrow was arched and she was staring at him in a way he found totally distracting.

"Do we make coffee or love?" she said.

"It's got to be coffee first." He turned the pages. He heard her sigh, then run water into the coffeepot. The sheets in front of him contained details that were cold, sparse, colorless. You could not build a rounded character from the chill of these photostats. He tried to remember Burckhardt's face. He got nothing. Just that handshake, the strength in the fingers, the clap on the shoulder. *Chin up.*

He read through the pages. The details of a career, a life. Somewhere in all this there were the reasons for self-destruction, somewhere.

Spouse: Anna Fleming. DOB 6.5.40.

Twenty years between them, he thought. They always said it makes a difference. Not at first, but later, when the man is closing on sixty and the woman touching forty.

Marcia set down a cup of coffee in front of him.

"If you're going to burn the midnight oil," she said.

"This won't take long—"

"I'm going back to Coleridge, who at least is a faithful old fucker."

He heard her go out of the kitchen. He heard her turn the pages of a book. He drank some coffee, stared at the file.

The war years were covered, pretty much as he remembered them. Liaison officer to General Clay. The congressional committee. Then Korea.

Wounded in action, 1952.

It didn't specify the nature of the wound nor even the nature of the action. Shot out of the sky? Thorne wondered. What exactly? Whoever completed these records and kept them up to date had had no eye for detail.

Promotion: Major General, 1954.

Marcia came back into the kitchen, opened the refrigerator, added some milk to her coffee, smiled at him, retreated.

Tattershall Air Force Base, England 1954-1957.

USAF Liaison Officer, Polaris Site, Garelochhead, Scotland, 1957-1959. Lowery Bombing Range, Colorado, 1960-1962. Naval Air Test Center, Maryland, 1962-1965. Griffis Base, N.Y., 1966-1967.

Dull, Thorne thought. What would somebody like Marcia be able to read between these dull lines? A career officer, a commitment. But Erickson had said: *Something of a radical.* How?

He turned to the final page.

An appointment to Aerospace Defense Command.

October, 1969, appointment to the staff of General Whorley, *Project Blue Book.*

Blue Book, Thorne thought. They had recently scrapped that, hadn't they? Tired of watching the night sky. Nothing out there.

Whatever, Burckhardt had been sent to Oscura, New Mexico, a classified site. His appointment there had apparently lasted for a year. In 1972, he had been posted to Escalante, Arizona, another classified site.

And that was it.

That was it.

Except for a handwritten note attached to the last page by a paper clip. Thorne set it aside, read it.

This officer is not recommended for further promotion.

Beneath the sentence there were the initials: *WHW.* General William Harold Whorley, Thorne thought. Who else? He stacked the papers together, closed the folder. Now, he thought. Why would Whorley block any future promotions for the old man? Too old? Too much of a *radical*? Why does a man drown himself? Why anything?

He yawned. He put the folder into his briefcase. He went into the living room. Marcia was still at her Coleridge.

"Any revelations, Sherlock?" she asked.

Thorne shrugged. "Dull City," he said. He was tired. He sat down on the sofa. "If I get myself a beret, could I become a poet too?"

"Eat it," she said.

He rubbed his eyes. He wanted to sleep.

The telephone rang. Marcia reached for it, then she covered the mouthpiece with her hand.

"It's for you, John. Female. Who do you know that talks in low, sexy whispers?"

Thorne took the receiver from her.

He heard a woman ask: "John Thorne?"

"Speaking," he said.

There was a short silence. Then the woman said: "My name is Anna Burckhardt. I think we should meet."

4:

Tuesday, April 4

IT WAS RAINING, A THIN, DRIFTING APRIL RAIN THAT covered the Eastern seaboard all the way from Providence to Savannah. The traffic on Interstate 95 was slow, crawling. Outside Alexandria a school bus had slammed into the concrete support of an overpass; a Volvo, unable to brake, had gone into the back of the bus and was smoldering now on the center strip. Tarkington, who had gone to a motel the previous night, leaving Lykiard outside the apartment complex, was driving alone in the Catalina. On waking, he had taken a couple of tabs of speed, white crosses, and he was beginning to feel them jangle the edge of his nerves. They always fucked him over, upsetting his stomach, making him shake, but on the plus side they guaranteed him alertness.

He passed the smoking Volvo carefully. The front of the school bus looked like crumpled yellow paper in the rain. There were a few kids with lunchboxes standing in the rain, an anxious driver, two or three cops, flashing lights, the whole bit. Up ahead in the fast lane he saw the red VW. He lit a cigarette, using the dash lighter, and he switched the radio on. Commercials, the jingles of salesmanship. Anything was better than Lykiard's company, he had to admit. The Greek never spoke unless it was to mumble some incoherency. It was Tarkington's feeling that the Greek had been in the field too long and needed a break. Like in a home for the criminally insane.

During the Second World War, Lykiard had strangled Nazis with his bare hands. Jesus. Where were they recruiting these babies from nowadays? Just sitting beside the Greek make him feel chilly.

63

He heard the voice of Dolly Parton. She sounded like a girl with a nylon rope stuck in her throat. Tits, though, you had to say that. And those glossy lips. Tits and lips.

He drove past the turning for Dumfries and Joplin.

The rain was constant, thin, and steady, the kind you could stand out in and not feel falling but that soaked you just the same. He glanced at his eyes in the mirror. Bags. They looked like small purple grapes. Quantico U.S. Marine Base. Somewhere to the west. Hemp, Morrisville, Remington. Where was Thorne going, anyhow?

A guy was getting a ticket for speeding just beyond the junction of 17. He stood beneath a golfer's colored umbrella while the cop wrote out the ticket. Automatically, Tarkington looked at his own speedometer. A quiet fifty. They hated it when you handed in traffic violations and asked for a reimbursement.

Suddenly he panicked. He had lost the VW. *He had lost the fucking thing.* No. Then he relaxed. He saw it slowing off the highway, going toward Fredericksburg.

Relax, he said to himself.

But the white crosses in his blood made his pulses and his heartbeat race in a wild way.

She was a woman who looked as though she were thirty-seven going on sixty. Her skin was pale, the lips pinched and almost colorless, and although she had made some attempt to comb through her thick hair Thorne noticed the unevenness of the parting. Her eyes were dark, dull, reflecting little of anything. When she had opened the door there had been no smile of greeting. A recent widow, Thorne thought. You had to make allowances for grief.

He followed her across a sparsely furnished sitting room and into a kitchen. For a moment he thought they were going to sit down to coffee, he could hear it perking, but instead she opened the kitchen door and they went out into the backyard, moving toward a broken-down gazebo. There were two deck chairs under the rusted roof. Sparrows flew up and toward the trees that surrounded the yard.

They sat in the deck chairs. Thorne could hear the rain harping on the roof. This better be worth it, he thought. Marcia had called in to say he had a cold. Farrago would have to do his own dirty work this morning. But he felt uneasy. Absenteeism in Foster's White House was something of an exception.

The woman lit a cigarette. Her fingers shook. She wore a plain wedding band. Her clothes were drab, a black wool cardigan, a pair of gray slacks, a simple necklace of amber.

For a moment, waiting for her to say something, Thorne looked across the lawn at the house. In the rain, the rear windows seemed opaque, almost as if there were no rooms beyond them, as if they had been painted directly onto the brick. It was a strange illusion. She played with her lit cigarette, moving it from one hand to the other and back again.

Finally he said: "I was sorry to hear about your husband."

She looked at him quickly. He noticed pale lipstick for the first time, a smudge of cosmetic shadow under the eyes, perhaps even a suggestion of rouge on the cheeks; but nothing took away from the pallor.

"My husband expected to die," she said.

Thorne sat back in the deck chair; he was beginning to feel damp. He was also beginning to suspect another aspect of lunacy. *Expected to die. Planned it all.*

"I don't follow," he said. "I'm sorry."

She looked quickly now toward the house, as if she were afraid of something inside.

"Just like I said. He expected to die."

"Well," Thorne said. "I guess it's something we all, uh, expect . . ." His voice faded. A large dark bird, a crow, floated bleakly in the rain.

"In the broad sense," she answered, and she smiled for the first time. Brief, uncertain. "My husband did not expect to be *allowed* to live. There's a difference."

Thorne shook his head. "I still don't see."

She flicked her cigarette away. She turned toward him and there was the slightest hint of the coquette in this gesture as though, out of long habit, she were continually projecting herself to men. He wondered how often the old man had left her on her own. His overseas postings, perhaps long periods apart, how could he know? The cloistered atmosphere of an air base, other husbands, unattached young men.

"His death wasn't suicide," she said. "He was a good swimmer. A strong . . . His death wasn't suicide."

In silence, Thorne watched the house. He had caught something from her, her nervousness, that indefinable sense of an edge, as if something quite unexpected were about to happen. The windows in the rain. The still drapes. The half-open kitchen door.

"Are you saying he was killed?" he said. "Who killed him? And why?"

"I don't have the answers," she said.

"Why are you telling me this?"

"He spoke highly of your father. When we lived together—"

"I don't follow that."

"Oh. We had been estranged for more than two years. Every Friday night he would call me. Like clockwork. Except last Friday."

Thorne put his hands into his pockets. He was cold, this rain had a chilling effect.

"I wasn't aware of your separation," he said.

She was silent, twisting her fingers together, turning her hands over and over. She could not be still.

"Your father was perhaps the only man Walt ever truly respected," she said. "He had met you, I believe, only once—"

"At the funeral," Thorne said.

"Of course. The funeral." She looked down at the grass, shifted her feet, rearranged her hands in her lap. "Something about you. He liked you. He thought he could trust you. I imagine he saw something of your father in you."

Thorne closed his eyes briefly. She was skirting the margins of something, touching on a nerve and then flitting away again.

"Why do you say he was killed?"

"They wouldn't let him live," she said.

"Who wouldn't? Who are you talking about?"

She faced him, her expression imploring: *Don't you know? Can't you work it out?*

He put his hand on her wrist and found her skin unexpectedly warm.

"Who?" he asked.

She shrugged and pulled her hand away from him and began to rummage in the pocket of her cardigan for cigarettes. She brought out crumpled Kleenexes, a couple of books of matches, a pack of Rothmans. She lit one, blew smoke into the rain, watched it drift.

"I can't answer you," she said.

"What do you expect of me?" he asked, conscious of a vague desperation in his own voice. Why had he come all this way? To confront a bereaved nut? A fruit bat? In his mind's eye he could see his empty office. A pile of newspapers. Farrago walking up and down, cursing him out.

"My husband thought you would know what to do," she said.

"His legacy to me was an attaché case filled with blank paper," Thorne said. "What am I meant to do with that?"

"He thought you would do the right thing—"

"The right thing? What *is* the right thing?"

She sighed, as if she were irritated. "He was afraid. Do you understand that? He wasn't a man easily scared, he was a brave man in many ways, Mr. Thorne, and although I had stopped loving him I never stopped respecting him. But he was scared."

"Scared of what?" Thorne was uncomfortable in the chair. He slumped back, watched the rain, wanting to leave. The major general had been scared. Okay. The major general had been killed. Okay. Why?

"But you wouldn't be interested in the personal history," she said. She smiled again, in a rather sad manner this time as though she were remembering some delicious moment from the past and suffering regret because nothing had worked out.

"He was at a place called Escalante." She looked at Thorne in an urgent way. "Something there scared him. That was what it was. Something at Escalante scared him. He told me very little. When he called me, the very last time he ever spoke to me, he said he was going to contact you. He had knowledge—"

"Knowledge?"

She nodded her head: "Knowledge he felt was important. But he didn't know what to do with it."

Thorne watched her fidget with her cigarette.

She said, "He told me that if anything were to happen to him, I was to tell you—Escalante."

Escalante, Thorne thought. A hard missile site. He turned the thing over in his head. You could come to the conclusion that the old man had gone soft, become pacifist, didn't like the missiles much anymore, wanted an end to the whole nuclear horror show. You could reach that one by an easy route. What then? He was going to blow the whistle on something? But what? A new missile? Germ warfare? Something, something he didn't like. He was going to blow the whistle and they didn't take kindly to that, so they put him away in a swimming pool.

Escalante.

"He also mentioned the Asterisk Project," she said.

He watched her face. She was gazing at him seriously. She sat back in her chair. The rain beat on the broken roof of the gazebo. A blackbird floated toward the trees. A pale column of smoke drifted from the roof of the house.

"What is it? What is Asterisk?" he asked.

"It's what they do at Escalante," she answered. "It's what troubled Walter. I don't know any more."

She stood up.

Is this it? he wondered. Is it finished now? He had come all this way through the rain—and for what? Puzzles? More unwritten manuscripts? He got to his feet and followed her across the lawn. The Asterisk Project. The mumbo jumbo of the thermonuclear mentality. Warheads capable of creating an Atlantis out of every continent. Project this, Project that, Project X.

On the threshold of the kitchen, she turned to him. "When we go inside, I'll pour you some coffee and we'll talk about the weather."

The weather, Thorne thought. The trouble with paranoia is that you no sooner open the door of one labyrinth when another unexpectedly beckons. She thinks the house is bugged. Who's mad around here? Her? Me? Or the late Walter F. Burckhardt?

He sat at the kitchen table. She poured coffee. There was a framed photograph on the wall. He recognized it. It was gray, a souvenir of another era, and it showed his father with a group of men, one of whom was the young major general. It was signed across the bottom: *This ought to bring back memories, best wishes, Ben.*

"I hope this rain doesn't keep up," she was saying.

"Sure," he said. It disconcerted him to find his father's picture here. The problem with having a famous father is what other people expect of you. The dead man's shoes that have to be filled. It had dogged him through school, university, it had harried after him when he had gone to work. People expected to see a carbon of the great man. Too many people, both in the House and in the Senate, had affectionate memories of Benjamin Thorne. After his death, one newspaper obituary eulogized: *We have lost a great American.* It brought them together, Republicans and Democrats and Independents, they had been for once unanimous in their sentiments. He turned away from the photograph. *The only man Walt ever truly respected.*

"I expect we'll get a little sun soon," she said.

She laughed, a strange little laugh that was brittle, smoky from too many cigarettes.

"We could do with it," he said.

He finished his coffee. He stood up, ready to leave. She seemed disappointed slightly, as if she wanted him to stay, as if perhaps suddenly she remembered something else she might tell him. Saying nothing, she walked with him to the front door. Outside, as he began to move to his car, she caught him by the wrist, her fingers hard and tight and desperate against his skin, she caught him and said: "Don't let him down. Please don't let him down."

2

The captain, who had not introduced himself, sat on the edge of his desk and swung one leg back and forth, forth and back, in a manner that was strangely stiff. Myers, handcuffed, had passed a sleepless night on a hard cot in a narrow room, conscious of the guard who sat reading back numbers of *Playboy* beneath a sixty-watt light bulb. They had taken his cigarettes, wrapped up his equipment, stashed his tent away, his tape recorder, books, camera, binoculars. And now they had brought him in front of the captain.

Myers did not care for the hard look in the man's eye. There was a certain savage dullness in there. Even the small gingery mustache suggested it would pierce your skin if you touched a single bristle of it.

"We don't get many bird watchers in this part of the world," the captain said.

"I guess," Myers answered. He was hungry. His stomach rumbled audibly. They might have had the decency to give him coffee at the very least. But when the coffee had come there had been only one cup, and that was for the guard reading *Playboy*.

"What kind of birds are you studying?" the captain asked. He was smiling. You could hardly call it that, Myers thought. It was a motion of lip, a show of teeth, utterly mirthless.

"The catcus wren, mainly," he said. "Look, I didn't know this place was off limits."

The captain had Myers' wallet open on his desk. A Bank-Americard, out of date, a social security number, a borrower's ticket for a public library in Baltimore. He turned the wallet upside down and shook it. A few pennies fell out. A paper clip.

"The cactus wren," the captain said. "An interesting bird, isn't it?"

"Really," Myers said. One fifty a week and Hollander hadn't even paid him yet. Fuck it, he thought. It isn't any skin off my nose.

"I didn't see any signs," he said.

"Maybe you didn't look hard enough," the captain said. "What other birds you expect to find around here?"

"Buzzards."

"Buzzards, huh?" The captain picked up Myers' social security card and stared at it. "Jackson Myers," he said. "Jackson Myers."

"Look," Myers said. "I don't want to appear, you know, pushy, but you don't have any grounds for holding me here. So—if you just let me have my equipment, I'll take off. No problem."

Stupidly, he found himself winking at the captain, as if between the two of them there might be some tacit agreement, a minor conspiracy. But the captain only stared; a look of frosted metal.

"Buzzards," he said to Myers. "And maybe you're also interested in the turkey vulture?"

"Sure, sure," Myers said. "Both kinds."

"Buzzards and turkey vultures." The captain sat down behind his desk, placed the tips of his fingers together, stared at Myers a moment, then said: "Bird-watching my ass."

"I don't get it," Myers said.

"Buzzards and turkey vultures. Two names. The same bird. Think again."

Myers looked at the ceiling. A bare light bulb burned. The room was windowless, formal, barren. He felt a moment of panic, fought against it, let it pass.

"I told you my specialty was the cactus wren," he said.

"And my specialty is the life cycle of the salmonella," the captain said. "Come on, Jack. Think again."

"Jesus," Myers said. "I told you. How many times do I need to keep saying it?"

"The cactus wren," the captain said, touching his mustache. "You crack me up, Jackson. You're a real stand-up comedian. I don't think you could tell a cactus wren from a pair of Jockey shorts."

Myers wondered if there was violence in all this. He was too old for the rough stuff. If they came on real strong he knew he would tell them anything; and more, if they wanted to hear it. He had had all that. This was meant to be a quiet outing in the desert, no sweat, two weeks in a tent. Think of it as a paid vacation. Hollander had said that.

"Who's behind you?" the captain asked. "Who's running you, Jackson?"

"Shit, I told you," Myers said. "I came out here in all innocence—"

"If you're innocent, I'm the Pope's wife," the captain said. "You might as well let it all hang out, Jack. Because we'll get it anyhow. One way or another."

Violence: was that implied here? Myers could feel the palms of his hands begin to sweat.

The door opened. The black MP from the chopper came in and put some papers on the captain's desk, then went out again. The captain looked at the papers quickly, then, as if they were a hand of cards and this a game of poker, he turned them face down.

He looked at Myers and laughed.

"Modern communications, wonderful things," he said.

Myers wondered about the papers. They've run me through. They've checked me out. *They know.*

So much for my feathered friends, he thought.

"So you retired in seventy-four," the captain said. "They put you out to pasture, huh? The usual pension."

Myers looked at the floor. Bare tiles. They suggested imprisonment to him.

"Operated in Turkey." The captain turned the papers over and looked at them. "Bangkok. London. A stint in Korea. Well. You certainly moved around, Jack. I guess you saw a lot of birds on your travels, huh?"

Myers said nothing. They had him. They had him cold. He was the dunce made to stand in the corner wearing the conical hat of humiliation. *Christ, what now?*

"When did you change sides, Jackson?" the captain asked.

"I never changed sides—"

"No? You were just hanging out there with your field glasses for the benefit of your health? That it?"

"You can't fucking accuse me of changing sides."

"I didn't realize you were so sensitive, Jack. Take it easy. I'll put it another way. When did you enter into a contract of gainful employment with a certain foreign power who, for the present, shall remain nameless?"

"I did none of that," Myers said. "You can't fucking hang that on me."

"That so? You're freelancing? You're solo? Where's the bread coming from? A rich aunt in Connecticut just named you in her will and you thought, Hey, I'll take a jaunt in the desert and check out one of our military installations? That it? Come on, Myers, I didn't sail up the fucking Potomac on rubber wings. Who's behind it?"

Myers got up from his seat. Awkwardly, he scratched the tip of his nose with his handcuffed hands.

"You've got to be working for them," the captain said. "Otherwise, where's the sense? Where's the profit motive?"

"You got a key for these fuckers?" Myers asked. The metal was cutting his skin.

The captain took out a key, undid the cuffs. Myers rubbed his wrists. He shrugged. The cactus wren was shot to shit, and he wasn't working for the Russians. So what the hell.

He sat down and said: "Okay. You got me cold."

The captain smiled.

Hollander woke while the girl was still asleep. As he dressed he watched her. She lay lifelessly, arms spread; she might have been a marionette to whose strings someone

had taken a pair of scissors. Last night she had been full
of activity, yet it was mechanical; not cold exactly, not
that, going through the motions. He went into the small
kitchenette of her apartment and stared at the telephone
messages scrawled on the small blackboard beside the
phone. *Charlie 226-3354. Make it 3. 4:30. Hairdresser.
Karate class 7.*

He filled the electric percolator with coffee, plugged it
into the wall. Mechanical affection. Could there be such a
thing?

He watched the coffee spring into the plastic top of the
lid. She came into the kitchenette, yawning, naked; he
thought of his own daughter, a flash of her face, an image
of a snapshot he had received last Christmas in the mail. *I
love you, Daddy—Anna.*

"What's the time?" she asked.

He found his wristwatch on the kitchen table. "It's past
eleven."

"Already?" She yawned again, stretched, sat down at
the table. He poured two coffees.

He sat facing her, watching her as she sipped the coffee.
She smiled at him in a way that softened her features, as
if all at once she were offering him some glimpse of a vul-
nerability she preferred to keep concealed, then looked
around for a cigarette. He gave her an English Oval. In a
day or so, he thought, he would have to bring Myers back,
then debrief him. Debrief: he had caught himself at the ridiculous language of another time in his life. Traces remained, bits and pieces, the items of your history that
clung to you like lint to cotton. Debrief. The desert was a
drag, Myers would say. Pay me.

"Not bad," the girl said, tasting the cigarette.

He watched her face. It was young and yet in some
manner hard; it was as if she wanted to be older than
what she claimed to be. Even the dark roots that showed
through the fair hair suggested some valiant effort on her
part to make herself appear older, wiser, in some way
nonchalant. Nineteen years, he thought. He had loved
once. Maybe that was it, his share for a lifetime, maybe
you couldn't ever hope for more.

*You're married to the goddamn job, Ted. Where do I
figure? Where do the kids figure?* The lover had come
later, quiet drinks in the afternoon with Rowley, who was

a certified accountant and therefore safe, certain, predictable as the migratory passage of a lemming. Nifty little cocktail bars in the suburbs. The whole bit. I'll give it up, I'll quit. I'll resign. *Too late, Ted, too damn late.*

Rowley and me.

He laid his hand over the girl's bare arm. She looked at him, her eyes wide in some surprise, as if this touch were the last thing she expected, this curious tenderness stunning. She had glorious eyes, a mixture of colors, greens and grays that changed as the light changed. What am I getting into? he wondered.

"I woke feeling sentimental," he said.

"You ought to be careful of that," she said. She blew a stream of smoke directly at him.

He looked at his watch again. 11:30.

The girl inclined her head and let her lips touch the back of his hand. The gesture surprised him somewhat: it seemed somehow both subservient and yet proud, as if she were uncertain of her own emotions. He looked at the dark roots of her hair: now, instead of suggesting an attempt on her part to look older, harder, they made him feel a strange moment of pity for her, a passing thing. She raised her face, looked at him, then laughed.

He ruffled her hair with the palm of his hand. Then he stood up and went into the bedroom and looked around for his shoes. She came in at his back. She put her arms around him and, pursing her lips, blew lightly on the back of his neck.

"You know what that does to me," he said.

"I heard a rumor," she said.

He turned to face her: "When are you free?"

"After seven thirty," she said.

"I'll come back." He fastened his cuff links, knotted his tie in front of the mirror and experienced, as he caught her body in the reflection, an unusual desire. It wasn't the time, he thought. He had to think of Brinkerhoff now. He had to show Brinkerhoff a sample.

"Where did you put my envelope?" he asked.

"I'll get it for you." She went to the kitchenette and came back carrying a plain brown envelope with a wax seal. He took it from her. It felt cold.

"I kept it in the refrigerator," she said. "Under the vegetable tray."

"Pretty secure," he said. How had he come to trust her with this material? When had that happened?

"I figured nobody looks under vegetables," she said. "You'd have to be burgled by a rutabaga freak."

He smiled at her. "I guess you're right," he said. He took his overcoat from the wardrobe and put it on. She held it for him, helped him into it. He felt old, as if he were passing beyond that stage when he could get into an overcoat without a struggle, a rebellion of sinew and muscle and joint.

"You think I can't manage this by myself?" he asked.

"If I thought that, I wouldn't be tactless enough to help you, would I?" she said.

He turned, put his arms around her, kissed her on the forehead.

"I like you, Ted," she said. "I hate it when you call and I'm busy. Like last night. It makes me depressed."

"Years ago I might have been jealous," he said.

"Not now?"

"A little. A little."

He kissed her again, then left. In the elevator he tucked the brown envelope inside his coat. A single page: that would have Brinkerhoff's people humming. They would come around then. They would know this was real and not some blind, some sleight of hand. You had to make them look beyond the darkness of paranoia.

He felt the elevator fall. He looked at his own reflection in the metal plate that surrounded the buttons. Distorted, out of joint, like an image in the Hall of Mirrors. What was he? From the outside, sometimes even from the inside, it was pathetic: a retired intelligence officer who had found a Cause and whose only tenderness was directed toward three estranged kids and a whore with the impossible name of Davina. It was funny, funny-sad. But what else lay beyond it all except that familiar ocean of loneliness? You had to build dikes, all the time you had to build walls and barricades.

3

Congressman Leach was one of the Capitol's fixtures. Those who opposed him every two years did so with a kind of fatalism: you might just as well try to change

Mount Rushmore. When he rose from behind his desk to greet Thorne, Thorne realized, with something of a shock, that in the two years that had passed since their last meeting Leach had aged dreadfully. A certain vibrancy had gone out of him; his handshake was no longer firm but slack, slack and icy, and when he moved his limbs were stiff. He was wasting away; cancer? Thorne wondered. What else took such a quick hold and wasted a man so visibly? Leach smiled, dropped his hand, went back behind his desk.

"It's not often, John," he said. He was looking at his watch. Between committees, Thorne thought. A minute to squeeze in old Ben's boy.

"How have you been?" Thorne asked.

"Can't you tell?" Leach tilted his head to one side, raised his eyebrows. In the light that fell between the slats of the blinds the whites of the eyes were yellow, jaundiced.

"Have you been sick?" Thorne couldn't find a tactful way of getting to the question.

"What you're seeing is one of the pillars of the legislature crumbling," Leach said, smiling as if the act were painful. "I won't be running for office again, I can tell you that. Keep it to yourself. I don't want to read about my own retirement in the *Post* until I'm ready for it."

"I'm sorry to hear that," Thorne said. Washington without Leach would be a merry-go-round minus a horse.

"It comes to us all, John," Leach said. He coughed, took a handkerchief from his pocket, brushed his lips with it. "Can't hobble along forever. Not made that way."

Thorne was silent. If the old man was sick, then this visit was altogether wrong. Time running out; he would have affairs more pressing to attend to.

"How are things in the Big House?" Leach asked.

"Fast, furious."

"Fast furious Foster, eh," Leach said. "Between you, me, and the gossip columns, I don't trust that sonofagun. Like old Harry used to say about Nixon, I'm from Missouri as far as he's concerned."

"I only talked to him once," Thorne said.

"And?"

Thorne shrugged: what was there to say? The familiar smile was warm, the handshake firm, the first name assuredly used. You could not know what was genuine and what were just tricks of the trade.

"I liked him," he said.

"Well. One man's fish cake," Leach said. "He gets everybody around here riled up, I'll tell you that. He thinks we're a freeway and he's a damn bulldozer."

Thorne looked at the photographs around the walls of the congressman's office. There was one of his father and he wondered if there was an office in this whole city that didn't have a picture of the late Senator. Leach was rising, looking at his watch, wheezing slightly as he moved.

"John, it's real good to see you, but I've got a meeting in a few minutes, you know how these things are," he said. "Did you come to ask me something special? Or is this just a courtesy call?"

Thorne hesitated. The next step could be an impossible blunder. He held his breath. He rose from his chair and felt suddenly tense. Leach crossed the floor, walking awkwardly, like someone accustomed to a cane. He paused in front of Thorne and asked: "What's on your mind?"

"Is there anything you can tell me about the Asterisk Project?" he said.

Leach took out his handkerchief, coughed, spat into the folds of the handkerchief, put it away.

"The what project?" he said.

"Asterisk."

"Asterisk." Leach seemed to be thinking, remembering, searching his brain.

"It doesn't ring a bell, John. Sorry," he said. *"Should* it mean something?"

"It's just something I ran across," Thorne said.

Leach shrugged. "I wish I could help. But I never heard of it. Still, there's a whole lot going on around here that I never get to hear about. Half the time you're working with blinders on. You burn the midnight oil and you send your aides all over the whole goddamn place and then you find out the guy next door's been doing the same thing on exactly the same problem. The left hand and the right hand. You know how it is. But I never heard of—what did you call it?"

"Asterisk," Thorne said.

Leach shook his head. "Sorry."

He walked Thorne to the door. He was still shaking his head, as if he had forgotten how to stop.

"Thanks for seeing me at such short notice," Thorne said.

"Nothing," Leach said. "Anything for old Ben's boy."

The left hand, the right hand. What Thorne could not get out of his head was the look on Anna Burckhardt's face, her fear when she opened the kitchen door and they had gone back into the house. Could you work yourself into the state? Could you fabricate it?

Marcia said, "There's a great big stain where that creep who robbed us dumped the vase of flowers. It won't come out. I always thought water never left a stain. Mother's sage sayings, book one."

He watched her as she studied the mark on the rug.

"Anyhow, the lady I spoke to at the White House was very nice in a businessy kind of way," she said. "Hope John gets well quickly, so she said."

She sat on the arm of the sofa, one hand on Thorne's shoulder. In her other hand she held a yellow sponge which looked soiled and muddy.

"So Mrs. Burckhardt wasn't out to seduce you, huh?" She rubbed his neck. "Instead she wound you up and set you off on some clockwork conspiracy."

"Looks that way," Thorne said. "But she seemed so . . . Jesus, so fucking *upset.*"

"She just lost her husband," Marcia said.

Thorne shook his head. "Yeah, yeah. The *estranged* husband."

"So what? If I was estranged from you and you turned up dead in a swimming pool I wouldn't exactly die laughing at the idea."

Thorne got up from the sofa. He went to the balcony door and looked out. The same gray sky turning toward gray evening. The Asterisk Project. He thought about Leach. No. Leach hadn't known anything. That was a blank. He heard Marcia singing at his back.

"She said he was scared."

"Of what?"

"Of being killed, I guess." Outside, through the grayness of the cloud mass, there was a sudden weak watery beam of sunlight. It lasted a moment, then was gone. "Look, if he was being followed—"

"Okay. I'll play," she said.

"If he was really afraid, I mean, afraid of being killed, would he carry anything of value in his case?"

Marcia shrugged: "People do the weirdest things."

"Come on," he said.

"Okay. I guess he wouldn't."

"But he left the case for me, knowing there was nothing of value inside it, right?"

"Right," she said.

"Why?"

Marcia said, "Let me get my deerstalker."

"Be serious."

"Okay. I'm serious. The funny fit has passed. He left you the case because because because . . . He wanted to arouse your curiosity?"

Thorne turned to look at her. She was holding the sponge at arm's length, as if it were an offensive dead fish.

"Why not," he said. "He wanted me to know something."

"Yep," she said. "And years in the armed services had deprived him of straightforward speech. So he only knew the language of cloak and dagger, right?"

"Sometimes you're impossible," he said.

"In my perverse roundabout way I'm trying to help you, John," she said.

"And the burglary," he said. "It stinks. When you think about it, it really stinks."

"Burglaries do," she said.

"This one especially. Why this apartment? Why at that time? Why steal an utterly worthless attaché case? It smells."

Marcia stared at him. "Romantic poetry is less of a labyrinth. I've got work to do."

She went out into the kitchen and he turned once more to look from the window. Night over the Nation's Capital. Tourist attractions were being lit. Floodlights played on monuments. It was a great city of lights.

And dark corners, Thorne thought. Dark corners.

4

The food in the Greyhound station was *malicious*. Hollander could find no other word to describe the concoctions that lay before him. Hot dogs simmering in water, peas that had the appearance of tiny eyes plucked from the heads of extinct birds, cole slaw that was flaky and dry. Beside him in the line Brinkerhoff studied these things in a puzzled way. He passed them over and, like Hollander, settled only for coffee. They went to a table. A voice on the loudspeaker was reading off bus departures: Pittsburgh, Cleveland, Toledo, Chicago.

"You assure me that such food is eaten?" Brinkerhoff said. He was watching Hollander over the rim of his cup.

"Devoured," Hollander said. "With great relish."

The feeble pun was beyond Brinkerhoff, who was looking around the cafeteria at the faces of the various travelers obliged to spend thirty minutes or three hours between connections. Young people with backpacks and suntans returning from the South, foreigners who stood around with perplexing timetables and phrase books in their hands, solitary middle-aged men going out to visit married sons and daughters in Omaha or Sacramento. There were even a couple of freaks, *de rigueur* in Greyhound stations, Hollander thought, who mumbled to themselves.

Brinkerhoff put his coffee down and made a face. "It is remarkably similar to hot water," he said.

Hollander considered the sealed white envelope that lay in his coat pocket. He had taken it from the file and photocopied it in a post office, and now what he was about to give Brinkerhoff was a photocopy of a photocopy, a bad reproduction, but it would be enough. It meant nothing very much without the rest of the file, but if Brinkerhoff's people had any sense they would understand the significance of it. The rest of the file he had placed in a safe-deposit box in the vault of the First National. But as he thought of the envelope, he hesitated.

"You asked me for a little evidence," Hollander said.

"You have it?" Brinkerhoff's pale eyes moved slightly. There was a certain reptilian quality to the eyes, Hollander thought, in the way they were spaced, as if his vision were entirely peripheral.

"I have something," Hollander said. "A hint. That's all. A foretaste."

Brinkerhoff put his cup down, licked his lips. "This is going to take a little time, you understand that. Your . . . offering will have to be analyzed with some care, naturally. And then. Who knows?"

Hollander looked around the cafeteria. "I don't have time to waste," he said.

"Patience," Brinkerhoff said. "A day or two. I can't say."

Both men were silent. Hollander looked at his watch. It was 8:30. A day or two. He couldn't feel safe, he couldn't feel any sense of certainty in the outcome of this. He took out the envelope and slid it across the table to Brinkerhoff, who picked it up and put it in his coat pocket.

Pittsburgh, Cleveland, Toledo, Chicago. This is the last call for passengers for those destinations. Gate number three.

"Life in the Soviet Union will be somewhat different," Brinkerhoff said, smiling. "If it comes to that."

Hollander pushed his coffee aside. What would he be leaving? Greyhound stations and Pancake Palaces and the iconography of Colonel Sanders and Mickey Mouse watches and a democracy gone to the dogs? Maybe. But there were three kids. There was a girl called Davina. There was the solitude. Certainly that.

Brinkerhoff stood up. "I'll call when I have a response, Hollander."

Hollander watched him go quickly from the cafeteria. Then he looked at the faces of the passengers at other tables, thinking of how they appeared stranded, as if they too were uncertain of ever reaching their destinations. Moscow, he thought. None of them are going to Moscow. Moscow.

It wouldn't have happened except for the curious circuitry of history; there would be no Asterisk, no trip to Moscow, no defection. A working knowledge of Russian—by ironic courtesy of the GI Bill of Rights—and a postwar job with a company that sold—Christ—cardboard boxes to the countries of Eastern Europe. 1949. Trips, simple business trips: spiders' webs. Corrugated cardboard.

An illusion. *I had papers,* he thought, *papers I didn't even realize I carried.* Berlin, city of ruins. Death. *How was I to know the fucking papers contained CIA material? Coded bullshit identifying the principal operators of the* Komitet Gosudarstvennoi Bezopasnosti *in the Berlin area?*

The whole goddamn company, he thought. A CIA front. A stooge. The salesman as fall guy, stand-up comedian. *Did I ever tell you the one about the farmer's daughter?* So: slowly, unwittingly, you were recruited. The climate of the World. Red Peril. Frost of the cold war. You were recruited and thought nothing of it.

Covert operations. Everybody was doing it. The Soviets, the British, the Americans, the French. It was the fabric of the age. *Stop world communism. Stand up and be counted.* Then 1952, a continuation of the same pointless conflict; intelligence supplied to the United Nations Forces in Korea.

Gung fucking ho.

You're doing a good job, Ted. We think the world of you.

Washington.

I dirtied my hands, he thought. I got myself stained in the shit of McCarthyism, prime swine time, the madman from the heartland whose pulses palpitated at the thought of a Marxist in the State Department, who would have changed the color of his blood from red to something more American if he had had the power.

Name names.

That was the job: name names. Make it stick good.

Climbing the ladder, Ted.

Old newsreels. Guilty faces. Denials.

And that was your job: dig them out wherever they might be lurking—the State Department, Justice, even the army.

The ritual cleansing of the collective psyche.

Lives falling apart, crashing all around him.

You could continue to blame the times.

When the craziness was over he had gone to London for a year, coordinating the activities of Southern European intelligence from a tranquil office in Grosvenor Square.

But what was it? It was hollow, an empty shell, a surface upon which you rapped your knuckles and heard nothing come back but the echoes of yourself. Obscure fur traders in Stara Zagora had useless information to sell on the subject of Balkan intrigue; haberdashers from Smyrna, hungry for American residence, flew paper darts over the intelligence wires. A Bulgarian minister blows his brains out; a Turkish admiral is screwing his thirteen-year-old niece. Put it in boxes. File it. It added up to nothing. Nothing. It meant nothing, it made no mark, no indentation, upon the delicate equilibrium of the world.

Back home, he thought: a malicious deity had saved Cuba for last. Back home in time to see how all the deadly pieces on the checkerboard could be made to move when the stakes were for real. He was in a world of killers, a world in which only the most fragile of balances prevented the holocaust. They almost had you fooled, Hollander. They almost pulled the wool of patriotism over your eyes. But the darkness had been lifted and there was light and what you perceived was that borderlines and frontiers and properties and divisions didn't matter a shit because nobody was going to get off the old planet alive. Ah, Ted, Ted, Ted. Where was my brain? Sunk in the formaldehyde of nationalism; the preserve jar of insularity. America, America.

But Cuba was only an aperitif. Asterisk was the main course.

Asterisk.

New project for you, Ted. Security of a missile site in Oscura, New Mexico. Asterisk: it might have been the prototype of an advanced toilet tissue for all he cared: what did it matter? You were told to guard something, you guarded it. That was the cards they dealt you.

Breaking point. Shards. *I saw the file.*

I didn't mean to. I didn't want. But I saw the file.

Too easily, too simply, it came my way.

Blueprints, research rata, the whole schmear.

The thing they had christened Asterisk.

He heard the loudspeaker announce more bus departures. In another place at another time it would be a different voice: *Novosibirsk, Omsk, Magnitogorsk and all hellholes west.*

He stood up, gazing at the debris on the table.

There was an ache, a pain, far within him that he could not quite locate. There was an insistent pressure directly behind his eyes. My kids, he thought. My babies.

Moscow. Traitors' Row. It would be a different kind of loneliness there.

The piano was playing in a forlorn, broken way. Sharpe thought of a mongrel stumbling over the keys. What did they say about an infinite number of monkeys on an infinite number of typewriters? Dilbeck opened the conservatory door, Sharpe followed him out; the grass underfoot was damp and muddy. Dilbeck put his eye to the lens of the telescope, muttered to himself, then turned to Sharpe.

"I understand he went to see the widow," he said.

Sharpe nodded.

"What do you suppose they discussed?"

"The weather," Sharpe said. "Inside the house all they discussed was the weather."

"Ah," Dilbeck said. "Then she knows."

"I guess."

Dilbeck tutted, fidgeted with the telescope, put his eye once more to the lens. Inside the house, the piano stopped clunking. "Young Thorne's like the dog who will not let go of the bone," he said. "Even if there appears to be no meat on it."

Sharpe saw the conservatory door open and the daughter appear, a shadow with the light behind her.

"Phone, Daddy," she called out.

Dilbeck went toward the house.

Sharpe hoped the daughter would not join him. He tried to make himself inconspicuous on the lawn, lighting a cigarette, turning away, ignoring how she raised her hand in a greeting. He heard the conservatory door close. But he did not turn around to see if she had come outside or gone back in. He didn't want to encourage her. With that kind, it was the best course to turn your back and say: Fuck it.

He walked down to the trees, then strolled back to the telescope, the conservatory door opened, Dilbeck was coming out across the lawn. He was mumbling to himself, hurrying, as if something of the utmost urgency had taken place. Sharpe braced himself: visiting Dilbeck was like going to a dentist. You knew there would have to be a moment of pain.

"Damn," Dilbeck said.

Sharpe waited. He felt a single drop of rain on his face.

"Damn," Dilbeck said again. "You're going to have to do something about Hollander."

"Hollander? Ted Hollander?" Sharpe said. What was up now?

"Ted, yes," Dilbeck said. "Damn. You're going to have to do something there quickly."

He was silent a moment. His hand lightly lingered on the shaft of the telescope.

"In this business, Sharpe, it never rains without truly pouring," he said.

They gave Myers a meal of fried chicken and mashed potatoes and green beans and apple pie; he understood he was being, in the fashion of the Pavlovian creature, rewarded. He ate hungrily. The captain watched him. What happens to me next? Myers wondered.

When he was through eating, he sat back and lit one of the cigarettes that had been returned to him. They had deprived him of nicotine all day long. He looked at the captain, who was smiling.

"Well, Jack," the captain said. "Feel better?"

"Much better," Myers said.

"It looks like we're going to have to keep you under wraps for a day or two," the captain said. "But you'll eat okay. You'll sleep okay. And you won't have to go around looking for birds."

Under wraps? Myers wondered. They made him sound like something you have to throw a tarpaulin over.

"I'm a prisoner?" he asked.

The captain clapped him on the shoulder. "No, Jack. You're not exactly a prisoner."

Myers looked at his empty plate. And he thought of Hollander; a sinking feeling. He had never been very close with Ted, but they had trusted each other. Now he knew, he knew beyond doubt, that he had landed Ted in something of a mess. Sometime in the future, he thought, he would have to say that he was very sorry.

5:

Wednesday, April 5

IT WAS THREE MINUTES PAST MIDNIGHT AND RAINING. AN upper-floor window of the embassy building was lit, a thin glow behind drawn drapes. Inside the room, Brinkerhoff was walking up and down and pausing now and then to peer through the drapes as if to reassure himself that the world outside did not cease to exist even if he was not perceiving it.

The undersecretary, a stout man whose present relations with the Politburo were outstanding and who therefore could not be crossed, was seated behind his desk and drawing swastikas on his blotter pad. The scientific attaché, whose relations with the Politburo were equally shining, sat slumped in a chair with his legs crossed. On his lap there was a sheet of paper; he was writing something, stopping every so often to suck the end of his pen or to run his fingers, in an agitated way, through his thinning hair.

"It's beyond me," he said finally.

"I don't understand," the undersecretary said. "What is beyond you?"

"This . . . this information," the scientific attaché said.

"The question is not whether it defeats your brain," Brinkerhoff said. "The problem is one of its possible authenticity."

"It isn't in my field," the scientist said. "It would have to be examined by experts."

"Like who?"

"Berganin would be the best," the scientist said. "It's his sphere of interest."

"Berganin is in Moscow," the undersecretary said.

86

"It would take days," Brinkerhoff said. "I don't think Hollander is a man of much patience. He's going to pressure me soon. I have to tell him something."

The undersecretary yawned. "I should wake the ambassador," he said.

"The ambassador is doing what he knows best," Brinkerhoff said. "He's out. He's at a party. And even if he were here he would leave the decision to you, you know that."

The undersecretary yawned again. He looked at the scientific attaché. "Is it conceivable? Answer me that."

The scientist sucked his pen. "Anything's possible—"

"Don't give me answers from the ether," the undersecretary said. "I'm an idiot. Explain to me as you would answer an idiot."

The scientist shrugged. "It's possible. I don't understand it. But it's possible. The consequences, if this were true, would be devastating."

Brinkerhoff turned from the window. He had been watching the rain fall through the streetlamps. "Then we must act on Hollander, because even if there's only the slightest possibility—"

"Look, this is one sheet of paper out of many. We would need the rest."

"Which we will get when we have made certain commitments to Hollander," Brinkerhoff said.

"It smells," the undersecretary said. "He wants to defect. I don't buy it."

Brinkerhoff said, "I don't think he *wants* to defect. If he stays, he's a traitor. If he leaves, he's a traitor but alive. It's simple."

"And if he's a plant?" the undersecretary asked. He was wearing pajamas under a dressing gown. American pajamas, American gown, Brinkerhoff noticed.

"If he's a plant then what have we lost?"

"Your reasoning is wild," the undersecretary said. "A plant is a danger."

"A *disposable* danger," Brinkerhoff said. "There's nothing to lose and much to gain." He looked at the scientific attaché. "Am I right? Am I being reasonable?"

"Reasonable," the scientist said. "If this is a part of Asterisk, then it's very reasonable."

"Asterisk," the undersecretary said. "I wish I had a dollar for every time I've heard something about this marvelous Asterisk."

Brinkerhoff said, "Asterisk or not, do we act on Hollander?"

The undersecretary shrugged. "I can't take the responsibility for this on my own. It needs to be cleared."

"You're talking again of days—two, perhaps three, days."

"This Hollander," the undersecretary said. "I don't like the *sound* of it. He thinks his information is going to make the world safe—"

"Perhaps," Brinkerhoff said. "All this information can be evaluated later. His personality can be dissected. But I urge you to act now, Secretary. But not by diplomatic bag."

The undersecretary stared at his rows of penciled swastikas, then reached for the telephone. "I will make a call. Then we will see."

Brinkerhoff sat down. He placed the tips of his fingers together. Everything was so slow, so slow.

The meeting had gone on too long. Dilbeck was very tired. The air in the conference room was thick with tobacco smoke; papers were strewn across the surface of the long table, ashtrays crammed, people yawning. He looked across the faces, waiting for an opportunity to bring the meeting to a close. Burlingham, the man from the RAND Corporation, was still holding forth. The problem with Burlingham was you couldn't easily shut him up. Dilbeck sighed. Some people were in love with their own noises, just as his daughter, bless her, thought she was really making progress with her music. Noise, everything was noise. It was what the modern world manufactured best of all. The six people of the Asterisk Project Committee were especially adept. Through the lens of a telescope you could sense the peace of space, that was something, even if a freeway droned in the distance. And plants; plants grew silently, patiently. He wanted to go home.

He stood up and tried to bring the thing to order. He had considered bringing up the subject of Thorne before the committee, but if he could contain that for the time being it would be best. Thorne was, as yet, only a small nuisance. And besides, the real reason for this meeting was Ted Hollander.

Burlingham, finally, had stopped talking. Dilbeck looked around the room. Marvell, of the National Security Agency, sat with his necktie undone and, in his shirt-sleeves, had the appearance of a hotshot newspaper reporter hanging on a dramatic deadline. Whorley of Aerospace Defense Command looked his usual alert self. Razor-sharp, Dilbeck thought. You could imagine cutting yourself on Whorley. Nicholson, from the U.S. National Space Board, was gaunt and ghostly. You could see him suddenly fading away around the edges.

"I don't think we've really touched on the *reasons* for Hollander sending a man out there," Dilbeck heard himself say. He was hoarse now; the smoke was in his throat. "I've heard a great deal of wild speculation—"

Burlingham interrupted: "You're in charge of security, Dilbeck. Let's hear it from you."

Marvell sarcastically slapped his hands. "What's your feeling, Dilbeck?" he said. "Let's have it."

Dilbeck closed his eyes. Security, he thought. You tried to sit on something, keep the lid closed: but it was the first law of security that nothing in the world was airtight. This is what the others did not understand. They thought you could create a vacuum, a perfect vacuum.

"Hollander had charge of intelligence, as you all know," he said. "For personal reasons, as he put it, he quit. Who knows why?"

"Why wasn't there an investigation?" Marvell asked.

"He quit," Dilbeck said. "The strains of the job, I daresay. His wife found somebody else. Divorce. That kind of thing tells on a man."

"This is history," Burlingham said.

"History," Dilbeck said. Could he ever get Emily married off? he wondered. Fatigue: the most random thoughts came in like birds. "History," he said again, feeling for threads. "Hollander's history is important here. For one thing, in the course of his job, he might have stumbled across some information. We can speculate further and say that he *must* have. Otherwise, why send a man out to that godforsaken place? Why go to that trouble? So Hollander has some information on Asterisk. How much? And what does he plan to do with it?"

Marvell rolled his shirt sleeves up in the manner of someone who faces a long night ahead. Dilbeck watched him and thought: *No, I want to wrap it up, I want to go home.*

"There's nothing in his background to suggest any association with foreign powers," Dilbeck said. "His record is exemplary. I wish, in fact, we could find men of his caliber these days. Anyhow, somewhere along the way he discovered something about Asterisk—"

"And who do we blame for that?" General Whorley asked.

"Blame?" Dilbeck said. "Who do we blame for Major General Burckhardt? You people live in dreams. You think something like this is—is easily contained. You can put it in a box and tie it with a ribbon and nobody gets to look inside. But that's a fallacy. Hollander isn't a fool. The man is naturally curious. Some people take orders, don't ask questions, but Hollander—"

He watched Whorley get up and open a window a little way. Security, he thought. What did these people know? A little smoke and Whorley has to open a window. A mindless gesture. They were trying to pin every security breach on him, Dilbeck realized: I won't take the blame because there isn't any blame.

"Hollander," Nicholson said. "I just don't see any viable alternative in a situation like this."

Burlingham looked at his papers and nodded. "Nor do I," he said.

Whorley had returned to his seat. Cold, damp air was dissolving the smoke in the room. "Asterisk is more important than Hollander," he said. He had a way of saying things with finality, leaving no margins for argument. "And as far as Walter Burckhardt was concerned, I don't think that's my baby. I'm on record, I didn't want him to go any further, I wanted him out—"

"We're not discussing Burckhardt," Marvell said. "It's Hollander. I think it's a problem we can safely leave to you, Dilbeck."

Pontius Pilate, Dilbeck thought. He looked around the table. Hollander. He had always liked Ted. But that was the run of things. Death was no more significant than spitting a fishbone from your mouth. Nothing was permitted to get in Asterisk's way. Not even Ted.

Sometimes he felt he was scrambling up an impossible slope or being made, like Sisyphus, to fulfill a horrible task. You could not cover everything, you could not create a blueprint that would account for every single contingency. Poor Ted.

"I think we can assume that Hollander has some vital information on Asterisk," he said. "I think we can also assume that he means to go public with it eventually."

"Nobody would print such a thing," Nicholson, somewhat shocked, said.

"Wrong," Dilbeck said. "You have an underground press in this country, a fact that may have escaped your attention. You have alternative news media. If Hollander went public, he would find plenty of takers."

"You're ruling out the Soviets?" Whorley asked.

"In Ted's case, yes." Dilbeck felt his shoulders sag. He badly needed to be home, in bed, dreaming. Away from all this. Away. This was the moment he hated. "You're all agreed to leave this with me?"

The other faces nodded. Mob rule, he thought. The committee and the donkey. The whole and its parts.

He looked to the opposite end of the table. "Congressman?"

The congressman also nodded. As chairman of the House Science and Astronautics Committee he had some pull with this crew.

"I agree," he said. "Deal with it as you like, Dilbeck."

"I will," Dilbeck said. He turned his face away from the congressman. It had been obvious to him for some time that Leach was a dying man. So are we all, he thought, so are we all dying men.

"Thank you for your confidence," Dilbeck said in a hollow way, and gathered his papers together. The ball had been already set rolling; and even if they had disagreed he wasn't sure he could have stopped its momentum anyhow.

It made Tarkington sick. *Ted Hollander.* Not Ted Hollander. He had had to ask Sharpe three times if there was some misunderstanding. There was none. *Ted Hollander.* What the fuck was going on? He got out of the Catalina. Lykiard emerged a moment later, having taken a length of nylon rope from the glove compartment. They stood in the

rain outside the apartment building. This was no Nazi,
Tarkington thought. This was no funny Greek patriotic
business, dead of night, blow away a couple of Gestapo
babies. This was Ted Hollander.

He stared gloomily through the rain. Christ was not in
his heaven tonight. Jesus, he thought. Hollander had stood
by him during that whole London business when everyone
else was screaming for his head or his resignation, preferably both. Even Lykiard, with the soul of a barracuda, even
the Greek had to feel *some* twinge.

Holy fuck. His stomach was going to turn. He had
taken more white crosses and he was jangling, sick and
jangling. He beat his fist into the open palm of his hand
and watched Lykiard stick the sliver of rope into his coat
pocket. The fucking Greek, no feelings, nothing in his
heart.

The Greek nodded.

A car had drawn up outside the building. He saw the
familiar figure of Hollander get out, slam the door, move
toward the entranceway. According to Sharpe it was apartment number thirty-six. Hollander had some cutie stashed
away up there. Which figured, Tarkington thought. The
wife was long since gone. It was an emptiness that Tarkington, in a dulled way, understood.

I can't hack this, he thought.

The Greek had already begun to cross the street. The
rope in his pocket. Hand over the rope. Lykiard's eager-
ness was revolting, loathsome. *Oh, shit, Ted, what have
you done to bring this on yourself?* He put his fingers inside his jacket to the holster. Pray you don't need to use it.
Pray the Greek can do it fast with his nylon doodah.

He followed Lykiard. It was warm inside the building.
You climb the stairs, make believe it's a stranger you're
going to see. *To eliminate.*

Ted, sweetheart.

They used the stairway, reached the third floor.

"Lykiard, wait," Tarkington said.

The Greek paused. He turned to Tarkington, who saw
nothing in those eyes but hardness. He said nothing. He
looked up the stairwell. At the very top there was a black
skylight smeared with rain. A night like this, Tarkington
thought. Fuck it all. You had to feel sick.

They went along the corridor. Thirty, thirty-two, thirty-four.

Thirty-six.

Yeah, Tarkington thought. To be an insurance salesman right now. *Excuse this late call, my dear fellow, but your policy contains a slight anomaly.*

Your expiration date has been somewhat altered.

Christ on crutches.

"Wait," he whispered to the Greek. But the Greek wasn't much good at waiting.

She was asleep. Hollander bent over, kissed her lightly. He wondered how many had been here tonight. How many had come and gone? He took off his jacket. He hung it on the back of a chair. She didn't waken. He went into the kitchen. He turned on a light, looked at the messages on the blackboard. *Dave 12:30. Cancel karate. Susie's answering service 342/2050.* At least she didn't walk the streets, it hadn't come to that. What was the phrase they used? An escort service? Lonely businessmen burning with lust at conventions in slick hotels. Out-of-town strangers, carrying a telephone number furtively tucked inside their billfolds all the way from Reno to D.C. It was hardly more than one a night and, on some nights, not even that. What did it matter to him? He would have vanished out of her life soon enough. Time would pass. Things would continue. It didn't matter.

I knew him intimately, I didn't think he was capable of such an act. They would interview her. She might even make money. *I was a traitor's mistress.* He took off his shoes. He opened the refrigerator and found a half-empty bottle of retsina and he poured himself a small glass. It tasted sour. He would have to get used to vodka, there was nothing else for it.

The right thing, he thought. It was too late for doubt.

Too late for that.

He raised his face. Someone was on the other side of the door. In the corridor. He went quickly and quietly into the bedroom and woke the girl.

"Ted," she said. She put her arms around his neck. He drew away from her and put a finger to his lips.

"Sshh," he said.

"I don't understand," she said.

He put his hand over her mouth. *Say nothing.*

He went into the sitting room and sat in the darkness.

From the pocket of his pants he took out a switchblade knife and released the spring. He waited. He stared at the door. The girl appeared in the bedroom doorway, drawing a nightgown over her shoulders; a flimsy garment. It would flutter hearts in Cedar Rapids.

He motioned her away.

She stood, with the light falling behind her, and looked at him in a puzzled manner.

"Ted—"

He saw the front door handle turn. They were at the lock. He could hear the faint scratch of metal on metal, the tumblers of the lock clicking. He got out of the chair.

"Go back to bed," he told the girl.

She was staring at the doorknob. "Ted," she whispered.

The door opened.

He recognized the ropeman, Lykiard, and behind him, moving as slowly as ever, Billy Tarkington. Lykiard had the nylon taut between his two hands, the hands extended. The Greek was strong.

He came forward.

He stepped into darkness.

Grunting, Hollander thrust the blade upward between the ribs, dead into the chest cavity. In the bedroom doorway the girl was retching. The Greek went down on his knees and Hollander reached across the space in the dark and seized the hair and snapped the head backward, pushing Lykiard aside.

"Tarkie," he said.

Tarkington stood with his hands at his side.

"Ted, look," Tarkington said.

"Orders," Hollander said.

"Fucking orders," Tarkington said.

Hollander saw terror in the fat face.

"What's it going to be, Tarkie?"

Tarkington looked at the Greek. "I didn't want this, Ted."

"You take orders, that's all you do, Tarkie. Don't ask questions." Hollander felt a curious stabbing pain in his side, a stitch, he was beyond this kind of exertion. His lungs worked furiously. His eyes, there were dark spots floating before his eyes.

"I didn't ask for this," Tarkington said.

"No," Hollander said. "What's it going to be?"

Tarkington glanced at the girl. Hollander's cutie. She had her hand across her lips. He looked down at the Greek who was staining the rug. Old Ted; you had to hand it to him, he still knew the moves, coming up through the darkness before the Greek knew the time of day.

When he spoke his voice was shaky: "Ted, listen—"

"I could kill you," Hollander said. "Before you had time to reach your holster, I could kill you."

It was bluff, pure bull, Hollander felt weak, all his strength draining out of him.

"Or you could drag your dead friend out of here, go back, make up some convincing fiction, and give me a little time."

Tarkington had thoughts of death. The girl in the doorway moved, went out of his vision; he heard water run and a toilet flush. He could, he supposed, do what Hollander wanted. He could do that. It was a problem with Sharpe.

"What do I say to Sharpe?" Tarkington asked.

"That's your business," Hollander said.

Tarkington looked at the dead man. He was glad it wasn't Hollander.

"Make it up, Tarkie," Hollander said. "It wouldn't be the first time, would it?"

"No," Tarkington said. He reached down, felt for the Greek's pulse. Still and silent.

"Take him," Hollander said.

"Okay." Tarkington got down on his knees. He wasn't even sure he could drag Lykiard, never mind get him down several flights of stairs.

The alternative was to go for his holster.

But Ted: Ted was too fast. Ted still knew his stuff.

"Okay," he said.

"Go someplace, fire your gun a couple of times," Hollander said. "If Sharpe wants to know, you can always say you took a couple of quick ones at me while I was running away."

Hollander waited. He wasn't sure that Tarkington would go for it; he was counting on the fat man's inborn fear.

Tarkington straightened up, dragged the Greek by the heels toward the door. The toilet flushed again.

Hollander held the knife distastefully. In the doorway, Tarkington paused, sweating. He was already thinking of Sharpe, Sharpe's face, the whole fuck-up he would have to suffer through. *The holster*, he thought. *Would there be time?*

He knew there wouldn't be before Hollander was on him with the knife.

"Maybe," Tarkington said. "Maybe we'll run into one another again, huh?"

"I doubt it," Hollander said.

Tarkington looked down at the Greek a moment. "I'm glad you got him first, Ted. I'm glad about that much."

2

The *Post*'s editorial was sharply critical. Thorne cut it out and put it aside. Maybe, maybe not, he thought. It was headlined "Appealing to Nobody."

President Foster, in attempting to be all things to all men, runs the grave risk of being nothing to anybody. It would probably bring Bannerman down on his head, as well as Farrago, but he would send it up in his summary anyhow.

His telephone rang.

Farrago, on the other end, said: "Your cold better?"

"A bit," Thorne said.

"Guys like you," Farrago said. "You spend too much time on the nest. It weakens your resistance to germs. Take vitamins, John. Especially the B_{12} complex and a healthy dose of C."

"It works for you?" Thorne asked.

"Nothing works for me," Farrago said. "Including you. You finished yet?"

"Almost."

When Thorne hung up he called Sally Winfield in and raced through his dictation to her. At the last moment he included the *Post* editorial. There was some critical stuff from the *New York Times* and an article in the *Star* that wouldn't do Foster's blood pressure much good. He put them all together, added something pleasant he found in yesterday's *Phoenix Gazette. He may be a Democrat but he has the solid fiscal instincts of a conservative.* There, Thorne thought: your open-ended policy is paying off in the sticks. Next thing would be a letter of praise from Senator Goldwater.

When he had finished his dictation, he put on his jacket and went out. He told Sally he would be back in thirty minutes. He drove to the same seafood restaurant he had gone to before, the *Shrimp's Hideaway.* Erickson was already at the table, a cup of coffee in front of him. Fidgeting, looking somewhat like a nervy Clark Kent.

Thorne slipped into the seat facing Erickson.

"Did you get me the stuff?"

Erickson was flustered. "Man, you're going to skin me, I tell you no lies. This is the second favor this week. I can't keep this kind of thing up, you know that."

"I know," Thorne said. "I appreciate."

Erickson opened his briefcase and took out a bulky envelope. He slid it across the table, then picked up his coffee. "What the hell's going on anyhow?" he asked.

Thorne picked up the envelope and put it into his own briefcase, locking it.

"First it's Major General Whatsisname, now it's the heavy shit. What gives?"

"It's something Bannerman wants," Thorne said.

"You expect me to buy that one? Bannerman only has to pick up his telephone. He doesn't send out an errand boy. He doesn't go in for this kind of crap."

Erickson, narrowing his eyes in a look of both scrutiny and disbelief, finished his coffee. "Don't tell me anything. I don't want to know. Okay? And do me a favor."

"If I can," Thorne said.

"No more favors," Erickson said. "Store's closed. Gone to lunch. Savvy?"

"I'm with you," Thorne said. He watched Erickson rise and leave the restaurant. After a few moments he picked up his briefcase, went outside, unlocked the VW, drove away. A black Mercury that had followed him down Pennsylvania Avenue slipped away from the sidewalk and tracked him back to the White House.

In his office he found a telephone message on his desk. It said simply: *Senator Jacobson called. Call back.* He asked Sally to get him the senator's office. What did Jacobson want? Another old friend of his father's, Jacobson had

fitted neatly into the slots left vacant by Senator Thorne's
death. Politically, both men had been the closest of allies;
but whereas Ben Thorne had been open, gregarious, and
sometimes, according to his critics, indiscreet, Jacobson
was the kind of man who played whatever cards he held
in a furtive way. Thorne realized that he had not seen the
senator in more than a year—so why this call now?

He heard a woman's voice say, "Senator Jacobson's office."

"John Thorne, I'm returning—"

"Ah, Mr. Thorne. The senator wanted to know if you
would be free for lunch today."

Thorne looked at his desk diary. The day was blank. He
had intended seeing Marcia between her classes. But that
could wait.

"I think I am," he said.

"Fine. The senator has a meeting that ought to finish
around twelve fifteen, twelve thirty. Shall I call you back
when he's free?"

"Fine," Thorne said.

Senator William Jacobson: in cartoons he was always
characterized as having the collar of his raincoat turned
up, as if he had something dreadful to hide. He had an
oddly bland face, the kind you had to concentrate on to
remember. How does a man go so far in politics with such
a curious anonymity? He was in the papers a great deal,
usually in connection with Senate investigations of or-
ganized crime. He had published a book on the Mafia. Before entering politics, Thorne remembered, he had been a
professor of law at Columbia.

His telephone was ringing again. It was Farrago.

"I just had Bannerman chewing my balls off," he said.
"What the fuck are you playing at? Can't you find something in the fucking papers to cheer the Old Man up?"

"I'm doing my best," Thorne said.

"Try a little harder—"

"If I tried any harder, I'd be sending up obituaries,"
Thorne said. "In case you hadn't noticed it, the papers
aren't exactly falling over themselves to give the Old Man
merit marks—"

"Fuck," Farrago said. "Go back to sleep."

Thorne heard the click of a dead line.

He sat back, put up his feet, and thought about the

briefcase. It was tempting to open it here and go through Erickson's envelope—but that would be running a needless risk. Farrago could come in, or the oleaginous Duncannon, or even Bannerman himself on one of his irregular tours. Later, he thought. There would be plenty of time.

"Lykiard's in the fucking Potomac," Tarkington was saying.

But Sharpe was hardly listening; there was a time for excuses and a time for explanations, but right now was a time of planning what to say to Dilbeck. His anger was a slow fuse.

"I don't give that"—he snapped his fingers—"I don't give a monkey's fuck about the Greek. What I don't get is how two of you couldn't deal with Hollander. That's what I don't get."

Tarkington was trying to look through the slats of the blind. He wanted to believe it was daylight out there and not the continuation of some endless night.

"I might have wounded him," Tarkington said. "Look, he surprised us. He knifed the Greek. Before I could get my gun out . . ." He shrugged his shoulders. Was it going to wash? You could never tell with Sharpe. He was sitting behind his desk, his fists clenched.

"So where's Hollander now?" Sharpe said.

"I don't know."

"You know what you're good at, Tarkington? You know what?"

Tarkington waited, holding his breath.

"You're good at sweet fuck all," Sharpe said. "That's what you do best. You couldn't operate a pinball machine without the help of a Guide Dog."

Tarkington screwed up his eyes. There was sun out there. Over D.C., a flat white sun. A brand-new day.

"Okay," Sharpe said, rising from his desk.

"I said I think I wounded him," Tarkington said.

"By the same token, Tarkington, you might have been a fucking astronaut," Sharpe shouted at him. "You know what I'm going to do with you?"

Reykjavik, Tarkington thought. Ceylon, maybe. He had an overwhelming desire to get laid.

"I'm putting you back on Thorne as of now," Sharpe said. "Brandt's on him, but I want Brandt back here. You can't fuck up a simple thing like keeping an eye on Thorne, I guess."

It might have been worse, Tarkington thought. Surveillance could be a drag but Thorne didn't seem to move around a great deal so there was a chance to breathe, unwind a bit. It might have been goddamn Iceland. Or worse.

"Tell Brandt I want him in," Sharpe said. "Now get your ass out of my office before I puke."

Tarkington went out.

Sharpe unclenched his fists, noticing that the blood had drained from his fingers, that his fingers now looked the way they did after a long swim, white and drained and wrinkled. They were everywhere: you only had to knock once on the woodwork and there were incompetents everywhere. He would have to face Dilbeck again, maybe even the daughter.

Hollander, he thought. I ought to have known better. The old dog had learned all the old tricks. And he hadn't forgotten them.

It was a cheap hotel, a place for rummies, potential suicides, cut-rate whores, the unretreadable rejects of a Great Society. Hollander had checked in during the hours of darkness, noticing that the thin neon that burned outside had shed some of its letters, leaving impenetrable gaps in the sky: Hotel T j na. An inscrutable hieroglyphic, like something seen on the side of a passing boxcar. The clerk had been asleep at his desk. Hollander had paid in advance for one night, gone up to the fifth floor in an elevator he had last seen in a 1940s movie, locked himself in a room decorated in faded chintz, and fallen asleep. He slept for three or four hours and when he woke it was daylight and the sun was coming in beneath the brown blind. He woke thinking of Davina, how she had been sitting in a scared crouch in the corner of the bedroom, quite beyond explanations. Well. It could only have come through Myers, he thought. It could only have happened that way. But it was insignificant to him now, a trifle; it was enough for him to know that they had uncovered him.

They want me dead, he thought. It was quite a discovery to know that somebody had your number. But even that seemed unimportant. The only real thing was how

Brinkerhoff's people would react to his offering. How quickly they would respond. And then there was Escalante; the realms of endless speculation. Since they had failed to kill him, would they go to the trouble of moving it from Escalante? Would they go to that trouble?

He pulled up the blind. His body was stiff. There was a white sun over the tenements and, in the street below, a black in a long coat crossing the pavement with a brown bag clutched against his chest. The room smelled. The flowers on the wallpaper had long faded. There was a stain on the white sheets. It was a place you came to when there was nowhere left to go: a dead end.

But how much did they think he knew? Just how much? Enough, obviously, if they wanted him dead. Enough.

Did they know about Brinkerhoff? They couldn't, unless from time to time they exercised a little random surveillance. But he hadn't ever felt that strange intuition he always experienced when he was being followed. Maybe that meant nothing except the fact he was getting old, loosening up, letting his guard down.

No. They couldn't know about Brinkerhoff. If they did, they wouldn't have put out the death warrant. They would have hauled him in for questions. They would have wanted to know how much of it had gone to Brinkerhoff.

Reasonable. But this wasn't a place for reason.

If you started in on the hunt for reason, you wound up on a paper chase. I would have to look back into the crystal ball of my infancy, he thought, to understand why I'm doing what I'm doing. Selling out my country. Going over the wall. Giving things away, things they didn't want to give away, the Secrets. Later, they'll say: He must have been a communist, a red, why the fuck didn't anybody notice?

He smiled faintly. Streaks of light from the morning sun glinted on the windows of the tenements. In Moscow there would be snow. A cold wind coming off the Volga.

All I am, he thought, is the plus sign in a necessary equation.

Tired, he lay down on the bed. He had a picture of the Greek coming at him, the blade going in, the quick escape of Lykiard's breath from his open mouth and that look, that weirdly stunned look, in the eyes, like the astonished expression of a prizefighter who has walked straight into a sucker punch. It had been a long time since he had killed. What he hoped was that he wouldn't have to do it again. Ever.

They ate a lunch of lobster and salad. The senator talked small talk, a craft at which he was a master. Thorne imagined him moving with ease through fund-raising barbecues or cutting ribbons for new shopping malls. It was an art, this small talk. A part of it was how you paused, drew your breath, used your eyebrows during the silences; as if you were assimilating information of colossal import.

How have you been? What do you like about Foster? How is the work? Have you seen your mother lately?

They drank white wine and Thorne looked around the restaurant. It was the kind of place that made him uncomfortable; the waiters were gliding flunkies who seemed to approach your table on roller skates. And the senator had obviously developed a form of imperceptible semaphore with them; they came to the table even when it was not apparent to Thorne that Jacobson had called them. He felt somewhat suffocated by it all, the silent rugs, the heavy curtains, the burnished brass of the interior.

Over coffee, the senator lit a cigar and sat back in his chair.

"Are you happy with your work, John?" he asked.

"It's interesting," Thorne said. He placed an invisible "sir" at the end of each sentence he spoke, while he tried to keep in mind Marcia's distaste: *They're only interested in the freebies that go with the job, John. They're the number one fuckers of the democratic ideal.*

"You sound, ah, not altogether fulfilled," Jacobson said.

"I don't imagine myself doing it for the rest of my life, if that's what you mean," Thorne said.

"Of course not." Jacobson touched his spectacles. He was looking furtive all at once, turning his head this way and that; a world of potential eavesdroppers. "It's a start, not a bad start, some might say."

"It's a start," Thorne agreed. Where was this going?

"I daresay you entertain other ambitions."

"Well," Thorne said. "I guess."

"Politics?" The senator was smiling in a benign way.

"Maybe, I don't know."

"It isn't a bad life," Jacobson said. "If you've got the constitution of a buffalo, don't need much sleep, and don't court scandal."

Court scandal, Thorne thought. Quaint was the word for that one. This was Scandal City.

Jacobson blew a smoke ring and watched it drift off. Thorne was tempted to put his finger through it. From the corner of his eyes he noticed a waiter about to pounce on their table.

"There's a matter I've been asked, ah, to approach you about," the senator said.

Thorne looked suitably perplexed.

"It's not my province, of course. But since I know you personally, I agreed to speak with you—"

"Yes?" Thorne leaned forward, elbows on the table. What was coming next?

"Are you interested in running for the House of Representatives?"

"Do I hear you right?" Thorne asked.

"You do," said the senator. "I was approached, if that's the word, by a certain party. They sounded me out, so to speak. I told them frankly that I didn't know your feelings. This is all pretty much backroom stuff, John, and I'm not happy with it, but I think it's what your father might have expected of me."

Congressman Thorne, he thought. It would make a good TV series. He watched Jacobson relight the cigar with a slight flourish of his gold lighter. Why did everybody speak of his father as if they were talking about the pope? It was always the same reverential hush.

"The point is, Lindstrom is not running this year," Jacobson said. "And since that's your father's old congressional district, you can see how *useful* your name would be."

"I can see," Thorne said.

"Lindstrom's retiring. He would have been reelected anyhow. It would be a safe thing for you, I imagine." The senator stared at the tip of the cigar as if it suddenly irritated him. "If you're at all interested."

"I don't know," Thorne said. It sounded off somehow, it didn't ring true to him. What was behind it? Or was it just the family name? Was he catching that contagious paranoia that had begun, like some wretched virus, in a leather attaché case?

"Of course, it would mean full-time campaigning," the senator said. "You would have to resign from the White House."

"Of course," Thorne said.

"And other, ah, pursuits would be out of the question, naturally."

There it was. There. Laid on the line. Visible as all hell. Other pursuits.

Other pursuits.

"I don't think I follow," Thorne said. Push it, he thought. "Other pursuits?"

"What I mean is that congressional campaigning isn't just a matter of shaking hands." Jacobson laughed, as if at some intensely private joke. "It's demanding, it can be grueling, it consumes most of one's time. There just isn't the time for much else besides."

It was clumsy and obvious. Thorne felt awkward. He sat back in his chair and realized he was sweating, that his forehead was damp, his armpits moist. Diversionary tactics, didn't they call it that? You simply change the road signs around. They wanted him to change direction. Somebody else was sweating apart from himself.

"I'd like to think it over," he said.

Jacobson put out his cigar and looked apologetic. "I'm afraid it's not like that, John. There just isn't time. My party wants an answer immediately. I regret the haste of all this, but sometimes these things won't wait. What's it to be? Yes or no?"

He looked into Jacobson's eyes, saw there a blatant discomfort; it was as if he had a rash he was unhappy about scratching in public. He had been pressured. He had been pushed into this. It was all written on his face.

"No," Thorne said.

"Think again, John."

Thorne was silent for a moment. "I've thought," he said.

"Say yes, John."

Thorne got up from the table. "I'm too young for politics, Senator," he said. "But convey my thanks to your party, please."

He walked out of the restaurant.

The sunlight on the street was unexpectedly hot on his

face. He went in the direction of his VW. He unlocked it but didn't step inside immediately. He allowed the warm trapped air to escape, leaving the door open awhile. The United States Congress. What in the name of Christ had he stumbled into here?

He got inside the car, closed the door, remembered sitting with Anna Burckhardt in the rain and watching the back of the house as if there were unwanted strangers inside—that was the feeling he had now. That there were rooms you expected to be empty until you opened doors and crossed thresholds.

From the coin-operated telephone in the lobby of the Hotel T j na, Hollander dialed Brinkerhoff's number. He got a girl who spoke English as if she had devoured a phrase book.

"Brinkerhoff," he said.

"One moment, if you please," she said.

There was buzzing, static, then Brinkerhoff came on the line.

"Have you decided?" Hollander asked.

"These things take time," Brinkerhoff said.

"Time isn't what I've got," Hollander said. "They're on to me."

Brinkerhoff was silent a moment.

"How did it happen?"

"Does that matter?" Hollander looked along the lobby. A redhaired woman was talking to the desk clerk. She had her arm around the waist of a man who was so drunk that any sexual performance on his part would have been a minor miracle.

"They know about our conversations?" Brinkerhoff asked.

"I don't think so."

"Good."

"When can you come through?" Hollander asked.

"You must be patient. Bureaucracy is an elephant."

"You better start cracking whips, baby," Hollander said.

"Cracking whips?"

"I'll call you back." Hollander put the telephone down. The woman was helping the man into the elevator. He glanced in a bleary way at Hollander; momentarily, Hollander felt the edge of suspicion. I can be certain of nothing from here on in, he thought. Trust nothing, accept nothing. Out there, somewhere, they're looking for me.

"Our friend may very well be anxious," the undersecretary said. "It does not alter the fact that until the situation is clarified I can do nothing."

Brinkerhoff gazed up at the portrait of Lenin. The sun struck it, causing the glass in the frame to gleam.

"When can we expect this . . . clarification?" Brinkerhoff asked.

"I'm not a mind reader," the undersecretary said. "Does our friend think we just open our arms and embrace anybody who wants to defect? Does he imagine that just because he's an American we will be ecstatic to have him? A defector is an expensive commodity, Brinkerhoff. They don't come cheaply."

Brinkerhoff sat down. What could he do but wait? He chewed on a fingernail, then, annoyed with himself, put the hand inside a pocket where it might be safe from further mastication.

3

She was scared. It was not the physical punishment, it was the fear that came from not knowing how it would end, a terrible consciousness of dying. Over and over she had told them she knew nothing. She had screamed it at them. Now, while one of them stood in the bathroom doorway and watched her, she examined her own reflection in the mirror. Her upper lip was swollen, there was a cut beneath her eye, a bruise on her throat. She splashed cold water on her face. What was the other one doing? Going through the apartment as if he might still be here?

She turned to the man in the doorway: "Why don't you look under my bed?"

The man said nothing, watched her impassively.

She moved past him. He followed her into the living room. She sat down, took an English Oval from the pack he had left behind, lit it.

"You guys have really cramped my style, you know that?" she said. She could not keep the quiver out of her voice no matter how hard she tried.

The other guy came out of the bedroom and glared at

her. It was this one, the one with the square, clean looks of the hometown jock, who had hurt her the most. Now he looked as if he might hit her again.

"Are you jokers through?" she asked.

"One more time," the jock said. "He left no address. You don't know where to get in touch with him."

"Yeah yeah," she said. "I told you once, I told you like a thousand times. He went. Under the circumstances, I didn't expect him to hang around."

The man stared at her. She had rarely seen, even in her short lifetime of encountering kooks, such an open expression of violence. He could kill, she knew that at a glance. He could kill, go home, eat dinner as if nothing had even happened. Her lip really hurt. She would be out of work for days. She stubbed the cigarette, desperately trying to keep her hand from shaking. She didn't want them to know they had got through to the target, she wouldn't give them that satisfaction.

"Okay," the jock said. "You better keep your nose clean."

The two men went to the door.

She said, "Stick it, jack. Stick it up your ass."

The jock laughed, the other goon looked grim. They closed the door quietly behind them.

Hollander, she thought. You must have done something pretty bad in your time.

Sharpe let Dilbeck ramble on for a time, barely listening to the man's tirade. He lowered his eyes, like a schoolboy in trouble, studied the floor, shifted his weight around. Finally, when it seemed Dilbeck had run out of power, he said: "I lost a man, a good man."

"Do you want me to say my heart bleeds for you, Sharpe? You may have lost a man. But I've lost Ted Hollander, which is far more important—"

"Look," Sharpe said, shutting his eyes, fumbling around in the darkness of his head as if he were trying to locate an extra shot of strength; "Look, I have my people going through this town right now. I have them looking for Hollander. And if he's still around we'll find him. You can be assured of that—"

"Your assurances have a hollow ring, Sharpe, if I may say so." Dilbeck turned to a plant like someone seeking solace after a funeral. He picked up the pot, held the plant to the light. Something he saw on a leaf displeased him. He held it between thumb and forefinger, rubbing the tips of the two fingers together. "God, a mealybug. All I need right now is an epidemic of that."

"Listen," Sharpe said, thinking: Screw your mealybug. "I'm understaffed and underbudgeted—"

"Damn your budget. Appropriate what you want. Ask. Just ask. You'll get it."

"I don't need money, I need well-trained men," Sharpe said, his voice rising. "You know how long it takes to train a guy? It takes forever. These aren't the old days, if you don't mind my saying. We don't get men like we used to—"

"It's a familiar song," Dilbeck was saying. He had wandered off between the trestle tables, and it looked as if he was intent on examining every leaf in his search for the bugs. "It's a familiar song and it's rather late in the day to be singing it."

"Okay," Sharpe said. He wanted badly to sit. There was nowhere to sit. He felt a quick muscular pain in his left calf. "Okay, I agree. *But we're doing everything we can.*"

"With incompetents, clowns, and buffoons," Dilbeck said. He was reaching into a plant that looked to Sharpe like some kind of ivy. "Got you!" he exclaimed, rubbing out another bug.

The fucking plants. What was important here? Sharpe wondered.

"Then, of course, there's the problem of our young friend Thorne," Dilbeck said. "It won't go away simply by wishing. I've been reading your surveillance briefs. Why is he seeing Erickson? What's the connection there? Thorne is getting to be a bad nuisance."

"I've got him watched, twenty-four hours out of every twenty-four," Sharpe said.

"Watched," Dilbeck said, not without contempt. "I want a little pressure there."

"Like how?" Sharpe asked.

"I'll handle that end," Dilbeck said. "With all due respect, Sharpe, a certain *finesse* is needed."

Finesse, Sharpe thought. Sometimes the only finesse people understood was a five-pack in the teeth.

* * *

Thorne spread the papers on the kitchen table. Marcia stood behind him, watching. She put her hands on his shoulders and said: "More top-secret shit?"

Thorne said nothing.

"It looks like a computer printout," she said. "Is that what it is?"

"That's what it is," he said.

"Of what?"

"Secret," he said.

She wandered around the kitchen, poured herself a glass of milk, said something about calcium. She paused by the edge of the table.

"Why don't you think Jacobson was on the level? I mean, I don't want to see you in the crap of politics, John, but at the same time I don't want to see you on the long boulevard that leads all the way down to the schizo factory—"

"I'm not being schizo," he said. "I just don't like it when things don't add up."

"Nothing ever adds up," she said.

"Nothing ever adds up. What kind of grad-school mumbo jumbo is that?" he asked.

"Suit yourself, honey," she said. She went into the living room to her books.

He straightened the papers. They were stats of printouts from a Pentagon computer. They listed, one by one, the personnel data of the hard missile sites. He began to go down the list.

Adamson, Idaho
Badger, Montana
Caledonia, Nebraska
Davenport, Utah
Escalante, Arizona

He looked closer.

He skipped over the names listed under STAFF, SECURITY and went directly to those that came under the heading STAFF, TECHNICAL. At first, he did not believe what he saw; at first, it seemed to him that what he had discovered was just another enigma. If Escalante was a hard missile site, then these names made no sense. If, on the other hand, it was something else . . . But what?

He paused, raised his head, stared at the wall.

Then he looked back at the sheets again. He looked at the technical-staff data for the sites apart from Escalante. Predictable. Missile engineers. A nuclear physicist or two. But none of the other sites had anything that remotely approached the technical personnel at Escalante.

He walked up and down the kitchen for a time.

Why? Why?

He returned to the table and reread the listings again.

STAFF, TECHNICAL

MORGENTHAU, HAROLD S., PH.D.	CRYPTANALYST
FLYNN, WILLIAM K. B., PH.D.	LINGUIST
FORD, JASON L., PH.D.	LINGUIST
DANCE, TURNER M., PH.D.	ASTRONOMER

Beneath the list of these names, in the margin at the side of the printout, there was the character *. A footnote, Thorne thought. Somewhere there would be an explanatory footnote. He turned the pages. He found Zelda, Montana, the last listing. Then nothing. Nothing. The asterisk went nowhere. It led to zero. An asterisk that was not explained.

And those names, those Ph.D.s—Christ, what connection could they have with a hard missile site? A cryptanalyst, two linguists, an astronomer? Space, language, and space, codes to be cracked—what did that add up to?

He went into the living room.

Marcia was lying on the sofa, reading a book.

"Well?" she said. "What's the score?"

Thorne was looking along the bookshelves. "Haven't we got an old *Who's Who* somewhere?"

"Bottom shelf to your right," Marcia said.

He found it and gave it to her.

"I get to play?" she asked.

"I want you to check four names for me," he said.

She sat up on one elbow. He read the names to her. She checked each, reading the entries aloud. When she had finished, she looked at him curiously.

"Okay. What's what?"

"Those guys are listed as the technical staff at Escalante, which is supposed to be a hard missile site," Thorne said.

"And?"

"Come on—don't you think it damned odd? What kind of connection is there between a linguist, for example, and a nuclear missile?"

Marcia shrugged. "Listen, we live in a world where educated guys talk to dolphins—"

Thorne felt exasperated. "Think," he said.

"Well," Marcia said. "I noticed one tiny detail about the four."

"Yeah?"

"It's probably nothing."

Thorne closed his eyes. "Tell me."

"Unless I'm much mistaken," she said, and paused, "they're all over the age of sixty-five."

"Are they?"

"According to their dates of birth, they are."

He sat on the arm of the sofa, looking down at her.

"There isn't a young man among them," she said. "You might call that coincidence."

"You might," Thorne said. "Or there might be a reason for it."

"Like what?"

"I don't know."

Marcia closed *Who's Who* and put it down on the floor. She stared at Thorne for a time. He was thinking: Old men, all of them, all of them past the statutory age of retirement. Why? What was there about Asterisk that needed old men?

"John," she said, "ever since you got involved in this—shall I call it the Burckhardt affair—I've been worrying about you. Our sex life is practically dead. Which is bad enough—"

"It's easily remedied," he said.

"Not when you're spending all your time chasing around after loose ends and trying to fit the pieces together. You should take up painting by numbers, or something less strenuous."

"Come to bed," he said.

"And make love and know your head's filled with the old men of Escalante?" She stuck her tongue out at him. "I need total concentration—"

"No old men, I promise."

She raised her hand and he gripped it, helping her to

her feet. They went into the darkened bedroom. He undressed her, drew her toward the bed—but when he closed his eyes, when he sought that necessary dark, that sense of relaxation, all he could see were afterimages of the computer printout behind his eyelids—and it was a long time before they disintegrated.

"You're not concentrating, are you?" she said. "Sex should be savored. You're rushing it, lover."

"I wasn't aware of it—"

"Slow down, okay? There's no hurry. I'm not going anywhere. And your old men—well, they'll still be there in the morning, won't they?"

"I guess," he said. He put his arms around her and pulled her back toward him.

Brinkerhoff saw it come through on the IBM, 7 A.M. Moscow time. Decoded, from the difficult priority code, it read:

ACCEPT HOLLANDER INFORMATION REQUIRED AFFIRMA-TIVE ACTION URGED VASHILIKOV ACADEMY OF SCI-ENCES CODE ASSIGNED APRIL FIVE DASH NINETY DASH LETTER H M K L DASH TWELVE NUMBER 12 PRIOR-ITY ROUTE SIX NUMBER 6 URGENTLY SUGGESTED ZA-KUNIN MINISTRY OF SCIENCE

6:

Thursday, April 6

IT WAS THE SOUND OF THE TELEPHONE THAT WOKE Thorne. He sat up—conscious of the dawn sunlight coming into the bedroom, the sky beyond the window cloudless and blue and unspoiled—and picked up the receiver, fumbling it in his sleepiness. He expected to hear his mother. She was given to the eccentric habit of making calls at odd hours from wherever she might be; an addicted traveler, she had called in her time from Tokyo, Edinburgh, Munich, unaware of the subtleties of chronological differences.

But it was not his mother.

"You better get in here," Farrago said.

"Jesus," Thorne said. "What time is it?"

"Six on the morning of the sixth," Farrago said. "Did I interrupt you at your . . . activities?"

"What's going on?" Thorne said.

"Bannerman wants you to come in. Like now."

Thorne watched Marcia. The telephone had not wakened her. She slept deeply, her mouth slightly open, her breathing regular.

"Now?" Thorne said.

"This is the White House," Farrago said. "The White House never sleeps. Didn't you know that?"

Thorne pushed the sheets aside, hung up the telephone, went into the bathroom, and gazed at his own puffy image in the mirror. Ungodly hour: what did Bannerman want with him at this time of the day? He washed his face in cold water, dressed, didn't stop for coffee. "Now" was ten minutes ago in Bannerman's lexicography. He went out of the apartment building into a dawn that was sunlit and

113

cold. He shivered, turned up the collar of his coat, looked across the rows of parked cars that had begun, in dull reflections, to catch the first glimmer of sun. He went to the VW, got inside, drove out of the parking lot.

There was something he found especially lovely about this town at this particular time of day. The emptiness of streets, the silences, the appearance of buildings as they emerged from darkness. A street-cleaning vehicle, spraying water, rotating its huge brushes, was moving along the edge of the opposite sidewalk. The only other vehicle in sight was a green car some way behind him; he saw it in the rearview mirror. A beautiful morning altogether, a time of day in which you could not imagine darkness and perplexities and conspiracies, you could see only a certain clarity.

Inside the White House, he went directly to Farrago's office. Bannerman was sitting with his chair tilted back against the wall. Thorne looked at both of them quickly. Farrago in his usual droopy bow tie and plaid suit, rimless glasses, his hair untidy; like a professor of classics from another age. Bannerman was dressed in a black suit with a pale-gray vest, across the front of which there hung a gold watch-chain. It was not the kind of suit, Thorne thought, in which it would be easy to sit down; it looked curiously brittle, as though it might crack. Bannerman's face had its customary expression of despair, something in the way the jowls hung; he was a man with global puzzles on his mind.

"Sorry about getting you in this early, John," he said. Now he rose; Thorne watched the chair tilt forward from the wall, released from Bannerman's substantial weight. *He's apologizing*, Thorne thought.

Thorne glanced at Farrago, who was staring at his blotter pad. In one hand he held a paperweight; the kind that contains an igloo and, shaken, produces a snowstorm in miniature.

"Sometimes things happen," Bannerman was saying. He had gone to the window and was looking out. Thorne realized, inexplicably, irrationally, that he was afraid of something here, something in this room, something that was about to happen.

"You know," Bannerman said, turning with that quick, famous smile for which he was notorious: on and off, off and on, an electric beacon. "Time becomes, well, precious."

"The thing is—" Farrago said.

"The thing is, we're promoting you, John."

Promotion? Thorne thought. First the House of Representatives, now promotion: where did they draw the line?

"I realize it's going to be unsettling at first," Bannerman said, "But I read your file and it says your French is excellent, so you shouldn't have any problems in acclimatizing yourself."

"French?" Thorne said. "You're losing me. I'm sorry. I just don't follow."

"You're going to the embassy, John. Paris, France."

Thorne watched Bannerman: the smile flickered. He saw the chief of staff's hand go out for a congratulatory handshake, and he raised his own to meet it, he raised his own slowly, before he had time to think.

"Now, wait," he said. "I still don't think I understand any of this."

"Paris, France," Farrago said. "You're going to the embassy."

No. They would pull somebody out of State if there was an opening in Paris. They would pull out one of the career diplomatic boys. How far did this thing go? Where was the end of the line? This trumped-up promotion to Paris, where did it end? It was wrestling an octopus.

"To do what exactly?" Thorne asked.

"To be Cunningham's attaché," Bannerman said. He was grinning, an expression that had begun to infuriate Thorne. "The opening cropped up, as these things do, and Cunningham asked for you personally."

"This is all very well," Thorne said. "But I don't want to go to Paris."

"Ah," Farrago said.

"I don't want to work for the ambassador. I'm quite happy right here."

Bannerman's smile began to radiate a warmth that Thorne found distinctly chilly. He was still clutching Thorne's hand, as though he were determined never to release it.

"You're going to Paris, John," he said.

Thorne dragged his hand away. "It's not my line. You know that. Max, you know that."

He looked at Farrago for support but Farrago had his face turned toward the window. The room was silent now. Thorne heard the sound of an electric motor, maybe that of a lawn mower, from outside. He shut his eyes: Paris, he thought. It wasn't an altogether unpleasant prospect; and in other circumstances, maybe, just maybe, he would have accepted. But not like this.

Bannerman said: "You're going to Paris, John."

Thorne looked at the chief of staff. The eyes were determined and cold; you wondered how many had tried to cross his path on his climb up the ladder and what had become of the victims.

"No," Thorne said. "Thanks a lot, but no."

Bannerman laughed. He had taken a small nail file from his vest and was working on his fingers. "I don't think I'm getting through to you, John. You see, you don't exactly have a choice."

"What do you mean by that?"

Bannerman was silent. Thorne looked at Farrago.

"Max. What does he mean? *You* tell me."

Farrago raised one hand in the air in the fashion of one giving up on a problem; don't ask me, it's too hard, I can't find a solution.

"Max," Thorne said. He listened to the lawn mower. He imagined he could hear it vibrate in the room. So, it reached this far. Asterisk reached this far. It was the same damn wall, the same goddamn thing. He felt angry all at once, angry at the thought of being pushed, manipulated, dispensed with—like an errand boy sent home, no more deliveries for the day.

"Don't look at me," Farrago said.

"John understands," Bannerman said. "Don't you, John?"

Thorne stared at the chief of staff. "No, I don't understand. Suppose you spell it out."

"Is that necessary?" Bannerman was no longer smiling. He was gazing at his nail file. "On your desk, John, you'll find an airline ticket for the midday flight to Paris. Today. You understand me? *Today.*"

"No," Thorne said. "No way."

"Is this display of stubbornness a family trait?" Bannerman said. "As I recollect it, your late father had a stubborn streak some miles wide."

Thorne walked around the office. This reference to his father: it was clear, it was plain enough, he was to understand that some enormous favor was being done for him courtesy of a man who had been fifteen years dead. He was to understand the not very subtle implication involved: that without this family connection he would have been dealt with in a more abrupt manner. His immediate reaction was one of disbelief and behind it, taking flame, a deeper sense of anger. Dear Christ, he thought. Why don't I just lie down and roll over like some good old dog and lick their goddamn hands? The hell with that.

"John," Bannerman said. "I want to wish you the very best in your new position. I'm sure you'll find Paris stimulating and Cunningham a good man to work for."

The chief of staff looked at his watch, walked to the door. There he paused, swung around, and added: "Be on the flight. Okay?"

He went out.

There was a silence in the room for a time. Farrago, politely making a funnel of one hand and pressing it to his lips, cleared his throat. Then he said: "Well. Congratulations."

Thorne went to the window. He saw the lawn mower below, flakes of clipped grass flying behind the driver of the vehicle.

"Congratulations?" he said. "What's behind it?"

"Behind it?"

"I didn't ask for it, did I? And you never said you were unhappy with my work here. So what the fuck's behind it?"

"Like the chief said, John, it's a promotion for you—"

"Promotion my ass." Thorne turned to look at Farrago, who suddenly appeared pathetic, ineffectual, fingering his floppy bow tie with a gesture that suggested nervousness succumbing to panic.

"France, Jesus," Farrago said, smiling in a watery way. "Wish I could get over there."

"Go in my place then," Thorne said.

He slammed the door. He went down to his own office.

There weren't the usual newspapers piled on the desk.

There was an airline ticket in a blue envelope. He

picked it up. Paris, midday flight, one-way. He twisted the thing in his fingers. Then he sat down behind his desk, laid his hands on the bare surface, and noticed a cardboard box in the corner of the room. He went to it, looked inside.

His desk had been cleared out. The pictures had been taken down from the wall. Everything had been shoved into the box. Jesus, they wanted him out of the way fast. On top of the box there lay the photograph of Senator Thorne. The face seemed darker than before, more stern, as if some disillusionment were beginning to move across the features. Thorne took out his address book and flipped through the pages. His hand was shaking as he dialed a telephone number; anger, fear, some bad combination of the two—he wasn't sure. He called Leach's home number. There was no answer. He tried the congressman's office. A girl asked his name, then said the congressman was in a meeting. Be on that flight, Thorne thought. He shoved the telephone down. In a pig's ass. Okay, try Jacobson. What could Jacobson tell him? He dialed the senator's home number in Fairfax. Mrs. Jacobson told him that the senator was attending a conference in Wichita. He put the telephone down, then he sat back, thinking, thinking of the moves.

They wanted him gone, that much was visible in the scheme of things. They didn't want to damage him, so it seemed, but just to get him off to the sidelines. Why? Because he was asking too many questions, because he hadn't been particularly discreet: because of Asterisk. Okay. It made some kind of sense: it was the logic that told you that the scrambled bits and pieces of the jigsaw could be made to form a whole . . . if you had the plan, the overall pattern. But he had no such matrix. A few facts, a couple of hints, a couple of puzzles. His inadequacy suddenly irritated him; his ignorance distressed him. *You're the kind of person who cringes at the thought of having lint in your navel.* Maybe. But this was worse. This was like stepping inside a room that you knew intimately but one in which something has been moved, something so small as to be almost imperceptible—but it would drive you mad as you looked for it. He rose from his desk and walked to the window. Well, he thought. You can at least say, with some degree of certitude, that you know roughly where you stand.

He watched the lawn mower make a wide arc across the grass.

Someone had been knocking on his door during the night. He had ignored it, tried to sleep; there had been footsteps in the corridor, the voice of a drunk singing. Now, the sun streaming into the room under the brown blind, he got out of bed and dressed. He went into the corridor. Here and there a few bare light bulbs were lit, bleak little nimbi. He got into the elevator and rode it to the ground floor. The desk clerk was reading a paperback book entitled *Improve Your Word Power*. He was mouthing words silently to himself. *Psychasthenia*, Hollander thought. Is that what I suffer from? The inability to resist self-questioning. To put doubts away.

He picked up the telephone and dialed the number he had been given by Brinkerhoff. It rang only once, then it was answered, as if Brinkerhoff had been waiting beside the receiver.

"You will be pleased to know that a clearance has been given," Brinkerhoff said. "There are arrangements to be made, but you must be prepared to leave at a moment's notice."

Pleased? Am I pleased? Hollander wondered.

"The remainder of your information is necessary," Brinkerhoff said.

"Naturally." Hollander gazed at the desk clerk. *Emunctory*, he thought. Was emunctory in the book? Or nescience?

"Where do we meet?" Brinkerhoff asked.

"I always found the Pancake Palace a treat," Hollander said. "It has a certain nostalgic ring."

"In one hour," Brinkerhoff said.

Hollander put the telephone down. He was going. He was going. He looked at the desk clerk, who had bad teeth.

"I'm checking out," he said.

"Got your key?" the clerk asked. He put his paperback aside. Hollander put his key down on the desk. The clerk picked it up, handling it as though it were explosive. Going, Hollander thought. *What did it really mean?* He pictured Davina, wanted to call her, say something: a word of farewell. The language was inadequate. Then he thought of his kids. They would have to live with this too. *Do you know what your daddy did?*

What is it, he wondered, this urge to say goodbyes?

He smiled at the clerk, who was already buried back in his paperback. Yes: sooner or later his kids would be haunted by this. How could he ever make them see that he was doing it—when you got to the bottom line—for them as much as for anyone?

He left the hotel, stepped out onto the sidewalk.

Sunny D.C. morning. He walked a little way, went inside a coffee shop, drank coffee and ate a doughnut. Just think: it may be your last American honey-glazed, custard-filled special. He did not imagine they would have such delicacies where he was going.

The waitress was smiling at him. It was as if she had never seen a defector before.

* * *

Thorne left the White House at ten. He went to his car, drove down Pennsylvania Avenue. At a gasoline station he tried to call Erickson. It was useless. He was being fenced, boxed in; and he knew that Erickson could tell him nothing. When he got through to Senator McLintock's office and asked for Erickson he was told that Erickson had quit. Quit, he thought. Overnight. *Just like that.* He hung up, returned to his VW, sat inside motionless. He was cold. The sun on the windshield was like frost. He watched the station attendant at the pump; then he drove off in the direction of the airport. There were jets in the sky high above the Potomac, vapor trails. He parked his car at the airport and went through the terminal building to the observation deck. Think. *Think.* Escalante. Asterisk. Fuck Paris. They could stick Paris. He had something to do here. They couldn't just wash him away as if he were a speck of grit blown randomly into someone's eye, an irritating touch of sand. It was this as much as anything that he hated, it was this presumption that he could be bought and sold by the power brokers if only he would learn how to stifle his curiosity and sit still in quiet corners and ask no questions. A man is killed in a swimming pool. A terrified woman thinks her house is bugged. A group of strangely unrelated, weirdly incongruous scientists are apparently dredged out of retirement to work at a missile site. The walls of silence. The offers of goodies. It wasn't enough.

It was pure shit.

He watched an American Airlines flight take off at the end of the runway. It was followed almost at once by a TWA jumbo. The sky was filled with activity. *They expect me to smile*, he thought. Nod my head, be grateful. He looked upward into the sun. A wind blowing in across the tarmac made him shiver. Where did he turn now? what was he left with?

You're on your own, he thought.

He went back into the terminal building. The girl at the TWA desk was uncertain about the possibility of a refund at this late stage. Thorne said it wasn't that important anyhow. It was something he didn't have to do, he could simply have become, in the parlance of the airlines, a no-show, but it gave him some small, tight feeling of pleasure to watch the girl remove his name from the passenger list and punch this deletion into her computer.

"I hope we can serve you again sometime," she said. She had toothpaste teeth, a manicured smile, her eyes were glazed with artificial delight.

"Maybe," Thorne said.

He went back to his car.

The undersecretary was not absolutely pleased with the decoded cable; he had an inbred dislike of American intelligence. He enjoyed the country and hoped his stay would be a protracted one, but so far as intelligence went he had all the feelings of a pheasant who smells a fox on the downwind. He wasn't even happy with the way Brinkerhoff had become convinced by this Hollander. But what could he do except give it his stamp of approval? Vashiljkov, Zakunin: you did not trifle with these names.

"I meet him in one hour," Brinkerhoff said.

The undersecretary sighed. It had to be important. They hardly used Route 6 unless it was something unusual.

"I have already arranged the transportation," Brinkerhoff said. "I took the liberty of assuming your approval."

"Very efficient," the undersecretary said.

Brinkerhoff looked at his watch. The undersecretary noticed, with a slight pulse of envy, that it was one of those watches you had to press before the time lit up. He wanted one for himself.

"You will travel with him?"

Brinkerhoff nodded. "Yes. Yes, I will travel with him."

The undersecretary got up from behind his desk. It was and absurd desk anyhow; it made him feel like some wretched dwarf. He stared at the folders that lay across the surface. The constant chatter of intelligence reports. The file on Hollander. Everything checked out. That was what worried him.

"Brinkerhoff," he said, in a confidential manner. "You really *trust* Hollander? Really?"

"I hedge my bets," Brinkerhoff said. "At first I imagined him to be stupid. Now I think perhaps. Perhaps. It's a gamble."

"A gamble," the undersecretary said.

"The odds are even."

The undersecretary watched Brinkerhoff press his watch again and look at the time.

"How does that work?" he asked. "Could I see?"

Out to the airport. Back again. In to the White House. Out again. The guy maybe had ants in his pants today, Tarkington thought. He was wracked by fatigue. He was thankful when he saw the red Volkswagen pull up outside Dunkin' Donuts and Thorne go inside the shop. He got out of the Catalina and, though this wasn't strictly by the book—but when you were this tired you didn't need to be told what to do by any goddamn book—he followed Thorne inside. He sat six stools away and ordered a black coffee. He wondered about Thorne. Well-dressed (yawn: Jesus Christ), clean-cut, you would have put him down as an up-and-coming young lawyer, something like that. The strangest people broke the rules, though. The most unlikely dudes did all the wrong things. He sipped his coffee. Hollander, for example: never in a million years would he have thought of a warrant coming down for Ted Hollander. Ah, well, it was beyond him. He had become too accustomed to unanswerable questions. After a time, you didn't even want to ask.

Thorne went outside.

Tarkington finished his coffee. Here we go again, he thought. Here we go again. Wearily, he got behind the wheel of the Catalina and slipped into the lane behind the red bug.

Dilbeck received a telephone call from the congressman, which he took on the conservatory extension. He was deeply concerned with the mealybugs, deeply so; it was a regular blight. What really irritated him was the prospect of chemical killers because no matter how good they claimed to be he knew they did some damage to the plants. Still, you had to go sometimes with the lesser evil for the greater good.

"Our boy just isn't biting," Leach said. His voice was barely a whisper.

"I didn't think he would," Dilbeck said. He suspected Thorne had some integrity. It would have disappointed him to learn otherwise.

"Is there some other way you can deal with this?" Leach asked. "Like yourself, I would prefer not to involve the other committee members. A little containment would be a good thing."

"I can deal with it," Dilbeck said. He watched a bug, looking like a slow-motion drop of spit, cross the back of his hand.

"Without, uh, needless violence," Leach said.

"Of course," Dilbeck said.

The congressman wheezed into the line. For a moment, Dilbeck held the receiver some inches from his ear.

"You had better keep me posted on Hollander too," Leach said. "I wish . . ." His voice trailed off as if there were some unspeakable regret in his mind.

"You wish the way I wish," Dilbeck said.

"Dammit," Leach said. "Ted Hollander. *After all.*"

When Dilbeck had put the telephone down he went into the house. He climbed the stairs to his study. He passed the closed doors of his daughter's bedroom. Her stereo was playing Prokofiev's Seventh Piano Sonata. He listened for a moment. It was cacophony to him, as if someone were dropping stones on the piano keys from a great height. He climbed the second flight and when he reached his study he was out of breath. He went inside the room, locked the door behind him, opened a green metal filing cabinet, fiddled through the files, took out the one that had been hastily assembled on John Thorne.

Now, he thought. Sharpe would never have understood this approach. With Sharpe you had two solutions: money or the gun. If it was too expensive to buy somebody off, you had to resort to the pistol. Well, it worked for some. Dilbeck preferred other avenues. It was a difference in philosophies. He opened the file.

She was a pretty girl. A very pretty girl. A long time ago you might have waved a bottle of acid under her face. She had long dark hair, expressive eyes, *intelligent* eyes, a soft mouth.

He looked at the photograph for some minutes. Then he closed the folder and laid it on his desk.

2

Mrs. Rowley Salladin hated marketing. Of all the chores that were involved in the smooth running of a five-bedroom house in Arlington, marketing was the worst. It was not so much the actual *visit* to the supermarket, no, it was the unpacking of brown bags when you finally got home. She stashed the new spices on the rack, the paprika, the cracked black pepper, the bay leaves. Into the freezer she put the cans of orange juice, the waffles, the lamb cutlets, the bag of ice cubes. She emptied carrots, a lettuce, a bag of tomatoes, a bunch of celery, into the vegetable tray. When she was finished she poured herself a cup of coffee and sat at the kitchen table and looked around the glossy waxed kitchen, as if she were suspicious of the existence of some dirt speck in a place she could not see. Only the other day she had found a cobweb in a high corner of the upstairs bathroom and, at its center, a large spider. She had gone for the Raid, sprayed the spider—horrified by the way it twisted, curled, dropped out of its lair—then knocked the web out with the end of a straw broom. She tapped her fingers on the table. The house was silent. Now, she thought, what was her project for the day?

The yard. She wanted to plant corn for this year. Yes, she would do something with the yard. She already had the seeds.

She finished her coffee, rinsed the empty cup, set it to dry on the yellow plastic rack.

The telephone was ringing.

The sound quite startled her, breaking as it did into the silence of the large house.

She picked up the receiver.

After all these years his voice was a shock to her.

"You shouldn't have called," she said. "You shouldn't have."

He was silent. Had he changed? What did he look like now? Was he different? She felt an unexpected longing in her heart; it was as if she had never stopped loving him, as if he were always somewhere in her mind, and all the rest of it, everything else, was a form of emptiness you had to get through. This large waxed kitchen, her spotless life. She remembered how they had loved and she felt the sickness of a great loss.

"You shouldn't have called," she was saying.

"I had to," he said. "It's the last time."

"I don't understand you," she said. "What do you mean?" She was conscious of her own weird hysteria; of herself, seen as if from a height, a blob of a figure in a glossy, shining kitchen. She was herself a stain, something spilled and about to spread.

"I'm going away," he said. "I wanted to say goodbye."

"Where? Where are you going?"

"You'll hear about it, I guess." He paused again. "I suppose the kids are in school?"

"Yes," she said. "Ted, where are you going? You make this sound so . . . *final*."

"That's the word," he said. "Final would be a good word for it. I want you to tell the kids that I love them. I want them to try and understand."

"Please," she said. She was crying, despite herself she was crying, clutching the telephone as if afraid that it might, like some horrible kite, be tugged from her hand and blown with the wind. The cord was twisted around her wrist. She couldn't see, her eyesight was blurred.

"Please, Ted," she said. "I don't understand you. Tell me what you mean. Tell me."

But the line was dead and she was talking to nobody and it all might have been some dream, something that came in the depth of the night to touch her and make her wonder if, all those years before, she had made the mistake of her life.

Folly, Hollander thought. Sheer folly. But you don't take your leave without making a sound of some kind. He put the telephone down and stood with his face pressed against the glass inside the booth and felt the movement of a pain inside him. Then he recovered, the moment passed, he wasn't the father of three children again, he was Hollander about to defect. He could have called Davina. But they would have her telephone bugged by this time, expecting him to call her. He wasn't even sure of Mrs. Rowley Salladin's phone; a slight chance, maybe not much of one, not after all this time.

He went into the Pancake Palace.

Brinkerhoff was already at the table, picking gloomily at a blueberry waffle. Hollander sat down. He hoped they would understand, when it all came out he hoped they would not think too badly of him.

Brinkerhoff smiled. "I urged our undersecretary to use a telephone," he said. "He isn't a telephone person, Hollander. He enjoys writing notes. It gives him time to wait for replies and think up countermoves."

Hollander ordered coffee.

Brinkerhoff waited until the waitress had gone, then he said: "I hope you're ready for some protracted travel."

"I'm ready," Hollander said.

"We will drive early in the afternoon to an airfield near Damascus—"

"We?" Hollander asked.

"I would not let you travel alone, would I?" Brinkerhoff smiled; it was mirthless and yet Hollander saw, obliquely, some clumsy attempt at friendliness. Brinkerhoff trusted him, wanted to know him: he could see that now.

"Then what?" Hollander asked.

"Havana."

Passports, visa, the necessary vouchers for foreign travel: Brinkerhoff appeared to have the means of transcending these nuisances.

"After Havana, Moscow," Brinkerhoff said. "How do you feel now?"

"I'm ready," Hollander said. A shadow crossed his mind, it floated through then was gone, a sense of doubt—could he step away from all this now? Could he stand back and free himself from the route he had chosen?

Did he want to? He noticed Brinkerhoff's funereal hand pass across the cuff of his coat.

"I understand," Brinkerhoff said. "I don't think I entirely understand you, Hollander. But to leave your own country . . . I understand that."

"It's not just the leaving," Hollander said, feeling a somewhat unexpected warmth toward the other man. *Your only ally now,* he thought. *Your only comrade.* "It's the knowledge you can never come back."

Brinkerhoff stabbed his fork into the blueberry waffle, as though he were killing some domestic pest. "Yes," he said. "Yes. There's that."

"But I made the choice, didn't I?"

"You made the choice," Brinkerhoff said. "Nobody made it for you."

Hollander was silent now. The waitress approached their table, smiling, ready to please. He tried to remember what he had heard or read about service in Soviet restaurants. It was bad, nonexistent.

"Now," Brinkerhoff said. "The remainder of your documents. Do you have those?"

Hollander finished his coffee. "I have to go to the bank before we do anything else," he said.

Brinkerhoff looked at his watch. "We have plenty of time."

Hollander ordered a second cup of coffee. He watched the waitress—Barbara Ann—cross to the coffeepot and pour. He looked up at the illuminated menus that hung on the walls. A word of waffles, pancackes, doughnuts, all lit in scrumptious color. Havana, he thought. Then Moscow.

"You're tense," Brinkerhoff said. "Don't be."

"I'm trying," Hollander said. He shut his eyes. *When did you first feel you could save the world?* I don't know, Doc. *Have you always wanted to sacrifice yourself?* I don't know, Doc, I don't know. *You really think what you're doing will help sustain the balance of power?* I wish I could be sure, I wish I could be sure. *Hollander, I think you're a fool.*

He was aware of Brinkerhoff watching him.

He was trying to be sympathetic, understanding, he was stretching every fiber in a heart unaccustomed to feeling so that he might make Hollander be at ease.

"I'm fine," Hollander said. "Don't worry about me."

Sharpe took the call when it came: he had been lying on the office sofa, trying to catch up on his sleep, idly watching a game show on the colored TV he had recently fetched from his apartment. It was called *Wheel of Fortune*. Contestants spun a wheel and got to buy prizes. Sometimes they went bankrupt. *I'll have the his and her dressing gowns*, a woman was saying, a faceful of avarice. *I'll have the Gucci travel bag. I'll have the rest in a Tiffany gift certificate*. The wheel spun. The telephone rang. He was thinking, somewhat detachedly, of giving up the apartment and moving full time into the office. Think what you'd save. He reached for the receiver.

It was Richard F. Drucker. An old cold-warrior. He saw commies under the lids of saucepans and thought the long-dead senator from Wisconsin America's only modern saint. But Drucker was good with the electronic stuff; he had been born to eavesdrop.

"I've got something for you," Drucker said.

Sharpe, watching the wheel of fortune spin, listened. When he got off the line, he called Dilbeck. From here on in it was a matter of speed.

In the public library Thorne opened the atlas at a table in the reference room. American states, American states. Arizona. He ran his finger down the list of cities and towns.

> *Eden   89*
> *Ehrenburg   93*
> *Elfrida   700*
> *Elgin   247*
> *El Mirage   3258*
> *Eloy   5381*
> *Escalante   72*

Seventy-two, Thorne thought. It was your original one-horse settlement.

> *Escalante   72   C4*

He checked C4 on the map.

Escalante lay somewhere between a place called Congress and a place called Dixon. He estimated it to be about a hundred and twenty miles northwest of Phoenix.

He closed the atlas.

He had been running all day, he had been scrambling like a thing caught in quicksand. Now he was tired and hollow. He massaged his eyelids, blinked, looked around the library. Empty tables, a middle-aged woman on a step-ladder, piling books on a high shelf, a clerk behind the desk stamping something on paper. There was a profound silence in here; you could not imagine noise, save for the whisper of turning pages. A fat guy was standing at the stacks of crime thrillers. To Thorne, he looked remotely familiar, a fact he dismissed from his mind.

Three, four days ago—it was like ancient history to him now. Three, four days ago, there had been a normality, a sense of things being in their right place. Not now. What could you say to describe the now: an awareness of flux? He thought of the midday flight for Paris. By now they would know he hadn't gone. *They.*

Things in the woodwork of Washington.

The termites that nibbled on the timbers of your life. *They.*

Who were they?

More significantly, who were they *not?*

He laid his hands on the cover of the atlas. The fat man by the crime stacks was leafing through a book. He wasn't reading; he had an abstracted, distant expression on his face.

The doughnut shop!

Unless he was badly mistaken, he had seen the same fat man inside the doughnut shop a while back. It would make sense. They would have somebody watching him.

Thorne closed his eyes and wondered: *Have I gone mad?*

Is this lunacy? People following you, men drowning in swimming pools, wives afraid of their own kitchens, blank pages on a manuscript, a burglary, sudden unemployment. It had all the connected elements of a dream.

Somebody else's dream. Not his own.

He got up from the table and went outside. He crossed the parking lot and sat inside the VW, watching the library steps. The fat man came out a moment later, walked in a leisurely way down the steps, turned his head this way and that, looked at the VW, then lit a cigarette. It figured, Thorne thought. He wasn't very good at it. But maybe there were ramifications to that too, maybe he was supposed to know he was being followed because—because? Because of what? There might be more than one. There might be another he didn't know about. He was meant to notice the fat man, a kind of diversion that would keep him from spotting the other.

If there were an other.

Dear Christ, he thought.

They have me going in circles.

He started the engine of the VW. The man went to a pale-green Catalina. Yeah, Thorne thought: it was the same car that had picked him up just after dawn. The same damn car.

He drove out of the parking lot.

After a moment the Catalina followed.

He watched it in the mirror. It was as if the sight of it were the only tangible proof he had that he wasn't going completely out of his mind.

"It defeats me," Dilbeck was saying. "It doesn't make any sense."

"Why doesn't it make sense?" Sharpe said. "He called his former wife, sometimes a guy does that kind of thing—"

"It's ridiculous," Dilbeck said. "Hollander knows the methodology, Sharpe. He knows the operation, the *modus operandi*. He knows we're looking for him. He must know we put the taps on all the numbers he's likely to call. He isn't a stupid man. Why call his wife?"

Sharpe was silent. He felt the sunlight beat down on his scalp, wished he had worn his hat. He watched Dilbeck look down in the direction of the trees; a slight breeze made the stalks shiver, the branches shift.

"Going away," Dilbeck said.

"That's what he told her."

"Going away," Dilbeck said again. "He calls to say goodbye."

"Like he's never coming back," Sharpe said.

"Mmmm," Dilbeck said.

Mmmm, Sharpe thought. The sound of wisdom.

"But he *knows* he's going to be tapped, dammit." Dilbeck waved vaguely in the direction of the house. Sharpe swung around, expecting to see the daughter, but the old man was simply gesturing in an idle way.

"Maybe he doesn't know," Sharpe said.

"No," Dilbeck said. "It's almost as if he wants us to catch him."

"That doesn't make any better sense," Sharpe said.

Dilbeck shrugged. "You traced the call?"

Sharpe nodded. He smiled as if to say: *We're no slouches.* Dilbeck put his hands in the pockets of his jacket.

"He wants to be caught," he said, more to himself than to Sharpe. Then he looked at Sharpe. "It isn't all just black and white, Sharpe. Sometimes the colors run and you've got indeterminate grays."

Sharpe looked away. He hated this feeling he always got that Dilbeck was trying to lecture him on the subtleties of life.

Dilbeck looked inexplicably sad all at once. "Grays," he said again. He wasn't thinking about Hollander now: he was thinking about John Thorne and his girl. Pretty girl, pretty name. It was sometimes a pity what you had to do.

3

Fredericksburg. The Catalina had been behind him on I-95 all the way. Thorne tried to accept it: it was a fact of life, a stubborn Catalina that would not be shaken. He parked the car in a side street in Fredericksburg and went into a bookstore; he browsed, seeing nothing, among a pile of glossy, hardbound, cut-rate novels. The fat man came in, the bell above the door tinkled, and Thorne rushed abruptly past the guy back into the street, noticing the look of surprise in the plump face, the raising of eyebrows, the way the mouth was suddenly distended in anxiety. Outside, Thorne walked quickly along the street, turned, turned again, found himself hurrying across a small park where kids played on slides and built castles in a sandpit. He moved under the shadow of the trees, sat down on the grass, looked back the way he had come. The kids screamed. The fat man was nowhere. Running in a panic through the streets of Fredericksburg. Thorne closed his eyes: all he could think of was Anna Burckhardt. It was as if he had all the pieces save the final one without

which nothing would make any sense at all. Anna Burckhardt. Why did he think she knew more than she could
tell? The face filled with dread, the motion of a cigarette,
the rain on the broken-down roof of a gazebo. Frightened.
Scared unto death. *She had to know more. She had to
know more about Asterisk.* He had no other cards to play.
He had an empty hand except for Anna Burckhardt.

He stood up, still looking back the way he had come.

There was no fat guy. The kids playing, the mothers
of Fredericksburg patiently watching, sitting on sunlit
benches and talking among themselves and God's in his
heaven. He crossed the park. The sun was warm now. He
walked along streets that suggested picture postcards of a
lost America: thirty miles and a hundred light-years from
Washington. People sat on porches, watched the street, the
occasional passing car; the sidewalks were lined with trees,
nothing altered here, the patterns remained the same regardless of the occupants of the White House coming and
going, regardless of change. There was a magnificent indif-
ference here, Thorne thought. Save in one particular house
where a scared woman sat at a kitchen table and mourned
the passing of something . . . Thorne hesitated at a street
corner. A kid leaning against a fire hydrant looked at him,
shading his eyes from the sunlight. Thorne crossed the
street. Faintly, a breeze blew through the trees. He could
hear birds. He suddenly thought of his own childhood,
summers at the Cape, the precious times he spent with his
father. My father, he thought. The genetic attachment, the
freak whim of nature. Another man's son wouldn't be here
right now, wouldn't be doing this, wouldn't be ensnared in
any of this.

He stopped outside Anna Burckhardt's house. It was
still, it had the appearance of emptiness, the windows
blind and unyielding and drapes drawn across them. He
looked up and down the street. Nothing. No Catalina, no
fat man, nothing. He went on to the porch, rang the door-
bell, waited. She didn't come. He rang again, nothing. He
tried to look in through the windows, through the spaces
in the drapes, but he saw only dimness and the outlines of
furniture. He went around the back of the house. The
kitchen door was closed. He tapped lightly on the glass.
Something moved in the gazebo; spinning round, he saw a
crow rise from the rotted roof and fly into the trees. He

tapped a second time. She didn't come. Why did he have this feeling that she was inside?

"Mrs. Burckhardt," he called out. "It's me, John Thorne. Please open your door."

He peered through the windows of the kitchen. He tried the kitchen door. It opened. The house smelled musty, stale, old perfumes trapped and decayed.

He crossed the floor. There were dirty dishes in the sink. Saucepans, knives and forks, glasses. The faucet dripped. He tightened it.

"Mrs. Burckhardt," he said.

His own voice came back in a dull echo. He stepped into the living room. He stopped.

Whatever he had hoped to find here was lost to him.

He sat down, his hands shaking.

Whatever she knew, whatever it was, belonged in a realm he could not enter.

She lay face down on the sofa. A bottle that had once contained pills or capsules lay on the floor, just under the fingers of her dangling hand. Her skirt was bunched up at the back. She had worn no underwear. He got up, pulled the garment back in place, but he did not turn her over to look at her face. The room had that queer vibration of recent death, as if some singular element of life, having failed to escape, remained trapped between the walls. He stood over her. Suicide, of course. *Estranged wife depressed over husband's recent death.*

He didn't buy a word of it.

It was a fabricated headline that might convince forensic medicine, a coroner's court. But he knew she had not died from her own hand. He was sickened, sickened by the needless waste, another life gone.

He sat down, turned his face from the sight of the woman, found himself thinking suddenly of Marcia. Of how it would be if he stepped into his apartment and found her face down on the sofa, the empty bottle of pills, the pallid skin—

Marcia.

It would be so simple for them.

Marcia.

He got up and went out through the front door and walked quickly to his car.

He noticed the Catalina idling a little way down the street.

They came out of the First National Bank, Hollander with the envelope in his coat pocket. Beside him, Brinkerhoff walked in an oddly stiff manner, as if he were afraid of the contact of concrete on the soles of his feet. They paused at the edge of the sidewalk, waiting to cross. The light was against them. Traffic flowed past in a hundred reflections of sunlight. Hollander glanced at the buildings on the other side of the street.

The last time, he thought.

My country, 'tis of thee— What did he feel? Why couldn't he fetch the feelings up from inside himself, examine them, attach labels to them? This process of emotional regurgitation appalled him: he had reached his decision, there was no way of changing it now.

The very last time.

A smell of fried food floated out of a nearby franchise. He looked at the tinted windows of the restaurant, at the silhouettes of diners, the white ghosts of girls moving between the tables with trays of hamburger, french fries, carbonated drinks in waxy containers. The last time, he thought: should I feel a sudden bleak regret? He was numb. He experienced nothing now.

He felt Brinkerhoff's hand on his elbow. Maybe, Hollander thought, maybe he expects me to run. A failure of nerve at the very last hurdle. He watched the shadows in the buildings. Metropolitan Life Insurance Company. Would he find life insurance in Moscow? A department store. A window filled with dummies in raincoats and a banner that said: *Be Ready for When Those April Showers Come Your Way!!!* A woman selling flowers on the corner. She sat hunched over colored petals in the manner of someone at prayer. Hollander looked at the signal change. WALK DON'T WALK. WALK. He crossed to the other side, Brinkerhoff still attached to him by the elbow.

Their car was parked a little way down the street. They had jettisoned Hollander's; wherever they were going they were going in Brinkerhoff's black Fiat. He felt edgy again, the movement of his nerves; it isn't something a man does every day of his life, he thought. It isn't every day you decide to go over the wall.

Stop, he thought.

Stop.

The face in the parked Chevrolet. The face behind glass, turned away from him slightly, but it was a face he knew. He walked quickly, Brinkerhoff striding beside him. How had they picked him up? He knew the answer to that one. He knew he had been trapped by his own sentimentality. It was falling to pieces all around him.

"Quick," he said.

Brinkerhoff unlocked the door of the Fiat. Hollander got inside. Brinkerhoff steered the car away from the sidewalk.

"Is something wrong?" he asked.

"Something is very wrong," Hollander said.

Brinkerhoff bit his lower lip. "What have you seen?"

Hollander felt the shadows of the tall buildings fall across his face, the occasional stabs of sun that burst between the concrete.

"What have you seen?" Brinkerhoff asked again.

Hollander turned around in his seat.

The Chevrolet was behind them. It was Brandt. Brandt, human flypaper. Brandt whom he had once sent to Mexico City to dispatch a man called McLean in a hotel room. He remembered: *It has to look like he did it himself, Brandt.*

I can make it look any way you like, Ted.

McLean, Hollander thought. McLean and all the others who had died on account of Asterisk.

He felt he was looking into a cracked mirror; and what he saw there was bloodless and without life.

Thorne entered the apartment; what he wanted more than anything else was a drink, something stiff and bracing.

"Marcia," he said.

The apartment was unlit. Outside, the afternoon was giving way, the sun going.

"Marcia," he said. She wasn't on the balcony. He saw her books in a neat pile on the desk. An unusual sense of order, no sprawl—

He was horrified. It was so atypical, so totally uncharacteristic, that he felt a sudden falling sensation in the center of his chest as though his heart had slipped abruptly from its mooring. He saw Anna Burckhardt's face again.

"Marcia," and his voice was hoarse.

There was no answer.

He walked across the living room.

"Marcia." He heard his own feeble cry. This wild apprehension, the leap of his nerves, a pulse laboring beneath his eyes: Marcia.

He found her in the kitchen.

She was sitting at the table. There were suitcases on the floor beside her. She looked pale, pinched, there was something altogether spaced out in her appearance; the glazed expression in the eye he had come to associate with the times when she smoked dope.

"Marcia—"

"I thought it over, John," she said. "I don't see any future for us."

What

He laughed, relieved that nothing had happened to her and simultaneously shocked by her sentences, by the sight of the cases, the way she looked, the chill in her voice.

"It's no joke, John," she said. "I'm leaving you."

She got up from the table.

"There's a cab coming in a minute or two."

"Wait a minute," he said.

"Please, John, don't make it difficult for me—"

"Where the hell do you think you're going?"

"Please," she said. She dragged one of the cases out of the kitchen. He followed her.

"Marcia, listen—"

She would not look at him. The perfect stranger.

"Marcia, listen—"

"Look," she said. "Don't say any more, okay? It's finished. I wanted to be gone from here before you got back, I didn't want to see you again. You follow me?"

"Marcia—"

"It's changed, John. It's not the way it was before you got into this stupid business with your major general, your missile sites. I mean, you're not a working journalist any more running down some hot story, are you? It's just changed so much—"

He held her by the arms and forced her to face him. He saw it now. "Who was here? Tell me! Tell me who came here!"

"Nobody came here, John. Nobody. I can make up my own mind, okay? This isn't working out. That's all."

"Don't fucking lie to me—"

"I'm not lying—"

"Marcia, somebody came here, somebody must have threatened you somehow—"

He suddenly realized he wanted to hit her, he wanted to strike her out of this state of mind, he wanted the truth. She pulled away from him, stepped back, brushed a loose strand of hair out of her eyes.

"I must get my other case," she said.

She went into the kitchen. He followed after her, trying to keep her from moving.

"Somebody threatened you, didn't they? How? Tell me how. God damn it, tell me!"

"Please, John." She hauled the other case out of the kitchen and into the living room.

"You can't speak, right? Is that it? They've bugged this place, right? They planted their shit here—"

She looked at him in a rather sad manner. "It's been fun, John. It's been nice. I'm sorry it hasn't worked. Okay? Can you let that sink in? It's finished."

"I can't let this happen," he said.

"You can't stop it, John. It's too late."

"Marcia, just tell me, okay? Just tell me."

She looked down at the rug. "The only thing we've got to talk about now is what happens to our stuff. That's all."

"Our stuff? What the hell does that matter?"

"Some of it's yours, some of it's mine, and I guess some of it's jointly owned."

"I don't believe this," Thorne said.

She went on, her voice a monotone he had never heard before. "The prints are mine. The furniture is mostly yours. What I can't remember is who owns the refrigerator. Can you? Did you buy it? Did I buy it? I can't remember."

Thorne sat down on the sofa. He felt weak, enfeebled, as if he had been traveling a long time on a craft that had not been created for rough oceans. He looked at her and thought: There isn't a thing they can't do. There isn't a single thing. With a signature on a piece of paper, with a furtive telephone call, with an act of surveillance—it didn't matter, they could do anything they liked. It didn't resemble anything he remembered from his father's fervent lectures on the brilliant nature of American life and values: this was something else, a place on the dark side of the moon, perhaps a place his father had never suspected, almost as if the words of the constitutional document he had held so precious threw perverse shadows of themselves, produced counterfeits, opposites, so that for every truth there was a concomitant lie.

He clenched his fists in frustration. At least it hadn't been Anna Burckhardt's fate. At least there was that.

"I guess we can work out who owns what," she said. "Especially with the refrigerator."

The refrigerator? he thought. It wasn't the time to be babbling.

From outside there was the sound of a car horn.

"I guess that's my taxi," she said. She looked at him and there was a very faint smile on her lips. "Goodbye, John. I'm really sorry. Really."

4

He had Brinkerhoff driving in circles, but the tan Chevrolet remained behind, unshakable, dogged. You could say that of Brandt, Hollander thought: he had no intellect and little intelligence, but when you told him to do a thing he would do it, no questions asked. He would have a Colt .45 converted in the shoulder holster; he would have radio contact with whoever was running him. Sharpe, somebody else, the question did not matter now.

Beyond Rockville, Brinkerhoff asked, "Who is he? Someone you are acquainted with?"

"More than acquainted," Hollander said. When something looked like breaking with Asterisk, who else had he turned to but Brandt? He could see the bland, rather innocent face; passing it on the street one might have thought of smalltown football games, a hero of the rah-rah-rah girls, a touchdown that saved the trophy in the final minute. One might have thought of the college hero, Big Man on Campus. But the façade was nothing. Inside, Brandt had the heart of an ice cube. *Leave it with me, Ted. Don't worry about a thing.*

"Are you armed?" Hollander asked.

Brinkerhoff nodded. "One hears so much about the possibility of being mugged in American cities—"

"This isn't your average mugger," Hollander said.

The highway was choked with the traffic of a late sunlit afternoon. Commuters getting out of D.C. as early as they could and hurrying home to red-brick houses, wives, perhaps the obligatory martini in a chilled glass, stories of what Johnny had done in school and how much coffee prices had gone up and whether there might be a vacation this year. It was as if these were pictures he perceived on a receding tide, reflections on wave crests, mere illusions.

He twisted round in his seat.

The Chevrolet was tucked in behind.

Brinkerhoff was looking for an opening in the fast lane. There was a Mayflower truck, followed by a refrigerator monstrosity that blew black smoke and had upon its side panel the motto BIRDS EYE. As far back as Hollander could see both lanes were tightly sealed.

"Give me your gun," Hollander said.

Brinkerhoff glanced at him doubtfully.

"This isn't the time for any of that," Hollander said. "Give me the gun."

"The glove compartment," Brinkerhoff said.

Hollander took out a Colt, a Police Positive. It surprised him somewhat; he had expected a Czech or a Soviet handgun, if anything.

He checked the weapon. Brandt wasn't like the Greek; he wasn't slow-moving, he wasn't uninventive, and he had more native cunning than the late Lykiard. He looked at Brinkerhoff. He was calm, he had himself together; it was as if there were no possibility of danger. He might have been one of the commuters pondering his hard day at the office, wondering about this account or that one, planning how he could get ahead in the ratrace.

Once more Hollander looked back.

The tan Chevrolet was there. Steady. Brandt never lost that quality known as cool, because he had none to lose. He ran like perfect clockwork once you had set him in motion. *I'm going to have to kill again*, Hollander thought. *Or be killed.*

Was anything ever worth that?

They passed the exit ramp for Germantown. Brinkerhoff

appeared to know where he was going now that the maze
of Washington was left behind them.

"Pull over," Hollander said.

"What?"

"Quickly now. Don't signal."

Brinkerhoff drove the Fiat onto the shoulder.

The Chevrolet went past.

He saw Brandt's face, the look of astonishment as the
tan car continued in the inside lane.

"Now get back into the traffic," Hollander said.

Brinkerhoff found an opening between a truck and an
ice-cream van. A temporary maneuver, Hollander thought.
For the time being.

"It's better to be behind than in front," he said.

But Brandt would simply fall back, allow himself to be
overtaken; then they would play the slow game with one
another until Brandt had got the Chevrolet in back once
again. It was breathing space, nothing more.

Hollander watched the passing landscape a moment.
There were billboards looming up, monolithic slabs of advertising detritus: *Quaker State Oil, When in Hagerstown
stay at the Holiday Inn.* It was strange to him, alien; as if
for the first time he had come to feel that he was a for-
eigner in his own country.

Between his gaps in the traffic up ahead, he could see
Brandt's car. He thought: *I've got to get out of this place,
I don't belong here anymore.*

Thorne found the note pinned inside the refrigerator,
which explained why it had seemed she was babbling in-
consequentially; she had been trying to tell him. She had
thumbtacked it to an egg carton and it was folded over in
such a way that at a casual glance one would have over-
looked it. He opened it and read:

> They said they'd kill you if I didn't
> leave. I love you. Gone to Mothers.

He ripped the paper up and took it into the bathroom
and flushed it away. What had begun in anger had turned
to something else: a dumb, unfeeling sensation, a cold realization that they could fuck with your life any way they
liked. They could create chaos and destruction, kill as they

pleased, frighten as they liked—and all because of what? Because of what? Darkness and denial, cajolement and menace, surveillance and threat: and what appalled him now was his suspicion that you could never quite penetrate the heart of it. It was the core of an impossible onion. The arrogance implicit in it all was stunning; it transported you beyond what was right and wrong, what was moral and what wasn't. It took you into a nebulous region where any kind of act, so long as it had the sanction of the powers that ran the game, was in itself correct.

Dear Christ, he thought. They had come here to frighten Marcia, because they wanted to show a little more of their muscle—if any further demonstration was necessary. They had come here to scare her because they wanted to isolate him, they wanted to set him apart, they wanted him to see how simple it was for them to disturb and unravel the fabric of his life. They could take away his job, scare his girl, do whatever they deemed necessary.

Outside it was practically dark. The sun had almost gone; a few reddish traces in the sky, that was all, like colors spilled carelessly from a palette. He stood on the edge of the parking lot and looked across the neat rows of parked cars. He had the feeling of needing to *do* something: he was angry again. He felt it as one might feel a palpitation in a nerve, a tic or pulse beneath the skin that would not stop bleating no matter how hard you rubbed.

At the far end of the parking lot he saw the green Catalina. Jesus, he thought. They don't know when to draw the line, when to stop and say they had done quite enough, put an end to wholesale damage. He walked to his VW, hesitated, stuck the key back into his pocket, and looked in the direction of the Catalina. He saw the face of the fat man behind glass. He was filled all at once with a sense of violence, of vengeance, of getting even for how Marcia had been treated. Why not? Why not? He owed himself something, after all. He hesitated, then walked to the green car.

The fat man looked at him oddly, as if this confrontation were the most unlikely thing in the world. Slowly, watching Thorne, he unrolled his window.

"What's up, buddy?" he asked.

Calm, Thorne thought. Keep cool, be patient. What good is anger?

"Get off my ass," Thorne said.

"I don't think I follow you," the fat man said.

"Get off my case, okay?"

"Listen, buddy, I'm waiting here for somebody—"

"Like you waited in the library, like you waited in Fredericksburg—just get off my ass."

The fat man leaned down to roll his window up, doing the offended citizen bit. Thorne thrust his hand through the space, pulling the man forward by the lapel of his jacket, pressing his face against the edge of the glass. He was strong, he wrenched himself away, he looked like somebody suppressing an urge to violence.

"Listen," he said.

"I don't need to listen," Thorne said. He opened the door of the car and the fat man slid away across the bench seat.

"I'll call the cops," the guy said.

"I'm going to tell you something and I want you to listen," Thorne said. He was aware of his own rapid heartbeat, the pulse in his wrist: it was the kind of fear you could not draw a circle around and push aside. He was afraid of himself all at once and of what he might do; it was like stumbling across some dark capacity you never knew you possessed, a capability of killing.

His own voice sounded oddly thick to him: "I'm going to get inside my car, okay. I'm going to drive out of here. If I see you behind me, I'm going to kill you."

He wondered how it sounded to the other man, if it carried any weight. The fat man started to laugh.

"You're going to kill me?" he said.

"You got the message," Thorne said. "You're quick."

The fat man covered his mouth with his hand, trying to contain his laughter. Thorne couldn't tell; was the laughter one of fear, of ridicule? He didn't know.

He slammed the door of the Catalina shut.

He walked to his VW and got inside and drove out of the parking lot.

Tarkington took out his gun and held it flat in the palm of his hand. The fucker, he thought. *Who does the fucking joker think he's kidding?* He would have killed him there and then. He would have blown him quite away. But Sharpe, goddamn Sharpe, hadn't given him the green light for an act like that. So you have to sit and be humiliated and look like you're scared and pretend. It was downright embarrassing. It was a pain in the ass.

He drove out onto the street. Now what? Did he go back to Sharpe and say his cover had been blown? Or did he keep on the tail of this young clown? An order is an order.

Vigilance at all times.

An order. The kid-glove crap.

What was so important about this joker anyhow that he couldn't be blown away like anybody else? Tarkington ran into the same old wall of puzzlement. It was like trying to understand the circuitry of a pinball machine. You were in a maze of circuits and colored wires. When the lights flashed, they flashed. When they didn't, they didn't. The random transistor. Vigilance. There was a high place where everything originated, an Olympus; only you were on the foot of the slope and trying to look up and there were clouds, great mothers of clouds, everywhere.

I'm a sap, he thought. But I don't like being threatened. And I just don't take easy to humiliation.

He was sweating.

He followed the red VW to the end of the street, shrugged his shoulders, and continued after it when it took a right turn.

Thorne parked outside a Safeways market and went to a telephone. It hadn't worked; he had known it wouldn't work but he had done it more for his own sake than to get the fat man off his track. He felt pretty good about it. Even as he saw the green car cruise across the parking lot, he felt good.

He closed the door of the booth, dialed Marcia's home. Her mother answered. She had one of those clipped New England voices that sound as if they are coming from permafrost. She had never approved of her daughter's co-habitation with Thorne. He heard the receiver being clunked down on the table, the distant sound of a TV droning. He looked through the dirty glass window of the booth. The supermarket had a special on Mineola oranges and another on pork ribs. He tapped his fingers, stared in the direction of the green car. Its headlights were dimmed.

"John?"

"That was quite an act you put on," he said. "Just for a moment, you had me almost convinced."

"It was terrible," she said. "He was an old guy, very pleasant, oldie-worldie charm, but you could smell something nasty—"

"Did he have a name?"

"Count Dracula, I guess."

"What did he say?"

"He hummed and hawed a bit but what it boiled down to was that if I didn't get my ass out of there you were a dead duck."

Isolation, Thorne thought. He might have been carrying around some deadly germ, a new strain of *Mycobacterium leprae*.

"He had this young guy with him, who was very creepy. He spent his time wandering around touching things. He did something to the telephone—"

"Yeah," Thorne said. "It figures."

He was silent for a time. He watched a family get out of a station wagon and walk toward the supermarket. Mom and Dad and the whole tribe. The ordinariness of it depressed him somewhat. He imagined them sifting through the vegetable racks, feeling tomatoes for firmness, scrutinizing squashes, examining eggplants. Doing plain straightforward things.

"Look," he said. "Stay at your mother's place—"

"Is that going to keep you alive?"

"It just might," he said.

She paused, then said: "A few days ago wasn't everything kinda normal? Refresh my memory—"

"It was normal," he said.

She paused again. "This thing you're into . . . is it worth any of this?"

"I never asked you if Coleridge was worth all the trouble, did I?"

"Oh, screw Coleridge. I don't like going to the funerals of loved ones, you understand? I get quite weepy and out of control."

He said, "It isn't going to come to that—"

"John. Why am I a little bit scared?"

"You don't need to be—"

"Hah! Someone just steps in and says, Hey, the man you love is going to be offed and you tell me not to be scared like it's something that happens every goddamn day of the week?"

He stared at the green car. "Take it easy—"

"I don't like playing traditional waiting roles, John. It just isn't my scene. I could never have been in love with a sailor or somebody like that, you know, hanging out waiting for his return—"

"Just sit tight, okay? I'll be in touch."

"And what I don't want," she said, as if she weren't listening to him; "what I don't want is some stranger calling me in the middle of the night to say you got in the way of a truck or you decided on a midnight swim."

"Don't worry about me." What else could he say? *Be terrified for me?*

"I love you, John Thorne," she said.

"It's a feeling I share, kid," he answered.

He hung up, went back to his car. The Catalina followed him out of the parking lot.

"Your friend is persistent," Brinkerhoff was saying.

The tan car was behind them again. They had come off Highway 240. They were going toward Damascus. Hollander turned around in his seat. He had the Police Positive in his hand. You had to admit: Brandt was good with the car, neither too risky nor too careful. But he had managed to get in back of them once more.

"How far is it to the airfield?" he asked.

"Seven, eight miles," Brinkerhoff said. "You have a suggestion?"

"I'm playing it by ear," Hollander said. Brandt would be on the radio constantly, reporting the positions, waiting for instructions. And he would not be alone in this. There would be others. The radio would bring them in when the positions were reported. How many? Two? Three? It would depend on who was in the field now.

He turned back around in his seat.

The headlights cut a broad band in the dusk ahead.

It was a small apartment of the kind sometimes advertised as "an efficiency unit," which meant that the rooms were small and the kitchen narrow. When the congressman came to the door, he had an expression of pained surprise.

"John, this is unexpected—"

Thorne stepped inside. It was a place of white walls and few decorations, Leach's spartan Washington domicile.

"One question," Thorne said. "What is Asterisk?"

Leach looked puzzled. He moved very slowly to the sofa and sat down. He wheezed as he moved; the impression of a man waiting patiently to die. For a moment, Thorne thought he should feel some pity for the old man, some sense of sympathy, but he could not overcome outrage.

"We've been through this," Leach said.

"Let's run through it again," Thorne said.

"I'm sorry, John. I can't help you." Leach reached for his walking stick. He raised himself to a standing position with obvious strain, his face the kind of white Thorne associated with the dead.

"Asterisk, Congressman, that's all I want to know."

"I said it before, I can't help you—"

Thorne rubbed his face wearily: "I think you can—"

"No," Leach said.

"People have died," Thorne said. "Beginning with Major General Burckhardt. Add his wife to that—"

"The names mean nothing to me," Leach said.

The congressman walked to the window, looked out a moment, then let the drape fall back in place. Momentarily, Thorne wondered if perhaps there were someone outside, if Leach were signaling something. It would make as much sense as anything else.

"Asterisk," Thorne said.

Leach turned around to look at him: "John. Let me give you a word of advice. Drop it. Leave it alone."

"I'm not prepared to do that now," Thorne said.

"I knew your father pretty well, John. I always liked him, always did. Sometimes, politically, we were poles apart, but I had a lot of time for him. If he was alive now, he would be telling you just the same as me. *Leave it alone.*"

Thorne shook his head. "I want some answers."

"What makes you think I'm in a position to give you answers?"

"I figured it out," Thorne said. "It isn't hard. After I approached you, I was suddenly offered the chance to run for Congress. Out of the blue. Just like that. I walked away from it. Next thing, I'm being sent to Paris. I walked away from that too. Suddenly I'm out of work, suddenly my girl friend is threatened—you don't have to be clairvoyant to recognize when strings are being pulled, do you?"

Leach hobbled around the room on his stick for a time, saying nothing.

Thorne licked dry lips; all at once he realized he was tired, as if he had reached some limit to himself. But he wasn't going to let this slide, not now, he wasn't going to walk away from it.

"Asterisk," he said. "What is Asterisk, Congressman? Why is Escalante listed as a missile base when the kind of staff it has obviously has nothing to do with missiles?"

Leach stared at him; his skin reminded Thorne of a crumpled white handkerchief.

"You're a fool, Thorne. You're a plain old-fashioned fool. I didn't think they made fools like you these days. People have been trying to do you favors you don't goddamn deserve. You're too blind to see your own position. But people don't have the patience of saints, Thorne. It's not a limitless supply, you understand that? It comes to an end."

There was a harsh note in the voice, something ugly in the way Leach sounded and, as he turned his face full round, in how he looked. This wasn't an expression you ever caught in newspaper pictures; here the mask was off, the defenses down. And then, just as abruptly, the voice became friendly again.

"John, John, John. You don't need to be involved. Believe me. Trust me. You don't need any part of this."

Thorne sat on the arm of the sofa. Why was he perspiring like this? He stared at the palms of his hands, saw the crystalline sparkle of sweat in the lines.

"Look, Congressman. Somebody — some*thing* — fucks with my life. I don't like it. I don't care for it. I don't even know what it is. And you ask me to leave it *alone*?"

Rather shakily, the congressman extended one hand as if he were making an uncertain plea, like a lawyer on behalf of a client he knows to be guilty as hell.

"There's time to walk away, John."

Thorne shook his head. "No. Not that easily."

Leach sat down a moment, fell into silence, then he rose and, clutching his cane, went into the kitchen. Thorne could hear a faucet running, the sound of ice cubes in a glass. He walked to the kitchen, stood in the doorway. Leach was pouring two glasses from a bottle of Laphroaig.

"Probably sacrilege to put ice in this," he said. "Probably there are Scotchmen turning in their graves." He looked at Thorne, smiling.

Thorne swallowed a little of the malt whiskey. It burned in his throat and chest.

"Cheers," Leach said, and drank.

Thorne watched him: the smile was still there, but it was untrustworthy, wily, concealing things.

"Play ball, John. Play ball."

"And if I don't?"

The congressman shrugged. "We don't have Siberias in this country."

"No?" Thorne put the glass down.

"You're a young man, John. Bright. What I hate to see is a waste of potential. You only get one quick shot at life, John. Grab what you can while you can. Don't throw it away."

We don't have Siberias, Thorne thought. No, we have killings that look like suicides. We have secrets and conspiracies and God help you if you try to puncture the bubble. God help you.

"Just think, John. Just pause and ponder a moment."

Thorne shook his head. "It's gone past that stage."

"John. For the sake of your father's memory—"

"That won't work," Thorne said.

Leach was silent for a time. Thorne moved toward the door.

"Wait," Leach said.

Thorne hesitated in the doorway.

"If you won't give me your word that you'll stop this, I can't do anything more for you. Do you understand that? I can't do anything more."

Thorne looked at the congressman for a time. The pale, pathetic face: was Leach actually sorry? was he truly sorry?

"Thanks for what you've done so far," Thorne said. "Whatever it is."

He went out, closing the door.

In the corridor, which was empty, lit by bright fluorescence and almost startling in its unbroken white gleaming, he paused: the fear was coming in at him again and this time it wasn't a fear of his own capabilities. It was a strange emptiness: a terror.

Nobody would raise a finger now to help him.

There was nobody.

He looked down the white corridor. It might have been the kind of passageway—clinical, stark, unshadowed—you would expect to find in a hospital for the incurably insane.

Dilbeck hated Sharpe's office despite the surprising domestic touches of the floral sofa and the colored TV. These were superficial things: take them away and you were left with your standard bureaucratic sterility. Sharpe was in the communications room, sitting behind a row of receivers, when Dilbeck came in. A radio operator was filling his pipe with tobacco as if he had all the time in the world. If anything, this room was more hideous than Sharpe's office. The gadgetry, the consoles, the dials—here you ran smack into the technology of it all and you knew it was for real.

"I didn't want to drag you in," Sharpe said.

Dilbeck waved the apology aside. "It doesn't matter."

"Hollander's in a Fiat with somebody else—"

"Do we know who?"

Sharpe was silent a moment, the radio crackled, there was a disembodied voice of the kind one might expect to hear at a fraudulent seance.

"It's an airstrip," the voice was saying.

"Do we know who the companion is?" Dilbeck asked.

"I had the license plate checked out."

"And?" Why was Sharpe being so reluctant?

"It's registered to someone called Brinkerhoff—"

"Do we know this person?"

"You want me to fetch his file?"

Dilbeck was becoming irritated. Brinkerhoff. What did that name mean?

"Instructions requested," the voice was saying over the radio, a cold voice that might have emerged from an android.

"Never mind the file," Dilbeck said.

"Brinkerhoff is attached to the Soviet embassy," Sharpe said.

Dilbeck felt as if he had been struck.

He sat down and stared at the dials.

And he had told them. He had told the committee. He had come right out and told them that there was nothing in Hollander's background to suggest any association with a foreign power. *He had said that.*

It was a matter of record now.

He shut his eyes.

"I'm awaiting instructions, for God's sake," the voice was saying.

"Who's out there?" Dilbeck asked.

"Brandt," Sharpe answered.

"Alone?" Dilbeck asked. He opened his eyes.

"I've got Rupert Mulholland coming in from Baltimore," Sharpe said.

"But Brandt's on his own?"

Sharpe nodded.

"What in the name of God kind of tinhorn operation are you running, Sharpe?" Dilbeck tried to still his anger. It did his blood pressure no good and, besides, he knew he was projecting his own stupidities, taking his own flaws out on Sharpe. *I swore by Hollander at that meeting,* he thought. I put my own damn head on the chopping block.

"There's a light aircraft of some kind," the voice was saying. "*Please instruct me.*"

Twenty minutes ago Leach had been on the telephone. Thorne. Thorne-in-the-side. One thing at a time, he thought. Be logical. A question of priorities.

"*Please instruct me—*"

Sharpe looked at Dilbeck. "Do I finalize this? Have I your authorization?"

Dilbeck saw the shadow of a noose dangling on a scaffold of his imagination. "You not only finalize," he said calmly. "You pulverize."

Sharpe pulled the microphone toward his mouth.

"Green," he said.

"Got you," the voice said from the other end.

Sharpe smiled. He looked at Dilbeck as if for approbation now; Dilbeck wondered what Socrates felt with all those inquisitive pupils sitting at his feet.

Across the airfield there was a Turbo Centurion sitting behind a darkened hangar. Brinkerhoff drove the Fiat alongside the aircraft, braked, threw his door open at once.

Hollander turned in his seat. The headlights of the Chevy came burning toward them, glowing, growing, bearing down on them with the speed of some unavoidable impact. Hollander opened his door. He glanced up at the cockpit of the Centurion. There was a shadow behind the thinly lit glass. He saw Brinkerhoff moving out of the beam of the Chevrolet. He moved behind the Fiat. He had the Police Positive in his hand; kneeling he took aim, fired, the tan car swung to the side as if to avoid collision. It ran up against the side of the hangar, its headlights out. He heard a door slam shut.

"The plane," Brinkerhoff said.

"Get down," Hollander said.

There was a flash in the dark from alongside the hangar. Brandt, he thought. It was what he had been trained for; survival. The propellers of the Centurion began to spin. He felt Brinkerhoff at his side. They crouched beside the Fiat. Where is Brandt? Where is he now? He peered across the dark at the hangar.

"The plane," Brinkerhoff said.

"Stand up now and you're dead," Hollander answered.

He heard the propellers.

There was another flash through the dark. It cracked the windshield of the Fiat. Hollander could hear the safety glass splinter. Brinkerhoff made to rise. Hollander tugged at his coat.

"It's only a few yards," Brinkerhoff said.

"A few yards is all he needs."

"In this darkness?"

"In this darkness," Hollander said. He had seen Brandt on the practice range: lethal. One of the best.

"We sit like this for how long?" Brinkerhoff asked.

Hollander said nothing. He thought of the envelope in his pocket. He was giving them Asterisk. He was giving them a plain brown envelope. He was giving them everything. The doubts again—when would he learn that there was a time and a place for everything? When would he grow up?

The propellers whistled. He felt the draft they created. He looked once more up into the cockpit and he knew what he would do in Brandt's place. The pilot. A certain target. A sitting duck. He would take the pilot out of it. But Brandt was programmed, his movements and urges preordained. He had not been told to get the pilot. The pilot did not figure in any of this. Hollander, only Ted Hollander. *Destroy*.

Across the airfield there were the lights of a second car. They were bringing up reinforcements now, Hollander thought. It was what he expected. He watched the car come across the field. It had come in from the Baltimore side. Who was working out of Baltimore these days? McKay? Mulholland? Old-timers, maybe they had been retired, put out to pasture, maybe this was one of the new crew.

He watched the lights as they came closer.

He took aim with the Colt, fired at a dark place between the lamps, as if the lamps and the head of the unseen driver formed the points of a triangle. The car went into a spin and then, like something run by a remote-control device gone berserk, went on running into the hangar. He heard glass shatter, the engine run, the sound of wheels going nowhere as they spun around and around on concrete.

"We could make it to the plane," Brinkerhoff said.

Brandt was out there still. What to do with the man?

"Stay down," he said. The Russian obeyed.

Hollander moved around the side of the Fiat. The goddamn darkness. Brandt could play a waiting game. He could afford to. Before long there would be more reinforcements. He raised the gun and fired a shot randomly in the direction of the Chevrolet. There was an immediate response. He saw the glare, the sudden glow; he fired quickly toward it. In this dark how could you tell? How could you know you had hit anything?

He heard Brinkerhoff sigh.

You take a chance, Hollander thought. You have to.

He stood up. He held the gun between his two hands. The old nerves. The old sharp sensation in the head. The same old need for the electricity of clarity.

He began to walk toward the hangar.

He had written the book on this. And now he was breaking his own rules. He had a sudden flash of his family, as if he saw three young faces smiling out of a snapshot done in garish color. Going soft, he thought. Nothing is like what it used to be. Change, flux, uncertainty—say what you wanted to, nothing remained still for very long.

He would give them Asterisk.

Then they would be equal all around.

The world would be safe—not for democracy or for totalitarianism, but for three kids whose faces came to him as he walked toward the darkened hangar.

He heard Brandt move. He heard a sliver of glass slide and snap under a foot. He threw himself down on the concrete, remembering the manual, remembering how he had written the book. He saw the flare and he fired directly at it.

Silence.

A great silence came in at him.

"Hollander."

It was Brinkerhoff calling to him across the darkness.

"Hollander."

He heard Brinkerhoff come across the tarmac toward him.

He saw the Russian bend over him.

"You've been hit," Brinkerhoff said.

Hollander was dizzily conscious of having passed one perilous moment only to encounter another. He thought of the envelope. The pain started to hurt him.

"Where is it?" Brinkerhoff asked.

The wound or the envelope? Hollander wondered.

Brinkerhoff was kneeling now. He could feel the other man's fingers undo the buttons of his coat.

"How bad is it?"

Hollander said, "It hurts like hell."

Brinkerhoff was silent for a moment. It was as if he were considering something important; it had fallen into his lap. He could take it, he could take it and leave, he could leave Hollander where he was.

Do what you're going to do, Hollander thought.

Whatever it is.

In the darkness, he could not see Brinkerhoff's eyes.

"The plane," Brinkerhoff said after a moment.

He helped Hollander up; it was like a needle now in the center of his chest. He twisted his body this way, that way, trying to alleviate it. It would not budge. He groaned: his shirt was moist.

"You could take the envelope," he said. "I couldn't stop you now."

Brinkerhoff said nothing.

Hollander looked at the shadow inside the cockpit.

He was aware of the night all at once, the stars overhead, the moon that had the appearance of something newly minted in some impossible forge. He was aware of his consciousness seeping away from him as a tide finally ebbs. He barely felt himself being helped onto the Centurion. And by the time it had taken off and swung eastward toward the great impenetrable dark of the Atlantic, he was conscious of nothing.

"Buffalo Nine," the communications man was saying. "Buffalo Nine, are you reading?"

He had a pipe between his teeth and a look of incurable placidity; Sharpe imagined the only thing that might shake him would be the thought of falling behind in his mortgage payments.

"Buffalo Nine," he went on saying. He was silent a moment, glanced at Sharpe, then went back to his microphone. "Marvin, are you getting this? Are you getting any of this?"

Sharpe turned to look at Dilbeck but averted his eyes at the last moment, for he knew the expression of hollowness he would encounter there. Neither Brandt nor Mulholland was answering his signal. He wanted to think there was some electronic failure somewhere, a blown terminal or a broken circuit or, at the least, the existence of some geographical obstacle—a mountain, a hill—that had caused this state of affairs.

Dilbeck, who considered the failure of machines and devices personal affronts to him, leaned forward in his chair and said, "Well, Sharpe. Well. What now?"

Sharpe dropped his hands. "Brandt's last message was something about a plane—"

"I heard," Dilbeck said. Ted Hollander, he was thinking. You could not put one over on Ted. You would have to be up very early to catch Ted.

"So now we assume that Hollander and his Russian friend have flown," he said.

"It looks that way," Sharpe said.

"Okay." Dilbeck rose from his chair. There was the

most curious smell in this communications room, he thought. It was like burned rubber. "He takes a flight with his chum. Where?"

"I hate to think the rest," Sharpe said.

"So do I, Sharpe, so do I—but what else is there?" Dilbeck blew his nose, rolled the handkerchief up, stuck it away. "They have five or six routes they use in these situations. So far as I know, they use Mexico City, Toronto. They've used Montreal before now. Where else?"

Dilbeck tried to bring to mind old intelligence dossiers.

"And Havana," he added.

"Which is it to be?"

"All of them, of course. All of them. Alert every air base and control tower within a three-hundred-mile radius of—what's it called?—Damascus? We want one unauthorized flight—"

"We don't even know the type of craft," Sharpe complained.

Dilbeck stared at him. There had lately been a whine in the man's voice he had grown mightily to dislike. "I don't give a tinker's shit if we know its serial number, make, year of production and the personal names of the spot welders who put it together—every unauthorized flight must be brought into radio contact and its credentials ascertained."

Sharpe turned to his communications man. "Get your ass on that, Vic."

"It's going to take all night," the communications man said.

"You haven't got all night."

The communications man opened a drawer and brought out a manual of call signals: he began to flick through the pages.

"Get other people in here, Sharpe," Dilbeck said. "Delegate this operation. Use telephones. Use the radio. But for Christ's sake, get on it!"

Dilbeck left the room and sat down on the sofa in Sharpe's office; he was very tired. He felt a sense, too, of emptiness, and on the edges of consciousness the uneasy knowledge that he would have to explain all this. They would not understand. He could not get them to understand, not ever. The Soviets. Who would have thought it of Hollander? Airtight boxes, sealed pigeonholes, the inside of a camera. They thought you could bottle everything. *They* thought. Well, Whorley hadn't exactly been able to keep his old major general in tow, had he? Let *him* try to cast the first stone.

God, he hoped they could bring that plane out of the air, preferably into the sea somewhere so that it might never be found save for some fragmented items of wreckage that might one day wash up on obscure beaches for the puzzled delight of holidaymakers. Yes, let that happen.

He sat with his eyes closed. In the other room he could hear telephones ringing, the radio chattering; it all sounded so hideous and unreal.

And now his tired mind came around to Thorne.

Even Leach was agreed. They had gone as far as they could with that young man. *Ball's in your court, Dilbeck, I wash my hands of him.*

He rose, called Sharpe out of the communications room, then closed the door as Sharpe, chewing a toothpick, stepped into the office. He looks haunted, Dilbeck thought.

"Finesse isn't getting us anywhere," Dilbeck said.

Sharpe, as if he understood nothing, stared dumbly.

"Thorne's your baby now," Dilbeck said.

He once more closed his eyes. He was thinking of the Russians. If they had their teeth in Asterisk, courtesy of friend Hollander, they would worry it like a dog with a marvelous bone. When would his colleagues learn that there was not a hope in hell of forever containing something like Asterisk?

The sound of the telephone on Sharpe's desk startled him. *Brrrnnng. Brrrnnng*—it was like some fresh alarm. He watched Sharpe pick it up. Sharpe listened a moment, frowned, then covered the mouthpiece with the palm of his hand.

"Our young friend's at the airport," Sharpe said.

"Intending to travel?" Dilbeck asked.

Sharpe shrugged.

"Nothing would astonish me," Dilbeck said. "Put a lid on it. Put a very tight lid on it, Sharpe."

5

In the men's room Thorne caught his own ragged reflection and, for a moment, it was as if the face he saw in the glass were not his own. There were new lines under the eyes; the pallor of his skin reminded him of the weird bleached quality of a newspaper that has lain too long in bright sunlight. He turned on the cold-water faucet, splashed his face, combed his hair, but he did not check the results of these efforts in the mirror. One look had been enough. There are days, he thought, when what you see is a fool staring back at you.

Over the intercom, the sound of which echoed in the tiled bathroom, he heard a girl's voice lisp: *Passengers for Rome are presently boarding through gate number six.* Rome, Thorne thought. I could go to Rome and do as the Romans do, whatever that might be.

He let the cold water run across his wrists and fingers.

The door opened. A uniformed man came in, went inside a cubicle, closed and locked the door. In the space under the door Thorne could see the pants being dropped around shiny black shoes.

Even pilots have needs, he thought.

Even pilots.

He dried his fingers on a towel that had come to the end of its tether and lay strewn across the floor like a flag of defeat. Sullied, soiled, ashen.

There was the noise of a toilet flushing.

The pilot came briskly out of the cubicle and went to a washbasin, rolling his sleeves up. He moved with the quick economy of a man who lives every day of his life with decisions of importance.

Thorne opened the door.

He walked through the main lounge, past the vacant, vaguely anxious faces of those who waited for flights or for arrivals. He went inside the cocktail bar and sat up on a stool and ordered a Bloody Mary.

The bar was crowded. There was Muzak playing. Early Beatles hits processed through the Muzak factory and sounding now like the death throes of Lawrence Welk. He looked around the bar for a sign of his fat friend, but he wasn't around. Maybe he clocked out at a certain time? Could you hope for that? Maybe he simply went off duty and slept and then, like a toy made to function by a spring, rolled out of bed next day and got back on the job.

There were a couple of beautiful people standing next to him at the bar. She was in dark-green pants and white blouse and carried her expensive jacket casually over her shoulder. He wore a blue jean suit and a white ruffled shirt open to the navel and brown-tinted glasses. He had seen them in the pages of *Vogue*, those asexual glossy demonstrations of what was up to date in the world of fashion. What is it tonight? Thorne wondered. A quick jet to Vegas? A jaunt down to New Orleans to enjoy some latenight fun in the French Quarter? Her face was made up in an immaculate manner; she talked as if she knew she was being observed, an actress's flair. He hung on every word, or so it seemed, but there was a glaze across his eyes and a dead quality in the way he laughed at the right moments.

She: *I don't believe Alexis has house-trained her mutt.*

He: *How so?*

She: *I found a little pile of poop in the master bedroom.*

(Laughter)

Their heads inclined at the same time as if set on a collision course.

Thorne finished his drink and once more saw his image, this time reflected in the mirror behind the bar. A young man who has had too many late nights. A little worn around the edges. A blunt instrument. The Beatles played on as if they had been wrapped in cellophane. *Penny Lane you're in.*

He signaled the barman, ordered a second drink, turned around and looked across the bar. *Passengers for Rome. This is the last call for TWA flight . . .* Where is he? Thorne wondered. Where is the fat man?

He sipped his Bloody Mary.

She: *Alexis always thinks she has a way with dogs.*

He: *What makes you think so?*

She: *My dear, look at the men she's been married to.*

(Laughter)

Thorne picked up his glass, moved away from the bar. He went to the back of the cocktail lounge and, screened by people, watched the front door.

Escalante—

He was dreaming. In a moment he would wake.

Marcia would be sitting on the edge of the bed.

He would get up. Have coffee. Dress. Briefcase. Car. Office. Home. Marcia.

This part is the dream, he thought.
You play ball, John.
My dear congressman
You scratch my back
How could he
Pictures, flashes, Anna Burckhardt lying face down in
that sleep from which there is no awakening, an old man
floating in a pool, Marcia hauling her suitcases—
Last call for passengers for
Through the open doorway of the bar he saw a straggle
of newly arrived passengers drifting across the main
lounge. Texans, garrulous men in garish leisure suits,
broadbrimmed hats. Their women looked as if they should
be carrying white poodles.

And there, across the lounge, sitting with a newspaper
folded in his lap, there he was. The fat bland face, the expression one of a complete lack of curiosity such as you
might expect to see in the eye of a profound retard.
Thorne heard the ice cubes click in his Bloody Mary.

He stepped back against the wall.

The beautiful woman brushed past him on the way to
the toilet, leaving a trace of perfume in the air. He
couldn't imagine her pissing. He couldn't, by the same token, imagine her breathing the air he breathed. He saw the
fat man get up, leave the newspaper on the sofa, and walk
to a glass case that contained a replica of Washington in
the year 1876. Fastidiously modeled dwellings in miniature. Tiny people in the streets, stuck, going nowhere.

He went to the telephone and pushed in coils and dialed
a number; his hand adhered to the receiver. He heard
Erickson's voice at the other end, a note of irritation. The
beautiful woman passed him again, the perfume stronger
now, cloying, like the scent of a thousand sick petals opening for one final outrage.

Erickson, understandably, was not pleased.

"I'm sorry about the job," Thorne said.

"Yeah," Erickson said. "No more sorry than me. They
said nothing. There was just this note from McLintock.
Thanks a lot, here's your check, goodbye, sorry it didn't
work out. I know better."

"It was because of me," Thorne said.

"What else is new?" Erickson said. "If you want nothing

more than to proffer your apology, Thorne, then excuse
me while I get back to the help-wanted column—"

Thorne said, "Wait."

Erickson was silent.

"Have you ever heard of Asterisk?"

"It doesn't ring any bells."

"Are you sure?"

"Sure I'm sure."

"You'd tell me if it did?" Thorne asked.

The fat man's nose was pressed to the glass case.

"I don't like how you sound," Erickson said. "Go home
and lie down in a darkened room, man."

"Erickson, listen to me, they've been following me
around for God knows how long—"

"John, give me a break."

"Erickson, please listen. It's because of the Asterisk
Project. You understand? That's what it's all about, that's
why Burckhardt was killed—"

Erickson was silent.

"Are you listening to me?" Thorne asked. *I sound perfectly insane*, he thought. A disembodied voice gone crazy
on a telephone line.

Erickson was still silent.

"Burckhardt was killed because of it—"

The line went dead. Thorne held the receiver in his
hand, put his forehead against the wall, he could feel the
perspiration on his brow stick to the paneled wood. You
couldn't blame Erickson, you couldn't blame him. He put
the receiver back in place, finished his drink, and realized,
with a start, a consciousness of horror, that he had just left
Erickson with the verbal equivalent of twenty-five pages of
blank manuscript. Only the word Asterisk had been added.
Just that.

He put his hand to his forehead.

Passengers for Chicago are boarding at gate number

Marcia, he thought.

The fat man was scratching a jowl.

Thorne put his empty glass down beside the telephone.

I expect to die, he thought. Is that what I expect?

Funny, Tarkington thought. Funny how people will go
to all the trouble of making a replica like this. He couldn't
personally see the point to it. All that work and then you

stick it in a glass case and people come and they look a
while and they go away and they forget. All that work for
nothing. Making those tiny models. I never had a hobby,
never had the time for it.

He turned his face in the direction of the doorway of
the cocktail lounge.

There was one joker who wouldn't humiliate him again.

* * *

Expecting to die. No. One more death. What difference.
Passengers for Chicago. Another drink. Two beautiful
people in embrace. Phony. Didn't fit. Look right. What
would you have done, Senator Thorne? What would your
solution have been? Dying of brain cancer. Incoherent in
the last months. The brain gone. No more committees,
meetings, policies, no more thoughts. John, is that you? Is
that you? I can't see, headaches blind me, come closer.
They've been watching me, John. Did I ever tell you? It
started in the war with Stalin. He isn't dead. Did I ever
tell you that, no? He's still alive. They put a wax doll in a
coffin so the people could pay homage, but he's alive.
Stalin sent the order down on me personally, John, personally. His own hand. I had a copy of the order. Watch
Thorne, it said. I lost the paper. Come closer, John.
Closer. Who are you? You're not John. You're too old.

Passengers for Chicago.

Thorne gripped the edge of the bar, finished his drink.
Was it a genetic thing? Did it pass from father to son like
some inexorable poison? This *fear*.

No.

The fat guy is out there. You couldn't make that up. A
solid fact, a thing in the real world.

He put his empty glass down.

He went out into the main lounge.

He passed the airlines desks, the pretty girls who stood
in gleaming rows and made out tickets or surveyed the
weight of baggage on scales. There was a good-looking
one behind the Air-India desk; she had her hair pulled
tightly back, accentuating the height of the cheekbones, as
if in drawing the hair back she had also somehow
tightened the skin.

The old man losing his grip during those last months,

the profound deterioration that took place—it was utterly pathetic. He looked up at the fluorescent lights on the high ceiling. The Air-India girl was smiling at him. He was conscious of the fat man, some fifty feet behind.

He went toward the exit.

The fat man followed.

Outside in the darkness he began to sprint toward the parking lot, surprised all at once by what his own body was capable of performing. Then he could no longer feel himself. He was no longer aware of the complex moving parts of the mechanism. This dislocation—was this the fear of death? Had Anna Burckhardt felt something like this? And her husband?

The night sky was alive with lights.

An airplane just beginning its climb; roaring along the runway, ascending, looking like some massive silvery sword. He felt the ground vibrate beneath him. Another plane was descending, a DC-10, he saw its lights grow brighter, brighter, as it came whining toward the runway.

The VW.

He couldn't remember where he had parked the VW.

There were thousands of cars, row after row after row. Thousands. Where had he left the bug?

He stopped running a moment and tried to catch his breath. Across the spaces of darkness he could hear the footsteps of the fat man. Trying to run, to keep up.

Tarkington went from one car to the next. His lungs felt oddly raw. You put too much strain on the old pump, he thought. Kaput, just like that. He had seen it happen before. He remembered old Bill McWilliams, who always looked strong as an ox, and how, suddenly, just like that, just like a snap of your fingers or the crack of a straw, old Bill had keeled over in the heat of Istanbul. A massive coronary, they said. Now, leaning against the side of a car, straining to catch his breath, he saw himself as if from above: a mass of jelly quivering. Steam rooms, the rubber suit, he would have to find time to work this burden off.

He felt dizzy a moment. There were spots, rather like frail mosquitos, darting around in front of his eyes. This guy Thorne was young, looked fit and healthy, he could never outrun Thorne no matter what.

A white station wagon went past slowly, looking for a

space. Tarkington saw the silhouettes of a crowd of kids in the back of the vehicle. Noses pressed flat and grotesque against the glass.

Then he looked across the parking lot. Thorne would be going for his little red car. Tarkington went in that direction.

Thorne continued to run. When finally he saw his car he remembered all along where he had left it; squeezed between a Continental and a Honda Civic; it looked to him like three generations of automobile sizes, as if the large one had spawned the VW and the bug, in turn, had put forth its own progeny. He fumbled his keys, found the lock, hauled the door open, got inside. When he put the car in first, nothing happened.

That clutch—

You procrastinate, you always pay for it.

He got it into second, and it shuddered as he moved it forward. He turned on his full beams. He saw the fat man coming down through the bright lights toward him. He was like a toad, an astonished toad. He was reaching inside his jacket for what could only be a gun when Thorne put his foot down on the gas pedal and thrust the bug forward straight at the guy. The fat man, as if he could not believe the testimony of his own eyes, hesitated a moment, then sidestepped, and Thorne could hear the whistle of his tires as he turned the bug away from the other parked cars at the last moment. *Kill*, he thought. You want to kill. They've brought you to this, finally.

He slowed the car at the cashier's booth, watched the barrier rise to let him through after he had blindly shoved some bills into the cashier's hand. Now, where now?

He had the feeling that he no longer controlled his own actions, that his destiny was something which had been preordained, set in motion by forces and events he could not comprehend; that he was no more than a glove puppet at the ultimate mercy of whoever's fingers were making him dance. And he could not answer the question of Where? Where now?

Dilbeck had gone home. He thought he might sleep. He thought that if anything happened, if anything changed, he would be wakened by telephone. But his daughter was clattering the piano keys like a lunatic. When he went inside the living room he sat for a time before the fire she had lit in the fireplace, and he closed his mind to her playing. There was an innocence and a naïvety in what she did that he did not want to touch him. She finally stopped and crossed the room and sat on the rug at his feet.

"You look worn out, Daddy," she said. "And miserable."

"It's been a difficult day," Dilbeck said, his voice flat. He felt a thickness at the back of his throat like a clot of mucus.

She stared into the firelight.

He looked at her face and wished she had been pretty and wondered why it was easier to love someone who looked good. After all, what were appearances? He put his hand on her shoulder.

"I'm learning 'The Merry Peasant,' " she said brightly.

"Really," he said.

"You know it?" She began to sing it for him; her voice was a close approximation to her virtuosity on the keyboard.

"I think so," he said. When could he get her married off? Why didn't young men call on her? She had been born to put forth babies and make a home for some man; some women perceived that as their destiny, others did not. Emily did.

She stopped singing. She touched his knee with her fingers. She was smiling at him in her openmouthed way. She had begun, he realized, to irritate him. It was not a feeling he enjoyed. He got out of his chair and went into the conservatory and closed the door behind him.

The last place left, he thought.

He switched on the lights and had the strange feeling he had just missed something that had been moving around in the darkness; it was as if he had caught the tail end of a perception of something scuttling off into shadows. He moved from plant to plant, as a surgeon moves from one bed to the next of those he has recently operated on.

Shit, Dilbeck thought.

There were mealybugs everywhere. Everywhere he looked.

The green car was behind him on the Jefferson Davis

Highway. He turned on his radio. There was a cheerful voice that came to him from another world. It eulogized Alberto VO-5 hair shampoo. And then there was a country singer. He switched the radio off. He peered through the darkness at the lights coming toward him in the opposite lanes. He was going south, toward 495.

And to whatever lay beyond.

Whatever.

Congressman, he could say. *I'm sorry. You're right.*

He could say that.

He could pull over into some gasoline station and go to the telephone and call Leach and presumably some magic wand might be waved and the pile of shit transformed to gold, Leach had the power, the personal alchemy that could transmute violence into serenity. If that was what he wanted. He could do it easily.

Congressman, I've reconsidered, he could say.

Or: Senator, that offer we discussed the other day.

Or: Paris might be rather fine this time of year, Mr. Bannerman.

Options: they yawned like caves in front of him.

He glanced in his mirror, saw the green car.

It seemed he had spent his life being followed.

To hell with them, he thought. To hell with them and their needs and desires and conspiracies and their wretched compulsions to secrecy.

He put his foot down hard on the gas.

He turned onto the Beltway, drove past Andrews Base, turned again where Pennsylvania Avenue led toward Chaneyville and, beyond that, the mouth of the Potomac and Chesapeake Bay.

Yes, to hell with them all.

Tarkington had a small furry mascot dangling from a string inside the windshield. It had belonged to the Greek. Lykiard had considered it lucky. Fat luck. Now it bounced like some spider against the glass, imposing itself between Tarkington and his view of the taillights of the red bug. That dipshit—Tarkington had almost come undone when he had seen the red car coming straight at him. But now he knew his man was running scared—knowledge that was a decided advantage in the survival stakes.

*   *   *

Somewhere he had crossed the Calvert County line and was traveling the leg of land that led south to Cove Point and Chesapeake Bay—and beyond that, he realized, there was no place left to run. He had a picture of Marcia sitting by the telephone in her mother's house in Alexandria, waiting, waiting. Lives just fall apart; they break in the whirl of chaos. How had she pictured their lives? Growing old and frail and bound together by memories and snapshot albums?

Goddamn.

The VW was slowing to a halt.

He shoved his foot down on the gas pedal.

The gasoline gauge registered empty. The needle had fallen beyond the reserve capacity. He had nothing left.

Goddamn.

He pulled it over onto a grassy verge.

The moon was concealed by trees. He could see it, a translucent disk sliced by bars. The trees, he thought. What else? what else is left?

He began to run again.

From behind, he heard the door of the green car slam shut. He ran. He ran toward the moon as if he were a moth magnetized by an irresistible light. Branches of trees slapped against his face. The air was clear, cold, it reminded him of a night of impending frost, one of those autumnal nights that fall just before the dark of winter. His heart seemed to slide back and forth against his ribs. His lungs burned. He could hear the undergrowth break beneath the feet of the fat man and he was conscious of a flashlight feebly penetrating the black around him. A gun, a flashlight, what would he have given for those items now? He stopped running, he had been zigzagging between the trees, now he ached. *Take up tennis*, Marcia had told him. *You'll go to the dogs real quick unless you exercise.* He had asked: *Doesn't screwing count?* The voices belonged, like facetious echoes, to a past he had drifted away from, and he was scared again, he was scared and adrift and insubstantial. Through the dark he heard the sound of a frightened bird flap, he imagined the tips of feathers brushing the topsides of branches. He had to run again. He saw the pencil-thin beam of the flashlight through the trees. He had to run again.

The trees yielded to a clearing of some kind.

He saw an abandoned truck in the clearing. It had been left to rot. The vandals had come. Tires gone, hubcaps gone, windows smashed, doors yanked off. He leaned against the truck a moment, straining for breath, conscious of the smell of rust from the vehicle, the scent of damp upholstery, aware of the moon high above the clearing. Beyond he saw more trees. Looking back the way he had come, he saw the trembling light of the flash.

There was a sound suddenly.

In moonlight, he had become a perfect target.

He heard the violent, abrupt rap of metal on metal. There was the echo of an explosion. It receded backward through the trees, sucked away. There was another shot. He lowered his head, he ran awkwardly around the side of the truck and into the trees again.

Whenever he paused he could hear the fat man doggedly coming forward. Fight, he thought. Ambush. Quit running. He came out of the trees.

He was standing on the black edge of the river.

Fight, then what? If I win, what then?

He heard the water swirling past and in moonlight saw some illuminated scum float toward the bank. The pollution of the world. The disgorgement of some chemical detritus floating on out to sea. He could swim the river, get to the other bank, and hope that the fat man could not make it.

What then?

He was aware of the stars overhead. They had the sharply real appearance of theatrical props.

He waded into the river.

The water smelled. It was as if he had disturbed something long rotted, broken the hard surface that had grown over ancient excrement.

There was an outrage of light through the dark.

He heard the water around him whip briefly up, a quick circle of foam erupting in the manner of some tiny aquatic volcano. He lowered his head, fell forward, began to swim.

The fat man had reached the bank. He was flashing his light over the surface of the water. He fired his gun twice. Thorne felt the air crack around his head. He fired again. Asterisk, Thorne thought. You reached a point where you were devoured by your own curiosity. The water stung his eyes and tasted vile in his mouth. He was gasping, striving for the opposite bank. The fat man fired again. Thorne felt his clothes suck at his flesh. Devoured, he thought. Swallowed whole, nothing left to spit out. *Asterisk.*

The fat man was silent for a time.

He was swinging his flashlight back and forth.

Thorne pulled his face beneath the water and, feeling that his heart might burst open in his chest, let the undercurrent carry him downstream.

Tarkington played the beam over the surface of the river. The light rippled like some slight, illuminated fish emerging. No sign of Thorne. No sign now. Tarkington put his weapon away. I got him, Christ, he thought. I got him with the last two shots. Because then his head had vanished and he had gone under and out of the glare of the light. Tarkington sat on the bank, following the motion of his flashlight. There was no Thorne. Scum, eddies of foam, no Thorne. He would wash down the river past Solomons, then past Point Lookout, then down through the waters of the Chesapeake Bay, drawn by tides and currents down past Tangier Island, Cape Charles, past Cape Henry Lighthouse, and finally what was left of him, the bleached remains, would wash on out into the dark Atlantic.

Tarkington had no more uncertainty.

It was hard to breathe, and his body ached, but he felt he had done something right.

Dilbeck was wakened from a dream of starlings by the sound of his telephone ringing. He had been watching a flock of the birds coming across a rather strange, flat landscape. He had been watching them grow and knew they meant him some meance—but now he reached for the receiver and he heard Sharpe's voice on the other end of the line.

Sharpe had a somewhat needless *gloating* quality to his tone. "Thorne's finished," he said. He might have been rubbing his hands in glee.

"That's something," Dilbeck said, yawning. "And the other thing?"

Sharpe hesitated. "We're still working on the other thing," he said at last.

"Typical," Dilbeck said. "You solve the minor problems and leave the major ones undone. You sometimes remind me of the man who's insulating his attic while rats are gnawing at the timbers in the basement."

"Believe me," Sharpe said. "We'll work all night if we need to."

"You may need to," Dilbeck said and hung up. He waited a moment, then he dialed a number.

"Congressman," he said.

He heard Leach's distant, fragmented response.

"Our young friend is out of it," he said to Leach.

"I'm glad to hear it," the Congressman said. "I'm also sorry to hear it."

"Nobody is ever entirely happy with this kind of thing," Dilbeck said.

"Why should they be?" Leach asked. "But they happen. From time to time."

"From time to time," Dilbeck said. He put the receiver down. He was thinking of Thorne's girl now, a lovely young thing. It was no tangible consolation to think that, at least, they had not made a widow out of her. But that was it nowadays; young people did not perceive marriage as his generation had done. They *shacked up*. She would move on, of course. She would move on, and the memories would grow more and more feeble. He knew.

7:

Friday, April 7

HE DID NOT KNOW HOW LONG HE HAD LAIN ON THE BANK after coming up out of the river. He was exhausted, the current in places had been strong, pulling at him, drawing him away, and the struggle against it had left him drained. He lay with his eyes open and looked up into the night sky and he thought: The longest day of my life is just finished. The stars were hard and bright. The moon burned on his blurry vision. When he closed his eyes he thought of the whole nightmare as though it had happened to someone else. He was becoming detached from the experience; or was this detachment simply a consequence of how he had come to accept events? Nothing else could happen to him now. Could it? could it? He lay on the bank and looked at the sky and he laughed. Damn right it could, he thought.

When he climbed up the bank away from the edge of the river, he found himself walking through trees. He paused. He was sick. The amount of the river he had swallowed came back up in quick spasms. He sweated a cold sweat. He was shivering, suddenly feverish. What was in that fucking river? The rejects of some factory manufacturing tetrasodium pyrophosphate or some other chemical of the kind Marcia always said they put in food to kill off the American public? He leaned against a tree. When the sickness had passed, he continued to walk.

He reached the highway after about thirty minutes. His clothes stuck to him, his shoes were waterlogged, he could taste in his mouth the garbage of the river once again and thought he was going to throw up another time. The moment passed. He walked along the edge of the empty highway. But he stayed as close as he could to the trees, as if out of the fear that the fat man might make a reappearance or that the green car would emerge from nowhere. He kept walking. He had no notion of time: after midnight? It was as if the calendars had fallen away from him, and day and time were left without significance. His mind seemed to have frozen over like some calculating device he could not get to work. An amnesiac moment. Why was he walking here? Why wasn't he back home in the apartment with Marcia? But all that had changed, hadn't it?

He stopped, took off his shoes, shook them out, then walked a little way in his socks. A truck came rumbling past. He turned to face it, stuck his thumb out, and it vanished into the dark ahead. Would I give *myself* a ride? he wondered. You see a miserable, drenched figure in the night; do you stop? No. You think an escaped convict, maybe a lunatic, and you just keep on driving. He kept walking. The cold seemed to have reached his bones, gotten into the marrow. Another truck slid on past, followed by a car that was not a green Pontiac. Maybe the fat man thinks he killed me, Thorne thought. Maybe. Maybe right now he imagines I'm slipping down the river and out into the ocean. It was a slender prospect. But it consoled him a moment.

He walked for what seemed like an hour, two hours, he couldn't be sure. He tried to get his brain to work but it was like the first gear of the abandoned VW: it kept slipping and slipping and it wouldn't engage. How far had he walked? It was still dark, dark in a fashion that suggested there might never be a morning. You couldn't imagine a dawn coming up through this. It was stars and moon, the whole celestial gallery of constellations and clusters burning away out there, how could you foresee a morning?

He reached the outskirts of a town. The sign said REVENUE, POP 980. It was an odd name for a town, he reflected. Revenue. He walked. He passed some houses. Silent front porches. Unlit windows. Where was Revenue in relation to anything else? He saw a darkened shopping plaza of the kind one sees on the edges of small, anonymous towns, a supermarket, an ice-cream store, a small department store, a crafts store. A few machines were lit outside the supermarket. He walked toward them to see what they had to offer. Chocolate milk. Ice water. Chicken noodle soup. He found some wet coins in his pants and pushed them into the machine for the soup. It was probably a chemical facsimile of the metabolism of a dead hen, Marcia would have said that, but it was hot and wet and he drank it down quickly. Then he felt sick again. He crumpled the cardboard cup and went back across the deserted plaza to the highway. There he paused, checked his wallet in the reflection of the glimmer of a streetlight. Wet credit cards, his ID, about forty dollars in cash. He put the wallet away and continued to walk.

Revenue Motor Lodge.

The sign was unlit and it was a rather grandiose name for a couple of wooden chalets but he went toward it. The office was shut. He rang a bell. Nobody came. He rang again. He heard a noise from within the office and a light was turned on and through the lace curtain at the window he saw a woman in a dressing gown coming to the door.

She looked at him coldly.

He said, feebly, that he had fallen in the river.

"Your boat capsize or something?" she asked. She had the kind of face in which you find written a thousand dark suspicions after a lifetime of guests who stole lamps, paid with bad checks, vomited in toilets, threw empty beer cans from windows.

"Yes," he said. "I almost drowned."

She held the door open a little way and he stepped inside the office. She took a key from a rack and asked him to fill out the registration slip. He did so. *Dead; would they think that?*

"Chalet four," she said, smiling a quick, brittle little smile, as if she were reluctant to give anything human away. "Lucky you didn't drown," she added.

"Lucky is right," he said. He took the key, left the office, found chalet four. He unlocked the door and went inside, took off his wet clothes and looked for the dial that would bring heat into the room. He found it and turned the thermostat up to seventy-five and laid his damp clothes next to the hot air vent to dry. He showered, which did nothing to revive him, and then he fell on top of the bed and slept.

It was light when he woke. The sun was shining into the room through the open drapes. He heard a car outside the window and for a moment he thought of the Catalina. He rose from the bed and looked out. A pickup truck was idling in the parking lot. The driver was delivering something to the motel. He carried an obviously heavy cardboard box in the direction of the office. Thorne drew the curtains and sat for a time on the edge of the mattress.

Now, he thought.

Now.

You do the obvious thing. You do the obvious *stupid* thing. What else is there left to you? Somewhere at the heart of all this you committed yourself, didn't you? Somehow you reached that core.

No, he thought. No

He felt his clothing. Slightly damp still but he could wear it and his body heat would take care of the rest. He picked up his wallet.

He looked at the telephone. He knew that the telephone beside which Marcia might now be sitting, half asleep, would be tapped. They would have done that. They would want to be sure of things. Tapped telephones, he thought. He had stepped through into some other dimension from the one that was familiar to him. It was as if he had opened the locked door to that room he had long considered empty, only to find—what you find, whatever it is.

He dressed slowly. There was the faint smell of the river hanging to his clothes. How could he contact Marcia?

I can't, he thought. There isn't a way.

He left the chalet. He went to the driver of the pickup, who was emerging from the office. He was a small, skinny man with the face of a hatchet and he wore an incongruous Mexican-style mustache which gave him the appearance of some battle-weary revolutionary. He was suspicious of Thorne almost at once.

"I need a ride," Thorne said.

"Where you going fella?" the driver asked.

"It doesn't matter," Thorne said. "My boat, my boat capsized in the river last night and I'd like to get to—"

"I'm headed for Richmond," the driver said. He squinted his eyes and scrutinized Thorne. "It'll cost you, though. Company policy says no riders. Taking a chance. It'll cost you."

Company policy, Thorne thought. "I'll give you ten," he said.

"Ten's fine," the driver said. "Hop in."

Thorne, conscious of the river in his clothing, got into the cab of the pickup. The driver climbed up behind the wheel.

"Boat turned over, you say?"

"Right," Thorne said. "I nearly drowned back there."

"You fishing or what?"

"Just cruising," Thorne said, and realized how odd this might sound.

"River's full of shit, I hear."

"You better believe it," Thorne said.

The driver was silent. The chalets of the Revenue Motor Lodge receded, the highway flattened itself out in front of the truck. It was a gorgeous morning, Thorne thought. It was the kind of morning on which you might be justified in thinking that all kinds of promises were about to be fulfilled. He closed his eyes, listened to the rhythms of the truck.

"Anyplace special in Richmond?" the driver asked.

Thorne thought a moment. "The airport," he said finally.

"Yeah," Tarkington was saying. "Through the head, twice. In the river. I guess maybe he's out somewhere in the Chesapeake Bay right now."

Sharpe put his coffee down and looked across the desk at Tarkie's face. Why was the fat man laying all this on him now? Was he looking for praise?

Tarkington took a cone of water from the cooler and lit a cigarette. His eyes shining, he looked at Sharpe, then in a coy way, as though he were a child who had done something that deserved to be rewarded, lowered his eyes to the floor and scraped his feet back and forth.

"Yeah, magnificent," Sharpe said. "Truly stunning."

He gazed at some papers on the desk. Thorne was one thing, sure, one problem less, but the night had not yielded up the plane and that was the biggest headache right now. He picked up the report of Strachan and read it a second time:

To: Control
From: Vernon P. Strachan
April 7, Friday; 0216 hours

Investigation of Damascus airstrip revealed the

deaths of both Brandt and Mulholland. The latter had been shot through the head. His car is written off. Brandt had been shot in the chest. Mulholland's gun had not been fired. There were three rounds remaining in Brandt's gun.

Further investigation reveals Damascus airstrip owned by one Thomas Surr but there are no records relevant to his ownership obtainable locally and no knowledge of his whereabouts. According to local sources the airstrip is used only by the North Maryland Flyer's Society and then only on an irregular basis.

Sharpe let the flimsy paper fall from his fingers. When he had sent the name of Thomas Surr through the data banks, the answer had come back: *Unknown.* So there was a blind; and who knew where that plane which Brandt had reported might be by this time?

Poor Brandt, Sharpe thought. Poor Mulholland.

He couldn't keep losing men at this rate. He looked at Tarkington, who was still beaming, and he wondered: Why hadn't he lost Tarkie instead of somebody like Brandt?

He got up and went to his window and opened the slats of the blind. He stared up into the morning sky. Up up and away, he thought. Like Ted Hollander.

Thorne got out of the pickup at Richmond Airport. He booked a seat on the next flight to Phoenix: Eastern Airlines to Dallas, the connection from Dallas to Phoenix by American. He used a credit card which the girl behind the desk looked at for a time as if it might be a forgery. She consulted a booklet, a list of credit cards reported lost or stolen or otherwise useless. She checked the number of Thorne's card and he wondered if they had managed to do this too, if they had somehow contrived to invalidate his charge cards. He watched the girl's face. She was without expression. She checked the number, seemed satisfied in an uneasy kind of way, then she wrote out his ticket for him. He took it, looked at the clock, realized he had an hour to kill before the Dallas flight. He went inside the cafeteria and halfheartedly picked at some scrambled eggs, ate a slice of dry toast, drank two cups of coffee. His hand trembled perceptibly. *You don't have to try and go through with this*, he thought. *You don't have to make an attempt that can end only in futility.*

After all, who do you owe anything to?

He thought of Congressman Leach again.

You could call him. Take it all back.

Swallow it.

It would have the taste of the river to it.

He finished his coffee. How much chance did he have anyhow? Was there a hope in hell he could even make it to the fence.

Madness.

When he heard his flight number being called for Dallas he hesitated, conscious of the ticket that lay in his pocket with the immediacy of a weapon. If you step away from this, he told himself, how can you ever bring yourself to look at anything else again?

A week ago, he thought.

He was aware of his powerlessness, his inability to turn clocks back to an earlier and better time, to that point where ignorance begins to shade into knowledge. A little knowledge, he thought. A dangerous thing.

When he boarded the airplane and tightened his seat belt he realized that he understood now how the major general had felt waiting in the cocktail lounge with his worthless attaché case.

Sheer futility.

He felt the plane begin its run. He closed his eyes as he always did during takeoff. It was the sensation of rising and the possibility of falling that, in their hideous combination, bothered him.

Sunlight came back, in sharp glints of light, from the wing of the craft.

I can't pull this off, he thought.

During the layover at Dallas he did two things. He arranged to rent a car in Phoenix and he sent a telegram to Marcia care of the Department of English at George Washington. The message read:

SOMETIMES YOU HAVE TO TAKE A LITTLE SUGAR IN SPITE OF IT ALL—THE PHILISTINE

2

Dilbeck's consciousness of dread had been deepened by Sharpe's telephone message and now, as he hesitated outside the conference room, he imagined the clamor of his colleagues. They would want blood for this one. They would want heads to roll.

He opened the door and saw the faces at the table turn toward him. Whorley, in uniform, was standing at the window lighting a cigar. Burlingham, the man from RAND, was absentmindedly debating the baseball season with Marvell and Nicholson, his spectral self, was scribbling something in a notebook. Leach appeared half asleep, drawn into himself with sickness and fatigue.

Dilbeck looked around the room.

They're waiting for me, he thought.

They want to know why I called this meeting.

He went to his chair and put down the manila folder he had been carrying. It contained Ted Hollander's file and a sheaf of reports from Sharpe and his people, all neatly held together by a bulldog clip. This won't hold so neatly together, Dilbeck thought.

This is going to fall apart all around me.

He opened the file, cleared his throat. He could not even begin to salvage anything from the fact that Thorne had been terminated because this was something he shared only with Leach. The others knew nothing of Thorne.

"We have a problem, Gentlemen," he said.

Silence.

"It appears that Edward Hollander has defected to the Soviet Union."

Silence.

And then, as he had known it would, the room seemed to explode.

"Dear God," Whorley said.

Nicholson stood up and thumped his fist on the table. "How much does he know? God damn it, Dilbeck, what has he taken with him?"

Dilbeck, swaying slightly on his feet, closed his eyes. He could hear them out there squabbling, shouting, banging on the table.

"Gentlemen, please—"

The congressman raised one hand for silence, which came after a minute or two. He was staring straight at Dilbeck but addressed him in such a way as to suggest that Dilbeck was present in only the grammatical third person, like a shadow of a real self.

"Perhaps Mr. Dilbeck will inform us as to the extent of his knowledge concerning Hollander's information," Leach said, patiently, quietly.

"That isn't known yet," Dilbeck answered.

"When will it be known?"

Dilbeck didn't know the answer to that either. There were hours of research to plow through, masses of intelligence reports that would be flowing in over the next few days; there could not be a complete picture until everything had been studied.

"I'm not certain, Congressman," he said.

"Will we ever know what Ted Hollander has given to the Soviets? Will we *ever* know?" Burlingham asked, his voice almost hysterical, like the grinding edge of a saw on a recalcitrant length of wood.

"Yes, I'm sure," Dilbeck said.

There was more furor over the table.

"What can we do to the stable door now that the horse has bolted?" the congressman asked.

Dilbeck shrugged. "Very little. I'm sorry, but there you have it."

"Sorry!" Whorley was walking around the room. "Do you understand the consequences if the Soviets have Asterisk? Do you?"

"I do," Dilbeck said. "In my own defense, I might say that I'm not responsible for the weaknesses, such as they are, in Ted Hollander's psyche—"

"You went on record, if I may remind you, as saying he had no connection whatsoever with the Soviets," Nicholson said.

"And that was my mistake, I agree," Dilbeck said. "But there was nothing in his record—"

"Records mean little," Marvell said.

Burlingham, with a steady hand, was lighting a pipe. "How do the Soviets know Hollander is on the level?"

"They check, then they double-check, then they check again," Dilbeck said. "And even after that they run another check, just as we do ourselves—"

"Asterisk," Whorley said, his voice low and hushed, as if what he were pronouncing were the secret name of the Holy Grail, something arcane and strangely solemn.

There was another silence in the room.

Dilbeck coughed. His head was swimming; he was peering at things through some viscous substance. He looked across the faces; there was the kind of silence in which you might hear the growing of grass.

"I will, naturally, resign forthwith," Dillbeck said.

The congressman was on his feet. "No. I don't believe we can accept your resignation. I speak for myself, sure, but I think you've done some valuable work here and I don't think any blame for Hollander's idiosyncrasies can be attached to you."

Dilbeck looked down at the table. Burlingham concurred; Marvell, too, sided with the congressman. Nicholson, after a moment, came round to the same way of thinking. Only the general appeared upset with the whole business of Dilbeck staying on the job. A vote was taken. Dilbeck retracted his offer to resign.

"Thank you, Gentlemen," he told the committee. "Now I think we wait on the intelligence data that we can expect in the next few days from the Soviet Union, which, together with a complete picture my people will put together, should give us a clear idea of what Hollander has taken over with him."

The room was silent again.

Dilbeck picked up his folder.

He went out into the corridor. It was a close-run thing. For a time there they had really wanted his head; only the congressman had brought the situation around. Momentarily, he felt a conspiratorial affection for Leach.

It was midafternoon, mountain time, when the plane carrying Thorne arrived in Phoenix at Sky Harbor Airport. There was a bloody-looking sun in the sky, a strange coppery tint to the air, a slight wind blowing through the palms. Inside the terminal he went to the Avis desk for his car rental; the girl led him outside to a Pinto and handed him the keys. He drove out of the airport to the nearest gasoline station, where he obtained a map of Arizona. Next, he went to a shopping plaza and in a department store purchased a dark three-piece suit, a pair of black shoes, a white shirt, a conservative tie that was black with pale-gray stripes. He used his credit card, expecting all the while that the salesman would refuse to accept it. A touch of deeply rooted paranoia, Thorne thought. He had felt it even inside the changing rooms when he had been trying the new clothes on and had looked at the door handle almost as if he expected to see it being turned. A clear mind, he thought. Clarity. Calm.

He sat down in his new clothes at the cafeteria in the department store and drank coffee, studying his map. Two hours, he reckoned. Two hours to Escalante. He took his wallet out of his pocket. He looked at his security clearance pass, which was stamped WHITE HOUSE PERSONNEL. Did it still have any power? was it still useful? He looked at the photograph of himself and he was seeing a younger man, the light of some optimism in the eyes, a firmness to the mold of the jaw: a face of some strength or what, more quaintly, was called character. He didn't look like this anymore. He put the pass back into the wallet and realized that he was both nervous and afraid; whose, that the lines between these sensations had blurred to the point where there wasn't a difference. Calm, he said to himself again. You can only pull this off with some kind of cool, an impertinence, a quality he wasn't sure he had in any abundance.

He walked outside to the Pinto. *No green Catalinas,* he thought. Not now. He drove, following the map, in the direction of Interstate 17, then he took the turning for Highway 60. He was traveling in a northwesterly direction out of the city. The midafternoon traffic was heavy. The highway, burned by the unexpectedly strong sun, shimmered in front of his eyes. The buildings of downtown Phoenix went past, a scattering of skyscrapers in the desert. He could see through a haze the mountains to the north, ragged, lunar, like a landscape you might encounter only in some dream of alienation. There were great pockets of shadows, like caves, in the sides of the mountains. He drove past ramshackle collections of trailer parks, shantytowns that existed under the shadow of the highway, boxcars stationary on railroad sidings, scattered factories, brand-new industrial estates. They had taken the desert and turned it into another form of wilderness. Marcia, he thought; what would she have had to say about all this?

The ecological substructure was being, quite simply, ripped away.

Marcia

He glanced in the mirror. It had become habit. A truck was in behind him in the slow lane. He saw the driver's face in silhouette.

Then the urban sprawl yielded to a few sparse dwellings, a small township, a hamlet, and finally to the desert itself. It was strange: he had the feeling that he had stepped out of a bleak Eastern spring into the riot of summer all in one day. He saw the saguaros, monsters beyond the highway; he saw rocks and rubble and cholla as if they had been deliberately placed in position centuries ago by some divine act, a cosmic hand, and had not been changed since. Everything cast long shadows.

Towns came and went as he drove.

Wittman, Morristown, Wickenburg. They passed, seeming little more than traffic signals and a few dwellings with a temporary look to them. He had the unsettling sensation that one day the desert would finally take back everything that had been wrested from it. It was a feeling that suggested violence, some implicit force. An earthquake, a drought, a cataclysm of some kind—and then there would be only desert and nothing else.

To the west there were mountains which, according to his map, were known as the Vulture Mountains. He imagined gulleys, and dry washes containing bleached bones, birds of prey moving in the cool of shadow and silences, great quiet wings drifting.

Birds of prey, he thought.

The birds of Escalante.

He squinted into the weakening light of the sun.

Before dark, he thought. I want to be there before night comes.

3

Sharpe took Drucker's call, listened to the man a moment, and then said: "What's it supposed to mean?"

"I only pass on the messages," Drucker said.

"It sounds like a code, doesn't it?"

"I only pass on the messages," Drucker said again.

"Let me write the goddamn thing down." Sharpe took out his pen and asked Drucker to repeat the words.

Drucker did so.

Sharpe stared at the words for a while, willing them to yield some kind of sense. When he had tried to stoke his tired brain into activity, when the message seemed finally meaningless, he picked up his receiver and dialed Dilbeck's number.

Dilbeck said: "Unless this is important, Sharpe, I don't want to know. I just had a hard time with my colleagues concerning our Flying Dutchman and—"

Sharpe cut in: "We intercepted a telegram that was sent to Thorne's girl."

"Telegrams aren't uncommon," Dilbeck said, a yawn in his voice.

"This one's weird," Sharpe said. "I'll read it to you."

Sharpe read it. There was a short silence.

"It came out of Dallas," Sharpe said.

"Dallas?"

"Fourteen hundred central time."

Sharpe could hear the sound of a pencil or pen being tapped on a wooden surface.

"Thorne's dead, isn't he?" Dilbeck asked finally.

"Yes," Sharpe said.

"I'll be in touch."

Sharpe listened to the cut in the line. *Thorne's dead.* Why did that have such an ominous sound? He rested his face in the palms of his hands, thinking of Thorne, of Drucker in the field—Drucker who was one of the best interceptive technicians Tech Serv had ever had, Drucker who was so far to the right of the spectrum that he thought the senator from Wisconsin America's only twentieth-century saint—he thought until everything became something of a congealed jumble in his mind. Failure had such an empty ring to it, like the sound of a hollow silver dollar falling on wood.

The afternoon sun was going down and hung low now in the Western desert. It was a flare finally burning out. On the edge of Escalante, he slowed the Pinto. It was barely a town; he passed a bar called Lucky's, a hardware store, a grocery, a few scattered houses, a couple of trailers with TV antennae appended to them. A girl on a swing watched him pass. She raised her hand in a quick shy greeting, smiled, then let the hand fall. Thorne drove through the place. There were a couple of jets in the darkening sky, hardly more than points of red light from which scarlet vapor trails hung in various stages of disintegration. Smoke signals, Thorne thought. He stopped the car, spread his map out on the seat, ran his finger over the name of Escalante. Six, seven miles out into the desert there was the mapmaker's symbol for a military reservation, a curious red hieroglyph. A military reservation: it could cover a multitude of sins. He drove the Pinto off the road and into the desert, stopped once more in the kind of terrain this small car hadn't been engineered to withstand, and consulted the map again. Six miles maybe. He drove on slowly, avoiding rocks, pitfalls, while the suspension system of the car whined underneath him.

The landscape became more hostile.

He had to steer the car upward through a dry wash and push it in second gear over a slope that was crumbling beneath the tires. It was no place in which to be stuck. He made it over the incline and then were cautiously down the other side. The Pinto stalled, he started it again, it stalled a second time. He switched the ignition off and sat for a time looking through his window and thought: You're a couple of miles from a road, from the threads that link one fraction of the civilized world with another, and suddenly everything's different. The sun was dropping behind the mountains. He turned the key in the ignition, the car started, and he maneuvered it the rest of the way down the slope. At the bottom there was a path of sorts. He could see tire treads in the scrub, flattened cholla, and—as he turned the car on to the path—a sign that said: U.S. MILITARY ESTABLISHMENT: ESCALANTE BOMBING & GUNNERY RANGE. UNAUTHORIZED PERSONNEL FORBIDDEN BEYOND THIS POINT. Bombing and gunnery, he thought; and something else besides. He drove on past the sign.

He had the car at ten miles an hour. The path was rutted and broken, crumbling and dry, and some kind of irrigation ditch ran on either side of it. They might be waiting for me, he thought. They might be expecting me.

Unless.

Unless I'm already dead.

Not only unauthorized, but dead into the bargain.

He passed coils of barbed wire and a second sign that repeated the first. Waiting, he thought. Waiting for me to show.

Then what?

Then he knew the answer to that very well.

Dilbeck saw her come out of the building, walk down the steps, and cross a stretch of grass. He got out of his car and went toward her. Lovely girl, he thought. The long black hair, the knowing look in the eyes, a perfect mouth. She walked with a long stride, self-assured, comfortable with herself, even slightly arrogant.

He intercepted her. When she saw him the expression on her face became one of fear, her eyes turned cold and distant, her skin suddenly pale.

"Miss Emerson?" He took off his soft hat and held it an inch above his skull.

She stopped, saying nothing.

"I hate to interrupt you," he said. He watched her put her hands in the pockets of her black velvet pants. There was a book beneath her arm; the title had the word *Lamp* in it, he couldn't see the rest of it.

"Well, you *are* interrupting me," she said.

He put his hat back on. He smiled at her.

"Look, I don't think I've got anything very much to say to you, Mr. Whatever-your-name-is—"

She turned and began to move away.

He put out his hand, gripped her by the arm.

"That hurts," she said.

"I am sorry," he said. Such a lovely girl, he thought. Perhaps it would have been better all around to have had her killed. Perhaps. "You see, the gravity of this particular situation shouldn't be underestimated, Miss Emerson."

"Let go of my arm, okay?"

He took his hand away. "I think perhaps you don't see the seriousness very clearly. A matter of national security is involved—"

"What else?" she said.

"Don't make it tough on me." He watched a group of students come from a building, walking slowly, books beneath their arms, walking with the casual detachment of the young; so sure, so very sure of themselves.

"Okay," she said. "Suppose you tell me what you want?"

"I wonder if you've heard from John Thorne."

"Do you think I'd tell you if I had?"

The defiance of it; Dilbeck felt a slight glow of approval about her. He liked her spirit.

"I doubt it," he said. "I would hope so, but I doubt it. Do you know where he is?"

She smiled, her confidence apparently growing.

He let her savor her moment and then he said: "Why does Thorne call himself the Philistine?"

She crumpled, momentarily she looked as if she had been struck, but she recovered with the composure of an actress. "You're mistaken," she said, her voice a little hoarse.

"Let's not beat about the bush," he said. "You know and I know that he sent you a telegram from Dallas today. We read it probably before you did, Miss Emerson. Let's not beat about the bush, eh?"

She was silent. She bit her lower lip hard. Fine, large white teeth.

"Why does he call himself the Philistine?"

She looked up at the sky, blinking against the light, and then she stared down at the ground. Dilbeck watched her.

She said nothing.

He looked at his wristwatch. Then he said, "Well. I think you've told me what I need to know."

"How? I haven't told you a damn thing!"

"Just by your reaction, Miss Emerson. That's all. You see, I wasn't sure it was from Thorne before, but I'm pretty sure now. Thank you."

She permitted a small flicker of anger to alter her features. It lasted a moment, then passed. "Pig," she said. "Pig."

"The Philistine," Dilbeck said. "It's an intriguing nickname. If we had more time then maybe you could explain the reason for it to me."

He raised his hat once more.

"Goodbye."

He walked in the direction of his car, conscious of her standing motionless, motionless and shocked, behind him.

He got inside his car, saw her image reflected in the

mirror, then drove away. He drove until he came to a call-box, went inside, dialed Sharpe's priority number.

"One of your people has fucked up again," he said. "Thorne is still alive."

Sharpe was silent for a long time.

Dilbeck said, "I want you to pull out all the stops, Sharpe. Understand? I want every available item of information analyzed. I want you to follow through on the fact that we know he was in Dallas. And I want you to work on the assumption that he is on his way to Phoenix. Have you got that?"

"Yes," Sharpe said quietly.

Dilbeck hung up. He yawned, seeing his own image in the mirror inside the box. His bones, even his bones, felt weary, as if in the hollow cylinders of his skeleton the marrow were beginning to melt.

Sharpe started to make telephone calls to the various field offices that might help him in this matter. He was having a hard time keeping himself in control. He was having a very hard time. Sweat soaked his shirt, the palms of his hands, the soles of his feet. He got through to Dallas. He asked for a check. Within ten minutes he had it. He got the Poenix number and asked for another check.

Thorne, he kept thinking.

John Thorne. You couldn't go on living a charmed life, sonny.

Within twenty minutes of making his calls he had pieced together a picture of John Thorne's movements. He called Dilbeck back. When he was through talking with Dilbeck, he dialed the number of Tarkington's motel.

Tarkington answered, sounding cheerful.

"I am sorry to trouble you," Sharpe said. "But I'd like you to come in to the office."

"What? Now?"

"I don't think it can wait, Tarkie. I don't think it can wait."

When he had hung up he went to a map that was pinned to the wall. He began looking at the most unlikely places. Yeah, he thought. Why not? Turner, out in Ashkhabad, was badly in need of replacement. Why not?

Ashkhabad sounded very fine.

* * *

"Laphroaig," the congressman said. He handed the glass to Dilbeck, who sniffed the drink before sampling it.

"Very fine," Dilbeck said.

He looked round the kitchen. It was the first time he had been in Leach's apartment and he was surprised a little by the absence of life signs. It was as if nobody lived here.

"The goddamn bungling is staggering," Leach said.

"Indeed," Dilbeck said.

Dilbeck was silent. He watched Leach move around on his cane. He grunted, wheezed, as he moved; he was coming apart at the seams in that final process of disintegration that life can no longer stall. A few more months, Dilbeck thought. Another funeral to attend.

"We know that John Thorne booked a flight from Richmond, Virginia, this morning. The same John Thorne reputed to be a corpse."

"Bungling," Leach said again.

"However, Thorne has something of a cash-flow problem apparently, because he's traveling everywhere with credit cards, which makes it no great problem to keep track of him," Dilbeck said.

Leach drained his glass and set it down.

"He rented a car from Avid at Phoenix," Dilbeck said. "The rest is elementary."

"Escalante," Leach said.

"Of course." Dilbeck looked into his glass.

"What a reckless young idiot," the congressman said, lifting the bottle of malt whiskey as if to pour himself another drink, then setting it down again. "What will happen to him at Escalante?"

"It's already taken care of, Congressman."

"And that will be the last of him?"

"As you say."

Leach sat down, propping his walking stick against the wall. "Old Ben Thorne was a stubborn old fart. A good man, but dynamite wouldn't shift him if his mind was made up."

"Like father, like son," Dilbeck said.

"I guess."

Both men were silent in a manner that suggested a moment of rumination, the passage of a memory, something shared.

"First Hollander, then Thorne," Leach said.

"Two different problems, I fear."

"Yes," Leach said. "I wonder if Asterisk is worth anything now."

"It remains to be seen," Dilbeck said. "It remains to be seen."

It was almost dark when he saw the perimeter fence. He drove the Pinto toward it. Now, he thought. Now. He turned the engine off, sat for a moment, trying to keep control, trying to hold together the delicate balances of himself. A failure of nerve—and it would fall apart like a house of dominoes. He got out of the car, slammed the door and, as he did so, he heard the click of an automatic weapon from behind the fence. There was a uniformed guard pressed against the wire. He had an M-16 clutched to his side, leveled directly at Thorne.

From behind he heard the sound of a motor. He turned, saw a jeep come up alongside him. The driver wore the helmet and armband of an MP. Thorne did not move; he had the feeling that if he moved he would be shot. I'm sorry, he might say. I'm sorry, I just lost my way in the dark, didn't know this was Uncle Sam's property, ha ha, you know how it is, fellas.

The MP got down from the jeep.

He looked at Thorne. In his hand he held an automatic pistol which, in the dying light, did not look remotely real to Thorne.

"What the fuck you think you're doing?" the MP asked. He made a gesture with the pistol. Thorne stared at the gun, mesmerized; it would blow me away, he thought. He made to reach into his jacket for his wallet. The MP waved the gun again.

"Keep still," he said.

"I only wanted—"

"Just keep still," the MP said. He frisked Thorne, took out the wallet, flipped it open.

"My clearance is—"

"Very fancy," the MP said, looking now at Thorne's pass and the WHITE HOUSE PERSONNEL stamp. He could feel himself sink, a sensation of falling, his nerves beginning to snap like rubber bands drawn to their extremities. *No, control, control, the only way.*

"So what brings you all the way out here?" the MP asked.

"I can't discuss that with you," Thorne said. Good, excellent, the voice was firm. He was pleased with himself. "I have to see the officer in charge."

Inside, he thought. Once inside you can play this by ear because there's no way of taking into account contingencies, possibilities. *I must get inside.*

"Can't discuss it with me?" the MP said. He looked in the direction of the guard beyond the wire fence. "Chuck, you got any instructions concerning this guy?"

The guard did not answer immediately.

"No," he said eventually. "None."

They weren't expecting me, Thorne thought. Have I been written off in Washington? Account closed? Dead? He waited.

There was a long silence, then the MP said to the guard: "Get the captain on the phone, Chuck. You better clear this with him." He looked at Thorne again. "We get instructions concerning these things," he said, shrugged his shoulders.

Thorne watched the guard go to a telephone that had been installed inside the fence. The guard picked up the receiver, pressed a button, and spoke in a low voice. Thorne stared at the low white headquarters, the two or three outbuildings, white stone turned gray in the twilight. He tried to hear the guard's voice, but he caught nothing. Control, he told himself again. He looked back at the MP, who was still holding his gun in the manner of a man who would not care if he were instructed to fire it. Thorne shut his eyes briefly. The air was still warm, but he could feel the edges of a chill that would come in with the desert night.

The guard put the receiver down.

Thorne waited.

He heard the guard come back, the fall of his boots on concrete, then the slight noise of his weapon touching the wire fence.

Now

The guard coughed.

"You get the captain?" the MP asked.

"Yeah," the guard said. "He'll see Thorne."

No, Thorne thought. This easy. This simple.

He heard the gate in the fence open.

"Go ahead," the MP said.

Thorne went through the gate, aware of the MP at his back. Aware of the gun. He glanced at the guard, a man with red hair and freckles, a small-town boy by the look of him, something clumsy in the way he held the gun and how he stood, as if he were unaccustomed to this.

"Go on," the MP said. "Chuck, you lead."

They crossed the concrete. They passed the outbuildings. Thorne saw a jeep, a black car, more piles of barbed wire. Why was it this easy? Why? He was scared. He could feel the nerves again; it was as if telephones were ringing insanely inside his head. *I took a wrong turning, fellas. If you could just point the way back to the highway.*

A door was opened. He followed the guard into a dimly lit corridor. A few weak light bulbs, an empty desk, walls of white-painted brick. More signs. NO UNAUTHORIZED PERSONNEL BEYOND THIS POINT. NUMBER TWO CLEARANCE NEEDED. They went down the corridor. Thorne sensed something about to collapse within himself. A string snapping. A cord breaking. *Hold, just hold.* The fear, what did you do with the fear?

And then he realized something odd, something funny. Something that didn't fit.

The guard had said: *Yeah, he'll see Thorne.*

What was it?

But he had not heard the MP give the guard his name.

He hadn't heard it—

He was dizzy, some darkness pressed in on him, he felt a pressure immediately behind the eyes. *They were waiting for me.* They knew. They knew everything. Didn't they?

Another door was opened. Thorne was conscious of a smell in the building, antiseptic and crisp and sharp in his nostrils. He followed the guard into the room beyond the door. It was a small office with the same brick walls of the corridor, the place was barren, undecorated, it was how he imagined the inside of some terrifying vacuum.

They had me from the start, he thought.

The man behind the desk stood up, smiling.

"Thorne," he said. "My name is Church. Captain Church."

He had a small reddish mustache. *It looks fake,* Thorne

thought. Unreal. Like the gun. Like everything. Run, he thought. Run. No place to run.

"May I see your ID?" Even the smile was false.

Thorne passed the wallet to the captain.

The captain opened it, looked at the little plastic squares, glanced at Thorne, checking photographs against the real person that stood before him.

Thorne heard the door close behind him.

Trapped

He stared at the captain. The masquerade, he thought. Nothing else is real here anyhow.

"The White House sent me here," he said. It was a voice that was not his own. It came through some distorted bullhorn.

"Indeed," the captain said.

A game

He's playing a game

Thorne looked back at the closed door. The guard was there still, holding the M-16 down and away from his body as if he were afraid it would go off. The MP was gone. He turned back to the captain.

"And what does the White House want, Mr. Thorne?"

Thorne felt a dryness in his throat.

"My brief is high-level security," he said. "Do you have that clearance, Captain Church?"

The captain would not stop smiling.

"I think we can cut through this bullshit, don't you?" he said. "I think we can shove it aside."

Aside, Thorne thought.

Just like that.

The captain's smile.

Thorne swung around.

Desper—

He caught the young guard off balance. He was conscious all at once of several things. The guard falling. The automatic weapon scuttling across the floor. The captain fumbling for his pistol. Opening the door. Going into the corridor. The weak lights. A siren going off. The piercing echo of the alarm ringing through the building. The captain's voice. The sound of gunfire. Running running running. The siren wailing. Running. The end of the corridor. Turning. Still running. The sound of footsteps behind him.

You wanted this, he thought. This is what you asked

for. This is where you *needed* to come. The alarm went on and on and on. He heard doors close. Another round of gunfire. A voice across a loudspeaker system.

The intruder must be stopped and if necessary killed

If necessary.

He kept running. A door opened in front of him. A soldier with a pistol raised in his hand stepped forward and Thorne pushed him aside before the man could fire and he kept running, he kept running, running through the siren and the loudspeaker voice and the sound of gunfire.

He was going down steps.

Conscious of going down.

Trapped.

There was a lower level. Another brick-walled corridor.

Space.

The corridor came to an end in an elevator.

Good Christ. Good Christ. Get me out of this—

He slammed the elevator door behind him.

The sound of gunfire again. He was going down. It was dark. There wasn't a light in the elevator. He couldn't find a fucking light. Voices from above. *Alert lower-level duty officer!* Why didn't they stop the alarm? Why?

The elevator clanked to a halt. The automatic door slid open. There was another corridor. Run. He had no breath left. No energy. He only understood that he had never been this afraid before in his entire life.

Another elevator did all these corridors end in elevator shafts did they all lead down through a desert honeycombed with passages and shafts and rooms and darkness

He stepped in. Closed the door.

Going down.

The siren was louder now in his ears.

He felt it would pierce the shell of his skull, split him open.

The elevator hit bottom.

The door opened.

He stepped out.

He was in a corridor lit only by a red light bulb, a strange glow, a red bulb that threw no shadow and looked like something left from an old Halloween. Unreal. He stopped running. His side ached. He stood against the wall, staring at the bulb, trying to catch his breath. He couldn't stay here. He couldn't stand still. He heard the elevator hum, going back up. Then there was the noise of footsteps clattering on stairs somewhere.

Hurried, urgent—

He ran again.

The red light receded.

NO PERSONNEL BEYOND THIS POINT

The corridor turned. Up ahead there was another red light, this one blinking on and off rapidly in a hallucinogenic fashion. A strobe.

He could hear footsteps from behind.

Where? he thought. Where now?

He continued along the corridor, passed through a door, found himself in a gallery where a large tinted window looked down into a chamber.

He stopped, startled.

Asterisk

He put his hands flat against the glass and stared into the chamber beneath him.

Asterisk

An enormous disk, perhaps five or six hundred feet in diameter, was raised up on a platform and tilted slightly away from him. He stared at the glistening expanse of metal, the seamless stretch of an underside, yellowy gold even under the cluster of red lights, a sequence of what looked like portholes slit into the side of the object—and he wondered, he wondered, what kind of faces had looked out from behind that glass? What kind of eyes had perceived? what kind of brains? The night sky, the appearance of lights, the mysteries of what came and went across the reaches of darkness and space—

Asterisk—

There were footsteps in the corridor.

Thornel

And then there was a roar in the dark that might have been a plane taking off, it might have been the sound of a comet falling out of a moonless sky, the rush of a shooting star or a meteorite or some other astral body hurtling toward the vulnerable surface of the planet. But it was none of these things.

The glass panel in front of his face shattered.

He was running again. Running. He had always been running.

More footsteps in the corridor. His lungs worked madly.

He imagined them as two pale jellyfish pulsating in his chest.

Asterisk—was that what he had really seen?

Was it

He was standing at the bottom of a metal spiral staircase. He started to climb. He could hear shouts echoing down the halls and corridors. The alarm still whining. God. God. Get me out of it. Out. He pulled himself up the spiral, dizzy, not caring to look back down.

Thorne!

Then the stairway opened out into another corridor.

Running. When would it stop?

On either side of him now there were doors, metal doors, uniformly green and closed. He passed them in a blur, pursued by the alarm, by the noise of boots over steel.

The corridor

A dead end a trap a blank wall a fucking blank wall nowhere left nowhere else left to hide

A door to his left swung open.

A man appeared in the frame, an old man in a white coat. He made a gesture and Thorne understood: He's beckoning to me. Why?

Thorne went toward the door, stepped inside the room. The man shut the door and slid a bolt. It was a tiny room, a cell, windowless. There was a bunk in a corner and a table covered with books and papers. The old man had spectacles pushed up on his skull.

The mad room, Thorne thought.

The place where it all ends.

The alarms, deadened a fraction by the closed door, still sounded. Thorne, leaning against the door, aching for breath, eyes watering, saw the white coat, too long for the old guy, touch the floor.

He looked at Thorne.

The room where it all ends.

Where else? Where else could it end but the place where they had the thing called Asterisk? Logical. Perfect. A closed system. He put his hand to his brow: cold, no sweat. Why? The old man was standing only a few yards away from him, pulling his glasses down over his eyes. He wore a blue plastic name tag on the lapel of his clinical coat. The letters, like a dye running, meant nothing to

Thorne. Inscrutable. Marks on papyrus. An alphabet of incomprehension. Why not? Why would there be any understanding here?

Act, he thought.

In the name of Christ, *act!*

The sirens still. The alarms. All hell.

"You saw it?" the man asked.

Thorne tried to answer, couldn't.

"Who sent you here?"

"Sent me?" It was not his own voice; it came from a dark place in his head, some muffled source. He stared at the man's name tag. The letters formed the name MORGENTHAU, H.

Morgenthau. *Who's Who.* The computer printout.

The cryptanalyst.

"Why did you come here?"

Sit me down, Thorne thought. Lay me on a couch. Analyze the shit out of me. The alarms. Running men. Some other time over coffee, he thought, some other time, some other place, you and me can sit down and you can put your cryptanalytical brain to work on my psychic puzzles.

"How do—" His voice went again, broken.

"How do you get out of here?" the man asked.

Why did he move so fucking slowly? why?

"There's a way," Morgenthau said. He turned his face toward a door at the other side of the room. Why is it all slow motion now? The flawed sprockets of a projector. "There's a way."

Thorne was aware: he was meant to follow Morgenthau to the door across the room. The old man had already begun to move in that direction.

He was opening the door.

It gave to another corridor, this one of badly lit red bricks. They must have run out of steel, Thorne thought. Inane. Move. Move.

Morgenthau closed the door and was moving into the corridor.

He paused and, as if there were all the time in the world, said: "You know what they've got here?"

Thorne nodded his head: know? what did he know?

The old man sighed, gesturing for Thorne to follow him along the corridor. Leadenly, dreaming a dream, dreaming a long dream, he saw Morgenthau walk ahead of him. He caught up with him: the alarms sounded distant now.

The hand, covered with fine white hairs, touched Thorne's sleeve: "How did you get here?"

Major General Burckhardt. It's a long story. Thorne saw the reflections of pale lights glimmer on the man's glasses. Water in the pool.

"Walter." The man's voice was dry and Thorne realized that he must have spoken a thought aloud. "Walter," Morgenthau said again.

"They killed him," Thorne said.

"It's as easy for them to kill . . ." Morgenthau was leading him from the corridor into a narrow, low tunnel. There was the smell of something rank, putrescent. The old man stopped, crouching. "You've seen what they've got here. You know what it is."

Thorne looked down the darkness of the tunnel. What Wonderlands lay ahead of him down there? He could feel Morgenthau's breath on the side of his face.

"If you know what it is then you know what it means," Morgenthau said. "And if you know that, then you see the importance . . ."

The importance, yes, Thorne thought. Why was the old man rambling? was he deaf? didn't he hear the noise of the sirens? didn't he know the jeopardy?

"It doesn't add up," Morgenthau was saying. "They don't want us to see what they've got here . . . and yet they don't prevent us from stumbling into that gallery. It doesn't add up."

There were echoes all at once and Thorne realized that the old man's words, rising from a whisper to harshness, were coming back out of the tunnel. Addddupppp. Adddduppp . . . He gazed into the blackness of the tunnel.

"Walter," the old man said, as if this were a spare moment in time for grief, for eulogizing, for putting the ghosts to rest. "I knew he would try to blow it. I knew he had the courage for that."

Thorne moved away from the old man, feeling the dark and the cold of the tunnel engulf him.

"Five hundred yards," Morgenthau said, coming back to the present. "I don't know how much good it's going to do you. If they don't get you in here, they'll get you out in the desert."

Thorne wanted to say something, a word of gratitude, anything. But Morgenthau was already moving away from the tunnel. Five hundred yards, Thorne thought. And then what?

He turned from the light, from the opening that Morgenthau was slowly disappearing into, and he began to run again. It was dark, darker, the farther he ran. And then he could see nothing in front of himself. In the blackness he suddenly encountered a dead end. A trap, that was it, that was all it was, a trap—but this time one without doors, exits, loopholes. Morgenthau had sent him into the tunnel knowing there wasn't anyplace else left to go. That was it. It made sense. Pretending some fondness for good old Walter, pretending some compassion, a longing to help, feigning a tiny act of courage, all he had done was to send Thorne into a blind place—

He shoved his hands into the dark in front of him.

Metal. Cold cold metal.

But what?

There it was. Some kind of handle that felt it had the shape of a small wheel. He gripped it, twisted, hearing the grind of joints, of tumblers turning, the freeing of an unused lock. The hatch swung slowly away from him and he stepped through and he saw, way overhead, the night sky, the millions of stars spread across the galaxies in a way you never saw above the pollution of a city, the shape of the moon hanging with enormous clarity. Morgenthau, he thought, thank you: thank you.

He began to run. The terrain was rough, crumbling under his feet, and although the sky above was illuminated, incandescent, the desert itself was dark. He moved sightlessly, he moved blindly, he stumbled through this darkness. Once or twice he fell, once or twice he lost his balance or tripped over some debris beneath his feet.

When he could finally run no further, when his lungs felt dehydrated and his heart sore, he lay face down in what seemed to him in the darkness a gulley, an arroyo, and he pressed his body close to the ground. He closed his eyes, listening, listening for the sound of pursuit. But there was a deep, primeval silence, the night windless, still, seemingly bereft of all life.

It lasted only a moment.

He heard the motor of a vehicle not far away. And then

something more ominous, something that vibrated through the darkness, sending waves of brushed air across the silences. He raised his head. The helicopter had a lamp rigged to its cabin. The light was stunning, a solid white beam that illuminated everything for yards around. He got to his feet. He began to move again, more slowly this time, away from the light. But it came on after him, like the eye of some ancient predatory thing. It burned up the sky and the desert below. He moved toward a clump of sparse bushes which afforded him very little cover. And the light kept coming, the chopper whirring in the air, the light swinging this way and that, mesmerizing desert moths that flew in its path like particles of metal drawn to a magnet. He moved out of the bushes, found himself going down a slight incline—

There was a sudden yellow light like one that might have been created by an exploding candle and he understood, he realized that they were dropping flares, that the whole desert was lit. He felt totally vulnerable, laid bare, and even as the flare was falling and disintegrating he was running again, scrambling on his back down the slope, knocking stones and rubble as he went. He lost his footing, slipped, slipped and went spinning over and over and over, reaching the bottom of the slope, understanding that he had somehow twisted his arm, that the arm was becoming numb. He got up, swayed, the pain was bad, he got up and dragged himself forward through the dark. He wasn't thinking. His mind was a void. He was conscious only of a physical self, a thing, an object he had somehow to protect.

The helicopter behind him.

The light.

Fragments of the desert lit up, throwing unnatural shadows.

More yellow flares. The sky seemed to scream. The jaundiced lights briefly tore the darkness apart. They must see me, he thought. They must see me. They must.

He kept going forward.

From behind there was the sound of voices.

He stopped, pressing himself to the side of the arroyo he was passing through. The helicopter, like some killing bird, was almost directly overhead. He could almost feel the warmth of the beacon on his skin.

He looked upward.

Someone was firing from the cabin.

He heard the whine of a bullet, the sound of metal slamming into the rock face around him. He slipped forward, started to run, seeing the chopper swing in an arc above him. It was coming in again. Another flare was fired. He was a bull's-eye, a target, how could they miss him now? He covered his face with his numb arm, the light was bright, terribly bright, blinding. He heard the explosion of a gun. Fragments of smashed rock flew up in a quick rain around him. The chopper hovered. The beam was going back and forth as if momentarily the person controlling the light had lost him. He scrambled down the dry wash. More flares, flare after flare, the *whoosh* of the flare gun, the explosion of sparks and light.

He was running, rushing away from the scalpel of light. When he could go no farther, when his strength had the texture of threadbare fabric, he fell down on his knees, closed his eyes, wanted to sleep. Muscles don't function, he thought. Connections severed. The millions of messages, impulses, codes, that constitute that thing known as volition—fucked. But the great bird was still coming, it was still coming after him. Get up. Had to get up.

He rose, went forward a few more steps, fell, rose again, moved on.

Can't make it

Must

Can't

Yes

He reached an area of flat land. Shadows of saguaro, thrown by the helicopter light, created great flat pools of dark. He ran across the flatness. When he couldn't run he scrambled, going on all fours, moving like some injured mammal. *They'll get you out in the desert.* Morgenthau and the major general. Had they whispered together about what to do with Asterisk? Had they conspired feebly in the cells and corridors and underground vaults of Escalante? The major general; the dead man's reach. Had Morgenthau been scared of the consequences? Burckhardt hadn't, had he?

Get up, Thorne. Get up. Go.

Ahead of him he saw lights, different lights now.

They're coming from all directions now, he thought.

Front. Back. Above. He turned his head, watching the illuminated helicopter hover: a great mantis with a firework
for a heart. But it wasn't moving. It was still, hanging. It
wasn't moving.

And suddenly Thorne realized that the lights he saw
ahead of him were those of vehicles on the public highway
he had left no more than an hour before. Cars, trucks, a
thin stream of commonplace traffic—

He had come back to the highway.

The helicopter was still.

Waiting? Waiting for what?

Instructions?

Thorne ran in the direction of the highway. It was as if
the mundane constructions fabricated in Detroit offered
him now a thin thread to safety, to the known. He looked
back again. The malevolent light in the chopper was lit.
He's on the highway: do we pursue? He was beset by the
illusion that there was nobody inside the thing, that it was
programmed, remote-controlled, that the appearance of
traffic on the highway had fucked its circuits. Kill me in
the desert, he thought, and there's nothing to explain. Kill
me on the highway and that's a whole new ball game.

He reached the edge of the road.

The helicopter was still hanging in a state of suspension
a half mile behind him. He had a sudden urge to turn
around, to gesticulate, taunt the goddamn thing. But he
didn't. He looked down the darkened highway, hearing
from behind the distant slashing of blades.

There was more traffic coming from the south. South,
north, it didn't matter to Thorne; all that mattered was
getting away from this place before the powers that coor-
dinated the movements, the killing impulses, of the chopper decided a death on a public highway was something
that could be hushed up any old time.

A truck was looming up: he watched the headlights
grow. He moved into the highway and raised his arms, his
face caught in the full beam of the lamps. He thought:
The United States has in its possession a flying saucer; a
UFO.

Asterisk.

From the corner of his eye he was conscious of the light
in the chopper going out and a sudden dark covering the
grounds of Escalante.

8:

Saturday, April 8

IT WAS RAINING IN WASHINGTON; RAIN CLOUDS COVERED the whole way from Tidewater up to Baltimore, massive gray banks that lay in the sky like swollen Zeppelins going nowhere. There was no sun: it was the kind of day that suggested there might never be a sun again. From the window of the conservatory Dilbeck watched the rain fall across the telescope. He laid his face against the glass, conscious of Sharpe standing at his back, conscious of his daughter moving around upstairs, shifting furniture in her bedroom in one of her frequent urges to change her environment. He put his hands in the pockets of his tweed jacket; he heard Sharpe clear his throat and he turned around to face him.

"You were saying something about the young man leading a charmed life, I think," Dilbeck said.

"Yeah," Sharpe said.

"I admit he's been more than lucky," Dilbeck said. He had a throbbing pain in the center of his skull; six aspirin had done nothing to diminish it. He looked at one of the trestle tables on which lay the flimsies of the reports that Sharpe had brought him. More than lucky, he thought. One could say that again. The young man had contrived to get inside Escalante and then out again—which indicated that, beyond luck, a certain amount of pussyfooting was going on out there. Later, he thought. Later I will deal with the matter of this delicacy of conduct. And Thorne—after all, there was one box from which even Houdini himself had found it impossible to escape. The last box of all.

Sources indicated that he had caught a plane from Flagstaff sometime before midnight; in Denver he had apparently waited for several hours before catching another flight for Washington. The problem was, Dilbeck thought, that although they could keep track of his movements because of his credit card activity, the reports were always several hours behind now; they were running late, just too late. Now if he were back in D.C., then he was lying low. Sooner or later, he would naturally try to contact the girl; that much was obvious. It was going to be a waiting game.

"You've got a couple of men keeping the girl under watch?" Dilbeck asked.

"Yes—"

"Good men, I mean?"

Sharpe shifted his weight, one foot to the other. How shabby he looked, Dilbeck thought; jaded, washed out, his skin like the texture of an old dollar bill.

"Good men," Sharpe said, his voice quiet.

Dilbeck looked back toward his telescope. The reports indicated that the young man had seen Asterisk. Too bad. Too damn bad. Still, he had presumably satisfied his curiosity even if it left the huge question of what he intended to do with his knowledge. The telescope seemed forlorn to him, rainwashed, like an item of an ancient technology recently excavated, whose function has defeated all expert scrutiny. If I were Thorne, he thought, what would I do with it? Try to go public? He whistled something tuneless between his teeth a moment. And then he thought of Edward Hollander: the bird had flown, the nest was empty, but nevertheless . . . ah, poor Ted. Poor old Ted. Wherever he was, he was not quite beyond the revenging claw. Not quite. All that was needed now was to keep the wires quiet for a long time, to confuse, to let nothing out. Make the Russians dangle, let them hang.

Hollander & Thorne: he had come to think of this pair as the bastard offspring of some ungodly mismatch. Or a firm of undertakers. Nine lives of the cat. Where was Thorne now?

"Can I make a suggestion?" Sharpe asked.

"Go ahead—"

"Bring the girl in—"

"Then what?"

"We keep an eye on her until we turn Thorne up—"

Dilbeck smiled patronizingly, rubbed his head, tried to

locate the pain center. He stared at Sharpe who, doglike, was waiting to see if his suggestion was to receive approbation. Dull, Dilbeck thought. No imagination. None.

"I don't think so, Sharpe," he said. "If the girl is left at liberty, then Thorne will try to contact her. If, on the other hand, we lock her up somewhere, where's the lever we have to bring Thorne into the open? What advantages do we gain?"

Sharpe looked at the floor.

"Well," said Dilbeck. "I must admit I admire his tenacity. I thought he was simply stubborn and foolish, with a sprinkling of integrity, but he's turned out to be a somewhat more formidable opponent than I'd first imagined."

Sharpe coughed lightly, raising a handkerchief to his mouth. After a moment, he said, "We're still trying to piece together the amount of information Hollander had in his possession. We don't know yet. We haven't touched the base on that one."

"Keep at it," Dilbeck said. "I think I need to take a short nap. Call me if anything turns up. Okay?"

Sharpe went to the door. He looked out into the rain as if he were afraid of stepping outside, catching pneumonia, and dying. Dilbeck stared at his plants.

"It will work out in the end, Sharpe," Dilbeck said. "It always does."

Sharpe opened the door, turning up the collar of his raincoat. Watching the door close behind him, Dilbeck reflected on the paucity of truly imaginative men; he reflected on what he considered to be a famine. Ah, well, he thought. You do the best with what you've got. Even if it isn't always enough.

Hollander had wakened in an unfamiliar white room; there were flowers on the window ledge and between their colorful foliage, bars of deep-blue sky. He experienced a brief amnesia. He looked down at his bandaged chest and remembered slowly, remembered the turbulent flight over the ocean and how the small plane had rocked back and forth, the long raking gashes of an electric storm sizzling in the Atlantic darkness. Then nothing. Nothing until now. He sat upright, feeling a sharp pain in his ribs.

The room in which he lay was small and bright. A crucifix hung on one wall, a tiny elaborate Jesus bemoaning his fate, though whether the look of misery was attributable to the pain of nails or to the subsequent idolatry and iconography, Hollander wasn't sure. There was a bedside radio which he switched on. A sonorous voice was speaking in rapid Spanish. Havana, he thought. Havana. He turned the radio off. He struggled with his pillow, propping it up behind him.

The door of the room opened and a nurse came in, a slender dark-haired young girl in white costume, white shoes; everything, even her smile, was white, as if she were seeking some camouflage against the walls of the room.

He looked at her and asked if she spoke English.

Smiling still, she shook her head. Her smile was wonderful. She checked his pulse. Her fingers were warm. He felt the relief of his return to humanity, to consciousness. She poured some brown medicine into a spoon and lifted it to his lips. It tasted ghastly and he made a face as he swallowed it. She laughed. She took his temperature by placing a thermometer under his arm. When she was finished, she went out.

He tried to turn over on his side, but the pain was too great. The brown liquid, whatever it was, had begun to make him feel a little drowsy. Morphine extract? he wondered. The subtle drug. He closed his eyes and when he opened them some time later Brinkerhoff was sitting beside the bed.

"How are you?"

Hollander's mouth was dry. Brinkerhoff helped him swallow some water.

"I guess this isn't Moscow, huh?"

"Not yet," Brinkerhoff said. He was silent. He watched Hollander as if he were trying to figure something out.

"When do we make the next leg of the trip?" Hollander asked.

"In a day or so. When you're better."

"The pain's still rough—"

"Of course," Brinkerhoff said. "The surgeon, a very fine one I might add, and a Russian into the bargain, took a bullet out that was lodged very close to your left lung. I think you've been fortunate, Hollander."

Hollander looked at the window, the yellow sunlight on the flowers. I'm alive, he thought. I don't know where I'm going, but I'm alive. Then he turned his face to the Russian. Fortunate, he thought. Lucky to be alive. And yet something wasn't quite right.

Something was awkward; there was an uneasiness.

"Is there a problem?" he asked. "Is there a problem about going on to Moscow?"

"Should there be?" Brinkerhoff said. He smiled in a vague way and made a dismissive gesture with one hand.

"No, I can't think of one," Hollander said. Why then, why this sensation of unease? Imagining things, he thought. Imagining things. That's all. A little morphine goes to your brain and no mistake.

"I think you should sleep for a while," the Russian said, "You'll need your strength."

"If you say so," Hollander said. He closed his eyes, he heard Brinkerhoff go from the room, he heard the sounds of footsteps fade in the corridor. From outside there was the noise of some kids screaming. Kids, he thought. My kids. Don't think. Let it slide. Don't think about them. Gone. He began to drift into a hypnagogic state, neither fully asleep nor wide awake, but beyond pain. Well beyond pain. He was floating downstream now, floating through the tributaries of himself, and it wasn't a bad feeling at all.

2

The Flophouse of the August Moon, Thorne thought. A bed at $2.50 a night and one free bowl of cornflakes in the morning wasn't such a bad deal when you were in that conditon of being a beggar who is unable also to be a chooser. It was a large, square dormitory with cubicles and high, narrow windows. The graffiti cut deep into the wooden partition of his own cubicle were like a testimony to the passing sadnesses and sorrows of the men who had come and gone before him. *Dave from Denver Passing Through, Only Got One Good Shoe, Where Can I go And What Can I do?* Or: *Anybody who knows where Hank Schimmel can be found please call at the Greyhound station in New Orleans and ask for Benny at the shoeshine stand.*

He had bought an overcoat, used, at a Salvation Army thrift store for three dollars; it was shabby, but it covered the tears in his suit. His shoes were scuffed, he hadn't shaved in days, he looked every inch a bona fide denizen of the flophouse. When he had arrived in the early morning, bussing in from the airport to the horror of the early commuters who saw the kind of face that should not belong in any America of the suburban consciousness, he had come upstairs at once to the cubicle and had tried for a few hours to sleep; but even though his fatigue had begun to feel like a heavy sack he was doomed to carry on his shoulders, sleep evaded him, he drifted from one shallow darkness to another, scouring the shoals of sleep but achieving only a brief satisfaction. His mind was working as if adrenaline, not blood, were running in the veins. A decision, he kept thinking. One way or another. A decision. But even more than his need for a scheme he wanted to see Marcia.

His first priority.

Marcia.

Closing his eyes brought back pictures of the long desert night, the ghostly yellow flares, the helicopter, the truck ride to Flagstaff, the lights.

Closing his eyes also brought back Asterisk.

For a moment he was convinced he had hallucinated the sight, some nightmare projection of his own that had happened to assume the shape of a monstrous disk, but he knew better, knew he had seen it, knew it was real and no yellow-red chimera shining behind glass.

It stunned him; it made him strangely afraid.

He had never subscribed to the idea of flying saucers; he had considered those who had reportedly seen them to be victims of their own fancy, extreme cases given to the wishful thinking that the human species wasn't alone in the universe—

But now—

Asterisk. He had seen it. He had seen it.

He lay on the bed in the cubicle a long time, thinking, remembering. Strange lights. Unexplained sightings both in darkness and in daylight. People who swore they had seen UFOs, others who claimed—like George Adamski—they had actually taken trips on the things. Were they telling the truth? He didn't know, he knew only what he had seen at Escalante; and he thought of the huge disk rotating across space, a bridge between star systems, intergalactic flight. Inhabited? Remote-controlled? The answer wasn't immediately important because the implication in either case was the same. Out there somewhere there was intelligent life. There was a life form more advanced than man.

Why did that frighten him?

The thought that suddenly the planet was vulnerable? The idea that if hostility came from space there was nothing, nothing, anybody on the planet earth could do about it? Or was it simply the notion of invisible observers drifting over the surface of earth, sometimes concealed in cloud cover, sometimes not, alien eyes watching, noticing, reporting? For what purpose? Whatever, he thought: it makes out lives seem insignificant in some way—planetary islands in the far constellations, oases in the star clusters of the night sky. A sense of your own limitations, your awful inferiority, the plain terror that comes from realizing your technology compared to theirs is as an abacus to a computer. No comparison, none. You floated in space, no longer alone, but suddenly vulnerable.

Then he thought: Whoever had Asterisk had the potential for almost anything. Whoever had Asterisk had the key to space and whatever else the disk might yield in terms of technology. And it all began to make a perverted kind of sense to him, the power play, the rush to understand Asterisk and keep it private and secret for purely logistical reasons as though it were nothing more than another indescribably powerful device on the route that leads down to doomsday. And the major general had died. Anna Burckhardt had died. There would have been others; others who thought it too important to be the personal preserve of a single nation. Others would have died along the way. This is what everything had been about: power. Power. Better ways to kill. Better ways to terrorize. A sick power. A control of space. Even new weapons, new circuitry, an entirely new technology.

It's more than that, he thought. *It has to be more than just that*. It has to be something that goes beyond the nuclear jingoism, something that doesn't simply usher in a new age of ballistic separatism.

No. A disk comes out of space. How it gets to earth isn't important—crashed, brought down somehow—none of that was important. What made sense was if you looked on it as some kind of gift, something that might bring a deeper benefit than the simple gratification of a military machine.

His head had begun to ache. He was being crazy: stop, think it over again, go back and look at the logic—what you're saying to yourself has something treasonable about it. Hasn't it?

He wasn't sure now.

How did you decide between x and y when y was your own country and x was some nebulous benefit for the rest of mankind?

The rest of mankind, he thought. The inflated phrase, the bloated turn of speech. He couldn't reduce it below rhetoric, no matter how he tried. He hadn't the language for it. It wasn't that simple anyhow. It was confusion, it had been confusion from the very beginning.

Go public, he thought. His instincts took him that way. No one nation had an exclusive right to this. It didn't make sense to assume so. Go public, get somebody who will write it up: somebody who will demolish the secrecy and blow it wide open. Yes. Yes. Was there another way?

He still wasn't certain.

He sat up on the edge of his bed.

From another cubicle he could hear the sound of a man drunkenly weeping, repeating the same word over and over and over. Life life life life life. A litany of desperation. He wanted to go to the man and offer some crumb of comfort, but it was Marcia he had to see first.

He left the flophouse. The street outside was a narrow passageway of decrepit tenements, forlorn figures sitting on steps and passing brown paper bags back and forth, seemingly immune to the slashing rain that, driven by a slight wind, fell in diagonal lines. He walked quickly up the street. He was looking for a telephone but the first one he came to, located outside a run-down gas station, had been vandalized. He continued to walk. His muscles ached. His strength threatened continually to ebb away from him and, weakened every so often, he would pause, lean against a wall, wait, as if he were hanging to some slender thread that kept him attached to awareness.

He found a main thoroughfare of small stores, pawnshops, a gospel church, cheap eating places where darkening chickens hung barbecuing in windows. There was a telephone box on a corner. He stepped in, shut the door, inserted coins, dialed Marcia's home number. He heard her voice and, as soon as he did, he hung up. Good, he thought. I know at least that she's home. He opened the door and stood for a moment in the street, looking this way and that, thinking: Nobody would believe that only a few days ago this bum was working in the White House. Nobody would buy that one in a hundred years. He began to walk. He considered the possible problems. Her telephone would be tapped, one; her place of residence would be under constant surveillance, two. Therefore, to get in touch with her he would have to circumvent these difficulties.

Okay, he thought.

Okay.

I've come this far. What's a few yards farther?

Dilbeck was wakened by the sound of his telephone ringing. He picked it up. Sleep hadn't eased his headache any; he felt he had been struck by a hammer on the cranium.

"I thought you'd like to be kept posted," Sharpe said.

Dilbeck said nothing. He could hear his daughter singing somewhere in the house.

"We know that Thorne spent several hours in one of those flophouses for down-and-outs—"

"Is he still there?" Dilbeck asked, hearing his own voice as if it were coming from his gut. He looked out of the window of his bedroom at the falling rain.

"No." Sharpe could be heard coughing. "A bus driver remembers dropping him off this morning in that neighborhood. I had my people do a door-to-door of hotels. I don't think we're far behind him now."

"Good," Dilbeck said. "Keep it moving."

Sharpe hung up.

Dilbeck put the receiver down. My head, he thought. He opened a bottle of aspirin that lay on the bedside table, spilled a few into the palm of his hand and swallowed them with a mouthful of stale water. Closing in, he thought. Closing in.

His bedroom door opened. His daughter stood there grinning.

"I've made you a poached egg for lunch," she said brightly.

"Splendid," he said, thinking: The last thing I need is a poached egg.

Thorne went inside the florist's, fully aware of the disdain his appearance would arouse in the smug face of the assistant. She was middle-aged, her face both self-satisfied and sour, as if life had come to her as an unwanted gift.

Thorne heard the tiny bell ring above his head as he stepped inside. The air was scented, heavy with a variety of perfumes. He selected roses, red roses, and carried the bunch to the counter.

The assistant stared at him. "You want to buy these?" she asked, as though the possibility of a man in a shabby overcoat having any need for such delicacies as flowers was quite beyond her comprehension.

"I want them delivered," Thorne said. "I understand you have a speedy delivery service."

"I believe that is what it says in the window," she remarked, touching the roses in such a way as to suggest that she suspected Thorne had contaminated them.

"I want them delivered immediately," Thorne said.

"Anything to oblige," she said, curtly.

"I don't expect to pay for sarcasm," he said.

She stared at him in a chilly way, then apparently chose to jettison his rudeness from her mind.

"You wish to write a card, *sir?*" she asked.

"I do." Thorne was given a small card and a pen. He thought for a moment, considered the risk, then wrote anyhow. *I love poetry and the places where poetry is read. But it is a cautious thing. I hate lint in my navel.* He slipped the card across the counter to the woman, having added the address. She scrutinized the message.

"How long will it take?" he asked.

"To that part of town?" She frowned a little. "An hour, perhaps less."

"It's very important," he said.

"It always is." She slipped the card into a small envelope and attached it to the wrapping around the flowers. "Cash or charge?"

"Charge," he said.

She appeared dismayed. He gave her a bank card, a driver's license, but held back his White House pass out of the fear that, given his appearance, she would consider him a total fraud and call the police. She made out the slip, he signed, she checked the picture on his driver's license against his face, and finally looked up his bank card account number in her book of lists.

"Thanks," Thorne said.

"Call again, won't you?" she said.

Thorne went outside, hoping the roses would be delivered, hoping Marcia would understand both the message and the terrible need for caution. He looked up and down the street. It was still raining hard. The street glistened, the gutters ran, litter and debris rushed in a crazy way to the drains. Now, he thought. The poetry room. Where, with his fingers crossed, he would wait for her.

3

Brinkerhoff picked up the telephone. The call that was coming through was long distance, his second of the day. He switched the scrambler button on and heard the undersecretary's voice on the line, although it was distant, fading, sucked away at times by static.

"I think you should know, Brinkerhoff, that since we last spoke, nothing has happened. Absolutely nothing," the undersecretary said. "How do you explain that away?"

"I'm not sure," Brinkerhoff said. He was frowning, and noticed that he had twisted his fingers in the telephone cord.

"Consider," said the undersecretary. "Consider the silences. Aren't they unusual? Consider, too, our previous experiences in situations similar to this one—"

"There haven't been situations similar to this one," Brinkerhoff said. He gazed up at the obligatory portrait of Lenin, then away, looking at the sunshine on the window.

"Defectors, man, defectors," said the undersecretary. "We've had them before. And in every case, every case, as soon as we had the defector safely in our possession our intelligence people began to pick up on the desperate attempts of the CIA to discredit the defector. Obviously, they would have to try to undermine the credibility of someone who has, so to speak, jumped the wall. It's a part of the game . . ."

The undersecretary was silent a moment.

Brinkerhoff stood up. He paced around the large room,

passed the overstuffed furniture, the trappings of a diplomatic mission. It was stuffy, the air stale, and he found difficulty in breathing.

"Why, then, have there been no attempts so far to discredit your Hollander? Why? Why this huge silence? Do you have an explanation?"

"No," Brinkerhoff said. "Of course, it's early, their machine may not have begun to work—"

"I don't buy that," said the undersecretary. "Their machine never stops working. No sooner do we have a defector than we start to receive reports, reports we are meant to intercept, of course, saying that the defector is a sexual pervert, or he's had electric shock therapy, or he hasn't got information that's any good or that he has a history of lunacy— So why haven't we heard anything on Hollander?"

Brinkerhoff was silent. He stared at his long white fingers, turning them over, as if there he might find written the answer he needed. The undersecretary, for once, had a good point.

"I ought to say that this is a special case," he said eventually. "When have we ever had someone like Hollander come across? When have we had this kind of information before?"

"Still, Brinkerhoff. Don't you think that would be all the more reason for them to grind up their propaganda machine? Don't you?"

"I don't know," Brinkerhoff said. "They may be playing it this way simply to throw us. Isn't that possible?"

The undersecretary was heard to sneeze twice.

"I want you to know, I want you to hear this for the record, I was never keen on Hollander from the beginning."

Brinkerhoff thought of the tape that would be recording this talk. The undersecretary liked to hedge his bets.

"What do you suggest?" Brinkerhoff asked.

"I suggest *you* decide," said the undersecretary. "You started this. You therefore finish it."

"I believe in Hollander—"

"And I don't. It smells to me. It's a dead fish."

"They're trying to confuse us—"

"We shall see. I believe that everything comes out in the wash, Brinkerhoff."

The line was dead.

Brinkerhoff, troubled, put the receiver down.

It was a double bind. Either Hollander was real or he was not. After all, hadn't he seen with his own eyes Hollander kill his own countrymen? Hadn't he seen that? But how could one explain the silence? Either the Americans erected this silence to imply that Hollander wasn't of any significance or they were doing it because he was. How did one choose? How?

Brinkerhoff sat down.

After a moment, he rose. He opened the bottom drawer of the desk, took something out, closed it again. Either/or, he thought. It was always either/or and their complicated twists, their complex ramifications, their elaborate little possibilities and perplexities. Sometimes, he thought, it would make more sense to toss a coin or roll a die. Sometimes, you simply could not fathom any of it on the basis of logic alone.

A florist's delivery van, embroidered with painted flowers and the slogan LET A FLOWER SPEAK FOR YOU drew up outside an apartment complex in the suburb of Chevy Chase. The driver got out, carrying a bunch of flowers, and went inside the building. In a parked car across the street, a man in a gray overcoat noted the arrival of the van. He stepped out of his car, waited for the delivery man to reappear. In the lane at the back of the apartment building there was another parked car, a black Marina. Nobody could enter or leave without being seen either back or front.

The man in the gray overcoat saw the van driver come out. This time he was carrying no flowers. The man in the gray overcoat walked quickly toward the van. He showed credentials which established him as a lieutenant in the District of Columbia police. The van driver, a small man with a reddish beard, appeared impressed.

"Who did you deliver the flowers to?"

"Second floor," the driver said. "Name of Emerson."

"Emerson?"

"Marcia Emerson, right."

"Was there a message?"

"I guess. I don't read them, you know."

"Where would the order have originated?"

"From the store—"

"Okay. You can go."

The driver got into his van and drove away.

The lieutenant went back to his parked car and spoke on the radio. He knew that a check would be made with the store where the flowers were bought. Then he switched his radio off and waited. He watched the apartment building.

Several minutes elapsed. Then a middle-aged woman appeared in the doorway of the building. She carried a shopping bag. She looked in the direction of his car. She crossed the street. The man with the police credentials prepared to open his door. He was ready. Whatever might arise, whatever, he was ready for it. The woman was good-looking, well dressed, respectable; a suburban matron.

She knocked on his window.

He unrolled it.

She spoke quietly. "I understand you're looking for John Thorne—"

"Where did you get that impression?"

"Please. There isn't time. My daughter just received a message from him. She's arranging to go and meet him, I think."

The man got out of the car. "You sure?"

"She said so," the woman said. "I told her to hand the message over to the police."

"You did right, lady," the man said.

He followed the woman into the apartment building. They went up to the second floor in the elevator. The woman, biting her lower lip, said: "My motive in doing this is simple. I don't like John Thorne. I don't like him associating with my daughter. Is that clear?"

"Clear," the man said.

"And I knew you were watching the building because you expect him to come here, don't you?"

The man shrugged.

The elevator stopped. He followed the woman along the corridor toward the apartment. She took a key from her bag and unlocked the door. They went inside.

"She's in the bedroom," Mrs. Emerson said. "I do believe she's locked herself in."

The man rapped on the bedroom door. "Come out," he said. "Come out. Don't waste my time."

She had used the service stairs. She crossed the foyer of the building quickly. Outside, in the rain, she ran to the corner, diagonally crossed the street, turned right, turned right again, and when she was sure she hadn't been seen she stopped running.

It was twenty minutes past two when Sharpe got the message. He swore, then with a feeling of the most acute reluctance, he was obliged to telephone his master. Banishing Tarkington—well, he thought, that was like simply taking a cancerous lung out of a body that had already succumbed to the ravages of the same disease in other organs. It was correct and it was futile. He listened to the telephone ringing.

4

Thorne was alone in the lounge when the door opened and she came in. She saw him and she started to cry. He put his arms around her and she cried against his shoulder for a long time. He smoothed her wet hair away from her forehead and thought how pale, how frail, she looked. There were dark circles under her eyes. When she had stopped crying she raised her face to look at him and then she began, with some small hysteria of relief, to laugh. She said his name over and over. He led her to a sofa and they sat down.

She regained her composure slowly.

"John, oh Christ," she said. "I thought, no, I don't know exactly what I thought. Then I got the flowers. I—"

"Easy," he said. "Were you followed here?"

She laughed again, brushing her eyes with the cuff of her raincoat. She shook her head. "I don't think so. My mother, I hope she won't get into any trouble, but when the flowers came she suddenly got this amazing idea on how to get me out of the building. I didn't think she had it in her or that she cared. Christ. I was scared. Really scared."

"Your mother helped?" Thorne asked. There was something melting in the New England frost.

Marcia laid her face against his arm. She said, "Your

sartorial taste is bewildering. Where are you shopping for coats these days?"

He kissed her lightly on the forehead, suddenly aware that with her presence his strength had come back, that the erosion of his spirit wasn't complete.

"The coat was necessary," he said. "I'll explain all that to you later, love. Right now, I need to talk with you."

The door of the lounge opened. A student, dressed in the bell-bottom jeans, complete with cuff embroidery of the late hippie period, stepped into the room. He went to the bookshelf, sifted through some periodicals, then sat down in the faraway corner of the room.

"Shit," Thorne said. "Is there someplace we can go?"

"There's my office—"

"It's out. As soon as they find you gone, they'll be swarming around your office—"

"Okay. Do you think you could drink some coffee?"

"Where?"

She stood up. "Come with me."

They went down into the basement of the building, using the stairs. There was a coffee machine in the basement corridor. Marcia put some coins in, selected two black coffees, then they walked to an empty classroom. They went inside, shut the door, sat down at a desk.

"Okay," Thorne said. "This ought to do for a time."

Marcia was smiling at him.

He looked at her for a moment.

Then he told her.

He told her about Asterisk.

She listened without interrupting, her eyes never leaving his face. When he had finished, she was silent for a long time.

She looked at him incredulously.

"Yeah," he said. "I know what you're thinking."

He paced round the room for a time, sipping coffee from the waxed cardboard container. She continued to watch him.

"Yeah," he said. "Yeah. I know how it sounds. But I can only tell you what I saw, Marcia. But it explains—it explains why Burckhardt was killed. He was sitting on information that was explosive, only he didn't know what to do with it, and because of his own sentimentality, because he thought of me as some carbon of my father, he imagined I'd know the best thing to do. Maybe he wanted it all brought out in the open, maybe he just wasn't sure."

She had her eyes closed. She said: "It's wild—"

"More than wild," Thorne said. "It explains that weird personnel list at Escalante. Jesus! I should have known. Linguists, a cryptanalyst. The possibilities of extraterrestrial life, language. It makes sense."

He crumpled his coffee cup and aimed it at the wastebasket. She was watching him now, as if she were observing the edges of lunacy.

"It's true," he said.

"Okay. Okay."

"I know what I saw."

She approached him across the room and held his hands a moment, looked at him sympathetically.

"Think," he said. "Think what it means. Just stop and think about it."

"I'm trying, John."

"It isn't simply a space revolution," he said. "Having asterisk, understanding it, how it got here, what made it move, how it communicated with its own base, there would be hundreds of technological details so advanced that any power possessing Asterisk would be—"

"I see that, John," she said quietly.

She leaned against the blackboard. There was a half-rubbed-out phrase written in chalk behind her: *The area of Sarawak in square miles is roughly equivalent to . . .* The rest was gone. I'll never know now, he thought.

Then he said: "The question is, what do I do now?"

"What do you think you *should* do?"

He rubbed his jaw, leaned against the desk, then he crossed the room and embraced her. He said: "I think it's too important to sit on. I don't think it's something that should be kept back from the rest of the world . . ."

"I had a feeling you'd say that," Marcia said.

He kissed her. The lips were cold, the hair wet still from the rain.

"And the consequences?" she asked.

"I can't predict them. All I know right now is that they want me dead."

"You'd make a God-awful corpse, Thorne," she said. "Even in your glad rags you look way too healthy."

"I have no intention of shuffling off just yet," he said.

"So the question right now is, what's the best way of proceeding? What's the strategy?"

"The newspapers?"

"Which newspaper? Who'd print it? Do you think anybody would believe me?"

"Sure," she said. "You've got some good contacts in the press. It would be the easiest thing in the world, my love, to find out your credibility quotient, no?"

"I guess," he said. He looked up at the rainy window. "What bothers me is that they're out there and they're looking hard and I can't keep running on my luck forever."

"Where do we go?" she asked. "Our apartment is obviously taboo, my office is off limits, my mother's place would be charming as a hornet's nest right now and we can't just hang out in here . . ."

Thorne thought for a moment. He thought of them tracking him and her through the wet city, the slow-moving cars, the radio communications, footsteps on stairs, the sound of knuckles on doors. His luck could not continue forever: crossing a street, waiting for a walk signal, catching a taxi, a bus, sooner or later they would see him. And now that Marcia was with him he felt doubly conspicuous.

"Where's the nearest telephone?" he asked.

"I guess outside the Student Union," she said.

"Let's go there."

He took her hand, they left the classroom together, climbed the stairs up from the basement and began to walk across the campus. The rain was constant, drumming, lashing across the university. They reached the callbox outside the Union. Inside, with Marcia crammed against him in the tiny space, he thumbed through the yellow pages of a rather dilapidated directory and found the number he wanted. He pressed in his coins, dailed, waited.

"Who are you calling?" she asked.

Before he could speak to her, the telephone was answered. A girl's voice. He asked quickly to be put through to Donaldson. The girl said that Donaldson wasn't expected back until five. He hung up.

"Who's Donaldson?" Marcia asked.

"A columnist. He has an amazing phobia about the present occupants of the White House. Total loathing would be more appropriate, I guess. If I'm going to talk to the press, it might as well begin with someone like Donaldson."

Marcia drew a shape with the tip of her finger in the steamed-up window. "What now?" she asked.

"We've got some time to kill before Donaldson is expected back—"

"It's five past three," she said, looking at her watch.

"Is there a movie house nearby?"

"If you're fond of subtitled lasciviousness I know the very place."

They left the phone booth and walked. Momentarily, Thorne wondered if what he intended to do was the right thing; he wondered about the validity of the old adage that concerned sleeping dogs and how they are best left to lie. But Burckhardt obviously hadn't thought like that, Burckhardt hadn't been deterred by that kind of doubt. And what was Asterisk finally but a discovery of such enormous importance that it couldn't be left, like some cheap secret, some minor advance in nuclear gadgetry, in the hands of a few militants whose patriotism was simply an extension of their need for adequacy? No, Burckhardt hadn't been irked by doubts like that. Whatever else Asterisk might be, it was something that had to be shared, something that had to be given to the world. Thorne was suddenly sure of this now, certain that what he planned to do was the right thing, finally the only thing.

They came to a street crossing, moving quickly to the other side against the don't-walk signal. A few hundred yards from the sidewalk, pale neons glimmering in the rain, was the marquee of the small cinema. *Adults adults adults!!!* An undiscovered French beauty, her photographed face tinted in a somewhat surreal way, stood in cardboard cutout with her legs splayed and her hands on her breasts.

"That's the place," Marcia said.

"You been here before?" Thorne asked.

"I wasn't always sweet and innocent, buddy," she said. "That only happened when I met you."

They began to run through the rain.

About twenty yards from the cashier's booth, twenty yards from the cardboard model, twenty yards from the security of the dark interior, Thorne suddenly stopped.

"No," he said.

It was all a question of plotting lines, rather like one of those puzzles kids did when you joined dots until you had a picture of a donkey, or an elephant, or a horse. These were more complex lines, of course, than in some simple juvenile drawing, but the principle was not vastly different. A florist, a cab driver, you used the memories of people instead of a pencil; you drew your lines on the basis of recollections. What it narrowed down to for Sharpe was the campus where the girl was employed. A taxi driver remembered dropping off a young man whose appearance was similar to that of the person who had ordered roses to be sent to the girl; and that person, according to the charge card, had been John Thorne.

Sharpe put the receiver down and, rubbing his forehead with the flat of his hand, turned to look at Dilbeck.

"I think we've got them," he said.

Dilbeck sighed. It seemed to him that it was a song he had been hearing for so long that its melody now was suggestive of a familiar lament.

"One of my people has seen them in the vicinity of George Washington," Sharpe said.

Dilbeck, his raincoat smeared with a moist film, his black scarf knotted tidily at his throat, picked up his gloves. He had a sudden overwhelming urge to look at John Thorne, to come face to face with the person who had caused them all so much grief. One quick look, that was all; a form of recognition. As if to say, Good try, too bad, it's been a long haul. He stood up and rainwater slicked from his coat to form an oily pool at his feet.

"Get your car, Sharpe," he said.

Sharpe seemed puzzled. "Why?"

"Let's see if we can prevent another fiasco."

Sharpe made a gesture of frustration: "But who's going to run control if I leave my desk?"

"Find somebody. It doesn't matter who. I think we have to be in on whatever's going to happen." Dilbeck moved to the door, pulling his leather gloves on. They were English gloves, he had bought them at a shop in the Burlington Arcade in London, in the year 1954; his second assignment to London, which he remembered just then with a slight touch of nostalgia, recalling his admiration for British cool, his enjoyment of their unflustered approach to things. He wished he had brought some of that home with him and imparted it to his own people; instead, what he had brought back was a taste for Typhoo Tea, marmalade on toast, and leather patches on the elbows of tweed jackets. He pulled the door open. Sharpe was fumbling into his coat.

"Let's go," Dilbeck said. "While the iron, as it were, is hot."

"Why aren't we going inside?" she asked.

He looked up and down the rainy street; then he grabbed her by the hand and, pulling her after him, walked away from the movie house.

"What's wrong?" she asked. "What's going on?"

He drew her into the doorway of a small crafts store. Raffia baskets, planters woven out of bamboo, Mohave rugs, hung in the window behind her head. He had seen a car pull up in front of the cinema, the door open, a man in a felt hat get out and go up to the cashier's desk. It might have been nothing, it might have been perfectly innocent, but the car was a certain green Catalina he had last seen driven by the fat man. He was sure of it. He was sure. He looked back down the street. A light from the window fell across his eyes. He blinked. Rain was falling from his hair, across his cheeks, his nose, a taste of chemical on his tongue. A green Catalina, a nightmare.

"We better get out of here," he said. "Fast."

He gripped her hand, then moved out of the shop doorway and down the street away from the theater. They came to a corner, turned, stopped beneath a dripping awning that hung above a bookstore.

She was rubbing rain from her eyes.

"What now?" she said. "What now?"

He tried to get his brain to work; but beyond, on the dark edges of his awareness, he was haunted by tiredness. He wanted all at once to sleep and wondered where he could find a further shot of energy. He put his arms around her.

"Let's get out of here," he said.

"I wish we would." She put her hand up to her hair, which, soaked now, hung like thick black strands of a fine metal.

They hurried along the street. And then it came to him, it came to him in a flash. Why not? he thought. It was nearby. It was only a few blocks away. The irony of it wasn't lost on him either. And besides, would anybody think of looking for them there?

He laughed in the rain.

"Don't flip out on me, John," she said.

"I don't intend to," he replied.

They continued to hurry.

A strong, violent wind was beginning to blow behind the rain, bringing cold, a touch of ice, a sense of winter at the heart of a sodden spring.

Dilbeck looked at the advertising neon hanging above the cinema. Trash, he thought. He was far from being puritanical, at least in his own eyes, but it seemed to him that the world was armpit-deep in garbage these days. The glossy mouth of a nude young woman beckoned to him from a photograph; she had her tongue upturned against her teeth. He glanced at Sharpe, who looked like a drowned ferret in this downpour. The third man, whose name Dilbeck didn't know, whose name Dilbeck didn't want to know right then, was holding a wet photograph of John Thorne.

"They didn't come in here," he was saying.

"But you saw them?" Sharpe asked.

"I saw them go down the block that way," the man said.

"Are you positive?" Dilbeck asked. He suspected that he was hearing, once more, the tune of a wild goose. A rude, atonal honk that, in his imagination, he thought resembled John Thorne's laughter at having slipped away once more.

"Okay," Sharpe said. He gave the man some instructions to put through on his radio concerning a search of the immediate area, then he looked at Dilbeck. "What now?"

"We follow in their footsteps, what else?" Dilbeck said.

Sharpe shrugged. He trailed behind Dilbeck as they walked quickly down the block. He was breathing heavily, occasionally pausing to spit out mouthfuls of dirty rain.

5

With the revolver in his jacket, Brinkerhoff went into the room where Ted Hollander lay. He closed the door quietly behind him, trying not to disturb the American; but Hollander was awake, alert, sipping milk through a straw. Hollander put his glass down on the bedside table and smiled. He thought that there was a curiously opaque expression in the Russian's eyes, as if something were badly out of place, something distressingly disjointed. Brinkerhoff sat on the chair by the bed.

"Okay," Hollander said.

Brinkerhoff looked at him strangely.

"What's bugging you?" Hollander asked.

"It's a small matter," Brinkerhoff said after a pause.

Hollander saw the misshapen lump in the jacket. It was unmistakable. *To Die in Havana,* he thought. It would have been a good drugstore title. He watched Brinkerhoff, wondering now why he felt no panic, no great desire to know what, if anything, had gone awry.

Brinkerhoff took the revolver out. He held it in the palm of his hand and looked at Hollander rather sadly.

"You're going to use that on me?" Hollander asked.

Brinkerhoff contrived a pale smile. "My undersecretary called. He is badly disturbed."

"By what?"

"By you. By this whole thing."

"You want to explain?"

"It's the total lack of response, Hollander. It makes him uneasy. In his experience, you see, people who choose to make the trip one-way from the U.S. to the Soviet Republic are usually the subject of considerable intelligence activity after the event. You know the kind of thing? It's an operation in undermining the credentials of the defector. The wires usually hum with all kinds of data. It's all perfectly standard in cases of defection."

"Yeah," Hollander said. He looked at the gun. He turned his face to the side, feeling the sunlight come through the window, warm on his flesh.

"In your case—" Brinkerhoff broke off.

"In my case you've heard nothing? Is that it?"

Brinkerhoff nodded. "It's odd."

"They're trying to throw you, isn't that obvious?"

Brinkerhoff got out of the chair and shrugged.

"That may be," he said. "But the risk is strong. You understand that?"

Hollander felt his hands become tight and, looking down, saw the upraised white bones of his bloodless knuckles. Go on, he thought. Use the gun, use it if you're going to.

"Our arrangement was for you to live in the Soviet Union," Brinkerhoff said. "In return for the information you provided. Customary in such situations as these. You provided the material. We were ready to keep our part of the bargain—"

"But now now?"

"It's too much of a risk, Hollander. How can I explain the silence from the Americans? Why aren't they singing about you? Why?"

"To confuse you. To make it seem like I'm not on the level—"

"We have the file. We can assess the information. But what do we do with you? What do we do if we find out that you are indeed a plant? My head would come rather swiftly under the ax. And the poor undersecretary, well, wouldn't he look bad? After all, he is my immediate superior—"

Hollander closed his eyes. "You want to save your own goddamn neck. And I'm just too much of a risk. Is that it? You don't trust me."

"Look, whatever my own feelings, they don't matter. They don't mean a damn thing. I do trust you, as a matter of fact. But the undersecretary has left this matter to my own discretion, a situation that doesn't mean anything very much. He is telling me that I need to protect myself. Do you see?"

Hollander stared at the Russian. Shit, he thought. Oh, shit, to come this far, to come this far and to get no further, to be slain like some bewildered animal in a hospital room miles from anywhere— He wondered what it would be like. To die. He wondered if there might be a moment when, in that last sharp echo of pain, there would be the outraged panic of knowing that you are slipping away toward a point where there is no return . . . He turned his face away from Brinkerhoff.

He had a misted image of his kids in the rainy park, Anna trying to feed chewing gum to a duck, Mark staring at him with an expression of hurt, Jimmy with his hands in his pockets. He was suddenly overwhelmed with love. He was abruptly pained by the depth of the love. It was as if he saw all the mistakes, all the losses of his life create a jet stream behind him, and he couldn't stand it. He couldn't take it. He had made it one huge, unholy mess and, in his book, you didn't get a second chance at things. He felt he wanted to weep. But his eyes were dry, his throat tight, his life—in any real sense—already over and dead.

He looked at Brinkerhoff.

He raised one eyebrow. He thought: It's going to make the surgeon's work redundant.

Brinkerhoff fired the revolver. Once, twice.

He watched Hollander slump down the pillow, his body turning to one side. There were enormous bloodstains seeping through the fresh bandages. Brinkerhoff put the pistol back into his jacket. He went to the door, opened it, stepped into the corridor.

He felt a touch of sadness.

It was waste, necessary waste.

Still, he had the file and what it all came down to in the long run was that documents were more important than people. He had the file; he had erased the risk.

6

Inside the apartment building Thorne remembered how he had last felt when he had walked down past the white walls, the sharp fluorescent lights; afraid, afraid, it all seemed such a long time ago now. He paused at a right-angled turn in the corridor and looked at Marcia. When he spoke he did so quietly. "That door over there," he said. "Number eighty-six."

She looked in the direction of the door. It was painted a dull gray, exactly like all its neighbors. There was a cloying smell of disinfectant in the air.

"I want you to go over. Knock. Okay? When he opens the door I'll be right behind you."

She moved toward the door.

Thorne, following, pressed his back against the wall and

nodded his head. When the door was opened, he wouldn't be seen immediately. The virtue of surprise. He watched Marcia, noticing how small she appeared, tiny and fragile and anemic beneath the silent fluorescence. He shut his eyes. Fatigue, out on the edge of his awareness, was like some relentless tide that came and kept coming, harrying him. He looked at Marcia again. She raised her hand, knocked on the door.

Nothing.

She glanced at him, then she knocked again.

There was a sound from within. A shuffle, something was dropped, there was silence. And then another shuffling sound. The lock was drawn back, the door opened.

"Good to see you again." Thorne stepped away from the wall.

The congressman swayed slightly, his stick fell from his fist, clattered on the floor. Thorne stepped into the hallway and, when Marcia followed him, he slammed the door. He pushed Leach softly against the wall. Then he picked up the stick and saw the congressman cringe, his shoulders stooping, some desperate fear in his eyes. Old, Thorne thought. Old and wasted.

"John," and his voice was barely a whisper.

They went into the living room. The congressman slumped into a chair, his head inclined forward: if you had wanted a picture that epitomized defeat, Thorne thought, this was it.

"I didn't . . ." Leach said, his sentence fading.

"You didn't expect to see me again?"

The congressman shook his head. "Nobody told me you'd come back. Nobody told me."

Thorne looked into the narrow kitchen. Then he glanced at Marcia, who had gone to the window. She reached up and pulled the drapes across. She turned on a lamp. The light in the room was pale. Like death, Thorne thought, watching the congressman. Like he was already dead.

"Nobody told me," the congressman said.

"When I walked out of here you thought that was the end for me," Thorne said. "Right? You said you wouldn't lift a fucking finger to help."

Despite the fatigue, the growing sense of numbness at

the center of his brain, Thorne felt an impulse to violence: *I want to hurt this wretched, sick old man. God help me.*

Marcia went into the kitchen, saying she would make coffee. Thorne heard the sound of a percolator being filled.

Leach raised his face and looked at Thorne wearily.

"What do you want? What the hell do you want?"

"To pass a little time, Congressman. Nothing more. Then I'll be on my way."

Leach took out a handkerchief and wiped his forehead with it. Thorne sat down on the arm of the sofa. He struggled out of his wet overcoat and threw it across a chair. The soles of his feet were damp, his shirt stuck to his chest, his hair was waterlogged now; a moment of dizziness passed over him, a moment in which his eyesight became blurred, his perception dim. Then it passed. It passed, but he felt weak.

He looked at the congressman, realizing his anger had undergone a change; the man was pitiful now, nothing more. Pitiful, beaten, standing at the very end of his life.

"I saw it," Thorne said. "I saw what you tried to prevent me from seeing. I got to it."

Leach looked at him. "I don't need to ask you what you're talking about, do I?"

Thorne shook his head. "I saw it, Congressman."

Leach stuffed his handkerchief into his jacket. He undid the top button of his shirt, frowned, reached for his cane.

"Where are you going?" Thorne asked.

"I need a drink," Leach said.

"Stay where you are," Thorne got up from the sofa and went to the entrance to the kitchen. Marcia was pouring coffee. "Somewhere you'll find a bottle of Laphroaig. Pour a little, would you?"

"Don't forget the ice," Leach said.

"The ice, right," Thorne said. "The sacrilegious ice."

He turned to the sofa. Leach, his head tilted slightly, watched him.

"So you saw it, Thorne. You saw it."

"Yes—"

"And?"

"What do you think?"

The congressman smiled; his eyelids flickered.

"I think it must have astonished you, yes?"

"To put it mildly," Thorne said.

"Suddenly you realize you know something that hardly anybody else in the whole goddamn world knows, something so far-reaching and so profound in all its implications that you didn't believe what you were seeing, right?"

"Pretty much." Thorne saw Marcia come in from the kitchen. She was carrying a tray with coffee and a glass of Laphroaig. Leach took his drink and raised it, in a somewhat mocking toast, in the air.

"I salute you, John. For your persistence as much as anything."

Leach sipped his drink, smacked his lips, then sat back in silence and stared inside the glass. Thorne took his coffee, wrapped his fingers around the warm china mug. He sipped some, feeling immediately revived, stoked back into awareness. He watched Marcia, who was standing at the window, smiling thinly, drinking her coffee in quick gulps.

"What now, John?" Leach said.

"It deserves to be made public—"

"I ought to have been able to predict that response," Leach said. The liquor appeared to have stimulated him; there were pink patches of color now high on his cheeks. "Given your early brainwashing I ought to have been able to predict it."

"Brainwashing?"

"Sitting at your dad's feet," Leach said. "Having the pristine visions drummed into you."

"Maybe," Thorne said.

"So. You go public, huh? A newspaper, maybe?"

"Yes," Thorne said.

"You think they'll print it?"

"It remains to be seen," Thorne said.

"I doubt it." Leach sipped from his glass. "I doubt it would ever see the light of day. Besides, it would make you look crazy. Have you thought about that? Suppose you go to a newspaper, suppose you find a writer who believes you, suppose you even get the support of that newspaper—what then? You haven't followed it through, have you? You haven't thought it all out. Where's your evidence? What can you show them? The whole goddamn world is going to break up about you. You'll be a minor nine-day wonder. Then instant oblivion. No, you haven't thought it through. You'll be known as just another nut, a conspiracy theorist, someone who's created his own Dallas, his own assassination, someone who sees faces in the patterns of trees and assumes some extra gunmen standing in the shadows. Ah, John. Don't you see? Don't you? You can't go anywhere. You can't take it with you."

Thorne put his coffee cup down. "If it's so easy to write it off as some lunacy on my part, why the hell did you go to so much trouble to put me away? Huh? Why did you do that?"

Leach rapped the tip of his cane on the floor, still smiling. The expression irritated Thorne, almost as if he knew that the congressman had some secret, something still to reveal.

"Little green men, John," Leach said. "You'd be known as the man who has irrefutable evidence of little green men except when anybody asks to see it you have to point all the way to Arizona, to some secret missile sites no less, by which time, as a precautionary measure, your flying saucer will have been moved. Back to square one, John. You haven't thought it through, John. You've been sloppy and hysterical. You've been hasty."

Thorne stared at Marcia. She was watching him carefully, as though she were waiting for him to counter the congressman's argument at one stroke, as though she were hoping that he might pull from his pocket a Polaroid snapshot of Asterisk.

"I'll take my chances," Thorne said. "I'll go to Donaldson—"

"A muckraker, a guttersnipe." Leach snorted, drained his glass, then looked at Marcia. "You look like an intelligent person, why don't you try to make him see the sense of what I'm saying?"

"Because I don't think *you're* making any sense," Marcia said sharply.

"Another one, eh? Thorne's converted you, I see. Okay, John. Maybe Donaldson would believe you. Maybe there's a faint chance he'd print your story. So what? You think people are going to credit the story when you fail to come up with evidence? Do you?"

"Like I said, I'll take my chances."

"Why would you want to do this, John?"

"I think it's too goddamn important, Congressman, that's why. You can't sit down on your fat asses on revolutionary stuff like this, you can't keep a thing like Asterisk to yourself—"

"Ah, the global argument?"

"Call it what you like," Thorne said.

"You're being an internationalist, an idealist, is that it?"

Thorne paused, conscious of how the situation here was changing, conscious, uncomfortably so, of how it had shifted since he had first entered. Leach was growing, Leach seemed to have gained the upper hand.

"I think a thing like Asterisk transcends any parochialism, any insularity," Thorne said.

Leach laughed in a dry way. "You would want our potential enemies to learn about Asterisk, would you?"

"Why not?" Thorne said. "I don't see why the information about Asterisk can't be—"

"Shared?" Leach gripped his cane, knocked it against the floor, looked suddenly angry. "You would want our enemies and our potential enemies to learn the secrets of Asterisk—the means of interstellar travel, the specifics of antigravity, you would suggest we just give this all away?"

"I don't see why information like that can't be used peacefully—"

"John, you're wet behind the ears, wet," the congressman said. "You don't know the game, and you don't know how it's played. We don't share things at this level. Don't you understand that? We don't go around giving our strengths away."

"People like you," Marcia said suddenly, "people like you, who've been on the whole shitty Washington merry-go-round for too long and who've become too stale, too stupid, and too self-centered, don't have a goddamn clue about how the world should work—"

Leach, once more, laughed. "I'm surrounded by idealists and fools," he said. *"Should work!* We're not dealing in *shoulds,* young woman. We're dealing in *things as they are.* Realities. Hard facts. Don't you see that much? Are you so goddamn dense—"

Marcia turned her face away. She opened the curtains with her hand and, in silence, stared out into the rain. Thorne did not move for a time. He was thinking of the disk, he was seeing once more the red lights burning on the disk's huge, smooth surface; and he was wondering if Leach were right. Was he being, as the congressman said, naïve? wet behind the ears? was he? Had the same kinds of thoughts occurred to the major general? He saw Anna Burckhardt lying face down on the sofa. The major general suspended in the bright-blue waters of a motel pool. He was thinking of lives trampled and crushed and he was remembering his father, he was seeing the light of belief in his father's face, he was seeing that again, feeling that again—and he asked himself: What would Senator Thorne have done with all this? Exactly what? But he was not Senator Thorne, he was another person, he was a different kind of man. He looked at Leach, who was sighing, shaking his head, and staring down inside his empty glass, knocking the melting ice cubes back and forth.

Thorne struggled now with a renewed fatigue. He was suddenly barely conscious of his own body; it was almost as if he were adrift, spinning, leaving himself. He watched Marcia: what is she thinking? he wondered. What?

He got up from the arm of the sofa and walked in silence around the room. He stopped by the telephone, looked down at it, touched it with the tips of his fingers. *No. I can't buy Leach. I can't operate in that way. I can't sell out. Everything's meaningless if I do.*

He picked up the receiver. He was conscious of Marcia turning at the sound. He saw Leach get up, propped by the cane, and cross the floor to a cabinet; he moved far quicker than Thorne would have thought possible. He reached the cabinet, opened it, and when he had swung around to look at Thorne, Thorne realized, with a sensation of suddenly sinking, that he had been too slow.

Leach held a small gun in his fist. It was neat, stainless steel.

"You can't call Donaldson, John," he said.

Thorne looked at the gun.

"You can't call him because you've nothing to tell him."

Thorne dropped the receiver, heard it fall back into the cradle, the dial tone cut. He had no more strength. No more left to fight with.

Leach was smiling, but this time in a sad way, as if all he felt now were some deep regret.

"What you saw at Escalante, John, simply doesn't exist."

The sun was hot against his closed eyelids. Unfamiliar

scents, sounds. Thousands of flowers opening in bright
light, fragile little birds hovering hundreds of feet above.
Not on such a day, Brinkerhoff thought. Not sorrow, not
now. He opened his eyes. Across the hospital grounds a
nurse was pushing an old woman in a wheelchair. Strains
of their conversation drifted toward him, soft, incompre-
hensible, interrupted by the occasional squeak of the
wheels turning. He sat upright, conscious of an orderly
moving toward him, a man in a uniform so white that as
he moved he created a sequence of tiny halos. Brinkerhoff
waited. The orderly's shadow fell across him; there was a
piece of flimsy paper. Brinkerhoff took it, knowing what it
would say, knowing already. And he thought of Hollander
slumping sideways in the bed. *Are you going to use that
on me?*

Brinkerhoff stared at the paper. It was the standard
stuff. It was predictable, unimaginative. Hollander had
been hospitalized in 1972: nervous breakdown. Yes, Brinkerhoff thought. A breakdown. He suffered from occasional schizophrenic delusions. What else? During his
hospitalization he had been treated with lysergic acid die-
thylamide. Sometimes he had flashbacks, illusions—there
was a history of paranoia. Of course, Brinkerhoff thought.
It had to be. There was nothing new under the sun, even
the Havana sun. Poor Hollander. Poor Ted Hollander. He
crumpled the paper and stuck it into his jacket.

He shut his eyes again. He thought that if he lived a
long life, if he lived to be a hundred, if he found himself
well and thriving through old age in the back country beyond his native Penza, he might never know the truth
about Edward Hollander.

But truth, he realized, had no real part in any of it.

The afternoon sky was prematurely dark, clouded over,
and rain was still falling in hard lines. Dilbeck felt it soak
through his coat, he felt his scarf at his neck as though it
were a sodden rope. Beside him in the rain Sharpe was
shivering.

"Lost them," Sharpe said.

Dilbeck wasn't so ready to give it up yet. He looked
along the street in which they stood; there were already
lights on the windows, bright against the bleakness of the
day.

Sharpe sneezed. "Thin air," he said. "Why don't we go back and dry out?"

Dilbeck shook his head and thought: No spirit, that was the trouble these days. No fire. Give in too easily. He stared up at the yellowy windows of the buildings. And then an odd thought occurred to him; he was prepared to dismiss it except for the fact that he had come to learn never to underestimate Thorne. It was the right neighborhood. Maybe, just maybe, a similar thought had occurred to Thorne. At the least, it was worth checking. At the very least, it was worth that.

"Let's check one more thing out," he said.

Sharpe, with a sigh of reluctance, shrugged. He followed Dilbeck off into the rainy darkness.

7

The small steel gun in Leach's hand was mesmerizing. It caught the light and threw it back in dull, broken lines. His hand was steady. Thorne put his arm around Marcia's waist, drawing her toward him, as if he might protect her from the line of fire if the gun should explode.

Leach drank the last few drops of water, left by the melted cubes, from his glass; then he put the glass down and jerked the gun in the air somewhat awkwardly. He saw Thorne flinch slightly.

"It isn't going to go off, John, unless I want it to," he said. "A double safety."

Thorne glanced at Marcia. He could feel her tremble against him and he wondered: Fear or cold? Something of both? He looked back at the congressman.

"If you want to understand all this, you need to go back about five years," Leach was saying. "You need to go back to the previous occupant of 1600 Pennsylvania. Before our good friend Foster had the luck to get himself elected."

Thorne heard rain on the window and thought: Death and rain. A grim combination somehow. But maybe you couldn't die in a rage of sunlight. Maybe this was the appropriate, the only, way.

"Five years ago we had certain intelligence reports that were dismaying to us," Leach was saying. "Are you listening, John? Don't you want to know, huh? Isn't your curiosity aroused?"

The voice seemed to Thorne to fade in, fade out; he tried to concentrate. Leach looked at the barrel of his automatic a moment.

"These reports told us that the Soviets were our equals in the arms race, if not exactly our superiors. It was, I might admit, a shock to some of us. But it had the effect of bringing certain heads out of the clouds. It was a taste of harsh reality, John."

The congressman—he looked suddenly smug, as though he were revitalized, all his sickness having left him. He was in control and enjoyed it. Thorne experienced a sense of hatred toward him. He caught Marcia's eyes. She was looking at him in a way that pleaded: *What have you gotten me into? What are we going to do about it?*

"A small select committee was formed, John. It consisted of the then president of the United States, his chief of staff, a high-ranking member of the National Security Council, the secretary of state and the head of the Joint Chiefs of Staff. I was the congressional member of the committee. Its purpose was to evaluate the arms situation. Our evaluation, though, was pretty gloomy. I remember . . ." Leach's voice trailed away; he was recalling something. He smiled to himself, then returned his attention to Thorne. "I can't tell you the precise moment when Asterisk was born because I don't exactly remember it. But at that period, if you recall, there was a lot of UFO activity around the world. The United States Air Force had lost a not insubstantial number of jets making interceptor flights. Only the tip of that particular iceberg was ever revealed. And Project Blue Book . . . well, that was Project Whitewash. We weren't alone in trying to intercept a UFO. No, considerable sums of money had been spent in the Soviet Union, Canada, the United Kingdom, the Benelux countries, in Brazil, in the Argentine, and, God knows, maybe even in China, all with one purpose in mind—to bring down an unidentified flying object. All this is a matter of record, John. A matter of fact."

Thorne was trying to concentrate. He had only a vague notion about where this was going, where it was leading; he felt suddenly anxious, but not simply on account of the gun or because of Marcia's fear.

"It was considered a great prize, John. Just think what the lucky country might achieve if it won the Big UFO

Lottery, eh? Well, I'm trying to tell you that this was the climate in which Asterisk was born."

Leach reached for his cane, pushed himself into a standing position, moved a little way across the room. He paused with his back to the window.

"It was decided at presidential level that the United States would possess its own flying saucer," he said. "Do you know what I'm saying? The great presidential mentality perceived a golden opportunity, John. Our own flying saucer—"

"I don't understand you," Thorne said.

"A simple scheme. I believe the modern phrase would be, we wanted to psych our enemies out. If they learned that we had a UFO, what would the effect be on them? Right? Do you think it's clever? Anyhow, this is what we did. *We built a flying saucer.*"

"You expect me to believe this?" Thorne asked.

"I hardly give a shit one way or the other, John. Don't ask me to care what you believe."

Thorne looked at the automatic.

"Anyhow, the UFO was duly built in a missile site at Oscura, New Mexico. A full-scale model, beautifully constructed on the basis of photographs and films. It was later moved to its present site. I won't go into the reasons for the transfer now . . . But it was built. The second stage of Asterisk was more difficult. Understand the high-level nuclear mentality, John. It's mainly fear and suspicion and total secrecy. You're with me?"

Thorne nodded.

"Good," Leach said. "Now try to imagine this. We want our Soviet pals to know that we have this . . . object. We want them to find out that it's real. It's not a mock-up, it's not a phony, it's the genuine article. And we want them to think this because we want to play on their fears of losing, of dropping so far behind in the Great Escalation that it's almost a joke. We have a goddamn flying saucer! You fellows can go shit in the river! That's the attitude, John. That the way the mind works at that level. So, how do we fool the Russians?"

Thorne, filled with disbelief, shook his head.

"We can't let the information fall into their hands just like that, can we? That stinks, John. And they're not idiots. They can smell a plant. So what do we do? Very

simple. We create an intense secrecy around Escalante.
We staff it with the most curious personnel you ever saw
on a hard missile site. Bit by bit, their intelligence picks up
on the weirdness of this personnel. We arrange for that to
happen. They're interested. But that's not enough. We
need to find someone who will feel so strongly about the
Asterisk that he'll want to defect to the Soviets. But that's
still not enough. We want it also to seem that we're trying
to prevent such a defection. The staff at Escalante is popu-
lated with people who might by any standards be called
security problems. Not risks, problems. Are you still with
me, John? Good."

Leach licked his lips, which seemed to have become dry.

"Good," he said again. "In the course of a few years,
one or two people want to make this Asterisk affair public.
A couple of humanitarian scientists who think it should be
universal knowledge. Types like yourself, John. They want
to go to the newspapers. This is too big, they say. They try
to get the information out. They're killed—"

"Killed?"

"Precisely," Leach said. "Remember—they can't be seen
to escape at the drop of a hat, can they?"

"Major General Burckhardt," Thorne said.

"Yes. Among others." Leach paused. He looked up at
the ceiling a moment. "But this *still* isn't enough. Killing
potential publicists, creating a strange personnel list, it
gives the Soviets something to go on, a bone to nibble on,
if you like. More is needed. An Asterisk Project Committee—APC—is created. Some of the best people, John, sit
on that committee and they have some information on Asterisk, some, *but I'm the only member of that committee
who knows Asterisk is a charade."*

"You expect me—"

"Don't ask me again, John, I'll tell you the same thing.
I don't give a damn if you believe me or not."

"But—"

Leach made a gesture with the gun. "Anyway, a couple
of potential threats, like Burckhardt, are killed. Now the
Soviets must know that something big is going on. After
all, we're killing our own men."

Thorne felt he was standing on the edge of a chasm of
total disbelief; it was as if he had been told that everything
he believed in was completely false, utterly hollow.

"You're asking me to believe that we killed our own people just because—"

"Ah," Leach said. "The cynicism in this thinking is bedazzling, John. The technical staff chosen for duty at Escalante were all dragged out of retirement and told they could pursue whatever research they liked. They were told nothing about any flying saucer. If they happened to see it, and if one or two of them thought they wanted to blow the thing open, well . . . they were old men, and pretty tired ones, and the waste wasn't anything really tragic—"

"Jesus Christ," Thorne said.

"The nuclear fear mentality," Leach said. "You're underestimating it."

"I don't—" He broke off, looked at Marcia, whose mouth was partly open, whose eyes now were without expression.

"Finally, a man came along who felt, like you, that Asterisk was too important for one country. He also felt, I guess, that the balance of power would be so distorted by our having this wonderful source of technology that he saw only disaster lying ahead. He defected. He fought our attempts to kill him—I'm glad to say—and two days ago he defected to the Soviets with a false file on Asterisk, a file that contains some specifications on antigravity and not much else. But now the Soviets think we've got something. And Asterisk, finally, is an unqualified success."

"Unqualified?" Thorne felt dizzy, light-headed, his weight cast off, as if he had swallowed some kind of soporific. He held Marcia tighter. There was a gloating quality in Leach's voice and a curious light in his eye; he looked like a man who has seen the realization of a dream which, in the first place, was demented.

"Yes. Unqualified," he said. "Doesn't it strike you that way? *Our enemies think we have a flying saucer, John.*"

Thorne looked at the gun again. Stall, he thought. What else? Try to stall. "What does Foster know about this?"

"Foster inherited the whole shooting works. He doesn't like it much but what can you do in the middle of a ball game? What can you do?"

"I don't believe Foster would support anything as murderous as this," Thorne said. And thought: But now, now you are prepared to believe almost anything. A UFO dreamed up by a committee of lunatics whose madness lay somewhere at the heart of a possible nuclear holocaust, whose idiocy stemmed from some disease of power. You can believe almost anything now. The sheer fucking waste of lives—you can believe even that. A man defects because he believes in the balance of a hideous power—and for what? Because he has been manipulated, he has become a toy in a game, a jagged fragment of glass in the kaleidoscope. And me, Thorne thought—what about me? What have I come through all this for? To die at the point of a gun? But what was his death, what was Marcia's—when you realized that others had been killed; when you knew that even the builders of Asterisk must have lost their lives? What were a couple more?

He watched Leach hobble across the floor. He felt the black depression of a cage. Trapped. They were trapped and there was going to be more waste . . . was there a point along the way, a clearing, a space in all this where it would stop? Stall: Jesus Christ, stall. Make time, make space. He watched Leach where he now stood in the doorway of the kitchen, the small gun in his hand. His eyes were barely more than two slits in the chalky face, his forehead grooved: the old pol and his last monstrous achievement. Time, Thorne thought. Make time.

"What would happen if the Russians said they've got a UFO of their own?"

Leach coughed slightly. "It isn't something we've ever discussed and I don't intend to debate it with you now."

"The whole scheme—" Thorne said: the whole scheme was what? What words did he have? What kind of inadequate language?

"The whole scheme worked," Leach said. "It *worked*."

"And that's the only criterion?"

"The only one." Leach leaned against the wall, looking at them. "Babes in the woods. The pair of you."

Thorne felt a dreadful dryness inside his mouth, as if his tongue were swollen and heavy, as if he might never speak again. He looked at Marcia: how in hell had he contrived to drag this lovely woman into such a lunacy? She was pale, her hair untidy as it dried, her lips cracked. She shouldn't have to die because of him. In his stupidity, in his naïvety, he had drawn her through the whole shit mess. Time, he thought. I must find time. He couldn't let this happen to her.

But the gun. The gun.

"So now you know," Leach said. "And now I'm going to have to kill you both because it doesn't make much difference any longer. I'm tired. The game has tired me. But I want this last thing to be a success. Do you understand that? I want this last thing to *work*."

Thorne caught the look on Marcia's eyes, couldn't define it: resignation? Had she reached that point? He had to get her out of all this. But what were you supposed to do? Go down on your knees? Pray? *Leach, I've been a bad boy and I'm very sorry and it won't happen again nosir Mister Congressman, sir?* He saw the light of a flickering determination on Leach's face and he thought: You can see the old guy in the smoke-filled rooms of legend, issuing patronage like rubber checks, you can see him slice a political opponent, banish his enemies to some bewildering oblivion, you could even see him pass down the orders that would mean death, death for some greater cause—but what you couldn't see was any appetite there for using the gun, as if—faced with the prospect of having to pull that trigger himself, face to face with physical victims—he were concerned over the mess on the rug, the disposal of flesh, the sounds that might disturb his neighbors. You could see that all this was real for him for the very first time, not some contract that passed across a desk, not a document he could rubber-stamp, not even an ugly whisper on a telephone line. It was real for him.

No: do I underestimate?

Beside him, he could hear Marcia's breathing, feel the insistent beat of a pulse in her wrist. You can't let it happen to her, Thorne: not for all the power plays and schemes and nuclear idiocies in the world. Leach had called it a game: okay, it was a game but it was wretchedly late in the day to be learning the rules for the first time.

Marcia sighed suddenly; Leach, in the manner of one who has arrived at an impossible conclusion, who likes the outcome, was smiling. The gun, Thorne thought. Go for the gun. Wasn't that what you were supposed to do? *They'll get you in the desert anyway*. He could hear echoes in his own head, voices coming back from all the shuttered rooms of memory. *Run for Congress. Go to Paris. I want you to send roses, red roses. Vital, vital. He*

didn't expect to be allowed to live. Faces: Burckhardt
standing in a cemetery, Anna gripping his wrist. Morgenthau leading him down a brick corridor to a tunnel. Somewhere in there, somewhere in that untidy grouping of
snapshots, there had to be an exit.

Major General Burckhardt

Major General—

Leach gestured with the gun, no longer smiling now.
The room streamed away from Thorne, appeared to tilt on
its axis, and for a moment he imagined he was going to
lose all balance, go down, lie there powerless to prevent
Leach from picking his spot, any spot. He held on to Marcia. *This is the most terrible room of my life.*

He will pull the trigger: he doesn't have the stomach for
it but he'll do it anyway. Old Glory. Stars and Stripes forever. The flag—*who named the flag, John? Who called it
Old Glory?* Said to be one William Driver, sea captain, of
Salem, Mass. *Correct. How many stars were there on the
original flag?* No, that's a trick question, a snare.

Burckhardt—

How did you get me into this?

An attaché case, right?

A blank manuscript, no?

Major General—

He looked at Leach. Was it a clock ticking? a faucet
leaking? the sound of coffee kicking against the lid of a
percolator? He closed his eyes a moment; a faint impression of Leach's face in the dark of his head.

"Congressman," he said. It wasn't his own voice. It was
distorted, maybe the sound of a flawed Dictabelt. *Truth is
the divine ventriloquist, dummy.* "Congressman," he said
again. Opening his eyes, he looked at the gun. There
wasn't a hope in hell of seizing it away. There were no
choices, no other routes now: this is where you committed
yourself to a course of action.

Leach was watching him: the look said, *I know what
you're doing, John. I know you have an eye on the second hand running down to the minute. I know.*

"Congressman—what I want to know is how you're going to save your own ass."

"Me? I think you're confusing things, John. I think
you've got it a little mixed up there."

"I don't think so," Thorne said. He wanted to sit; he

wanted to lie down. Suddenly it scared him to realize that he had stepped beyond caring now; he had arrived at some stage, some transcendental point at which dying no longer interested him personally. It was something you saw from outside; an event you witnessed as an observer. Fight it, he thought. Fight that one.

Leach said, "You can't try to shit me, John. Nobody's been able to do that in a quarter of a century."

"I'm not trying," Thorne said. Horribly, his mind was a blank: his mind was an empty cartridge, a dud. Something you fired but that didn't make a dent on any target.

"What the hell *are* you trying?"

"Major General Burckhardt—"

"Yeah?"

Pause: Marcia's pulse. "He left me an attaché case."

Leach laughed. "I heard."

"You heard?"

"Yeah." The congressman wiped his mouth with the corner of a handkerchief. Inside, from a deep point, he was coming apart; some central seam was unraveling.

"You heard about the case." Thorne looked at Marcia a moment. "He wasn't a great stylist, was he?"

Marcia shook her head. "Dangling participles and mixed metaphors, all over—"

Leach interrupted quickly: "John, John, John. I've been around too long. I don't have milk behind my ears. I have other people's bullshit, that's all."

It wouldn't work: but there was nothing else left to play. Thorne stared at the congressman: "Still, the man's grammar isn't what should interest you, Leach."

"What should I be interested in?"

"The whereabouts of the manuscript," Thorne said.

Leach paused a moment. "John, there were blank papers in that case. I *know*."

"No, Congressman. There were no blank papers except for the ones I put in there."

Leach smiled. You old shit, Thorne thought: you're suddenly enjoying yourself, getting off on all this.

"You're asking me to believe, if I can get this straight, that Burckhardt left you a manuscript?" Leach laughed again, then coughed, and went into his routine with the handkerchief, flapping it around his lips. "What was it,

John? The story of a flying saucer? Huh? Aliens from space?"

"Something like that." Thorne felt a chill, an emptiness of the heart. What more could he offer?

"Let me get it together, John. Burckhardt thought the saucer was for real. Okay? So even if I believe in this manuscript, and I don't, what could it be but the stupid ramblings of an old guy we'd have no trouble in proving was off the wall in no uncertain fashion?"

Answer that, Thorne thought: answer that. Lost at the crossroads. Mapless in bad territory. Which way did you go? A coin tossed in the air or a random sequence of bones thrown on the rug—what the hell difference did it make? There was no UFO: only Asterisk. Only the counterfeit.

But the sole logic here is that of survival.

The only valid syllogism is the one that concludes: *We're alive.* What else?

"Congressman," he said, "I don't believe I'm getting through to you. Burckhardt's papers—"

"Bull*shit.*"

"Okay. Okay." Thorne feigned a resignation he didn't feel. Have it your way, Leach. "I just wanted you to know."

"Tell me, John. Tell me what it is you want me to know about these—these papers."

"You're being obtuse, Congressman."

"How?"

"Names. Names and dates and places. That's how fucking obtuse you're being."

Leach motioned with the gun. "You're asking me to believe that when your young corpses turn up, or if you should suddenly vanish off the face of the earth, then this ridiculous manuscript becomes public? How? Donaldson?"

"You don't expect me to answer that, do you?" Thorne heard himself laugh, a high-pitched quirky noise. "The problem for you, Leach, is how to get your own ass out of it—"

"No," Leach said. "I don't buy it. If Burckhardt had left you anything but blanks, if he had left you this . . . let's jokingly call it information . . . why didn't you blow it before now?"

Easy, Thorne thought. The structure is weakening.

From somewhere in the building he could hear the sound of an elevator rising in its shaft.

"Why? Because I thought it was totally crazy, that's why. I wanted to check it. Wouldn't you?"

Leach said nothing.

Press it, Thorne thought. Go straight to the target. You could see the doubts begin. All you could hope for now was that the congressman was so far gone into a world of treachery, betrayal, and madness, a world in which truth values were assigned to phony propositions, in which lies were truths, in which conspiracy was standard behavior, so far gone into the demented mythology of power, that even a mythical manuscript would be believed. Play that card, he thought. It's Leach's world: turn it around against him, throw it back in his face.

"Names," he said. "Why do you think I came to see you and mentioned Asterisk? Why? You think I did that out of some weird coincidence, Leach? Names. Burckhardt's names. I was checking."

Leach looked at him a long time, as if he were calculating, sifting all the possible consequences. True or false, Thorne thought: the horror was that it didn't matter a shit. It was a lottery: it was your last chance at the big spinning wheel.

"Pull the trigger, Congressman," he said. "Pull the fucking trigger. Go on. What's stopping you?" He heard his own voice. Hysterical all at once. What am I doing? Why am I pushing this? why? "Go on, Leach. God damn you. Why don't you pull the trigger? Why don't you?" *Tempting. Goading.*

Leach stared at him in silence.

"Kill us. Kill us. Isn't that what you want?"

Leach looked at the small gun in his hand. "I don't think I believe you, John."

"No?"

The congressman shook his head slowly, side to side; he might have been looking down into an open grave at the funeral of some valuable old public servant.

"Then why don't you shoot?"

The silence. The elevator rising in the shaft. There was suddenly no air in the room. A vacuum now. *Believe it, Leach*, he thought. *In your world anything is possible, anything likely*. Trust in that universe of shadows and lies

that you helped fabricate yourself. The elevator rising in
the shaft. Believe that the shit finally hits the fan for
which it is destined. Why not?

"Blank pages," the congressman said. "All they found
were blank pages."

He was saying it more to himself than to any audience,
as if what he were looking for, and failing quite to find,
was a conviction in his heart. Thorne wondered what he
believed in; if he believed in anything. Of if you got down
to that last long haul which ends in a casket, a mumbled
eulogy, dirt falling with the inevitability of forgetfulness, if
you got down there and there was nothing at the end to
believe. Was that it for Leach? The paranoia that dictates
to you: *For every valid statement there is an opposite of
equal validity?*

The door. Get to the door. Get the fuck out.

He took Marcia by the arm and turned with her toward
the door. What did he anticipate now? the bullet in the
back? the slug in the aorta? Was that it?

I misjudged Leach, he thought.

He saw Marcia's hand go to the door handle.

He saw the handle turned, the stark corridor beyond.
He realized: It could come right now. You could have
your number called just at the point of the greatest optimism. From behind, he could hear Leach come across
the floor, his cane tapping rapidly.

"It can never be made public, John. You realize that,
don't you? True or false, Asterisk can never be made public."

Thorne wanted to say: There's nothing to go public
with. Nothing. A mythical manuscript. Nothing. Just like
Asterisk.

The elevator had stopped moving. The building was
silent. He stepped out into the corridor and he heard Marcia moan beside him.

Along the white corridor, by the elevator door now sliding shut, two men appeared.

He put his hand on Marcia's elbow. Burckhardt's hand
on his mother's elbow: death repeats itself. Leach's stick
tapped, tapped again, again and again. The snapping of a
hundred wishbones.

The older of the two had a vaguely pedagogic air: you
could see him give lectures on tree rings or microspores;

the other had the kind of face you expect to meet in the loans departments of stuffy banks.

And it was this one, the anonymous one, who had drawn a revolver from his raincoat and was down on one knee, holding the gun, police fashion, two-fisted.

No, Thorne thought

No

He heard the fluorescent tubes buzz above, as if their source of light were a million trapped fireflies. He heard Marcia's breathing, Leach's stick from behind, taptaptap

This corridor

Hadn't I felt I might die here

He looked at Marcia: her expression—something of an impossible bleakness. Coleridge couldn't help you in this shifting, haphazard world. Romantic poetry couldn't give you a sense of definition. You were defined by the appearance of a revolver held in the hand of some fucking stranger in a raincoat.

Forgive me, he wanted to say. Forgive me, Marcia. The unfinished thesis, the general wreckage, the ruins. He stared at the man with the revolver. What was he waiting for? Some flag to fall? The checkered square to drop? And the older one was smiling in some terrible way.

No more running, he thought.

This is it.

You come this far to find a gun in front of you and a madman with a cane at your back.

Taptaptaptaptaptap

He looked at the revolver. Twenty-five yards away. You couldn't miss.

Taptaptap

The noise of the cane stopped.

From behind, Leach was saying something.

He was saying, "No. No. No."

No no no: over and over.

The gunman, looking puzzled, lowered his weapon.

The older guy stopped smiling.

There was silence, silence.

9:

Sunday, April 9 a.m.

DAWN, THE FIRST STREAKS OF LIGHT WERE VISIBLE IN THE Eastern sky. Outside, an early bird was singing monotonously. All night long, unable to sleep, he had watched the night sky, the moon that had come out when the rain stopped—he had watched the stars, the dust of constellations, imagining that if you learned to read the patterns of the universe all kinds of questions would be answered. A cosmic shorthand. A celestial cryptogram.

He turned to look at Marcia, who was lying on the bed, staring at the ceiling. Ever since they had come to this hotel room she had gone inside the shell of some silence, some withdrawal. Was it fear still?

He walked across the floor, sat on the edge of the bed, lifted her hand: a deadweight. He wanted to say something. But what? After a moment he rose and went back again to the window. The stars were fading over Washington, a ritual extinction of light that would go on long after Asterisk was buried and forgotten. The same universal drift, the flux, the coming and going. Men made fumbling gestures to grasp some power: what did they amount to?

He heard Marcia suddenly say, "All for nothing. For shit. A zero. A stupid plan thought up by stupid men."

Hands in her pockets, he looked at her.

Yes: a zero. He suddenly remembered something of Roosevelt's his father had been fond of quoting: *This generation of Americans has a rendezvous with destiny.* He wasn't sure now if it was meant to be funny.

"A zero," he said.

He lay down on the bed beside her, closing his eyes. He could feel sleep; it was like the sound of wings brushing the walls of a room. A great disk from space, he thought.

Crossing the estuaries of darkness, spinning and spinning. And a zero.

"What good is it?" she asked. "I mean, what goddamn good?"

He could feel sleep.

She sighed: he barely heard her.

"We traded our silence for our lives," she said.

He wanted to say: Would you rather be dead? Would you?

"We played the same shitty . . ." Her voice seemed to come to him from a faraway place.

The same shitty game, yes: but there would be a tomorrow, a sunrise and a sunset, and none of these things would smell of betrayal and death.

She was silent now, as if turning over something in her mind: he could sense vibrations of concern, worry, from her. We're alive, he thought. What else counts? Silence, okay: you know what kind of world you're in, don't you?

"What if they find out there isn't a manuscript?" she asked. "I mean, what if Leach finally decides that it's a chance he's got to take?"

What if, Thorne wondered.

"John?" she said.

She repeated his name.

But this time he didn't hear, this time he had drifted off into sleep, into that darkness which has its own space, its own configurations and black holes and starry passages.

She said nothing for a time.

Then she switched off the bedside lamp and laid her face on the pillow beside him.

To nobody in particular she said: "Sweet dreams."

About the Author

Campbell Black was born in Glasgow in 1944 and educated at the University of Sussex. He has been an editor at two London publishing houses and a teacher of creative writing at Arizona State University and at the State University of New York, Oswego. A resident of the United States since 1971, he currently lives in Tempe, Arizona, with his wife and three sons.

Besides ASTERISK DESTINY, Mr. Black has also written one play and four other novels including the highly acclaimed BRAINFIRE, soon to be published in a Signet edition.